Library of
Davidson College

Music at the Aragonese Court of Naples

MUSIC AT THE ARAGONESE COURT OF NAPLES

Allan W. Atlas

Cambridge University Press

Cambridge
London   New York   New Rochelle
Melbourne   Sydney

Published by the Press Syndicate of the University of Cambridge
The Pitt Building, Trumpington Street, Cambridge CB2 1RP
32 East 57th Street, New York, NY 10022, USA
10 Stamford Road, Oakleigh, Melbourne 3166, Australia

© Cambridge University Press 1985

First published 1985

Printed in Great Britain at
the University Press, Cambridge

Library of Congress catalogue card number: 84-20039

British Library Cataloguing in Publication Data
Atlas, Allan W.
Music at the Aragonese Court of Naples.
1. Music – Naples (Kingdom) – 15th century – History and criticism
I. Title
780'.880621   ML290.8.N3

ISBN 0 521 24828 0

For Thone and Erik and the hill

Contents

List of Illustrations		page ix
A Note on Currency		x
Preface and Bibliographical Note		xi
Primary Sources Cited and their Sigla		xv
I	The Historical–Cultural Background	1
II	The Royal Chapel	23
III	The Composers in the Chapel and Other 'Illustrissimi' at Naples	58
IV	The Singers and Chaplains: An Inventory	87
V	Music for Secular Entertainment	98
VI	The Music Sources	114
VII	The Repertory	126
	Postlude	155

The Edition

Editorial Methods			159
1	O virgo, miserere mei	Johannes Tinctoris	161
2	Viva, viva, rey Ferranddo	Anon.	163
3	Missa L'homme armé	Anon.	167
4	Credo	Seraphinus	190
4a	Credo	Anon.	195
5	Magnificat [6th tone]	Bernardus Ycart	202
6	Adoramus te, Christe	Anon.	204
7	Christe Redemptor omnium, Ex Patre Patris	Franchinus Gaffurius	206
8	Pange lingua gloriosi	Anon.	209
9	Yerra con poco saber	Johannes Cornago	211
10	La pena sin ser sabida	Vincenet	215

11	[Textless]	Pere Oriola	218
12	Ora may, que forra·n ço	Anon.	220
13	La morte che spavento de felice	Anon.	222
14	Sufferir so disposto	Serafino dell'Aquila	223
15	Cavalcha Sinisbaldo tuta la note	Anon.	224
16	Fortuna vincinecta [Fortune, par ta cruaulté]	Anon. arr. of Vincenet	226
17	Je ne demande	J.p.	228
18	Falla con misuras [La bassa castiglya]	M. Gulielmus	230

Critical Notes to the Edition — 232
Bibliography — 239
Index — 255

Illustrations

Plate 1	Francesco Pagano (?): *Tavola Strozzi* (left portion) Museo di Capodimonte, Naples	page 14
Plate 2	Pisanello: Medal of Alfonso I, 'the Magnanimous', 1449 Museo di Capodimonte, Naples	15
Plate 3	Alfonso I's Triumphal Arch at the entrance to Castelnuovo	18
Plate 4	Domenico Gagini: Royal musicians (detail of Alfonso I's Triumphal Arch)	19
Plate 5	Domenico Gagini (?): Bust of Ferrante I (detail) The Louvre, Paris	21
Plate 6	Guido Mazzoni: Bust of Alfonso II as Duke of Calabria, c. 1489–92 Museo di Capodimonte, Naples	22
Map	The Kingdom of Naples	65

A Note on Currency

Payments at the Aragonese court of Naples were normally made in terms of ducats, tarì, and grani. The ducat was equal to five tarì, with each of these being worth twenty grani; thus: 1 ducat = 5 tarì = 100 grani, with 1 grana = 1/600 of an ounce of gold. Occasionally, payments are also recorded in terms of oncie and carlini. Each oncia was worth six ducats; one carlino was the equivalent of ten grani.

In general, the ducat used at Naples was on par with the prized ducat of Venice, as it was approximately with the florin used at Milan and Florence. Thus, comparisons of sums expressed in any of those denominations can, for the period in question, be equated on a rough 1:1 basis. As for the ducat–lira exchange, one may, at least for the period of Ferrante I, use a rate of 1 ducat = 3.2 lire.

Finally, there is the question of the relative value of gold ducats as opposed to ducats paid in 'money of account'. Throughout most of the period such ducats are approximately on par with one another. The largest discrepancy seems to have existed toward the end of the Aragonese period, when, in 1491, the ratio of the gold ducat to the ducat used in money of account was expressed as 1:1.15, the ducat of account thus being worth 15 percent less than its gold counterpart. (For further information and documentation, see the entries under Cipolla, Gnecchi, Grohmann, Martinori, and Salvati in the bibliography. My thanks to Dr. Alan Stahl of the American Numismatics Society for his help in these matters.)

Preface and Bibliographical Note

> Se vuoi delle liberali arte exempli, egli è qui in tutta perfetione, però che se o theologi o philosophi o poeti o huomini eloquentissimi et eruditi cerchi, qui ne è assaissimi et optimi; se medici o iuristi, qui ne è in gran copia et perfecti più che in niun'altra terra d'Italia. Se musici, sculptori, pictori, architecti, ingiegneri et de simili mestieri liberali, qui ne è in tutto colmo . . .
>   Francesco Bandini de' Baroncelli, *In laudes neopolitane civitis et Ferdinandi regis* . . .

These are not, as one might expect, the words of a Neapolitan praising his *patria*. Rather, the author was a Florentine patrician and member of Ficino's Academy, and he wrote the passage circa 1476 in order to justify to an unnamed friend his refusal to leave Naples and return to Florence (Kristeller, *Studies in Renaissance Thought and Letters*, 395). Nor was Bandini alone among presumably impartial witnesses in praising the cultural and musical life of Aragonese Naples. In 1450, the Florentine organist Antonio Squarcialupi, who had recently visited the court, wrote to Piero di Cosimo de' Medici, stating that he would tell him of the 'gran cose' that he had experienced there. It is hard not to think that music was among the things that had impressed the Florentine musician. And as late as circa 1513, with the Aragonese Kingdom of Naples now dead for a decade, Raffaele Brandolini, who, though raised and educated at the Neapolitan court, had long since departed for the humanist circle of Rome, could still speak of music at Naples in the most laudatory terms, even going so far as to tell Leo X that the latter's father, Lorenzo the Magnificent, had at least in part modeled the reorganized Florentine chapel on that of Ferrante I. And perhaps the Ferrarese, too, looked to the royal chapel of Alfonso I as a model for their own. In more practical terms, the esteem in which the musical life of Naples was held is evidenced by the numerous 'raids' on its personnel. Galeazzo Maria Sforza, especially, repeatedly sought singers at Naples, and the court became something of a hunting ground for its music-loving counterparts farther north. Indeed, with the likes of Cornago, Tinctoris, Gaffurius, Vincenet, and Ycart among the composers and theorists, with such secular performers as Laurenzo of Cordova (praised by Paolo Cortese as the finest clavichord-player of the day), the well-traveled English singer Madama Anna, and the improvisers Serafino Aquilano, Benedetto Gareth, and Aurelio Brandolini, with such short-term employees or just musical visitors as the singer Jean Cordier, the lutenist Pietrobono, or the dancing-master Guglielmo Ebreo, with organ-builders of international repute, and with a recruiting system that stretched its net first to Alfonso's native Spain, and then to the Franco-Burgundian territories as well as to those of the Emperor, it is little wonder that music at Naples greatly impressed those who were sensitive to the art.

Unfortunately, though, a truly detailed, 'last-word' documentary account of the musical life at the court cannot be written because of the devastating loss of archival materials. On 30 September 1943, students of medieval and Renaissance Naples were dealt a severe blow: a troop of German soldiers went to the Villa Montesano (about 30 kilometers from Naples), where the directors of the Archivio di Stato of Naples had stored the most precious of their documents for safekeeping during the war, and set both villa and documents ablaze. Lost in the flames were hundreds of volumes of the 'cedole della tesoreria', the account books that recorded the everyday expenses and activities of the court. Likewise destroyed that day were the remains of Ferrante's chancery, already badly depleted by earlier fires, earthquakes, and the like. Thus the very documents that would have formed the most important body of archival sources for our study were destroyed.

Yet there are two unified repositories of archival material upon which one may still draw, one at Naples, the other at Barcelona. At the Archivio di Stato, Naples, the postwar housecleaning turned up a number of fragmentary documents, both from the 'cedole' and from the chancery, that had not been sent to the unfortunate Villa Montesano and that had therefore escaped destruction. It was among these documents (inventoried in Jole Mazzoleni, *Le fonte documentarie*, and in the course of being published in the series *Fonti aragonesi*) that I concentrated my main archival efforts. And though the amount of material concerning music and musicians is relatively small, the fragments yielded important new information about Cornago and Oriola, the two outstanding composers in the period of Alfonso I, as well as further data on a number of other key figures in the chapel. Thus the notices added significantly to the 'cedole'-based research from before the war.

The other large collection of documents that pertain to the Aragonese court of Naples is housed at the Archivo de la Corona de Aragón at Barcelona. This material dates from the reign of Alfonso I, and consists of chancery records and correspondence – but not account books – that were sent from Naples to Barcelona upon Alfonso's death (since Naples would no longer be part of the Crown of Aragon). These documents formed the basis of the research by Anglés and, more recently, Gómez Muntané, and since my own wish to consult these sources never came to fruition I have relied heavily upon the work of the two Spanish scholars.

For the rest, there is the usual diplomatic and other correspondence that has come to reside at the archives that house the materials pertaining to the courts with which Naples had particularly close musical contacts, especially those of central and northern Italy: Milan of the Sforza, Ferrara of the Este, Mantua of the Gonzaga, and Medicean Florence. For the correspondence – usually one-sided in that it consists of letters from Naples to the other party – with the first three of these, I have relied wholly upon the published literature, the work of Barblan, Bertolotti, Lockwood, Motta, Prizer, and a few others being of particular value. As for the Aragonese-Medici correspondence, I have consulted the hundreds of such letters preserved in the *fondo* MAP of the Archivio di Stato, Florence. Although the yield with respect to music was small in quantity, the letters include important information about Laurenzo of Cordova, and help slightly to round out the important material about Florence–Naples already published by D'Accone. Still another small treasure trove of documentation at Florence has recently been made known by Leone and Galiano, namely two *Giornale* (pay registers) from the Neapolitan branch of the Strozzi bank. Long known to have bankrolled various endeavors of the Aragonese court, the Strozzi also made payments to a number of its musicians.

Finally, the Vatican archives preserve numerous documents concerning benefices for various members of the Neapolitan royal chapel. Here it has been my very good fortune to have enjoyed the generous help of Adalbert Roth and Jeremy Noble, both of whom shared with me their findings concerning Naples.

With the irretrievable loss of the 'cedole', which would have constituted the single richest repository of source material, the secondary literature necessarily takes on added importance, especially those publications that drew on the account books prior to their destruction. Five studies are of particular importance, those by Minieri Riccio, G. Filangieri, Barone, Van der Straeten, and De Marinis. The first four of these form a group of sorts, as they all date from the late nineteenth century. Minieri Riccio and Van der Straeten together provide us with the only four integral chapel rosters that we have. And the two of them, along with Filangieri (who also drew on numerous notarial acts) and Barone, included dozens of other references to individual musicians. Although the manner in which they present the documents – paraphrased, summarized, italianized (in Minieri Riccio, Filangieri, and Barone) – is at times faulty, we can only be grateful for the documentation that they left us.

De Marinis's study on the library of the Aragonese kings of Naples is now well known to musicologists. Though his work was not published until 1947–52, De Marinis had combed the archives before the war, and his hundreds of notices about the library contain a wealth of material about members of the chapel, their activities as scribes, and the preparation of liturgical books, including manuscripts of polyphony.

Between circa 1940 and 1960, two musicologists produced a series of articles that may be considered the musicological pathfinders on Aragonese Naples. (Minieri Riccio, Filangieri, Barone, and De Marinis had been interested in music only in passing, while one may speak in the same terms of Van der Straeten's interest in Naples.) Our knowledge of music at Naples would be much the poorer without the contributions of Anglés. Yet the very strengths of his work are at the same time its weaknesses. Anglés concentrated exclusively on the reign of Alfonso the Magnanimous – indeed, his subject is as much Alfonso as it is Naples, and he devotes as much attention to the Spanish realm as to the Italian – and, to judge from his citations, he drew only on the archives at Barcelona. Thus while his Spanish orientation complements the work that the first five scholars had done in the archives of Naples, and permits us to trace the continuity of certain musical traditions from Barcelona to Naples (and sometimes these seem stronger than those between Alfonso's Naples and that of his successors), we can only regret that he did not apply his musicological skills to the 'cedole' while they were still available. Alongside Anglés's work there are two noteworthy articles by Pope. Here too the Spanish element in the musical life of Naples comes to the fore, especially the contribution of Cornago.

Finally, there is a third set of studies, highly specialized in their orientation, that dates from the mid-1970s to the present: an edition–monograph on the Mellon chansonnier by Perkins and Garey; a similar study of the Montecassino manuscript by Pope and Kanazawa; Davis's edition of the works of Vincenet; Fallows's review-article on the three items just mentioned; Boorman's essay on the Seville/Paris chansonnier, which in part challenges my assertions about its Neapolitan provenance; Woodley's penetrating look at aspects of Tinctoris's career at the court; Cattin's discussion of sacred polyphony both at the court and at musically dependent monastic institutions; Galiano's survey of the entries pertaining to music in the *Giornale Strozzi* of 1473 and 1476; and my own contributions on the Neapolitan origins of the Berlin, Foligno, and Perugia manuscripts, as well as a note on the relationship between Alexander Agricola and Ferrante I. Taken together, this group represents a major contribution to our understanding of the musical life at the Aragonese court of Naples, especially because it balances the almost exclusively archival approach of the earlier studies with sound discussions of the musical repertory and the sources in which it appears. And it is on the solid shoulders of this recent scholarship, as well as those of the 'pathfinders' Anglés and Pope and the 'preservers' Minieri Riccio, G. Filangieri, Barone, Van der Straeten, and De Marinis, that the present synthesis of the musical life at the Aragonese court of Naples stands. (I cannot help ending this short bibliographic survey on a somewhat sad, if not bewildered, note. Where in the two massive tomes – 1,372 pages – of the recent *Storia di Napoli* that treat of the Aragonese period (Vol. IV, Pts. 1–2) is there even a glimpse of recognition that Naples was one of the leading musical centers of Quattrocento Italy? If only the balance of the second octave of Giovan Bernardino Fuscano's *Bellezze di Napoli* had been even partially taken to heart: 'E si la nobiltà di cose nostre,/si le faustose pompe e le bellezze,/si gli lavori vorai che ti mostre,/con gli ornati costumi e gentilezze,/il valor d'arme, di cavalli, e giostre/e l'armonie che avanzan le dolcezze/di cimbali, di voci, organi e lire,/piú materia che tempo avrai da dire' (Altamura, *La lirica napoletana del Quattrocento*, 219).)

As mentioned above, the loss of the 'cedole della tesoreria' makes it unlikely that a truly definitive documentary history of music at the Neapolitan court can still be written. However, some of the gaps in our knowledge still can – and, assuming a continued interest in the subject, no doubt will – be filled in. And I should like to suggest a few possible avenues of research. First, it seems imperative that the documents pertaining to Alfonsine Naples at the Archivo de la Corona be thoroughly explored once again. For just as Gómez Muntané has recently added to

Anglés's stock of documentation on Alfonso's patronage prior to his conquest of Naples, there can be little doubt that there is more to be found for the period 1442–1458. And though I doubt that any new documentation will radically alter our picture of music at Alfonso's court, even a small amount of new data on such people as Cornago, Oriola, Jaume Borbó, *et al.* or on the precise manner in which the chapel was organized and its various positions filled would be welcome. A second worthwhile area of investigation concerns the provenance of manuscripts. As I note in Chap. VI, of the eight polyphonic sources that I consider to be of Neapolitan origin, the provenance of only one – the Mellon chansonnier – can be linked directly to the royal court, while the origins of only one other – the Montecassino manuscript – can be determined with anything that approaches precision. As for the provenance of the other six, we can say no more than 'in or around' Naples, and there are some who might (unsuccessfully, I would maintain) even challenge that. Clearly, the final word about these manuscripts has yet to be stated. A third area that needs looking into is music in the churches and monasteries 'in or around' Naples and its relationship to the musical life of the royal court. As the manuscripts Montecassino 871 and Perugia 431 strongly suggest, the traffic was heavy and went in both directions. That my own investigation of documents concerning the monastery of SS Severino e Sossio has shed no light on the problem should certainly not deter others. Related to this question is that pertaining to music among the 'outside-the-court' nobility. And, finally, related to both of the last two subjects is the question of music in the 'provinces'. To what extent was there a flourishing polyphonic tradition in such towns as L'Aquila or Bari, for example, or even (to follow up some suggestive remarks in a recent article by Giulio Cattin) in so 'remote' a location as the Franciscan house in Ortona al Mare? Certainly, my own answers to some of these questions remain intuitive, and until such questions begin to receive convincing answers based on further research, our understanding of music at the Aragonese court of Naples – to say nothing of the kingdom at large – will remain incomplete. It is my hope that the present study will act as a stimulus in the search for further and fuller answers.

Finally, it is a pleasure to acknowledge the help, support, and, sometimes, downright scholarly charity (always given with a smile) of a number of institutions, colleagues, and friends. First, I must thank Brooklyn College of the City University of New York for a sabbatical leave in 1978–79. That year was spent as a Fellow at the Villa I Tatti, whose resources, stimulating atmosphere, and wonderful staff make it an ideal and idyllic place to work. Indeed, it was there that much of the research for the present study was accomplished. I am also indebted to the City University of New York, the Amerian Council of Learned Societies, and the National Endowment for the Humanities for grants that permitted me to make a number of other research trips to Italy. At Naples, the staffs of the Archivio di Stato – special thanks to Jole Mazzoleni – the Biblioteca Nazionale, and especially the Società per la Storia Patria were always exceptionally kind and helpful. On a more personal note, my sincerest thanks to Lorenzo Bianconi, Alexander Blachly, Ingrid

Brainard, Howard Mayer Brown, Salvatore Camporeale, Giulio Cattin, Gino Corti, John D'Amico, Stephen Davison, Dante Della Terza, Charmaine and Costanzo Di Girolamo, David Fallows, Alberto Grohmann, James Haar, T. Herman Keahey, Lewis Lockwood, Keith Larson, Jeremy Noble, Leeman Perkins, Isabel Pope, William Prizer, Adalbert Roth, Richard Sherr, William Sherzer, Alan Stahl, Eric Van Tassel, and Paul Watson, all of whom contributed in varied and valuable ways. And, of course, to Thone and Erik, who kept things going on top of the hill.

Primary Sources Cited and their Sigla

Archival Sources

ASF	Archivio di Stato, Florence
MAP	Mediceo avanti il Principato
Strozzi	Carte Strozziane, Ser. V, Vols. 27 and 32 (also cited as *Giornale Strozzi*)
ASN	Archivio di Stato, Naples
Misc.	Museo 99 A. 24, Miscellanea, I, No. 4
Priv.	Museo 99 A. 6–12, Privilegiorum, I—VII
TAF	Tesoreria antica frammenti, St. 227, Vols. I–XXXVIII
ASV	Archivio Segreto Vaticano
Lib. Annat.	Liber Annatarum
Lib. Resig.	Liber Resignationum
Reg. Lat.	Registri Lateranensi
Reg. Suppl.	Registri delle Suppliche
BNN	Biblioteca Nazionale, Naples

Musical and Other Manuscripts and Contemporary Printed Sources

Apt 16	Apt, Basilique Sainte-Anne, MS 16 bis (IV)
Barcelona 1	Barcelona, Biblioteca de l'Ateneu, MS 1
Berlin 78.C.28	Berlin, Staatliche Museen der Stiftung Preussischer Kulturbesitz, Kupferstichkabinett, MS 78.C.28
Bologna A 69	Bologna, Civico Museo Bibliografico Musicale, MS A 69
Bologna Q 16	Bologna, Civico Museo Bibliografico Musicale, MS Q 16
Bologna 596 H.H.2[4]	Bologna, Biblioteca dell'Università, MS 596 H.H.2[4]
Cancionero General	*Cancionero General de Hernando del Castillo* (Valencia, 1511; reprinted: Toledo, 1527; Seville, 1540; Antwerp, 1547)
Capetown 3.b.12	Capetown, South African Public Library, Grey Collection, MS 3.b.12
Chantilly 564	Chantilly, Musée Condé, MS 564
Dijon 517	Dijon, Bibliothèque Municipale, MS 517
Escorial IV.a.24	El Escorial, Real Monasterio de San Lorenzo del Escorial, Biblioteca y Archivio de Música, MS IV.a.24
Faenza 117	Faenza, Biblioteca Comunale, MS 117
Florence 3	Florence, Biblioteca Venturi Ginori Lisci, MS 3
Florence 27	Florence, Biblioteca Nazionale Centrale, MS Panciatichi 27
Florence 121	Florence, Biblioteca Nazionale Centrale, MS Magl. XIX.121

Primary Sources and Sigla

Florence 176	Florence, Biblioteca Nazionale Centrale, MS Magl. XIX.176
Florence 204	Florence, Biblioteca Nazionale Centrale, MS Palatino 204
Florence 2356	Florence, Biblioteca Riccardiana, MS 2356
Florence 2723	Florence, Biblioteca Riccardiana, MS 2723
Foligno	Foligno, Biblioteca Comunale, MS w/o signature
London 10431	London, British Library, Additional MS 10431
Milan 1, 2, 3, 4	Milan, Archivio della Veneranda Fabbrica del Duomo, Sezione Musicale, Libroni 1, 2, 3, 4 (*olim* 2269, 2268, 2267, 2266)
Milan 35 C sup	Milan, Biblioteca Ambrosiana, MS 35 C sup
Milan S.P.II.5	Milan, Biblioteca Ambrosiana, MS S.P.II.5
Modena α.M.1.2	Modena, Biblioteca Estense e Universitaria, MS α.M.1.2
Modena α.M.1.13	Modena, Biblioteca Estense e Universitaria, MS α.M.1.13
Modena XI.B.10	Modena, Biblioteca Estense e Universitaria, MS XI.B.10
Modena AS	Modena, Archivio di Stato, Biblioteca, MS w/o signature
Montecassino 871	Montecassino, Biblioteca dell'Abbazia, MS 871
Munich 352b	Munich, Bayerische Staatsbibliothek, Musiksammlung, Musica MS 352b
Naples VI.E.40	Naples, Biblioteca Nazionale, MS VI.E.40
Naples XII.F.50	Naples, Biblioteca Nazionale, MS XII.F.50
Naples XIV.D.20	Naples, Biblioteca Nazionale, MS XIV.D.20
Naples XXI.C.22	Naples, Biblioteca della Società Napoletana di Storia Patria, MS XXI.C.22
Naples CF.III.4	Naples, Biblioteca dei Girolamini, MS CF.III.4
Naples SM.XXVIII.4.22	Naples, Biblioteca Oratoriana dei Filippini, MS SM.XXVIII.4.22, part 5
New Haven 91	New Haven, Yale University, Beinecke Library for Rare Books and Manuscripts, MS 91
Oxford 213	Oxford, Bodleian Library, MS Canon. Misc. 213
Paris 476	Paris, Bibliothèque Nationale, fonds italiens, MS 476
Paris 676	Paris, Bibliothèque Nationale, Département de la Musique, Réserve MS Vm[7] 676
Paris 1035	Paris, Bibliothèque Nationale, fonds italiens, MS 1035
Paris 1069	Paris, Bibliothèque Nationale, fonds italiens, MS 1069
Paris 15123	Paris, Bibliothèque Nationale, fonds français, MS 15123
Paris 16664	Paris, Bibliothèque Nationale, fonds français, MS 16664
Parma 1158	Parma, Conservatorio di Musica Arrigo Boito, Biblioteca Palatina, MS 1158
Perugia 431	Perugia, Biblioteca Comunale Augusta, MS 431 (G 20)
Pesaro 1144	Pesaro, Biblioteca Oliveriana, MS 1144
Petrucci 1506[1]	Ottaviano Petrucci, *Lamentationum Jeremie prophete liber primus* (Venice, 1506)
Prague D.G.IV.47	Prague, Strahov Monastery, MS D.G.IV.47
Rome 14	Rome, Biblioteca Apostolica Vaticana, Cappella Sistina, MS 14
Rome 35	Rome, Biblioteca Apostolica Vaticana, Cappella Sistina, MS 35
Rome 51	Rome, Biblioteca Apostolica Vaticana, Cappella Sistina, MS 51
Rome 5170	Rome, Biblioteca Apostolica Vaticana, MS Vat. lat. 5170
Rome B.80	Rome, Biblioteca Apostolica Vaticana, San Pietro, MS B.80

Seville 5-I-43/Paris 4379	Seville, Biblioteca Colombina, MS 5-I-43/Paris, Bibliothèque Nationale, nouv. acq. fr., MS 4379 (part 1)
Trent 88	Trent, Museo Nazionale, Castello del Buon Consiglio, MS 88
Trent 89	Trent, Museo Nazionale, Castello del Buon Consiglio, MS 89
Valencia 835	Valencia, Biblioteca Universitaria, MS 835 (*olim* 844)
Venice 9 CCIV	Venice, Biblioteca Marciana, MS 9 CCIV (= 6879)
Verona 755	Verona, Biblioteca Capitolare, MS 755
Washington L 25	Washington, DC, Library of Congress, MS M.2.L 25
Zwickau 78	Zwickau, Ratsschulbibliothek, MS 78

CHAPTER I

The Historical–Cultural Background

Politics

On 6 June 1442 Alfonso V of Aragon (Alfonso I of Naples, called 'the Magnanimous') forced René I of Anjou from the city of Naples and thereby added the Kingdom of Naples to the Aragonese realm.[1] Since the two decades of turmoil that led to that decisive victory influenced not only the subsequent politics of the kingdom, but certain of its cultural developments as well, it is appropriate to offer a brief summary of the main events.[2] Alfonso (born 1396), who had succeeded to the Aragonese throne in 1416,[3] first came to Naples in 1421 at the invitation of Queen Giovanna II of the Angevin–Durazzo dynasty; widowed and without heir, she had chosen Alfonso as her adopted son and successor to the throne.[4] By 1423,

[1] Until then, the backbone of the Aragonese kingdom had consisted of the Spanish regions of Aragon, Catalonia (united with Aragon in 1137), and Valencia (added in 1232–1245 upon the victory over the Moors). In addition, the kingdom came to include Sicily, Sardinia, Corsica, and Mallorca and the Balearics. However, it was only in the early fifteenth century, during the reign of Martí I (see n. 3 below), that the concept of an Aragonese 'empire' became a reality. Before that time, many of the non-mainland territories were held in an on-again-off-again fashion or were semi-independent kingdoms ruled by junior members of the dynasty. On the Crown of Aragon, see Hillgarth, *The Spanish Kingdoms*, I, 233–86, 347–71; and, for a concise summary, Ryder, *The Kingdom of Naples*, pp. 16–22.

[2] There is no concise general history of Aragonese Naples in English. The closest thing to one in Italian is Archi, *Gli Aragona di Napoli*, which is sadly lacking in documentation. Far more important are the contributions in the *Storia di Napoli*, IV/1–2, by Ernesto Pontieri, 'Dinastia, regno e capitale nel Mezzogiorno aragonese', pp. 3–230, and Guido D'Agostino, 'Il Mezzogiorno aragonese (Napoli dal 1458 al 1503)', pp. 233–313. On the period of Alfonso I in particular, see the two important studies by Ryder, *The Kingdom of Naples*, which contains an extensive bibliography, and 'La politica italiana di Alfonso d'Aragona (1442–1458)', on which the present account is mainly based.

[3] Upon the death in 1409 of Martí I, the Catalan line of rule came to an end. The kingdom was then transferred by election to Alfonso's father, Ferdinando de Antequera, of the Trastamare dynasty.

[4] The Kingdom of Aragon justified its claim to Naples on the basis of two thirteenth-century marriages between the Aragonese and the Hohenstaufen rulers of Naples–Sicily. In 1209, Costanza, daughter of Pere I, married the young Frederick III, while in 1262, Pere II, son of Jaume I, married another Costanza, daughter and heiress of Manfred. However, Aragonese hopes of inheriting the southern Italian kingdom vanished in 1266, when Manfred was killed at Benevento by the forces of Charles I of Anjou, an event that led to the installation of the Angevin dynasty in Naples. And except for a very brief period after the Sicilian Vespers of 1282, when, at the invitation of the Sicilian rebels, Pere II occupied Sicily and crossed the Straits of Messina to Reggio Calabria, the Aragonese were not to realize their ambitions on mainland Italy until Alfonso's conquest. See Hillgarth, *The Spanish Kingdoms*, I, 234–44, 253–54, and Ryder, *The Kingdom of Naples*, pp. 20–21.

however, Alfonso had fallen out of favor, and Giovanna transferred the rights of inheritance to Louis III of Anjou, whose own claims to the throne had already been recognized by Pope Martin V in 1420. For the next eight years Alfonso bided his time, until in 1431 he returned to Sicily, where his display of naval power – including an attack on Ischia – persuaded Giovanna to name him as heir once again. Still, there was trouble ahead.

In November 1434, Louis III died, followed to the grave three months later by Giovanna, though not before the rather hapless queen had changed her mind yet again and bequeathed the kingdom to Louis' brother, René I. But with René held captive by Philip the Good of Burgundy and thus unable to enforce his claims, Alfonso pronounced himself king and set out for Naples. What should have been a relatively easy campaign given Aragonese naval strength began disastrously as Genoa, long an arch-rival of Aragonese–Catalan shipping interests, intervened on the side of the Angevins and defeated Alfonso at the Battle of Ponza on 5 August 1435. Yet Alfonso turned the military defeat into a political victory; taken to Milan as a prisoner, Alfonso persuaded Duke Filippo Maria Visconti to support his cause and so gained his first – and at the time only – Italian ally.[5] In 1438, with the war already three years old, René arrived on the scene, and there followed four more years of hostilities before Alfonso finally prevailed.[6]

No sooner had Alfonso gained control of 'il Regno', as the Kingdom of Naples was often called, than he moved his capital from Barcelona to Naples and entered the Italian political arena, making Naples one of the five major powers on the peninsula, along with Milan, Florence, Venice, and the Papacy. And though the following decade, from 1444 to 1454, was, as Mattingly calls it, one of 'peninsular fluidity',[7] with constant struggle and frequently changing alliances, Alfonso's foreign policy was both consistent and openly expansionist in tone. In general, Alfonso was determined to extend Aragonese sea power and gain influence in northern Italy. Having come to favorable terms with the Pope,[8] Alfonso maintained his old alliance with Milan and forged a new one with Ferrara, both of which were long-standing enemies of Venice, whose power Alfonso wished to challenge on the Adriatic.[9] Alfonso's other chief adversaries were Florence and

[5] Among the other Italian powers, both Florence, with its extensive commercial interests in Naples, and Pope Eugene IV sided with the Angevins, the latter actually lending military support. Venice remained technically neutral though its sympathies were with the French. In addition, a sizeable part of the Neapolitan nobility was pro-Angevin.

[6] The most thorough account of the conflict remains that by Faraglia, *Storia della lotta tra Alfonso V d'Aragona e Renato d'Angiò*.

[7] Mattingly, *Renaissance Diplomacy*, p. 71.

[8] Eugene IV had recognized Alfonso's sovereignty, ceded the papal territories of Terracina and Benevento to him, permitted him to control the clergy in the kingdom, and recognized the right of succession of his bastard son, Ferrante. Alfonso, in turn, pledged to support the Pope, fought in his name in the Marches against Francesco Sforza, and promised to supply naval forces in the event of war with either the Turks or the North African Moors.

[9] The Milanese alliance was broken and renewed a number of times, depending (at least while Filippo Maria Visconti was alive) on the duke's attitude toward Francesco Sforza, with whom Alfonso actually vied for the Milanese succession on the ground that Filippo Maria had promised the duchy to him in a secret agreement. Indeed, at the time of Visconti's death there was a considerable pro-Aragonese faction in Milan. These complications notwithstanding, the Nea-

Genoa, which, aside from their Francophile–Angevin leanings, stood in the way of his plan to secure a foothold on the Tuscan coast of the Tyrrhenian sea, from where he could challenge Florentine and Genoese commerce and control the sea lanes to Corsica and Elba. To this end, Alfonso embarked upon his first Tuscan campaign in 1447. But after failing both in the major battle of the campaign – the siege of Piombino, in September 1448 – and in his attempt to split the Florentine–Venetian alliance, Alfonso returned to Naples in November of that year with little to show for his efforts and his reputation sorely damaged. After still further military adventures in Tuscany during the war of the 'Milanese succession' in 1451–1452, Alfonso's policy of expansion was finally quelled by the Peace of Lodi and the formation of the Most Holy League, to which Alfonso was, notably, the last signatory among the major powers. And even after signing the treaty, Alfonso continued to do battle with Genoa right into 1458, the final year of his reign.[10]

If Alfonso's hopes for expansion on the Italian peninsula came to naught, he was more successful in his domestic policies, where, having taken over 'a very dilapidated edifice of state' he succeeded so thoroughly with his reforms and innovations as to bring about a 'revolution' in government.[11] By the end of his reign, Alfonso had managed to reassert the power of the crown, centralize governmental functions, build a bureaucracy staffed by professionals, and at least to some extent reduce the power of the barons, who had grown politically fat during the preceding century.[12] In short, Alfonso took a kingdom that had been in shambles and made it a power to be reckoned with.

Upon the death of Alfonso on 27 June 1458, the Aragonese realm was divided between his younger brother, Juan II, who inherited the Spanish territories and the islands, and his illegitimate son, Ferrante I (born 1 June 1423),[13] who received the Kingdom of Naples on the Italian mainland. Ferrante encountered difficulties immediately. In October 1459, Jean II of Anjou, then established at Genoa and supported by Pope Calixtus III, who had revoked Ferrante's right of succession on account of his bastardy, led his forces into southern Italy. With Ferrante fighting a

politan–Milanese alliance was a mainstay of Italian politics until the rise to power of Ludovico il Moro. The Ferrarese alliance was quickly cemented by the marriage in 1444 of Alfonso's eldest daughter, Maria, to Leonello d'Este, Marquis of Ferrara. In addition, Leonello's eldest son and successor, Borso, visited Naples in 1444–1445, while his two younger sons, Ercole and Sigismondo, were sent there in the Autumn of 1445 to receive their educations (see below, p.4 and n. 16). For Borso's 'Descrizione della città di Napoli . . .', an important source for the history of Naples, see Foucard, 'Fonti di storia napoletana nell'Archivio di Stato di Modena', I, 725–57.

[10] As Mattingly, *Renaissance Diplomacy*, pp. 74–75, puts it: 'Everyone, except perhaps Alfonso, . . . tired of the war'.

[11] Both quotations are from Ryder, *The Kingdom of Naples*, p. 367.

[12] For an especially critical assessment of the Neapolitan 'baronetti', see Benedetto Croce, *History of the Kingdom of Naples*, p. 63. On the important task welding together of Spanish and Italian institutions in the Neapolitan government, see M. del Treppo, 'The "Crown of Aragon" and the Mediterranean'.

[13] The year of Ferrante's birth is sometimes given as 1431; however, Pontieri, *Per la storia del regno di Ferrante I*, pp. 24–25, shows that it must be 1423. Our account of Ferrante's reign is drawn mainly from Pontieri's study, which, though not strictly speaking a biography, contains a series of essays that deals with the most important aspects of Ferrante's life.

war against rebellious barons – for many of whom the Aragonese rulers had never been anything more than illegitimate usurpers – in Calabria and thus unable to put up much resistance, Jean was able to occupy the capital. Only in 1465, seven years later, could Ferrante enter the city of Naples, the entire kingdom once again under his control. With his prestige now at a high point, Ferrante, as pragmatic a politician as there was in fifteenth-century Italy, set out over the course of the next decade to strengthen old alliances and build new ones by means of royal marriages:[14] in 1465, Alfonso, Duke of Calabria (Ferrante's eldest son and later Alfonso II), married Ippolita Sforza;[15] in 1473, Eleonora was wed to Ercole I d'Este, Duke of Ferrara;[16] while in 1474, Beatrice was betrothed to Matthias Corvinus, King of Hungary.[17] And as we shall see, each of these political ties opened the way to a flow of musical traffic between the centers involved. Conspicuously absent among the diplomatic–marital links was one with non-royal Medicean Florence, with which relations were still guarded. Indeed, in 1478–1479 the two states were again at war; and in December 1479, with Neapolitan troops pressing upon Florence, Lorenzo de' Medici undertook his famous journey to Naples in order to conduct personal negotiations with Ferrante. Lorenzo's diplomacy marked a turning point in Neapolitan–Florentine and Aragonese–Medicean relations; and from 1480 – a peace treaty was signed on 13 March – until both houses fell in 1494–1495, relations between Naples and the Medici were exceedingly warm, not only in the political and financial spheres, but also in artistic matters, where an extremely lively exchange was fostered. In fact, it is probable that without Florentine aid Ferrante would not have survived his two major political crises of the 1480s: the campaign against Mohammed II and the Turks, in which the Neapolitan forces under Alfonso, Duke of Calabria, won a clear-cut victory at the Battle of Otranto in September 1481, and the famous 'Congiura dei baroni' of 1485–1486, in which Ferrante had to contend not only with yet another rebellion by traitorous nobility, but also with the hostility of Venice and Pope Innocent VIII (of the Genoese Cybo family).[18] Again, Ferrante won a decisive

---

[14] Ferrante himself had married Isabella de Chiaromonte, daughter of the Prince of Rossano, in 1445, a union that had been arranged by Alfonso in an attempt to improve relations between crown and barons. In 1477, twelve years after Isabella's death, Ferrante remarried, now with his cousin, Juana of Aragon, sister of Ferdinand the Catholic.

[15] This marriage had already been planned in the final years of Alfonso's reign. The title of Duke of Calabria was traditionally vested in the king's eldest son.

[16] See n. 9 above, and Gundersheimer, *Ferrara: The Style of a Renaissance Despotism*, pp. 175–76, 218, who takes note of Ercole's strong Neapolitan orientation in both governmental and cultural matters.

[17] The politics of royal marriages were sometimes complicated. Previously, Beatrice had been offered to the son of the Duke of Sessa (1463) and then to Filibert, Duke of Savoy (1473); in addition, she was momentarily sought in 1473 by Louis XI for the then three-year-old Dauphin, the future Charles VIII. Before settling for Beatrice, Matthias Corvinus had rejected Eleonora. On the various marital proposals involving Beatrice, see Albert Berzeviczy, 'Les Fiançailles successives de Béatrice d'Aragon', pp. 146–65. Finally, we may note that in 1474–1476 Ferrante tried unsuccessfully to arrange a marriage between his second son, Federico, and Mary of Burgundy, daughter of Charles the Bold, this in order to reinforce the Neapolitan–Burgundian alliance.

[18] For the extensive Neapolitan–Florentine correspondence concerning the *Congiura*, see Pontieri, *La politica mediceo–fiorentina nella congiura dei baroni napoletani contro Ferrante d'Aragona, 1485–1492*.

victory, as the Duke of Calabria – now the prime target of the barons' enmity – led the Neapolitan troops to the walls of Rome, returning to Naples with a host of captured barons in tow in December 1486.

In the 1490s, events moved quickly and, in general, disastrously for Naples. Ferrante died on 25 January 1494. His successor, Alfonso II (born 4 November 1448), inherited a kingdom that was – despite the triumphs of the previous decade – in dire trouble. Not only were the Angevins once again pressing their claims to Naples, now with the support of Charles VIII and a contingent of anti-Aragonese Neapolitan barons exiled in France, but the political alliances that Ferrante had built so carefully over the years were crumbling, the crushing blow in this respect coming with the signing of the Pact of San Marco by Pope Alexander VI, Ludovico Sforza (il Moro), and Venice (together with such lesser powers as Ferrara, Mantua, and Siena) in April 1493, a treaty that left Naples politically isolated.[19] By the latter part of 1494, with political troubles mounting and Naples unable to find an ally to help stave off the approaching armies of Charles VIII,[20] Alfonso was called upon to abdicate, and in January 1495 he handed the throne to his son, Ferrandino (= Ferrante II, born 26 June 1467).[21] One month later, Ferrandino too was deprived of his throne, as the French army entered Naples in February. Though the French occupation proved costly, it was short-lived. By July, Ferrandino had re-entered the eastern part of the city; Castelnuovo was liberated in November and by the end of the year Naples was once again under Aragonese control. On 7 October 1496, Ferrandino died of natural causes and was succeeded by his uncle, Federico (younger brother of Alfonso II, born 16 October 1451), who was destined to be the last of the Aragonese rulers.

---

[19] On the hostility between Ferrante and Alexander VI and the events that led to the new alliance, see Pontieri, *Per la storia del regno di Ferrante I*, pp. 529ff. Naples had also lost two allies by natural causes. When Matthias Corvinus died in April 1490, his successor, Ladislas II, refused to accept Beatrice as his queen, thus rupturing the Naples–Budapest alliance. Similarly, the death of Lorenzo de' Medici in April 1492, and the ascent to power of his eldest son, Piero, could only weaken Ferrante's hope of future aid from Florence. The situation was well summed up in a letter of 12 October 1493 from Giovanni Pontano to Ferrante: 'L'Italia tutta è congiurata contro la potenza e stato vostro . . . A questo fine concorrono principalmente Fiorentini, sì per le cose hanno patite per la guerra fatta da vostro padre e da Voi, sì per essere da natura francesi . . . Del Papa non voglio dire altro, solo che de natura poco ve ama . . . Francia vi viene addosso; Spania vi tiene in mano, aspettando il tempo; e lo Duca di Bari [= Ludovico il Moro, to whom Ferrante had also given the title of Prince of Rosano] pur tuttavia pratica etiam con Tedeschi, li quali son poverissimi . . .'; for the excerpt quoted, see Pontieri, *op. cit.*, pp. 572–73; the entire letter is printed in Scherillo, 'Un uomo di stato del Rinascimento: gl'inizi e la vitalità di Giovanni Pontano', pp. 313ff.

[20] Charles had been invited to fulfill his ambitions against Naples by Ludovico il Moro, who had gained full control of Milan in October 1494, upon the death of Gian Galeazzo Sforza, husband of Alfonso II's daughter, Isabella. They had wed in 1489 in yet another of Ferrante's attempts to reinforce the Naples–Milan alliance. However, with Ludovico acting as regent, Gian Galeazzo never attained power. It was also Ludovico who prevented Ferrante from obtaining aid against the French from Maximilian and who derailed Neapolitan plans to arrange a marriage between Alfonso II's niece, Carlotta, and James IV of Scotland; see Pontieri, *op. cit.*, p. 556.

[21] Alfonso spent most of the remaining months of his life in an Olivetan monastery in Sicily; he died at Messina on 18/19 November 1495. For the final years of the Aragonese reign, see especially D'Agostino, 'Il Mezzogiorno aragonese', pp. 263–97.

By now, Naples had become a plaything of international politics. In 1498, Louis XII renewed French claims to the kingdom, while Ferrante's cousin, Ferdinand the Catholic, pressed Spanish claims. Though the two rulers planned for a while to divide the kingdom, differences between them resulted in war, with Gonsalvo de Cordova ('el gran Capitano'), who had driven the Moors from Granada in 1492, leading the Spanish armies to victory at the River Garigliano in 1502. In the following year, Ferdinand proclaimed himself King of Naples, and in 1522 Naples and Sicily were integrated into the Spanish empire, of which they would remain a part for the next two centuries.

The Humanist–Literary Tradition

When Alfonso defeated the Angevins, he gained control of a kingdom whose intellectual life had been moribund for a century. Thus it was one of Alfonso's great accomplishments that he revived the cultural life of Naples and made his court one of the leading centers of the humanist movement.[22] Already by the mid-1430s – first on Sicily and then at the temporary capital, Gaeta – Alfonso began to surround himself with the nucleus of his eventually large humanist circle, attracting to his court both Lorenzo Valla and Antonio Beccadelli, called 'Panormita'. Valla was at Naples from 1435 through 1447 and it was there that he spent the most productive years of his career, serving as Alfonso's secretary and court historian.[23] Since a number of Valla's works clearly reflect Alfonso's own literary interests and political aspirations, they may justly be considered direct outgrowths of his Neapolitan experience. Thus the *Collatio novi testamenti*, in which Valla compared Jerome's Vulgate with the Greek original,[24] and the *Emendationes sex librorum T. Livii* treat of Alfonso's favorite reading matter;[25] the *De falso credita et ementita Constantini donatione* of 1440, which constitutes one of

---

[22] Among the comprehensive surveys on the subject are Altamura, 'La letteratura volgare'; idem, *L'Umanesimo nel mezzogiorno d'Italia*; Croce, *La Spagna nella vita italiana durante la Rinascenza*; De Marinis, *La biblioteca napoletana dei re d'Aragona*; Driscoll, 'Alfonso of Aragon as a Patron of Art'; Gothein, *Il Rinascimento nell'Italia meridionale*; Santoro, 'La cultura umanistica'; Soria, *Los Humanistas de la Corte de Alfonso el Magnánimo*; Tateo, *I centri culturali dell'umanesimo*, pp. 28ff and 130ff; idem, *L'Umanesimo meridionale*, with an especially extensive bibliography for the period of Ferrante.

[23] The standard biography of Valla is Mancini, *Vita di Lorenzo Valla*; see also Fois, *Il pensiero di Lorenzo Valla*. A complete edition, with an introduction by Eugenio Garin, is available in the form of a reprint of the *Opera omnia* printed at Basel in 1540 (Turin: Bottega d'Erasmo, 1962). In addition, a number of Valla's works have recently appeared in critical editions based on earlier manuscript sources (see nn. 24 and 26–27 below).

[24] Perosa, *Lorenzo Valla: Collatio novi testamenti*. Alfonso's piety and knowledge of the Bible is attested by Vespasiano da Bisticci, *Le vite*, I, ed. Greco, pp. 84ff.

[25] Livy was the favorite author at Alfonso's regular 'ora di libro' and was read to him regularly, even during military campaigns. In 1444, Cosimo de' Medici presented Alfonso with a copy of Livy's *Ab urbe condita*, the so-called 'Codex Regius'. In 1451, Alfonso sent Panormita to Padua in order to retrieve what was believed to be one of Livy's bones; see Billanovich *et al.*, 'Per la fortuna di Tito Livio nel rinascimento italiano', pp. 250, 276–81. Others of Alfonso's favorite classical authors were Caesar and Seneca.

the earliest displays of essentially modern techniques of textual criticism, proved that the document purporting to uphold the Constantine Donation – and thus the temporal powers of the church – was a forgery and, whether directly provoked by Alfonso's own struggle with Eugene IV or not, provided at least inadvertent support for the king's claims against the church;[26] and finally the *Gesta Ferdinandi regis aragonum* constituted a history of the reign of Alfonso's father, Ferdinando de Antequera,[27] and was written by Valla in his capacity as one of the court historians.

It was this last work in particular that aroused the enmity of the two other humanists who most enjoyed Alfonso's favor, Panormita and his protégé, Bartolomeo Facio. Panormita (so called after his birthplace, Palermo), who had been a colleague of Valla's at Pavia, joined Alfonso's court on Sicily in 1434 and remained in the Aragonese circle until his death in 1471.[28] He had already gained a reputation in the mid-1420s with his *Hermaphroditus*, a collection of pornographic verses,[29] and was crowned poet laureate by the Emperor Sigismund in 1432. Trained as a lawyer, Panormita became one of Alfonso's chief legal advisors and diplomats and – unlike Valla and most of the humanists at the court, who enjoyed lives of subsidized leisure – spent most of his time laboring in the government bureaucracy.[30] By far the best known of his literary works is the *De dictis et factis Alfonsi regis* of 1455, an anecdotal account of Alfonso's wisdom and magnanimity that also sheds at least a small amount of light on the musical life of the court.[31] But most important, perhaps, was the role that he played as the head of the 'Accademia Alfonsina'; this, the first of the humanist academies, met regularly at Castelnuovo until Alfonso's death in 1458, at which time it moved to Panormita's home, where it became known as the 'Porticus Antoniona'. Eventually, the Academy would come under the aegis of Giovanni Pontano, under whose leadership it gained fame as the 'Accademia Pontaniana'.[32]

The third member of Alfonso's inner circle of humanists was Bartolomeo Facio (1400/10–1457). As were most of the humanists at the court, Facio was a

[26] For an edition, see Setz, *Lorenzo Valla: De falso credita et ementita Constantini donatione*. An Italian translation appears in Radetti, *L. Valla: Scritti filosofici e religiosi*, pp. 283ff. For differing opinions on the relationship of the work to the conflict between Alfonso and Eugene IV, see Camporeale, *Lorenzo Valla: Umanesimo e teologia*, p. 10, and Fois, *Il pensiero di Lorenzo Valla*, pp. 296ff, both of whom see a direct connection between the two, and Setz, p. 10, who does not.

[27] Besomi, *Laurentii Valle: Gesta Ferdinandi regis aragonum*.

[28] The basic study on Panormita is Resta, *L'Epistolario del Panormita*; see also the same author's article in the *Dizionario biografico degli italiani*.

[29] For an edition with the original Latin and an Italian translation on facing pages, see Ottolini, *Antonio Beccadelli: L'Ermafrodito–Pacifico Massimo: L'Ecatelegio*. There is some question about the date of the work; though it is generally assigned to 1425–1426, some would date it 1431–1432 (Ottolini, p. 10).

[30] On this aspect of his career, see Ryder, 'Antonio Beccadelli: A Humanist in Government'.

[31] First published at Pisa in 1485; the most recent edition appears in J. Gruterus, *Thesaurus criticus*, II (Palermo, 1739). For a partial translation into German, see Herzfeld, *Alfonso I./Ferrante I. von Neapel: Schriften von Antonio Beccadelli, Tristano Caracciolo, Camillo Porzio*, pp. 19–97.

[32] On the academy, see Santoro, 'La cultura umanistica', pp. 361–73; Minieri Riccio, *Cenni storici dell'Accademia Alfonsina*. Also useful for information on some of the less well-known academicians is Minieri Riccio, *Biografie degli accademici Alfonsini*.

'foreigner', having originally come to Naples as an ambassador of Genoa in 1444.[33] After entering Aragonese service as a tutor to the young Ferrante, Facio obtained the post of royal historian in 1446 or 1448, and in that capacity wrote his most widely known work, *De rebus gestis ab Alphonso primo libro X*.[34] Equally important is his small-scale *De viris illustribus*, which, with its biographical notices on Donatello, Ghiberti, Pisanello, Jan van Eyck, and other artists, is one of the first *Lives* to include information on painters and sculptors.[35] Yet Facio is probably best remembered – and frequently castigated – as the most vociferous of the anti-Valla faction at the court. Spurred on both by his own rivalry with Valla and by that between Valla and Panormita, Facio composed his *Invectivae in L. Vallam* in 1446, attacking Valla's history of Ferdinando de Antequera on stylistic grounds and trying at the same time to establish universal standards of historical writing.[36] It was this bitter dispute – Valla answered with his own *Recriminationes in B. Facium et A. Panormitam*[37] – that made Valla's last years at Naples unhappy ones and that no doubt caused him to give up the idea of his own history of Alfonso.

Though Valla, Panormita, and Facio were the three most important humanists to have enjoyed a close association with Alfonso, the court was host to numerous other figures of note: Gianozzo Manetti,[38] Giorgio de Trebizonda,[39] Aeneus Sylvius Piccolomini (the future Pius II), Pier Candido Decembrio, the young Giovanni Pontano (who arrived at Naples in 1448 at the age of nineteen after having joined Alfonso's entourage during the Tuscan campaign of the previous year), and eventually – during Ferrante's reign – Constantino Lascaris, who had tutored Ippolita Sforza in Greek at Milan and whose *Erotemata* was the first book entirely in Greek to be printed in the West (Milan, 1476).[40]

Notable as these figures were, a few qualifying observations on the humanist tradition at Alfonso's court must be made. First, it was largely an imported tradition; of the major figures, only the Sicilian Panormita was born within the confines of the kingdom. In addition, many of the humanists were merely transients, residing at Naples only briefly, sometimes (as with Piccolomini) on short-term diplomatic missions. Second, the literary output was largely one-sided, the major portion being devoted to the writing of history, a genre that would

[33] For a biographical sketch, see Rao, *Bartolomeo Facio: Invective in Laurentium Vallam*, pp. 13–25, and Kristeller, 'The Humanist Bartolomeo Facio and his Unknown Correspondence'.

[34] The work is printed in Gravier, *Raccolta di tutti i più rinomati scrittori dell'istoria generale del Regno di Napoli*, IV (1769).

[35] The only printed edition was published by Mehus at Florence in 1745. For the sections on the artists, see Baxandall, 'Bartholomaeus Facius on Painting', with the original text and an English translation on facing pages; see also his *Giotto and the Orators*, pp. 99–100.

[36] The work is edited in Rao, *Bartolomeo Facio*, pp. 61–124, which now supersedes Valentini, 'Le invettive di Bartolomeo Facio contro Lorenzo Valla'.

[37] A critical edition has been anounced by the Antenore Press of Padua.

[38] The Florentine Manetti, who had visited Naples a number of times, settled there permanently – a victim of voluntary exile – in 1454 after making the mistake of dedicating his *De dignitate et excellentia hominis* to Alfonso during the height of the Neapolitan–Florentine hostilities in 1451–1452; see Martines, *The Social World of the Florentine Humanists*, p. 185.

[39] On the Neapolitan activities of Trebizonda, who tutored Pontano in Greek, see Monfisani, *George of Trebizond*, pp. 114–36.

[40] See Geanokoplos, *Interaction of the 'Sibling' Byzantine and Western Cultures*, pp. 189–90.

heavily influence the whole of the Neapolitan literary tradition. Third, the development of a lyric tradition in Italian is conspicuously absent, this no doubt a result – and a reminder – of the status of that language at the court. Alfonso himself spoke Italian poorly, and the main poetic language was Castilian (as witness the many musical settings of Spanish lyrics), while the chancery and treasury used Catalan.[41] Finally, the humanist circle was a tightly closed one, centered at Castelnuovo, marked by a sharp competitive edge – which, at the daily 'ora di libro', must often have led (as Baxandall puts it) to a 'kind of scholarly showmanship'[42] – and devoid of any tangible effect on Neapolitan civic life at large.

The nature of Neapolitan humanism began to change with the succession of Ferrante; and signs of the newly placed emphases are already evident in the 1460s. In 1465, Ferrante, who was both less interested in either the classics or philology and more pragmatic about education than was his father, reopened and restructured the Neapolitan *Studio*, now with an increased emphasis on law. This was in keeping with his and the humanists' view of culture as an instrument of moral and civic education.[43] Naturally, the newly functioning *Studio* permitted learning to filter down beyond the narrow confines of Castelnuovo, and among the chief beneficiaries were the lower nobility of native Neapolitan extraction, who henceforth began to play an increasingly important role in Neapolitan intellectual life.[44]

The same decade also began to see a shift in – or at least a new element added to – the literary production of Naples. In 1467, the loquacious Loise de Rosa, 'mastro di casa' of a number of noble Neapolitan households, resumed work on his delightful *Ricordi* – begun in 1452, but interrupted soon thereafter – the first important prose work in Neapolitan dialect.[45] The third quarter of the century also witnessed the completion of Masuccio Salernitano's *Novellino*. Consisting of fifty *novelle*, often anti-clerical and anti-feminist in tone, Masuccio's work, which is modeled on Boccaccio's *Decamerone*, is the major fifteenth-century representative of the *novella* tradition,[46] and was published in 1476 at the Neapolitan press of Francesco del Tuppo, himself the translator of Aesop's *Fables* and possibly at one time a choirboy

---

[41] The court did foster a strong tradition of Spanish poetry and was host to a large contingent of Castilian, Aragonese, and Catalan poets. Indeed, prior to the unification of Spain, Naples was the main center at which the various Spanish regional literatures came together; see Croce, *La Spagna nella vita italiana durante la Rinascenza*, p. 45.

[42] *Giotto and the Orators*, pp. 99–100.

[43] See Santoro, 'La cultura umanistica', pp. 340, 347–60. On the Neapolitan *Studio*, see Cannavale, *Lo Studio di Napoli nel Rinascimento*; De Frede, *I lettori di Umanità nello Studio di Napoli*.

[44] Gothein, *Il Rinascimento nell'Italia meridionale*, p. 37, makes the interesting point that the extent to which the Neapolitan nobility participated in cultural activities was in inverse ratio to their political power. Thus, as their political influence shrank, they found an ever greater outlet in cultural affairs; see also Santoro, 'La cultura umanistica', p. 320.

[45] For an edition and commentary, see Altamura, *Napoli aragonese nei Ricordi di Loise de Rosa*.

[46] The judgment is offered by Wilkins, *A History of Italian Literature*, p. 170. An edition appears in Mauro, *Masuccio Salernitano: Il Novellino*; see also the important study by Petrocchi, *Masuccio Guardati e la narrative napoletana del Quattrocento*. For an English translation, see Waters, *The Novellino of Masuccio*. It is interesting to note that *novella* XXXIII contains the earliest appearance of the outlines of the story of Romeo and Juliet (Wilkins, p. 170).

in the royal chapel (see below, p. 35). Finally, it was in the 1460s that a generation of Neapolitan poets born between circa 1430 and circa 1445 began to develop a well-defined tradition of Italian lyric poetry, cultivating a style that was popular in tone and based on such forms as the barzelletta and the strambotto siciliano. That many of these were set to music is evidenced by their appearance in Neapolitan music manuscripts, especially those that were compiled in the 1480s (see below, p. 120). A representative collection of these poets' works appears in the manuscript Paris 1035, a canzoniere compiled for Giovanni Cantelmo, Count of Popoli, circa 1468;[47] and among the poets represented in the anthology are such important figures as Pietro Jacopo de Jennaro and Francesco Galeota.[48]

The 1470s witnessed a dramatic expansion of the Neapolitan lyric tradition, the signal event in its development being the Petrarchan influence imported from Tuscany. Right from the beginning of the decade, Neapolitan–Florentine literary contacts were intense. February–April 1471: the Florentine poet Luigi Pulci visited Naples on behalf of Lorenzo de' Medici and wrote at least one new canzona for Ferrante;[49] 1473: there appeared the first printed edition at Naples of Dante's *Divine Comedy*; September 1476: Federico d'Aragona, by far the most literary-minded of the Aragonese royal family, met with Lorenzo de' Medici at Pisa and discussed matters concerning vernacular poetry[50] (a product of this meeting was the so-called *Raccolta aragonese*, a veritable historical anthology of Tuscan poetry that was compiled as a gift for Federico by Lorenzo and Poliziano);[51] 1477: the first printed editions at Naples of Petrarch's *Canzoniere* and *Trionfi*. The Petrarchan influence was especially strong in the literary circles that enjoyed the patronage of Federico and Ferrandino, who was himself a poet. Thus the verses of such poets as De Jennaro, Giuliano Perleoni, called 'Rustico romano', Giovan Francesco Caracciolo, the young Sannazaro, and the transplanted Catalan Benedetto Gareth, called 'il Chariteo', who was also famous as an improvisator and whose *Amando e desiando io vivo* was printed in Petrucci's ninth book of frottole (1508), carried Naples into the mainstream of the vernacular lyric tradition.[52]

Finally, the Neapolitan humanist–literary tradition is crowned by the works of Giovanni Pontano and Jacobo Sannazaro.[53] Pontano, whose writings range

[47] There are two editions of Paris 1035: Mandalari, *Rimatori napoletani del Quattrocento*, and Altamura, *Rimatori napoletani del Quattrocento*. On the possible link between Cantelmo and the Neapolitan musical circle, see Atlas, 'On the Neapolitan Provenance of the Manuscript Perugia, Biblioteca Comunale Augusta, 431 (G 20)', pp. 54–55.

[48] On De Jennaro, see the excellent study by Corti, *Pietro Jacopo de Jennaro: Rime e lettere*; on Galeota, see Cianflone, *F. Galeota strambottista napoletana del '400*.

[49] De Robertis, *Luigi Pulci: Morgante e lettere*, pp. 963–72.

[50] Santoro, 'La cultura umanistica', p. 343.

[51] The literature on the *Raccolta aragonese*, copies of which may be found in the manuscripts Florence 204 and Florence 2723, is extensive; a summary of the scholarship appears in Maïer, *Ange Politien: La Formation d'un poète humaniste*, pp. 226–27.

[52] For general discussions of Petrarchism at Naples, see Corti, *Pietro Jacopo de Jennaro*, pp. xli ff, and Tateo, *L'Umanesimo meridionale*, pp. 110ff. On Gareth, who after Sannazaro was the major figure in the group, see Pèrcopo, *Le rime di Benedetto Gareth, detto il Chariteo*.

[53] The literature on Pontano and Sannazaro is especially extensive; the most recent bibliographies are those in Tateo, *L'Umanesimo meridionale*, pp. 73–75, 209–10.

from the lyrical to the didactic–philosophical works on social–political virtues and morality, was also active on the diplomatic front, serving as Ferrante's secretary of state and advisor and formulating policy as well as carrying it out. He was also, of course, the guiding spirit of the academy that came to bear his name.[54] Of far greater literary influence, however, was Sannazaro, whose *Arcadia*, begun in 1483 and published in its first authorized edition in 1504 at Naples, would be honored and imitated well into the eighteenth century. And though Sannazaro is most familiar to us for his cultivated language on pastoral themes, he could also don a local, more popular guise, as the following excerpt from one of his *gliuommeri* shows:

> La memoria felice   de re Andrea
> de la suppa navrea   si delettava,
> e spesse volta usava   gelatina,
> la salza gramillina   e le zandelle,
> e sopra alle crespelle   zafarana,
> pedeta de puttana   e maccaroni,
> con dui o tre caponi   sotterrati.[55]

Though Pontano and Sannazaro surely transcend the strictly local humanist–literary tradition – as this is exemplified by the works of a Panormita or the canzoniere of Giovanni Cantelmo – Naples is everywhere present in their works, whether in Pontano's *Dialogues*, which introduce his fellow academicians, or in his persistent use of the Partenope legend, or in Sannazaro's constant praise of the physical beauties of Naples and its surroundings; and it is with Naples that they remain closely identified.

Painting, Sculpture, and Architecture

In his famous letter of 20 September 1524 to Marcantonio Michiel of Venice, the Neapolitan humanist Pietro Summonte provides a veritable catalogue of art works that were then – or at least not too long before then – to be found in Naples.[56] After noting with pride the works executed by Giotto and his followers during the culturally brilliant reign of Robert the 'Wise' of Anjou during the fourteenth century,[57] he writes somewhat despairingly: 'Da questo tal tempo non

---

[54] After Pontano's death in 1503, the academy continued to function, first under the leadership of Summonte (on whom see below) and Girolamo Carbone, and then, from 1526 to 1530, under that of Sannazaro; it was finally suppressed by the Spanish Viceroy in 1542.

[55] *Opere volgare*, ed. Mauro, p. 301; quoted also in Tateo, *L'Umanesimo meridionale*, p. 188.

[56] The letter is printed in Pane, *Il Rinascimento nell'Italia meridionale*, I, 63–71, and Nicolini, *L'arte napoletana del Rinascimento e la lettera di Pietro Summonte a Marcantonio Michiel*, pp. 157–75. An earlier edition of the letter, by Fabriczy, 'Summontes Brief am A. M. Michiel', is not complete. As noted above (n. 54), Summonte was for a while the head of the Accademia Pontaniana and also published the first authorized edition of Sannazaro's *Arcadia*. On the Venetian Michiel, see Fletcher, 'Marcantonio Michiel: His Friends and Collection'.

[57] Giotto was active at Naples from at least December 1328 to April 1332; for the documents concerning Giotto's Neapolitan sojourn, see Previtali, *Giotto e la sua bottega*, pp. 151–52. Also

avemo avuto in queste parti, né omo externo né paesano, celebre, fino ad maestro Colantonio nostro napolitano, persona tanto disposta all'arte della pictura, che se non moriva iovene, era per far cose grandi.'[58] Then, after describing Colantonio's works and permitting himself a short digression on the art of Flanders, he continues: 'Ritornando dunque alli pittori nostri, dico che nullo pictor nobile avemu avuto qua poi Colantonio.'[59] Summonte's assessment is clear: in the course of some two centuries Naples had produced but one outstanding native artist, Colantonio, and as such he merits our attention.

Little is known about the artist's life. By 1438–1442 he had gained the attention of René of Anjou (Summonte: '. . . il re Raniero lo ritienne qua'), who seems to have been his patron. On this slight shred of evidence, Nicolini has placed Colantonio's birth at circa 1420.[60] Equally subject to guesswork is his date of death; perhaps he may be identified with the Colantonio who received payment on 26 July 1487 for having decorated a room in the Castel Capuano, though this does not square well with Summonte's remark that the artist died while still young.[61] Also open to speculation is the nature of Colantonio's relationship with the Aragonese court. Though he was not the official 'court painter', we shall see that some connection must have existed. Finally, Summonte writes that Colantonio was the teacher of Antonello da Messina, one of the great masters of the period, who was probably apprenticed to the older artist for some time between 1445 and 1455.[62]

Of the four Colantonio paintings described by Summonte, two are particularly important. The first is his *St. Jerome*, now housed at the Museo di Capodimonte (its original home was the sacristy of San Lorenzo Maggiore) and now thought to have been part of a larger work depicting St. Francis giving the Rules of his Order.[63] What is especially noteworthy about the panel, which shows Jerome in

present at Naples during the same general period were Simone Martini and Pietro Cavallini. The most comprehensive study on Trecento painting at Naples is Bologna, *I pittori alla corte angioina di Napoli*. There is no similar work for the Aragonese period; the major developments may be pieced together from Bologna, *Napoli e le rotte mediterranee*; Nicolini, *L'arte napoletana*; Rolfs, *Geschichte der Malerei Neapels*, pp. 85–174; Van Marle, *The Development of the Italian Schools of Painting*, XV, 345ff, many of whose attributions, however, are now contested.

[58] Pane, *Il Rinascimento*, I, 64–65; Nicolini, *L'arte napoletana*, p. 160.

[59] Pane, *op. cit.*, I, 66; Nicolini, *op. cit.*, p. 163.

[60] Nicolini, *op. cit.*, p. 202; see also Rolfs, *Geschichte der Malerei Neapels*, p. 90.

[61] Barone, 'Le cedole di tesoreria dell'Archivio di Stato di Napoli', IX, 623; Hersey, *Alfonso II and the Artistic Renewal of Naples*, p. 70, n. 65. Rolfs, *Geschichte der Malerei Neapels*, p. 90, sets the date of death at circa 1460; Nicolini, *L'arte napoletana*, stretches it to after 1472. It is surprising to find that the entry on Colantonio in the index of the recent *Enciclopedia universale dell'arte*, XV, 122, falls into a *Doppelmeister* trap and gives the artist's dates as 'c. 1352–1442'; on the problem, see Nicolini, *op. cit.*, pp. 199–201.

[62] Sciascia and Mandel, *L'opera completa di Antonello da Messina*, p. 83; Bologna, *Napoli e le rotte mediterranee*, p. 88, places Antonello at Naples first between 1450 and 1455 and then between 1457 and 1460. On the relationship between the artists, see also Giuseppe Fiocco, 'Colantonio e Antonello'.

[63] For reproductions, see Pane, *Il Rinascimento*, I, Fig. 23; Bologna, *Napoli e le rotte mediterranee*, Figs. 32, 34–35; Molajoli, *Il Museo di Capodimonte*, Pl. XII; Doria and Causa, *La Reggia di Capodimonte*, front cover and Pl. 47. The work in its entirety was reconstructed by Bologna in 1950 (p. 55) and attributed by him to Colantonio, and even this was challenged by Dimier, 'Colantonio et le Saint Jérome du Musée de Naples'. The question of what is and what is not by Colantonio is complicated by the difficulty of matching extant paintings with the descriptions given by Summonte.

his study, extracting the thorn from the lion's paw, is that it is generally agreed to have been modeled after a depiction of the same saint in the so-called 'Lomellini' triptych by Jan van Eyck, a painting that Alfonso kept in his apartments at Castelnuovo.[64] And that Colantonio based his painting on Van Eyck's underscores the frequently made point about the strong Flemish influence on Neapolitan painting of the period.[65] The second painting is the polyptych depicting the *Legend of St. Vincent Ferrer* in the church of San Pietro Martire, Naples.[66] This large panel, generally regarded as Colantonio's masterpiece, illustrates eleven scenes from St. Vincent's life and attests to Colantonio's relationship with the court – as does his access to Alfonso's Van Eyck – on the ground that the donor scene shows Isabella di Chiaromonte, Ferrante's first wife (who died in 1465), together with the young Alfonso, Duke of Calabria, and Eleonora in a setting that Pane identifies as the interior of the Cappella Palatina in Castelnuovo.[67] Finally, one scholar has suggested that Colantonio may have executed part of the well-known *Tavola Strozzi* (Plate 1), which provides us with the earliest known view of the topography of Naples.[68] In all, Colantonio stands at the head of the Neapolitan school and was fundamental for its stylistic development.

Though Naples itself failed to produce any other truly first-rate masters – by the time Antonello da Messina reached his artistic maturity, Sicily, his main place of activity, had been separated from the Neapolitan kingdom – it was the scene of a flourishing school of minor painters, who, following the lead of Colantonio, borrowed ideas and techniques not only from the art of Flanders but also from that of Catalonia–Valencia and thus developed what Van Marle has called an Hispano-Flemish style,[69] which, with its sharp realism, fastidious attention to detail, and lingering Gothic traditions, was an offshoot of the International Gothic so beloved of Alfonso.

Naples was also visited by a number of well-known foreign artists. In 1442, the Valencian Jaime Baço, called 'Jacomart' (c. 1410/17–1461), heeded Alfonso's summons to become the official court painter and two years later executed a panel (now lost) for the votive church of Santa Maria della Pace, which Alfonso had had constructed in order to commemorate his victory over the Angevins.[70] Jacomart, who remained at Naples – though with an interruption – at least until 1447, was

[64] Weiss, 'Jan van Eyck and the Italians', pp. 9–10; Pane, *Il Rinascimento*, I, 73. Only Bologna, *Napoli e le rotte mediterranee*, p. 62, questions the dependence of Colantonio's work on Van Eyck's, and rather unconvincingly at that.

[65] See especially Riccardo Filangieri, 'Les Origines de la peinture flamande à Naples au XVe siècle'; idem, 'La Peinture flamande à Naples pendant le quinzième siècle'; Castelfranchi Vegas, 'I rapporti Italia–Fiandra'; Van Marle, *The Development of the Italian Schools of Painting*, XV, 354ff.

[66] Reproductions appear in Pane, *Il Rinascimento*, I, Figs. 24–8.

[67] *Il Rinascimento*, I, 73ff. Doria, *Mostra del ritratto storico napoletano*, pp. 4–5, dates the work from circa 1460, two years after St. Vincent was canonized; see also Longhi, 'Una "Crocifissione" di Colantonio', p. 8.

[68] Causa, *L'arte nella Certosa di San Martino a Napoli*, p. 20, n. 17. The suggestion is dismissed by Pane, *Il Rinascimento*, I, 77, and Bologna, *Napoli e le rotte mediterranee*, pp. 195ff., who attributes the work to the Neapolitan painter Francesco Pagano.

[69] *The Development of the Italian Schools of Painting*, XV, 354ff.

[70] On Jacomart, see Post, *A History of Spanish Painting*, VI, 14–53; Bologna, *Napoli e le rotte mediterranee*, pp. 49–51 and *passim*. The church was destroyed by an earthquake in 1456.

Plate 1. Francesco Pagano (?): *Tavola Strozzi* (detail), left portion showing Castel dell'Ovo, Torre di San Vicenzo, Castelnuovo, and the Molo

Plate 2. Pisanello: Medal of Alfonso I the Magnanimous, 1449

instrumental in transmitting the style of the Catalonian–Valencian painters into southern Italy. Another official guest at the court was Pisanello, who was at Naples in 1448–1450.[71] And though he seems not to have left any paintings behind, he did execute three well-known medal portraits of Alfonso (Plate 2), which Seymour judges to be his finest works in that medium[72] and which reinforced the current of Roman classicism then present at Naples. Pisanello may also have played a role in the design of the Aragonese Arch (see below). Finally, the Venetian Antonio Solario, called 'lo Zingaro', was at Naples in 1495–1496

---

[71] Paccagnini, *Pisanello e il ciclo cavalleresco di Mantova*, pp. 243–44.

[72] Seymour, *Sculpture in Italy, 1400–1500*, p. 106. The medals have been reproduced many times: Paccagnini, *Pisanello e il ciclo cavalleresco*, Figs. 180–85; Pane, *Il Rinascimento*, I, Figs. 79–95, which include the sketches, and pp. 123–34 for an essay on them; Hill, *Italian Medals of the Renaissance*, I, 18, Nos. 41–43; Hersey, *The Aragonese Arch at Naples, 1443–1475*, Figs. 27–28; Pope-Hennessy, *The Portrait in the Renaissance*, p. 208. In addition to the medals of Alfonso, Pisanello struck one of Iñigo d'Avalos, the grand chamberlain of the court, and another of Pier Candido Decembrio, one of the resident humanists; these are reproduced in Paccagnini, *op. cit.*, Figs. 178–79, 186–87. Finally, there is also a medal of Alfonso by Mino da Fiesole; see Pane, *Il Rinascimento*, I, Fig. 97.

and perhaps began or at least planned his cycle of twenty frescoes on the *Life of St. Benedict* in the Chiostro del Platano of SS Severino e Sossio, a Benedictine monastery (today the seat of the Archivio de Stato) to which Alfonso II donated 15,000 ducats in June 1494 for construction and beautification.[73] The cycle represents the major work of its kind in Renaissance Naples.[74]

If Aragonese Naples failed to produce a major school of painting, it was certainly not owing to any lack of interest in the arts on the part of its rulers. Alfonso I was an avid collector of paintings – as he was of tapestries, illuminated manuscripts,[75] gems, cameos, antique coins, liturgical vestments and ornaments, and sundry curiosities from the Orient, all of which constituted a 'source of contentment and delight, not only to the senses, but to the spirit as well'[76] – and showed a decided preference for the art of the Flemish masters. Thus, he had among his treasures three paintings (now lost) by Jan van Eyck, whom he may actually have met in 1427, when the artist was in Valencia as part of a Burgundian embassy:[77] (1) a painting of St. George;[78] (2) the important 'Lomellini' triptych, which was probably purchased from Bartolomeo Facio's Genoese diplomatic colleague Battista Lomellini in 1444 and which, with its depiction of St. Jerome on one of its wings, proved extremely influential for Neapolitan painting:[79] and (3) an *Adoration of the Magi*. No doubt it was to one of these that Pontano was referring when he singled out a Van Eyck as being one of Alfonso's most cherished possessions.[80] In addition, Alfonso also owned tapestries designed by Rogier van der Weyden,[81] and on the occasion of Frederick III's visit to the court in 1452 ordered from Flanders a set of three tapestries with scenes from the story of Solomon and Sheba.[82]

The patronage of painting continued under Alfonso's successors, though seemingly with less refined taste: it was after all Ferrante who permitted Giotto's

---

[73] The dates of the cycle are a matter of dispute, and it seems that it was not completed until the second decade of the sixteenth century; see Pane, *Il Rinascimento*, II, 267–79 and Figs. 306–28; Hersey, *Alfonso II and the Artistic Renewal of Naples*, pp. 106–7 and Figs. 123–24. On Alfonso's donation to the monastery, see Jole Mazzoleni, *Il monastero benedettino dei SS Severino e Sossio*, p. 40.

[74] In closing this section on visiting painters, we may note that Bologna, *Napoli e le rotte mediterranee*, p. 67, conjectures that the French artist Jean Fouquet may have visited Naples circa 1444–1445.

[75] On Alfonso's collection of illuminated manuscripts and the Neapolitan school of miniaturists, see De Marinis, *La biblioteca dei re d'Aragona*, passim, and Putaturo Murano, *Miniature napoletane del Rinascimento*. For a very concise summary, see Diringer, *The Illuminated Book: Its History and Production*, pp. 356–60.

[76] Quoted after Driscoll, 'Alfonso of Aragon as a Patron of Art', p. 94; the original, from a letter to the Cardinal of Aquilea, appears in Croce, 'Una lettera inedita di Alfonso I d'Aragona'.

[77] Weiss, 'Jan van Eyck and the Italians', p. 9.

[78] *Ibid.*, pp. 11–12; Sanchis i Sivera, *Pintores medievales en Valencia*, pp. 69–70. The record of payment for the painting also records the purchase of four dulcimers.

[79] Baxandall, 'Bartholomaeus Facius on Painting', p. 102; Weiss, 'Jan van Eyck and the Italians', pp. 2–3, 9–10; idem, 'Some Van Eyckian Illuminations from Italy'. Van Eyck's depiction of St. Jerome spawned at least four works – in addition to Colantonio's – by artists either directly or indirectly associated with the Aragonese court; see the two articles by Weiss. All three Van Eycks are known only from references to them by Facio.

[80] *De magnificentia*, Book XIII; see the edition with Italian translation by Tateo, *Giovanni Pontano: I trattati delle virtù sociali*, pp. 117, 260. Tateo, p. 117, claims that Pontano's reference is to the *Adoration*, though there is nothing in the passage to indicate this.

[81] Baxandall, 'Bartholomaeus Facius on Painting', pp. 104–7; Nicolini, *L'arte napoletana*, pp. 162–63, 233–36.

[82] Hersey, *The Aragonese Arch at Naples*, p. 13.

frescoes in Castelnuovo to be painted over. But to an ever greater extent, beginning already in Alfonso's reign, it was the patronage of sculpture and architecture that came to the fore.

By far the two greatest artistic achievements in Aragonese Naples were, as Hersey points out,[83] the construction of the Triumphal Arch at the entrance to Castelnuovo and the ambitious, large-scale urban-renewal projects sponsored by Alfonso, Duke of Calabria. And such was the energy that the court committed to these works that Naples, not Rome, became the chief sculptural center south of Florence during the second half of the Quattrocento.[84]

It was Alfonso I's Triumphal Arch (Plate 3) that went up first. After a decade of planning, during which time Castelnuovo was being renovated,[85] the first phase of construction began in 1453, with the work continuing intermittently until the bronze doors, which commemorate Ferrante's victory over the Barons at the Battle of Troia in 1462, were set in place some quarter of a century later.[86] Unfortunately, much about the history of the Arch remains unclear, from the identity of the artist who was responsible for its overall design and sculptural program – among the chief candidates are Pietro da Milano, Francesco Laurana, Pisanello, Alberti, and even Alfonso himself[87] – to precisely which sculptured figures are the work of which artist. In this latter respect, music-lovers, at least, may take heart, for the one attribution about which all students of the Arch seem to agree is that of the royal musicians in the triumphal frieze (Plate 4) to Domenico Gagini.[88] The Arch itself is a monumental affair, full of iconographical and stylistic contradictions. Though its chief inspiration is clearly derived from the triumphal arches of Imperial Rome, the classical appearance of the Arch is countered by such elements as the round, medieval-looking Catalan towers that flank it,[89] the superimposition of one arch above another,[90] the contemporary-looking Virtues

---

[83] *Ibid.*, p. xiii.

[84] Seymour, *Sculpture in Italy*, p. 134.

[85] On the renovation of Castelnuovo, see Riccardo Filangieri, *Rassegna critica delle fonti per la storia de Castel Nuovo*, Vols. III and IV, and idem, *Castel Nuovo: Reggia angioina ed aragonese*.

[86] The Arch has given rise to an imposing body of literature. The most recent large-scale study is Hersey, *The Aragonese Arch at Naples*, which is particularly valuable for its bibliography. However, since Hersey is interested mainly in iconographical interpretation, the description of the Arch itself and the narrative describing its construction are frequently interrupted. For these aspects, the fundamental study is still Riccardo Filangieri, 'L'Arco di Trionfo di Alfonso d'Aragona'. Hersey's monograph also falls somewhat short with respect to its illustrations, which, though numerous, fail to make clear the visual–structural relationships between certain parts of the Arch. The reader dependent solely upon Hersey's illustrations would have difficulty visualizing the relationship between inner and outer arches on the lower level or that between the front of the Arch and its lateral sections, the latter relationship being especially important for the full scope of the triumphal frieze. The illustrations in both Filangieri, 'L'Arco di Trionfo', and Pane, *Il Rinascimento*, I, Figs. 147–81, are far superior in this respect.

[87] Pietro da Milano now seems to be favored; see Hersey, *op. cit.*, pp. 2, 34, 81.

[88] Among the other sculptors were Pere Joan and Guillermo Sagera from Catalonia, Andrea dall'Aquila, Isaia da Pisa, Guglielmo lo Monaco, and possibly Mino da Fiesole. Hersey, *op. cit.*, pp. 73–83, provides thumbnail biographies and bibliographies for each of the artists involved. On the special problem of Mino, see Pepe, 'Sul soggiorno napoletano di Mino da Fiesole'.

[89] We should note that the original design called for a classical-style free-standing arch in the center of the city; see Hersey, *op. cit.*, p. 21.

[90] The gaping void in the upper arch was originally intended to contain an equestrian statue, probably to have been commissioned from Donatello and similar in style to his Gattamalata at Padua; see Hersey, *op. cit.*, pp. 53–54.

Plate 3. Alfonso I's Triumphal Arch at the entrance to Castelnuovo

in the niches above the upper arch, and the juxtaposition of classical river gods and Alfonso's three patron saints (only one of which remains) on the chua that surmounts the entire monument. Yet these apparent instances of stylistic ambiguity or contradiction are explained both by the function of the Arch and by Alfonso's own artistic background and preferences; for the Arch is as much an entrance portal or gatehouse to Castelnuovo as it is a Roman-style triumphal

Plate 4. Domenico Gagini: The Royal Musicians (detail of Alfonso I's Triumphal Arch)

arch, while Alfonso was as much a product of Gothic Spain (as we will be reminded once again by the nature of his musical chapel) and medieval piety as he was of humanist, Renaissance Italy.[91] In all, the Arch, and especially the triumphal frieze, which represents Alfonso's entry into Naples on 26 February 1443 as a bearer of peace to a troubled kingdom, is monumental in its effect and stands today as the most impressive architectural–sculptural legacy of Aragonese Naples.

Whereas Alfonso I concentrated his resources about the Arch and Castelnuovo, his grandson, Alfonso, Duke of Calabria (Alfonso II), embarked upon a venture of artistic patronage of far broader dimensions. Beginning in the mid-1480s, and continuing until the French invasion a decade later, Alfonso set about to alter the face of Naples.[92] To be sure, some of the projects were more practical than aesthetic in character. Thus, in 1485, construction was begun on new walls (possibly designed by Alfonso himself) for the eastern edge of the city, while a similar project was begun in 1494 – though not completed until 1540 – for the western perimeter. Yet even such things as the walls were not built without an eye for beauty. The eastern walls were graced by Giuliano da Maiano's Porta Capuana – still the most beautiful entrance to the inner city – while for the western walls the architect's brother, Benedetto, began but never completed a sculptural project for the Porta Reale.[93]

Perhaps the high point of Alfonso's plan was the construction of the now-destroyed Poggioreale, designed by Giuliano da Maiano and completed by June 1489, when the 'villa-warming' took place. Alfonso intended Poggioreale as a country retreat to be used mainly for entertaining, and it was there that the royal family must have spent many an evening listening to music (see below, p. 102). Another of Giuliano da Maiano's projects was the smaller La Duchesca, built for Alfonso's wife, Ippolita Sforza – she died on 18 August 1488, before it was completed – in the gardens surrounding Castel Capuano, the Duke's official residence. Like Poggioreale, La Duchesca was eventually demolished. Finally, what would have been the grandest of the new structures seems never to have progressed far beyond the drawing board; this was Giuliano da Sangallo's design for the Palazzo dei Tribunali, intended to house part of the government bureaucracy. Had it been built, it would have been one of the largest civic structures of the fifteenth century.

That Alfonso entrusted the most important of his projects to the brothers Giuliano and Benedetto da Maiano and to Giuliano da Sangallo underscores the profound influence that Florence exerted on the Neapolitan renewal. And for the present-day visitor to Naples, this influence is best seen in a single monument, the church of Sant'Anna dei Lombardi – or, as it is more often called, Monteoliveto – with its three 'Tuscan chapels': (1) the Cappella Tolosa, possibly designed by Giuliano da Maiano and modeled after the Pazzi Chapel of Santa Croce; (2) the

---

[91] See Seymour, *Sculpture in Italy*, pp. 135–36, and the review of Hersey, *op. cit.*, by R. W. Lightbown, in *The Art Quarterly*, n.s., I (1978), 168–71.

[92] Our account is based on Hersey, *Alfonso II and the Artistic Renewal of Naples, passim*.

[93] See also Hersey, 'Alfonso II, Benedetto e Giuliano da Maiano e la Porta Reale'. On Giuliano's activities at Naples, see also Pèrcopo, 'Nuovi documenti su gli scrittori e gli artisti dei tempi aragonesi', pp. 575–79.

The Historical–Cultural Background 21

Plate 5. Domenico Gagini (?): Bust of Ferrante I (detail)

Cappella Piccolomini, again after plans by Giuliano and containing the tomb of Alfonso's half-sister, Maria Piccolomini, which was begun circa 1470 by Antonio Rosselino and completed by Benedetto da Maiano, its model being Rosselino's tomb for the Cardinal of Portugal in San Miniato; and (3) the Cappella Terranuova, with its *Annunciation* by Benedetto.[94] Thus, just as Petrarchism so heavily influenced the Neapolitan literary scene in the 1470s, so the genius of Tuscan architects and sculptors altered the very appearance of Naples in the decades that followed. The peace treaty of 1480 had opened the way for this heightened flow of Florentine artists, and Alfonso, though perhaps most comfortable in his more accustomed role of soldier, was artistically sensitive enough to exploit it. (Only in music, it seems, did the influence flow primarily in the other direction, from Naples to Florence.)

There remains one final aspect of artistic patronage, one in which a number of masterpieces were produced: portrait sculpture. To begin with – Pisanello's medals of Alfonso I have already been cited (see Plate 2) – there are the inscribed medallions with portraits of Ferrante by Girolamo Liparolo, the royal engraver of seals;[95] these are especially valuable in that they provide a measure against which one may compare possible portraits of the king that are not inscribed. And it is on the basis of such a comparison that Hersey has identified a magnificent bust of Ferrante in the Louvre (Plate 5). Far more controversial is Hersey's identification of a life-size bronze bust by the Modenese sculptor Guido Mazzoni that is housed in the Museo di Capodimonte, long thought to be a portrait of Ferrante: Hersey

[94] See Pane, *Il Rinascimento*, I, 229–44, and Figs. 237–77; Hersey, *Alfonso II and the Artistic Renewal of Naples*, pp. 109–18, and Figs. 128–53.

[95] Hersey, *op. cit.*, p. 27, and Figs. 25–27. Portrait sculpture is discussed by Hersey on pp. 27–43.

Plate 6. Guido Mazzoni: Bust of Alfonso II as Duke of Calabria, c. 1489–92

makes a convincing case for identifying it as a portrait of Alfonso II (Plate 6).[96] Another Neapolitan work by Mazzoni, dating from 1492–1494, is the intense, almost Baroque terracotta *Lamentation* in the Cappella del Sepolcro of Monteoliveto; here, an agonizing, spiritually defeated Alfonso II is portrayed as Joseph of Arimathea, while other members of the royal family appear around him.[97] Finally, there is the series of magnificent busts that Francesco Laurana – who had worked on the Triumphal Arch – made of three of Alfonso's female relations: Ippolita Sforza, his wife; Beatrice, his sister; and Isabella, his daughter.[98] Though far more intimate than the portraits of the male members of the dynasty, they were not executed without a thought to political motivations – both Hersey and Valentiner associate at least some of them with problems surrounding royal marriages – and thus served in their own way to glorify the power and virtue of Aragonese Naples.

[96] Hersey originally made the identification in 'Alfonso II, Benedetto e Giuliano da Maiano e la Porta Reale', p. 86. The vitriolic letter that it called forth from the well-known Neapolitan art historian Ottavio Morisani is probably best dismissed as an emotional display of scholarly chauvinism; see *Napoli nobilissima*, Ser. III, Vol. IV, p. 221.

[97] Hersey, *Alfonso II and the Artistic Renewal of Naples*, pp. 118–24, Figs. 169–74. Mazzoni also created a *Lamentation* for Ercole I d'Este in which the duke is portrayed as Joseph of Arimathea, and his wife, Eleonora d'Aragona, as Mary the wife of Cleophas.

[98] Hersey, *op. cit.*, pp. 27–43; Valentiner, 'Laurana's Portrait Busts of Women'.

CHAPTER II

The Royal Chapel

An Overview of its Development

If Alfonso I put Naples in the forefront of the Italian cultural scene in terms of the literary accomplishments of his court, he at least began to do the same in the field of music, collecting singers, instrumentalists, and, though to a lesser extent, composers as assiduously as he did humanists. And though the personnel of the royal chapel – whether under Alfonso or Ferrante – never matched that of the star-studded cast assembled by Galeazzo Maria Sforza at Milan in the mid-1470s,[1] the Neapolitan chapel must nevertheless be considered one of the major musical establishments of the period, with respect both to its size and – if we interpret the testimony correctly – to its quality.

Although there is evidence to show that Alfonso was accompanied by his chapel on his first expedition to Italy in 1420[2] and that he may have restructured or at least enlarged it sometime during his first stay at Naples,[3] and though there are a few scattered notices about members of the chapel in the late 1430s,[4] it is only

---

[1] For the Milanese rosters, see Sartori, 'Josquin Des Prés cantore del Duomo di Milano (1459–1472)', pp. 64–66.

[2] On 19 April 1420, Alfonso wrote to his protonotary Pere Raner from Viñalaroc: 'com nos vullam que ls capellans, xantres e scolans de nostra capella nos seguesquen en lo viatge per nos . . .'; see Gómez Muntané, *La Música en la Casa Real catalano-aragonesa*, I, 106 and 214, No. 271, where the letter is given in full. Just a few weeks later, on 23 May, Alfonso wrote to Pere Beger, his 'battle general' of Catalonia, from Mallorca: 'com nos per servir de la nostra capella haiam de gran necessari en Philippot, tenorista nostra . . .' ibid., p. 214, No. 272); other such letters could be cited. On Alfonso's chapel at Barcelona and on the singers and instrumentalists who accompanied him on his Italian campaigns of the early 1420s and early 1430s, see, in addition to Gómez Muntané, a number of important studies by Anglés: 'La Música en la Corte del Rey Don Alfonso V de Aragón'; 'La Música en la Corte Real de Aragón y de Nápoles durante el Reinado de Alfonso V el Magnánimo'; *La Música en la Corte de los Reyes Católicos*, I: *Polifonia religiosa*; 'Alfonso V d'Aragona, mecenate della musica ed il suo ménestrel Jean Boisard'; see also Baldelló 'La Música en la Casa de los Reyes de Aragón'. All of these studies draw almost exclusively on documents housed at the Archivo de la Corona de Aragón at Barcelona.

[3] On 9 March 1423, Alfonso expressed his desire to add three singers, then in Rome, to his chapel: 'Nos per fornir la nostra capella de bons xantres o cantors . . . scrivem de present an Guillaum Marti, Philipoto Foliot e Johan lo Coch, xantres en cort romana . . . pregnant los que vinguen de present en nostre servey.' The letter was written from Castelnuovo; see Gómez Muntané, *La Música en la Casa Real catalano-aragonesa*, p. 216, No. 275.

[4] We may cite the following: 28 March (?) 1437 – the singer Marsen received 16 ducats to buy a horse so that he could accompany the king (ASN, TAF, Vol. II, fol. 3ʳ); 30 October 1437 – both Guillem Blanch and Pietro de Mora are recorded as assistants to the chapel master (see Minieri Riccio, 'Alcuni fatti di Alfonso I di

from 1441 that the documents concerning the chapel become numerous enough and begin to show enough continuity with those from succeeding years to provide even a partial picture of the chapel as it was just shortly before Alfonso's final victory over the Angevins. The information for 1441 comes from a fragmentary payroll register – it covers only parts of January–February and September–December – that lists the expenses accrued by the court as Alfonso moved from one temporary encampment to another.[5] Altogether there are twelve separate notices that cite seven members of the chapel either individually or in groups of two or three. Among those who were already with Alfonso in the late 1430s (see note 4 above) are Mateu Tabaria,[6] Gonsalvo de Cordova[7] (who, unless he had a namesake from the same city, would serve the Aragonese court until at least 1481), and Domenic Exarch (who continued in the post of 'locumtenens' or 'sots capella maior').[8] The four singers who are apparently new to the chapel are Ffarrando,[9] Miguel Nadal,[10] Phelip Romeu,[11] and, most notably, the composer Pere Oriola, formerly thought to have entered the chapel only in 1444.[12]

The notices leave a number of questions unresolved. Could the fragmentary nature of the register, the references to musicians either individually or at most in groups of two or three (rather than to the entire group *en bloc*), and the failure to account for a 'capella maior' mean that we are dealing either with payments to individuals rather than to members of a chapel *per se* or at least with something less than the chapel in its entirety? The answer, though inconclusive, is 'Not necessarily'. First, the notices show that the payments were recorded at a number of different locations, some of which – Venafro and Miniano, for instance – served as campsites for no more than five and four days respectively. Perhaps, then, as Alfonso moved from one camp to another, he saw fit to take no more than part of

---

Aragona dal 15 Aprile 1437 al 31 di maggio 1458', p. 8); 9 November 1437 – Mateu Tabaria and Gonsalvo de Cordova each received 15 ducats for horses (ASN, TAF, Vol. II/1, fol. 1r); 20 May 1439 – the Cistercian Domenic Exarch is listed as 'locumtenens' of the chapel (Minieri Riccio, p. 21); 27 June 1439 – the chaplain Bartolomeo di Sicilia received some black Mallorcan material for his vestments (Minieri Riccio, p. 22).

[5] ASN, TAF, Vol. VI; the entire fragment – together with three others – is published in Jole Mazzoleni, 'Frammenti di cedole della tesoreria di Alfonso I (1437–1454)', *Fonti aragonesi*, I, 108–38. In the notes that follow, I cite both the folio of the original document and – in parentheses – the pages in Mazzoleni.

[6] 21 December: fol. 51^v (p. 124).

[7] 27 December: fol. 54^v (p. 128).

[8] 17 January: fol. 56^r (p. 130); 13 November: fol. 46^v (pp. 118–19); 21 November: fol. 47^r (p. 119); 3 December: fol. 48^r (p. 120); 12 December: fol. 50^v (p. 124). In addition, there is an entry for him for 1441 (with no precise date) in ASN, TAF, Vol. Ia, fol. 7^v; this volume, which bears the title 'Esiti delle cedole di cassa militare dal 1430 al 1597', is a fragmentary onomastic index to the now-lost account books. Although it lacks precise dates, it cites the year and sometimes sets boundaries within the year by naming the 'outside' months; at times it also specifies the person's position. Ryder, *The Kingdom of Naples*, pp. 84–85, following Faraglia, *Storia della lotta*, p. 255, n. 1, appears to be wrong in stating that Exarch had risen to the position of chapel master by November 1441. He is still listed as the 'loctinent de capella maior' on 3 and 12 December of that year (ASN, TAF, Vol. VI, fols. 48^r and 50^v).

[9] 17 January: fol. 57^r (p. 131).

[10] 10 January: fol. 56^r (p. 130); 21 November: fol. 47^r (p. 119); 17 December: fol. 50^v (p. 124); 27 December: fol. 54^r (p. 128).

[11] As in n. 10 above.

[12] As in n. 10, references for 21 November and 17 December. Detailed accounts of – and the documentation for – the activities of the composers in the chapel appear in Chap. III.

his chapel to any one location or even leave his singers behind altogether. In addition, though no single entry ever lists more than three singers, the chapel was not quite so splintered as might seem at first glance. Thus, while Alfonso was at Montesarchio from 3 to 17 January, he was eventually joined by at least four of the seven members of the chapel, while the same number were with him at Presencano during the final eleven days of December. And finally, the register does not necessarily account for less than the entire chapel on the ground that there are no payments to the 'capella maior'. The post of chapel master to the King of Aragon was traditionally held by the abbot of the Cistercian monastery of Santa Creus. When it became apparent that Alfonso was destined to remain in Italy, the abbot chose to stay in Spain and deputized Domenic Exarch as his 'locumtenens'.[13] Exarch, then, though nominally the assistant to the abbot, was in fact the highest-ranking member of the chapel as it was then constituted in Italy. In all, with Alfonso still at war and frequently on the move, the seven men for whom there is documentation in 1441 may well have represented the full force of the chapel, and as such would have approximated the number of singers that Alfonso had previously maintained at Barcelona.[14]

A second problem for which there is no conclusive answer concerns the references to the singers Miguel Nadal, Phelip Romeu, and Pere Oriola. Although they are referred to either as 'xandres' or 'xandres del dit senyor' – that is, singers of the king – in the entries for 10 January, 21 November, and 27 December, the record of payment for 17 December lists them as singers of 'don Fferrando' – in other words, of the eighteen-year-old Ferrante, then Duke of Calabria, who had arrived in Italy in 1438. And though Ferrante maintained a small retinue of his own,[15] there is no evidence that it consisted of a full-scale chapel, complete with singers of polyphony. It seems unlikely, therefore, that the three singers were officially part of Ferrante's household, especially since Romeu and Nadal had seemingly been in Alfonso's chapel for the previous eleven months and would be so listed once again in just ten days. Rather, it is more plausible that Alfonso, who was at Miniano – where the payment is recorded – for only four days at the very most (and this is the only entry made there), had gone there without his chapel, leaving the singers in the temporary charge of the young duke. Perhaps the payment was ordered at that time simply because the three singers had yet to receive their salaries that month.

A third question concerns the payments themselves. Whereas Nadal, Romeu, and Oriola seem always to be paid strictly on a salaried basis, that is, 'per lur provisio' or 'en acorriment de lur quitacio' (10 January, 21 November, and 17 and 27 December), three other members of the chapel – though sometimes paid on precisely the same days – are compensated only for having performed special services or as reimbursement for extraordinary expenses. Thus Exarch is paid specifically for having said Mass and for having made offerings on behalf of the

[13] Ryder, *The Kingdom of Naples*, p. 83.
[14] See Gómez Muntané, *La Música en la Casa Real catalano-aragonesa*, pp. 104–8.
[15] Pontieri, *Ferrante d'Aragona*, pp. 33–34; see also Ferrante, *Fonti aragonesi*, VIII, 32–33.

king; Mateu Tabaria and Ffarrando are reimbursed 'per compararsen calsses' (21 November) and 'per lo loguer de una bestia' (17 January) respectively; and Gonsalvo de Cordova was simply paid 'graciosament' on 27 December. The reason for what seems from the register to be a two-tier system remains unclear. Nor is it clear why Miguel Nadal and Phelip Romeu draw three ducats each in January, but only two in December (Oriola gets but one ducat that month) and just one in November (Oriola gets the same).[16] However, since the sum of three ducats received by Gonsalvo de Cordova in December matches that which had been paid to Nadal and Romeu in January, perhaps we may hazard that three ducats per month was their normal salary, with the smaller sums representing adjustments of one type or another. As we shall see, a monthly salary of three ducats will not be at all out of line with the earnings of those members of the chapel who were something less than superstars.

For 1442–1443, with the Aragonese Kingdom of Naples now a political reality, documentation is exceedingly sparse. Mateu Tabaria is accounted for once again from October 1442 to July 1443,[17] as is, for precisely the same period, Domenic Exarch, who has now been promoted to the rank of chapel master.[18] Yet another member of the chapel for whom there is documentation in these years is Johanne Dragonexo, who is listed as a 'scolà' of the chapel in April 1443, when he received 25 ducats in order to purchase a breviary.[19] His presence shows that Alfonso continued at Naples the Aragonese tradition of including boys in the chapel. Finally, there are notices concerning the chapel organists, Perinetto da Venezia and Joan Corbató. Perinetto, whose service at the court would extend well into the reign of Ferrante I, is mentioned on 24 June (his salary is listed at 120 ducats per annum) and 9 October, when he is listed together with the northern – perhaps Frisian – organ-builder *maestro* Rodolfo.[20] Corbató is recorded for the first time on

---

[16] The documentation for each of these three months seems equally complete.

[17] ASN, TAF, Vol. Ia, fol. 17ᵛ.

[18] ASN, TAF, Vol. Ia, fol. 20ᵛ.

[19] See De Marinis, *La biblioteca napoletana*, II, 227.

[20] The identification of Perinetto is at least somewhat elusive, and the Aragonese court may have had connections with two – or even three – musicians of this name. There is little doubt that the Perinetto of whom we speak here – and for whom there are records of his activity in Alfonso's chapel on at least the following dates: 24 June and 9 October 1443, 18 May 1450, 27 January 1451, and 8 November 1455 (Minieri Riccio, 'Alcuni fatti di Alfonso I', pp. 241–43, 256, 411–12, 439) – is the 'messer Perinetto Torsel orghanista' who is recorded at the court from January through July of 1473 and then again in February and May of 1476, when he was still earning 120 ducats per year. (The notices come from the Archivio di Stato, Florence, Archivio Strozzi, Ser. V, Vols. 27 and 32, these being registers of the bank that Filippo il Vecchio and Lorenzo Strozzi ran at Naples. Vol. 27 is published by Leone, *Il Giornale di banco Strozzi*. My own references to these registers are drawn from the recent study by Galiano, 'Nuove fonti per la storia musicale napoletana in età aragonese', p. 2 and nn. 5–9.) Galiano points out that the surname 'Torsel' is typically Venetian. (I am grateful to Professor Bianconi, who sent me the proofs of Galiano's article prior to its publication, for the opportunity to incorporate the findings of this important study.)

The Perinetto Torsel 'da Venezia' just cited might also be identified with the organist Perrinet Pronostrau (also cited as Perrinet Prebostel) who served Alfonso during the period 1423–1431; see Gómez Muntané, *La Música en la Casa Real catalano-aragonesa*, pp. 108–11, and Anglés, 'La Música en la Corte Real de Aragón y de Nápoles', pp. 982ff (Anglés's treatment of Pronostrau–Prebostel is often confused). Certainly, such an identification is in line with the migration of other of Alfonso's musicians and singers from Spain to

9 April,[21] and the two organists would serve together in Alfonso's chapel for at least the next twenty years (Corbató would leave in 1463), the employment of two organists reflecting yet another custom that had been established at Barcelona.[22]

It is obvious that the documentation for these years fails to reflect the true size of the chapel. First, the number of singers accounted for is actually smaller than it was in 1441, when the political situation was still unsettled; second, the known membership will increase about fivefold (not counting the organists) in 1444, and a steady increase makes more sense under the circumstances than does a sudden one; third, it is known that on 14 May 1443 Exarch countersigned privileges concerning the nomination of royal chaplains;[23] and finally, it is, as will be seen, reasonable to presume that at least Gonsalvo de Cordova, Pere Oriola, and Ffarrando – all of whom will be on the roster of 1444 – continued their service during these years, while some of the singers now recorded for the first time in 1444 had arrived at Naples a year or so earlier. In all, the chapel must have continued to grow during these two years: compelling evidence can be seen in the documented presence of two organists and boys, and in the filling of the position of chapel master by Exarch (in contrast to its previously having been held in absentia by the abbot of Santa Creus).

Given Exarch's position as the highest-ranking member of Alfonso's chapel, his career at Naples deserves attention, especially since it also exemplifies the way in which Alfonso treated the position of chapel master and furthered the careers of his favorite chaplain–singers. A Cistercian from the monastery of Santa Creus, Exarch came to Italy no later than 1439, when, as we have seen, he was 'locumtenens' of the chapel. During the final years of the war, he accompanied Alfonso from one place to another, often being paid 'per fer dir certes misses'.[24]

Naples. Nor does the identification raise a problem in that it indicates that prior to his journey from Spain to Naples he had traveled in precisely the opposite direction. For remarks on an Italian musician who served Alfonso in Spain – Xrispofol de Sent Steve, who is also referred to as being 'de Pisa' or 'fiorentino' – see Gómez Muntané, op. cit., pp. 108–9.

Finally, the identification of Perinetto with the 'Messer Pernecto, musico del Signor Re' who was at Ferrante's court in 1479 (Van der Straeten, La Musique aux Pays-Bas avant le XIXe siècle, IV, 31) and during the 1480s (Pèrcopo, Barzellette napoletane del Quattrocento, p. 11) is more difficult to sustain, since the designation 'musico' generally refers to the members of the secular musical establishment, whereas our Perinetto Torsel seems always to have been with the chapel (but see below the remarks about Gonsalvo de Cordova) and such an indentification would give Perinetto a career as a performing musician of some seventy-seven years (from circa 1423 to circa 1490).

On maestro Rodolfo, see also Riccardo Filangieri, Rassegna critica delle fonti per la storia di Castel Nuovo, III, 47. Rodolfo may well be identical with the organ-builder Rodolfo de Alemania recorded at Mantua on 9 July 1435, when he obtained a privilege to build organs for six years; see Bertolotti, Musici alla corte dei Gonzaga in Mantova, p. 7. He may also be identical with the Rodolfo di Frisia recorded at Ferrara in 1475; see Valdrighi, 'Cappelle, concerti e musiche di casa d'Este', p. 421.

[21] Minieri Riccio, 'Alcuni fatti di Alfonso I', p. 235; Gaetano Filangieri, Documenti, V, 139. Both scholars cite him as Giovanni Corbato; however, the spelling of his name in a letter of 1463 – at which time he was still at Naples – shows that he was a Catalan. Minieri Riccio's habit of italianizing the names of Spaniards will, as we shall see, cause more than a little confusion.

[22] Gómez Muntané, La Música en la Casa Real catalano-aragonesa, p. 109.

[23] Ryder, The Kingdom of Naples, p. 86.

[24] For instance, on 17 January 1441 (ASN, TAF, Vol. VI, fol. 56^r).

Shortly after the conquest of Naples, Exarch was given two chaplaincies in the Duomo (both of which he resigned in 1447),[25] and among his duties there was the responsibility of arranging masses for the past kings of Aragon. It was probably at about the same time – by October 1442 at the latest – that he rose to the rank of chapel master[26] – a post, however, that he would soon come to share with another Cistercian, Jaume Albarells.[27] And though it is not possible to define the precise manner in which Exarch and Albarells may have divided the responsibilities, that Exarch at least sometimes had charge of the discipline and education – presumably in part musical – of the boys in the chapel, whereas Albarells would in 1454 conduct a visitation of the royal churches in Calabria and otherwise look after other matters pertaining to churches and monasteries, might indicate that it was Exarch who supervised matters musical, while Albarells assumed responsibilities of a more administrative–ecclesiastical nature.[28] Whatever the exact division of labor may have been, Exarch was at least sometimes entrusted with the care of the liturgical books, vestments, reliquaries, and the complete furnishings of the chapel – on which Alfonso spent lavishly[29] – for in October 1444 he was paid to look after the transport of these items when the chapel accompanied Alfonso on one of his numerous excursions from the capital.[30]

In 1444 Alfonso tried to have Exarch appointed almoner of the monastery of Ripoll 'in commendam', while in 1445 the king was forced to use his 'juspatronatum' when Eugene IV denied Exarch another benefice that Alfonso had requested for him. Finally, Exarch capped his ecclesiastical career in 1451, when he became Bishop of Agrigento, a post that he held until his death in 1471. The bishopric, however, was 'in administrationem', and, as was typical of bishops in the Kingdom of Naples, Exarch did not reside in his see.[31] Rather, he remained in Naples, where he lived at the church of Santa Maria Incoronata, near Castelnuovo.[32]

---

[25] From here, the facts concerning Exarch's career are taken from Ryder, *The Kingdom of Naples*, p. 85.

[26] ASN, TAF, Vol. Ia, fol. 20ᵛ. However, he is once again referred to as 'locumentenent' in documents of October 1444 and October 1446; see De Marinis, *La biblioteca napoletana*, II, 229.

[27] Many of the important positions in the royal household were so shared.

[28] With respect to Albarells, see Alfonso's letters of 19 and 23 January 1452 printed in Jole Mazzoleni, *Il 'Codice Chigi'*, pp. 227–29, which show Albarells involved in matters having to do with the furnishings of a Calabrian monastery.

[29] For example, on 28 November 1441, Alfonso paid a goldsmith in Gaeta 100 ducats for a 'portapace' and two portable candelabras for the chapel; on 9 March 1442, the same smith was paid 80 ducats for an ampulla and two more candelabras (Minieri Riccio, 'Alcuni fatti di Alfonso I', pp. 28, 31). On the liturgical books for the chapel, see Chap. VI below.

[30] Minieri Riccio, 'Alcuni fatti di Alfonso I', p. 246; De Marinis, *La biblioteca napoletana*, II, 229.

[31] On this custom, see Hay, *The Church in Italy in the Fifteenth Century*, pp. 11, 20. We might note that, in general, incomes from episcopal sees were lower in Italy than in (say) France or England, and that in Italy those in the south were the poorest of all (Hay, pp. 10–11).

[32] In addition to Ryder, *The Kingdom of Naples*, p. 85, see Jole Mazzoleni, *Il 'Codice Chigi'*, pp. 331–32, where there is a letter of 5 June 1452 to the monks of the nearby monastery of San Martino, who ran the church and wanted Exarch out. Alfonso's answer: 'pertanto attento la comodita che nuy havimo delo dicto nostro cappellano maiore per la propinquita dela stantia al nostro castellonovo che nocte e iorno quando lo havimo mestieri, subito lo havimo et si stassi in altro loco non lo porriamo havere cussi presto et comodamente'.

The earliest known document to provide a roster of what is presumably the entire personnel of the chapel dates from 26 October 1444 and names the chaplain–singers in the course of enumerating the expenses – 370 ducats – for the purchase of nineteen horses and a mule that the members of the chapel would need in order to follow Alfonso when he traveled outside Naples.[33] Altogether, the notice provides us with fifteen names, while another document, from 2 October, states that the chapel also enjoyed the services of five boys.[34] The members of the chapel (not including the organists, who are not named in this document) in October 1444 were:[35]

> Fra Jaume Albarells
> Messer Fferrando Suval
> Messer Gonsalvo Garzia
> Messer Lambert
> Frate Antonio
> Messer Sancio Garzia
> Pere Oriola
> Messer Pascale
> Jaume/Jaime Santa
> Gabriele Alegre
> Giovanni Fenice
> Jaume/Jaime Sanya
> Bartomeu Figueras
> Fra Domenic Exarch – listed as 'locumtenens'
> Jaume Borbó – listed as 'master of the boys'

The roster warrants some comment. Since Oriola is the only member of the chapel who is known to have been a composer – he would apparently remain the only one until the arrival of Cornago a decade later – he must, at least from a purely musical point of view, be judged the most notable among Alfonso's singers. Perhaps next in that respect is Jaume Borbó, who still retained the post of 'maestro di canto' on 27 February 1451[36] and must have served temporarily as chapel master in 1450, for he is so designated in a notarial document of 27 August of that year.[37] In addition, Borbó was also active as a theorist and has left us two treatises, a fragmentary work on proportions and the *Illuminator* of 1453, which, however, is more concerned with rhetoric and poetics than it is with music.[38]

As for the other members of the chapel, we may risk some identifications: (1)

---

[33] The roster appears in Minieri Riccio, 'Alcuni fatti di Alfonso I', pp. 245–46, who, however, fails to give the precise date in October; it is supplied by Gaetano Filangieri, *Documenti*, V, 62.

[34] Minieri Riccio, 'Alcuni fatti di Alfonso I', p. 245.

[35] As stated in n. 21 above, Minieri Riccio habitually gives all names in their Italian forms, something that the original documents are rather unlikely to have done, especially during Alfonso's reign, when (as noted in Chap. I) the normal language of the treasury was Catalan.

Where the chaplain–singer seems beyond doubt to have been a Spaniard, usually Catalan or Valencian, I have restored his name to its probable Hispanic form (see Chap. IV). I have retained Minieri Riccio's 'Messer', though the original document may have offered 'mossen'.

[36] Minieri Riccio, *op. cit.*, 411.

[37] Gaetano Filangieri, *Documenti*, V, 44.

[38] On the treatises, see Gallo, 'Musica, poetica e retorica nel Quattrocento: L'*Illuminator* di Giacomo Borbo'.

Fferrando Suval is probably the Ffarrando who was with Alfonso in 1441; (2) Gonsalvo Garzia must certainly be the ever-present Gonsalvo de Cordova; and (3) Messer Lambert can no doubt be identified with the singer Lambert Azemar who had served in Alfonso's chapel in 1431 at Barcelona and then followed him to Messina and Ischia in 1432–1433.[39] While it is likely that Fferrando Suval and Gonsalvo de Cordova were with the chapel for the entire period 1441–1444, Lambert probably returned to Spain after the second Italian expedition and rejoined the king only after Naples was safely in Aragonese hands.

The roster also raises a question about the position of chapel master. What is one to make of Albarells's being listed first and Exarch's designation of 'locumtenens' after he had been recorded as chapel master for the period October 1442–July 1443? What may have happened is that when Albarells first came to Naples – and the roster of 26 October is the earliest notice for him – it was he who assumed the post of chapel master, with Exarch being temporarily demoted, and that only later – by 19 June 1445, when Exarch is once again listed as chapel master[40] – did Alfonso decide to have the two men share the responsibilities of the position.

Finally, one cannot help noticing that the great majority – no fewer than twelve of fifteen, and perhaps even all (see note 35) – of the members of the chapel are Spaniards, mainly, though not exclusively, subjects of the Crown of Aragon. Although the Aragonese court of Naples was quick to assume a somewhat international or at least Spanish–Italian character in terms of the poets, artists, and humanists who enjoyed its patronage, it was much slower to do so as regards its musicians. In the chapel – as in the governmental bureaucracy and the royal household, of which the chapel was a part – Spaniards would remain dominant throughout Alfonso's reign, and thus would always give his musical establishment a somewhat provincial tinge.

The second half of the 1440s has left us little documentation, and there are only a few new names that enter the scene; among them are Fra Giordi and Fra Ruberto, both of whom are paid on 13 December 1448 for services rendered during the preceding month.[41] The notices are especially interesting in that they record not only their salaries, but also the 'payroll tax' that was deducted. The entry for Fra Giordi reads as follows: 'A fra Giordi dela capella del Senyor Rey per la provisio sua del ppassat mes de novembre et son acompliment de vi ducats la resta per lo elatge . . . V d iii tr xvi.' Fra Ruberto was paid the same, 'per la dita raho'. In other words, though the two men earned six ducats per month, they actually received only 5 ducats-3 tarì-16 grani, the difference – 1 tareno-4 grani – having

---

[39] See Gómez Muntané, *La Música en la Casa Real catalano-aragonesa*, pp. 108, 220; Anglés, 'La Música en la Corte Real de Aragón y de Nápoles', p. 1013.

[40] Ryder, *The Kingdom of Naples*, p. 85.

[41] ASN, TAF, Vol. XIII, fol. 451ʳ. One can gain some idea of the fragmentary state of the documentation from the following statistics. As it now stands, this volume contains four references to musicians or other matters musical; yet an index drawn up before the dismantling of the volume, and now covering its final sixteen folios, includes eleven references to the 'capella del S.R.' and twenty-one to 'Musiche', etc., all of which appeared on folios that are now missing.

been deducted for the 'elagio' or 4 percent (approximately) tax to which all salaries were subject.[42]

Another figure cited for the first time in 1448 is Berthomeo Perez, a 'scolà' of the chapel, who was given 4 ducats-2 tarì on 29 December for offerings that he had made in the king's name on Christmas and the two days following.[43] Although nothing else is known about Giordi, Ruberto, or the young Perez, perhaps we may speculate that they were among the personnel recruited by Jaume Torres – chaplain, 'ajudant de cambre', and eventually custodian of the library (from 1451) – who went to Valencia in the Autumn of 1446 in order to find new singers for the chapel.[44]

One final activity concerning the chapel in the 1440s is the construction of organs. We have already seen that the chapel employed two organists – Joan Corbató and Perinetto Torsel (da Venezia), whose service may be presumed to have been continuous – and that the organ-builder Rodolfo was at the court in 1443. More significant, though, is the arrival at Naples of the Valencian Jacme Gil, whose association with Alfonso goes back at least to August 1420, when Alfonso had him build an organ for the chapel at Barcelona.[45] Just when Gil arrived is not known, but it was after 10 June 1444, when a letter was addressed to him in Valencia: 'En Juame Gil. Nos havem mester gran merce aci de vos en nostre servey . . .'[46] Like another builder of organs at the court some half century later, Giovanni Donadio di Mormanno,[47] Gil was both an organ-builder and an architect, for from June 1451 to May 1456 a Jacme Gil is cited as 'master of the works' – 'havent carrech dela obra' – of Castelnuovo, which was still undergoing renovations.[48] It seems unlikely that it is a simple coincidence of names. Alfonso's love for the organ would lead him to spend lavishly not only for their construction, but also for their decoration; and the sum of 25 ducats-3 tarì-18 grani spent on 30 December 1448 for 'los pintors que pinte los orguens dela cappela del Senyor Rey'[49] was but one modest outlay.

The next year for which there is ample documentation for the chapel is 1451, the most important notice being a complete roster dated 27 February that contains the names of twenty-one singers:[50]

---

[42] See Ryder, *The Kingdom of Naples*, p. 290. On the relative worth of a salary of six ducats per month, see the discussion of Cornago's career in Chap. III below.

[43] ASN, TAF, Vol. XIII, fol. 457v.

[44] Sanchis i Sivera, *Dietari del capellá d'Anfos el Magnànim*, p. xvii, nn. 1–2. For the letter of introduction that Alfonso sent ahead for the 'battle general' of Valencia, see Baldelló, 'La Música en la Casa de los Reyes de Aragón', p. 39.

[45] Anglés, 'La Música en la Corte del Rey Don Alfonso V de Aragón', p. 376; idem, 'Alfonso V d'Aragona, mecenate della musica', p. 767; Baldelló, *op. cit.*, p. 49; on the nature of the organ, see the discussion of Ycart's *Magníficat* in Chap. VII, p. 136 below.

[46] Anglés, 'La Música en la Corte Real de Aragón y de Nápoles', p. 1021.

[47] On Mormanno, see Ceci, 'Una famiglia di architetti napoletani del Rinascimento: I Mormanno', and Chap. V below.

[48] On Gil's activities in connection with Castelnuovo, see Riccardo Filangieri, *Rassegna critica delle fonti per la storia di Castel Nuovo*, II, 17–18; Hersey, *The Aragonese Arch at Naples*, 66–67.

[49] ASN, TAF, Vol. III, fol. 450r.

[50] Minieri Riccio, 'Alcuni fatti di Alfonso I', pp. 411–12; I follow the same procedure as for the roster of 1444 with respect to the names (see n. 35 above), usually accepting the hispanizations of Anglés, 'La Musica en la Corte Real de Aragón y de Nápoles', p. 1022.

Pirardo Taxamor – listed as tenor
Taxmet de Sancto Paolo – listed as tenor
Jaume Borbó – listed as 'maestro di canto'
Pere Martí
Joan Loret
Antonio Ponte (or, as a Catalan: Antoni Pont)
Blas Romero
Joan Soler
Luis Navarro
Joan Borbó
Antoni Dornis
Joan Trirades
Benet Miró
Joanet Rabaça
Genis Camptins
Joan Steve
Pere Regades
Matteo Ferrero (or, as a Catalan: Mateu Ferrer, and if so possibly a tenor: see Chap. IV)
Giacomo di Capua
Salvatore di Capua
Matteo di Capua

Add to this list the two co-chapel masters, Exarch and Albarells, and the singer Jaume Ynnya – documentation for all of whom is available for November[51] — and it is possible that at various times during the year the chapel had as many as twenty-four adult singers plus an undetermined number of boys and the organists Perinetto and Corbató, both of whom are named at the end of the above roster.

One can best appreciate the size of Alfonso's chapel by comparing its forces with those of similar institutions of the same period. Among the chapels of the great cathedrals of Italy, only that of St. Peter's in Rome, with eighteen singers in 1451,[52] was comparable in size. In 1459, the Duomo at Milan (the court chapel had not yet been formed) employed but seven adult singers, a number that was as large as most church chapels ever had until the mid-1470s.[53] Among the Italian secular courts of the time, only Ferrara could claim a noteworthy chapel, employing eleven singers in 1450, the year of Leonello d'Este's death.[54] Outside Italy, the court of Savoy retained ten singers in 1449, but averaged between fourteen and eighteen after 1450, reaching a high of twenty-three in 1460–1461.[55] The Burgundian chapel of Philip the Good, which maintained a roster of twenty-one singers from 1439 to 1467,[56] matched Alfonso's in size, while only

---

[51] See Minieri Riccio, *op. cit.*, p. 413; De la Ville sur-Yllon, 'La chiesa di Santa Barbara in Castelnuovo', p. 72. Ynnya was given 15 ducats on 10 November in order to purchase a breviary; see De Marinis, *La biblioteca napoletana*, II, 231.

[52] Haberl, 'Die römische "Schola cantorum" und die päpstlichen Kapellsänger bis zur Mitte des 16. Jahrhunderts', p. 226.

[53] D'Accone, 'The Performance of Sacred Music in Italy during Josquin's Time, c. 1475– 1525', p. 603, where figures for other churches are given.

[54] Lockwood, 'Dufay at Ferrara', p. 6. The Ferrarese chapel would decline sharply during the reign of Leonello's successor, Borso.

[55] Bouquet, 'La cappella musicale dei duchi di Savoia dal 1450 al 1500'. p. 250.

[56] Marix, *Histoire de la musique et des musiciens de la cour de Bourgogne*, pp. 243ff.

The Royal Chapel

that of Henry VI in England, which occasionally numbered as many as thirty-six adults and ten children,[57] substantially surpassed it. Thus at precisely the midpoint of the fifteenth century, Naples could boast one of the largest chapels in the musical mainstream.

As valuable as the roster is, it also raises some questions. Of the twenty-one singers named, perhaps as many as nineteen are cited only this one time: that is, there is no further documentation for them in either previous or subsequent years.[58] Although the scarcity of documentation and the references only to individual musicians throughout the late 1440s might explain the absence of the names before 1451, there is further documentation for 1452 and another complete roster for 1455; yet only Jaume Borbó and Joan Steve will be named on that list. The turnover in personnel, then, seems to have been great. And to confound the problem further, a number of singers – including such mainstays of the chapel as Oriola and Gonsalvo de Cordova – who were listed on the roster of 26 October 1444, but who are absent from this one, will be present once again in 1455. The questions of why they are missing and where they had gone will be dealt with presently.

Finally, is it possible to determine whether the chapel had grown gradually from a force of fifteen in 1444 to one of between twenty-one and twenty-four during the course of the late 1440s or had expanded suddenly at the beginning of the following decade? Though the answer is by no means clear, the second alternative may be ever so slightly more plausible. First, the expansion would follow closely another large-scale effort to recruit singers in Spain in 1450.[59] Second, it coincides with a general increase in other activities concerning the chapel. By May 1451, Alfonso had retained the full-time services of the Modenese organ-builder Constantino de Tanti, who was hired at a salary of 300 ducats per year.[60] There seems also to be at about this time a new emphasis on acquiring music books for the chapel; thus on 4 August 1451, the tenor Taxmet de Sancto Paolo was paid 30 ducats 'per comprar I libre de cant per la capella'.[61] Third, the expansion of the chapel in about 1450, together with a new sense of its importance as a cultural and even political asset, coincides nicely with a burst of activity in the visual arts:

---

[57] Bowers, 'London: The Chapel Royal', *The New Grove*, XI, 151.

[58] The exceptions are Jaume Borbó, Joan Steve, and perhaps Antonio Ponte (Antoni Pont?), who might be identical with the Frate Antonio who appeared on the roster of 26 October 1444, or with the Antonio Ponzo (=Antonio Pons franzese) who would serve at Naples in the 1460s–1470s. However, given the patterns that will emerge, it is equally possible that the Antonio of 1444 is the Antonio de Lenti who will be recorded in the chapel in 1455 (see below, p. 35). Obviously, it may also be that we have three different men. There is another citation for Taxmet de Sancto Paolo, but it dates only from later in the same year (see below).

[59] The expense, 960 ducats, was borne by Johan Canals, a Catalan merchant then residing at Naples; see Ryder, *The Kingdom of Naples*, p. 190.

[60] Minieri Riccio, 'Alcuni fatti di Alfonso I', p. 412. Alfonso had already taken notice of Constantino's work in 1449, when, in a letter of 14 April, he expressed a wish to bring him to Naples; see Baldelló, 'La Música en la Casa de los Reyes de Aragón', p. 48. On Constantino's activities in northern Italy in the 1460s–1470s, see Peverada, 'Vita musicale nella cattedrale di Ferrara nel Quattrocento', p. 29; Barblan, 'Vita musicale alla corte sforzesca', p. 813.

[61] De Marinis, *La biblioteca napoletana*, II, 231.

Pisanello's visit to the court (late 1448–1450), the refurbishing of Castelnuovo – as Alfonso, with the Tuscan campaigns now behind him, began to spend long, uninterrupted stretches at Naples[62] – and the beginning of work on both its arch and its Sala dei Baroni (1452–1453), and a new penchant for Flemish art, including the Van der Weyden tapestries.[63] All of these activities seem to show the court becoming increasingly aware of art as an expression of Aragonese wealth and power. And the building up of the chapel to a force that rivaled any in Europe would not only reinforce this display in yet another area but also add to the image of Alfonso as a man of deep piety, an image that he was always eager to cultivate. In all, a quick expansion of the chapel circa 1450, rather than a gradual one over the course of a half decade, fits nicely with other developments at the court.

If the chapel was an expression of Alfonso's wealth, power, and piety, it could also serve his political interests. And it appears to have done so in June 1451, when, in what was most likely an effort to improve the poor political relationship with Medicean Florence, the chapel visited that city and performed at the cathedral on Pentecost Sunday (13 June) and later that week at the Santissima Annunziata; there, on 19 June, they were treated to a feast of eggplants, white bread, fruit, and six flasks of Trebbiano.[64] It is also possible that the Neapolitan singers met the famed Florentine organist Antonio Squarcialupi.[65] If so, they would have been renewing an acquaintance made some eight months earlier, when Squarcialupi visited Naples. On 26 November 1450, Squarcialupi wrote from Siena to Giovanni de' Medici: 'è hora mai circa d'uno mese ch'io tornai da Napoli . . . volendovi rachontare di Napoli, et della mayesta del re e della sua corte, che veramente gran cose et magne sono a rachontare'.[66] And though the letter makes no mention of music at the court, it hardly seems possible that Squarcialupi did not hear the royal chapel; no doubt, it was one of the 'gran cose' about which he would report.

The documentation for the next three years, 1452–1454, is once again thin. Five new members of the chapel are recorded for 1452: Gerardo de Cimeterio, Giuliano Casanova di Napoli, Giovanni di Sant'Angelo, Angelo Recellani di Buccino, and Nicola de Rinaldo.[67] Further information about these new singers is restricted to Gerardo, who on 20 September 1452 received a benefice at the parish church of San Vito in the diocese of Suessa (near Terracina);[68] and that he took possession of the benefice is shown by the following entry from the one surviving fragment of the 'sigillorum' of Alfonso's chancery: '[9 November 1452] Gherrardi de Cimeterio cantoris Regii, lictera presentationis ad parrochialem ecclesiam Sancti Viti dioceses suessane regalis beneficii taxata tarenos XII.'[69] It is unlikely

[62] Ryder, *The Kingdom of Naples*, p. 54.
[63] See Bologna, *Napoli e le rotte mediterranee*, pp. 81ff.
[64] D'Accone, 'The Singers of San Giovanni in Florence during the 15th Century', pp. 317–18.
[65] *Ibid.*, p. 318.
[66] The letter is published in Gaye, *Carteggio inedito d'artisti dei secoli XIV, XV, XVI*, I, 160–61.
[67] ASN, Museo 99 A privilegiorum I; published in Jole Mazzoleni, *Regesto della cancelleria aragonese di Napoli*, pp. 5, 12–13.
[68] Jole Mazzoleni, *op. cit.*, p. 5.
[69] The document is preserved in ASN, Misc. I, No. 4, and is published in Bianca Mazzoleni *et al.*, *Fonti aragonesi*, III, 21.

The Royal Chapel

that the new chaplains increased the size of the chapel much; rather, their appearance serves to underscore the seemingly heavy turnover of personnel in this period, a conclusion that, as will be seen, derives support from the next complete roster, that from November 1455.

The signal event in 1453 is the arrival at the court of Joan Cornago by 6 April at the latest (a full two and a half years earlier than hitherto presumed),[70] while another new name is that of the Carmelite friar Nardello de Composta.[71]

Among the singers who seem to have left the chapel in the comings and goings of the early 1450s is the singer–theorist Jaume Borbó. Not only is he no longer recorded at Naples after 1451, but by 15 April 1454 the post of master of the boys was filled by Pere Brusca,[72] who would use the position as a stepping stone to that of chapel master, this by August 1465 at the latest.[73] And at least one of the boys in Brusca's charge may be identified: Francesco Tuppo,[74] who, as was noted in Chap. I, would publish Masuccio Salernitano's *Novellino* in 1476 and eventually produce and print – at Naples in 1485 – an Italian translation of Aesop's fables.[75]

The final roster from Alfonso's reign dates from 8 November 1455 and lists twenty-two singers and two organists:[76]

> Fra Martin Cortes – listed as chapel master[77]
> Messer Lambert Azemar
> Messer Gonsalvo Garisso (= ? Garzia)
> Messer Sancio Garzia
> Messer Pietro Furtado (or, as a Castilian: Pedro Hurtado)
> Messer Jaime/Jaume Sancia
> Messer Jaume Botells
> Pere Oriola
> Messer Francesco Roberto
> Fra Geronimo
> Messer Giovanni Ferrero
> Abate Antonio de Lenti
> Messer Ffilion Angerran

---

[70] The details of Cornago's service are given in Chap. III.

[71] He entered the chapel on 4 January: ASN, Priv. I; see Jole Mazzoleni, *Regesto della cancelleria*, p. 14.

[72] Both Minieri Riccio, 'Alcuni fatti di Alfonso I', p. 429, and Gaetano Filangieri, *Documenti*, V, 67, incorrectly give the name as 'Brusia'. The correct form appears in Anglés, 'La Música en la Corte Real de Aragón y de Nápoles', p. 1023, and is confirmed by many extant notices about him (see below).

[73] ASN, TAF, Vol. Ia, fol. 73ʳ. Woodley, 'Iohannis Tinctoris: A Review of the Documentary Biographical Evidence', p. 233, incorrectly confuses him with Joan Brusca (for whom there is no documentation until 1480) and errs in dating his appointment as chapel master from February 1466.

[74] Minieri Riccio, 'Alcuni fatti di Alfonso I', p. 429.

[75] The identification was made by Pirrotta, 'Music and Cultural Tendencies in 15th–century Italy', p. 132, n. 19, and gains support from the knowledge that the young Tuppo received his education at Alfonso's court beginning in 1445; see Minieri Riccio, *Biografie degli accademici Alfonsini*, pp. 35–37.

[76] Minieri Riccio, 'Alcuni fatti di Alfonso I', p. 439. On the forms of the names, see n. 35 above.

[77] Although Minieri Riccio lists Cortes as chapel master, four other documents – another from November 1455 and three from May 1457 – make it clear that he was the 'locumtenens' and was therefore only 'acting' as chapel master on 8 November; the documents are printed in Minieri Riccio, *op. cit.*, pp. 439, 456–57.

Gerardo de Cimiterio
Tassinot
Francisco Alos
Luys Adroner
Jaime Perez
Leonardo Egizio
Joan de Epila
Matteo Brandano
Joan Steve
Joan Corbató – organist
Perinetto da Venezia – organist

Two identifications may be ventured for singers who are cited for the first time. First, Ffilion Angerran is recorded as having been with Alfonso at Messina in November 1432;[78] he thus seems to have waited a decade longer than did Lambert Azemar, a colleague on Alfonso's expedition of 1432, to rejoin Alfonso at Naples. The second singer about whose identity we may speculate is Fra Geronimo, who may be the Jeronimo Milecto 'dicto Piovano' for whom there are notices in 1478–1481 (see below, p. 44). While the many new names – as many as fourteen of the singers seem to have no prior documentation[79] – underscore our point about the large turnover in the chapel, what is even more interesting is the reappearance of Oriola, Azemar, Gonsalvo Garzia (de Cordova), Sancio Garzia, and Jaime or Jaume Sanya, all of whom were present on the roster of 1444, absent from that of 1451, and now listed once again in 1455. It seems obvious that the sea lanes between Naples and Barcelona were well traveled by members of the chapel.[80]

For the final three years of Alfonso's reign, notices about the chapel refer only to individual singers. (Indeed, we now lack a complete roster until 1480.) Cornago, whose career at Naples is treated at greater length in Chap. III, is recorded once again in 1456–1457, when he continued to draw his salary of 300 ducats per year.[81] Just how good a salary Cornago earned may be seen by comparing it with the only other known salary for a member of the chapel in this period. On 27 April 1457, the tenor Jean de Bruxelles received one-third of his annual salary (no doubt covering the months January–April): 14 ducats-2 tarì,[82] which comes to 43

[78] See Anglés, 'La Música en la Corte Real de Aragón y de Nápoles', p. 1013, and idem, 'La Música en la Corte del Rey Don Alfonso V de Aragón', p. 375.

[79] Perhaps this number could be reduced by two if we hazard that Antonio de Lenti could be the Fra Antonio named on the roster of 1444 (though the latter could just as well be the Antoni Pont [Antonio Ponte? Antonio Ponzo?] of 1451) and that Matteo Brandano might be the Matteo di Capua recorded in 1451.

[80] It is not only that their names are missing from the roster of 1451; there is no documentation at all for any of them in between the lists of 1444 and 1455. It seems unlikely, then, that they stayed in Naples, and a return to Spain is the best explanation for their long absence. It is diffi-

cult to explain the absence of Cornago's name from the roster, but it is not owing to his having been sent to Rome, as is sometimes stated; see the discussion of Cornago's activities in Chap. III.

[81] 15 September 1456: ASN, TAF, Vol. XVI, fol. 43r; 8 January 1457: ASN, TAF, Vol. XVI, fol. 2v.

[82] Minieri Riccio, 'Alcuni fatti di Alfonso I', pp. 455–56: 'Fa pagare ducati 14 e tari 2 a messer Giovanni di Brusselle tenore della sua cappella, terza parte del suo soldo annuale.' Anglés, 'La Música en la Corte Real de Aragón y de Nápoles', p. 1024, and idem, 'Die Instrumentalmusik bis zum 16. Jahrhundert in Spanien', p. 1436, is incorrect in stating that the Flemish musician purchased a book for 80 ducats on that day. Anglés has conflated two separate notices.

ducats-1 tareno for the year. It is unfortunate that we have no record of the salary paid to Tinctoris in the 1470s–1480s. However, that Cornago's 300 ducats per annum matches the salary that Ferrante would offer to Alexander Agricola in 1492–1493 seems to indicate that 300 ducats may have represented the ceiling for singers' salaries – including that of Tinctoris – at Naples. In any event, no other member of the chapel is known to have earned more than Cornago.[83] Also present at the court in April 1457 was Lambert Azemar, who was given charge of a book of music for which Alfonso had paid 80 ducats.[84] The chaplain whose activities are most intensely documented in 1457 – even if for a span of only two weeks – is Martin Cortes, the 'locumtenens', who is shown performing a function that often fell to the high-ranking clerics in the chapel. Between 16 and 30 May, Cortes made offerings on behalf of Alfonso on three different occasions: 16 May, at the convent of Santa Maria di Romania, in honor of the consecration of the new abbess, Caterina Carafa; 18 May, at the Duomo; and 30 May, at the church of San Pellegrino.[85]

Finally, there is one more of Alfonso's singers who may be accounted for, the well-traveled Jachetto da Marvilla. His presence at the court is attested by a letter that he wrote to Lorenzo de' Medici from Bologna on 15 September 1466: 'Although I have been in the chapel of King Alfonso and then in that of King Ferrante . . . and although I have been in the chapel of the Pope . . . I have always wanted to live in Florence rather than in Rome or Naples.'[86] Unfortunately, Jachetto does not specify just when he was at Naples; nor does another of his letters, this one written to Francesco Gonzaga, Marchese of Mantua, on 25 March 1500 settle the matter precisely: '. . . having been trained by King Alfonso and by King Ferrante and by the illustrious Duke of Ferrara, and having been a singer in their chapels for a period of forty-five years, that is, twenty-nine with the illustrious Duke of Ferrara and the remainder with the house of Aragon . . .'[87] Clearly, Jachetto's memory has failed him, for not only has he forgotten to account for his service at Rome in 1469–1471 and a year at Milan, 1474, that interrupted his tenure at Ferrara, which had begun in 1473,[88] but his numbers simply do not work out. If his statement about his combined Neapolitan–Ferrarese service having lasted forty-five years is even close to being accurate, his association with Naples would have to have begun either at the very end of 1455 – he is not listed on the roster of 8 November – or in 1456. At the latest, though, Jachetto had to

[83] For a comparison of singers' salaries at Naples with those at other Italian courts, see the discussion of Cornago's career in Chap. III.

[84] Minieri Riccio, 'Alcuni fatti di Alfonso I', p. 456.

[85] Ibid., pp. 456–57.

[86] I quote the translation in D'Accone, 'The Singers of San Giovanni', p. 321. The original Italian is given in Becherini, 'Relazioni di musici fiamminghi con la corte dei Medici, nuovi documenti', pp. 96ff.

[87] '. . . per essere stato creato de Re Alfonso et de Re Ferrante e de lo Ill.mo Duca de Ferrara et essere stato a le loro capelle cantare per spazio di anni XXXXV Zoe xxviiij con lo Ill.mo Duca de Ferrara e lo resto con la casa d'Aragona . . .'; see Bertolotti, Musici alla corte dei Gonzaga, p. 10.

[88] See D'Accone, 'The Singers of San Giovanni', p. 324; Haberl, 'Die römische "Schola cantorum"', p. 327; Motta, 'Musici alla corte degli Sforza', p. 525; Valdrighi, 'Cappelle, concerti e musiche di casa d'Este', p. 421; Lockwood, 'Music at Ferrara in the Period of Ercole I d'Este', p. 119. Jachetto appears to have served at Rome on two different occasions: 1469–1471 and, according to his first letter, at some point before September 1466.

have left Naples by 1466, as witness his letter of that year to Lorenzo de' Medici, which also claims an otherwise undocumented period at Rome. Thus Jachetto's tenure at Naples, which the singer himself claims to have lasted sixteen years, could not have exceeded a decade or so, from approximately 1455–1456 at the earliest to the middle of the next decade at the very latest.

Far more significant, though, than the precise dates of Jachetto's service is the very fact that as Alfonso's reign drew to a close he had in his chapel three singers – Jachetto, Jean de Bruxelles, and, to judge from his name, Tassinot – who were of Franco–Flemish origin; at least one, Jachetto, would serve at most of the major musical establishments of Italy. Thus Alfonso was taking the first step in a process whose pace would quicken in the 1460s–1470s; he began – if only on a small scale – to seek singers from the North, just as the Medici and Leonello d'Este had done in the preceding decade and as was long the custom in the papal chapel.[89] However, to say that Alfonso was competing with those chapels in securing singers from the Franco–Netherlandish mainstream would be to overstate the situation. Alfonso never went that far, and his chapel never lost its 'provincial tinge', as I have called it. There can be no doubt that, despite his appreciation and procurement of works by Van Eyck, Van der Weyden, and other Franco-Burgundian artists, and despite his calling in Italian artisans to work on Castelnuovo, together with ultramontane craftsmen to build its organs, the royal chapel was for Alfonso something different, something with which he had everyday contact on a personal basis, and something that throughout his reign would remain primarily Spanish in character, staffed mainly – and always at the upper ecclesiastical–administrative levels – by his compatriots, with whom he no doubt felt most comfortable.

With Alfonso's death on 27 June 1458, the royal chapel passed to Ferrante, who quickly became embroiled in war, first against rebellious pro-French barons and then against the invading army of Jean II of Anjou. The extent to which the chapel was affected by the hostilities, which ended with Ferrante's victorious return to Naples in 1465, can only be guessed at, but there is at least some evidence that it continued to function. First, there is the testimony provided by Jachetto da Marvilla's letter of September 1466. Although it is evident that Jachetto has exaggerated with respect to the number of years that he was at Naples, it seems reasonable to assume that he at least knew – and would not dare lie about – which kings he had served. Since there is no documentation for Jachetto's presence at Naples in 1465 or any time thereafter, and since he had already left that city when he wrote the letter in 1466, his tenure in Ferrante's chapel must have come during the period of unrest. Second, on 30 January 1461, an otherwise unknown 'Abate Santillo delle cappella reale' was reimbursed for offerings recently made for the king.[90] The chapel, then, remained intact and was ready to move in new directions.

The second half of the 1460s represents a turning point of sorts for music at

---

[89] See D'Accone, 'The Singers of San Giovanni', pp. 314ff; Lockwood, 'Dufay at Ferrara', pp. 6ff; Haberl, 'Die römische "Schola cantorum"', passim.

[90] Barone, 'Le cedole di tesoreria', IX, 16.

Naples. Ferrante's prestige was at a high point. New cultural – and especially musical – ties were forged with Milan as a result of the wedding of Alfonso, Duke of Calabria, and Ippolita Sforza. In the area of secular music, local composers whose names are now lost to us began setting the numerous strambotti and barzellette that were being turned out by the 'Sunday' poets of the court. Chansonniers – some of them still extant (see Chap. VI) – with the latest songs of the Ockeghem-Busnois generation began to be copied. And the royal chapel also flourished. With the Kingdom of Naples now separated from that of Aragon, Ferrante began increasingly to look to the North, seeking to rid the chapel of its Spanish parochialism and entering the competition for the services of the prized Franco-Netherlanders. And though Ferrante was sometimes a loser in the musical sweepstakes, Naples was soon home to enough Franco-Netherlanders – singers, composers, and theorists – of international repute to make the chapel an outpost of Franco-Netherlandish musical culture.

The documentation for this development – and it consists almost exclusively of notices pertaining to individual singers – begins in late 1465, by which time Pere Brusca (the Spanish presence would never disappear entirely), formerly the master of the boys, had been promoted to the rank of 'cappellano maggiore'.[91] On 13 December of that year, Brusca was given charge of a book of polyphony recently copied by the singer Giovanni Campi.[92] As far as one can tell, Brusca would remain the chapel master until at least 1473, relinquishing the post only a few months before his death on 2 January 1474.[93]

In 1466 the documents mention four members of the chapel: in addition to notices about Brusca, there is one record of payment for Cornago, who was now Ferrante's chief almoner,[94] and others for two northerners, Fra Thomas de Alemanya and Ffelippo de Burgunya. The Dominican Fra Thomas – a later document, dated 17 February 1474, lists him as 'frare Thomas del Cayre del orde de sanct Domingo'[95] – is recorded as a 'tenorista' on 30 April; in addition, he was active as a chapel scribe, and was paid for having copied a psalter, an antiphonal, a collectar (all in 1466), and a dominical (in 1468), all for Ferrante's chapel, as well as a missal (in 1474) for the use of the duchess Ippolita Sforza.[96] It would appear that Ffelippo de Burgunya also functioned as a scribe, for on 7 May he was paid 2 ducats-2 tarì-10 grani for a 'libre de cant d'orgue . . . son notats diversos officis ecclesiastichs . . .'[97] As was the custom, the book of polyphony was consigned to the chapel master.

---

[91] ASN, TAF, Vol. Ia, fol. 73ʳ, where he is so listed for August–December.

[92] Barone, 'Le cedole di tesoreria', IX, 34.

[93] He is cited for the final time as specifically holding that position in July 1473, by which time he had been named – in 1471 – Bishop of Aversa (ASN, TAF, Vol. Ia, fol. 30ʳ). He is also given that title in the *Giornale Strozzi* for 1473 (Galiano, 'Nuove fonti per la storia musicale napoletana', p. 4).

The date of his death is so given in Parente, *Origini e vicende ecclesiastiche della città di Aversa*, II, 588–89; see also Galiano, *op. cit.*, n. 31.

[94] Barone, 'Le cedole di tesoreria', IX, 209. This position, like that of chapel master, was shared by two men.

[95] De Marinis, *La biblioteca napoletana*, II, 262.

[96] *Ibid.*, II, 247, 249, 262.

[97] *Ibid.*, II, 247.

In view of Ferrante's desire at this time to recruit northern singers of some renown, it is interesting to speculate about the identity of Ffelippo de Burgunya. Perhaps he is the well-known Filippet Dortenche, who seems also to have been active at Florence. The identification is reasonable since Dortenche was definitely at Naples no later than 24 July 1470: 'Felippi de Dortan, regii cantoris, littera passus, taxata nihil quia pro curia'.[98] It must have been later that year or early in the next one that Ferrante sent Dortenche to France for the purpose of recruiting singers, for Dortenche mentions the trip and the rewards gleaned for it in an interesting letter to Lorenzo de' Medici dated 27 May 1471:[99]

this year His Majesty the King sent me to France in order to bring some singers back here [Naples] . . . having been ordered not to speak a word of it to you . . . I returned but I was little rewarded for my services. This King nevertheless granted me ten gold ducats a month, five lengths of fine material for clothing, and thirdly 20 ducats . . . a year, besides which he gave me a captaincy in Calabria for one year from which I draw 50 ducats, and [he did] all [this] most graciously.

The letter is informative for a number of reasons. Not only was Ferrante recruiting avidly, but he was doing so on the sly, and thus setting the tone for the intrigue that would characterize his dealings with a number of musicians, both when he won and when he lost. We also learn the monthly salary – a very competitive ten gold ducats – of a fairly well-known singer of the kind who traveled the circuit of Italian chapels, one who was less than a 'star', but who must certainly have been a cut or two above the run-of-the-mill. In addition, we see one of the ways that Ferrante could augment the earnings of those members of the chapel who were not clerics and thus not able to receive lucrative benefices. Finally, toward the end of the letter, Dortenche expresses his wish to leave Naples and return to Florence, even if such a move entailed a reduction in salary. Although Dortenche's reasons for leaving Naples were of a purely personal nature – 'my wife is desirous of returning to her native city [Florence]' – they echo the sentiments expressed by Jachetto da Marvilla, who also wished to work at Florence rather than Naples. And though Dortenche remained at Naples – he is listed on a roster of 25 (?) October 1480 (see below) – his sentiments exemplify the difficulty that Ferrante had in trying to retain some of his better known singers.

By 1469 at the very latest, three other distinguished musicians had joined the chapel: the composer Vincenet, about whom we shall speak presently (see Chap. III), and the singers Antonio Ponzo (now known to be a Frenchman: see below) and Raynero.[100] Just when the latter two joined the chapel is not known, but by early 1469 they must have received an invitation from Galeazzo Maria Sforza to

---

[98] The notice, which appears in a *sigillorum* of the Summaria for 1469–1470, is published in Bianca Mazzoleni, *Fonti aragonesi*, III, 124.

[99] The entire letter, both in an English translation and in the original Italian, is given in D'Accone, 'The Singers of San Giovanni', pp. 325, 354. It is Dortenche's many references to Florence, another to his Florentine wife, and the rather familier tone – the singer addresses Lorenzo as 'Kar^mo chompere' – that leads D'Accone to assume that Filippet must have been active at Florence.

[100] In addition, there are notices for Brusca (all published in De Marinis, *La biblioteca napoletana*, II, 250–51, and Barone, 'Le cedole di tesoreria', IX, 222–23) and for three chaplains who are otherwise unknown: Alberto de Credencij, Fra Giorgio Marrotta, and Felippo Porcello (ASN, TAF, Vol. Ia, fol. 87r).

quit Naples for Milan, for on 25 March the two singers wrote back to the duke, stating that they accepted his offer but would not be able to leave before completing their duties during Holy Week.[101]

This was neither the first nor the last time that a member of Ferrante's chapel would transfer to Milan. The first known instance seems to have occurred in amicable circumstances. On 21 January 1463, Alfonso, Duke of Calabria, wrote to Francesco Sforza on behalf of Ferrante, saying that the king took pleasure in sending him the organist Joan Corbató,[102] who had served at the Neapolitan court since 1443. A second instance occurred around 1469 and involved the singers Antonio Ponzo and Raynero; to their credit, though, they did not desert the Neapolitan chapel until the 'busy season' of Holy Week was over. And if the Philipeto Romeo who is recorded as a 'cantorino' at Milan in 1469 is the same as the Phelip Romeu whom we found at Naples in 1441, he may have changed jobs at the same time. Yet another instance took place in late 1473 or early 1474, involved the peripatetic Johannes Cordier, and nearly caused a break in the already strained diplomatic relations between Naples and Milan. The precise date of Cordier's arrival at Naples is not known, but it must be sometime after July 1471, when he is still recorded at Rome.[103] Nor do we know just when he departed; but Galeazzo Maria was already referring to him as 'nostro cantore' in a letter of 2 July 1474.[104] The problem, of course, is that Cordier had been wooed to Milan in a most surreptitious manner and had left Naples without permission. In an angry letter of 12 July, addressed to Cordier at Milan, Ferrante or his agent (the letter is unsigned) takes the singer to task for his lack of gratitude toward the king and orders him to return to Naples together with a number of other fugitive singers (Romeu, Ponzo, and Raynero?).[105] Galeazzo countered by demanding the return of Don Constantino, who can probably be identified as the organ-builder Constantino de Tanti, who had been at Naples in 1451, had been active at Modena, Ferrara, Mantua, and Milan in the 1460s and early 1470s, and, if our identification is correct, arrived at Naples at about the same time that Cordier left.[106] Eventually, Charles the Bold of Burgundy was called upon to mediate; the decision went against Ferrante, and so far as is known Cordier never returned to Naples.[107]

---

[101] See Barblan, 'Vita musicale alla corte sforzesca', p. 820; on the activities of the two singers at Milan, see also pp. 826–28, 830, 836; and Motta, 'Musici alla corte degli Sforza', pp. 529–32. Ponzo, who appears to have been particularly friendly with Agricola at Milan, returned to Naples in March 1470 in order to pick up his wife (Barblan, p. 820), and returned again in August 1476 (if he can be identified with the 'Antonio Pons franzese' who was paid at that time: see below, p. 44).

[102] For a transcription and facsimile of the letter, see Barblan, op. cit., pp. 819, 821.

[103] Cordier joined the papal chapel in January 1469 after having sung in Florence. He is listed as a papal singer through July 1471. After a gap in documentation, his name is missing from a roster of 1473; see D'Accone, 'The Singers of San Giovanni', pp. 323–24; Haberl, 'Die römische "Schola cantorum"', pp. 230–31.

[104] See Walsh, 'Music and Quattrocento Diplomacy: The Singer Jean Cordier between Milan, Naples and Burgundy in 1475', p. 439.

[105] The letter is printed in Barblan, 'Vita musicale alla corte sforzesca', pp. 843–44.

[106] He was apparently still at Modena in early October 1473, for Galeazzo Maria wrote to him there on the 6th of that month; see ibid., p. 813.

[107] The entire affair is described in detail in Walsh, 'Music and Quattrocento Diplomacy', pp. 439–42, who sees as the basis for Charles's decision the duke's belief that Milan would in the long run be a more worthwhile ally than Naples.

The presence at the court once again of Constantino di Tanti draws attention to the organs of the chapel, and limiting ourselves for the moment only to the organs built expressly for use in the Cappella Palatina – the royal family's private chapel in Castelnuovo – in the late 1460s and early 1470s, we may note the activities of the following organ-builders: Antonello Sebastiani (June 1468, May 1470, February–August 1472), Giovanni di Gaeta (1470), Lorenzo da Prato (arrived from Bologna in June 1471), and Joan Oller (May–June 1472).[108] Certainly the best known of these was Lorenzo da Prato, who returned to Naples frequently in the decades that followed,[109] and who seems to have been responsible for the main organ in the chapel.[110] Equally important, at least in Naples, was Giovanni da Gaeta, whose organ for the chapel was decorated with the Aragonese arms in 1471.[111] Organ-builder, organist, and 'meste de fer lauts'[112] – he was also in charge of the king's 'chamber music' (see Chap. V) – Giovanni would leave Naples by February 1476[113] and, like Antonio Ponzo, Raynero, and Johannes Cordier, sought to find a position at Milan.[114] Finally, Naples was paid a visit by the famous organ-builder and organist Isaac Argyropoulos, probably in March or April 1472.[115] Apparently, Argyropoulos was not overly impressed with the technology of organ-building at Naples, for in a letter written just one year later, on 5 April 1473, he told Galeazzo Maria that a Milanese organ has recently been completed in which a pipe of seven spans was made in one piece, 'but in Naples they cannot do this in less than two or three pieces . . .'[116]

---

[108] See Riccardo Filangieri, *Rassegna critica delle fonti*, III, 7, 47; Barone, 'Le cedole di tesoreria', IX, 242. Further on Antonello, see Galiano, 'Nuove fonti per la storia musicale napoletana', p. 3, and n. 15.

[109] See Gaetano Filangieri, *Documenti*, VI, 8–9, where his presence at Naples is noted again in December 1481, January 1483, March 1485, and November 1492. One visit that Filangieri does not record must have occurred in March or April 1476; on 10 April of that year, Ferrante wrote to Lorenzo de' Medici from Sarni: 'Grandissimo piacere havimo prese de la venuta qua ad nui de mastro Laurenczo da prato, in modo che piu non ne potria essere piacuta. Rengratiamove de la opera che ad tale effecto havite facta, et ve ne remanimo obligati. Dicto mastro Laurenczo vederimo voluntieri, al quale per respecto de la virtu soe, et anco per amore vostro che tanto ne lo recomendati; non farimo mancare cosa che li bisognesse el che trovera in effecto' (Archivio di Stato, Florence, Mediceo avanti il Principato, Vol. XLVII, No. 123).

[110] Riccardo Filangieri, *Castel Nuovo*, p. 242. On his organ for San Petronio in Bologna, see Tirro, 'Lorenzo di Giacomo da Prato's Organ at San Petronio'.

[111] Riccardo Filangieri, *Rassegna critica delle fonti*, III, 7.

[112] On his function as a lute-maker, see Galiano, 'Nuove fonti per la storia musicale napoletana', p. 8 and n. 4.

[113] Just when he left Naples is not known, but it was after January 1473, when the *Giornale Strozzi* still record him at the court; see Galiano, *op. cit.*, p. 1. He is in Rome by 14 February 1476 (see n. 114 below).

[114] See the letters written by the Cardinal of Pavia (at Rome) to Galeazzo Maria on 14 February and 4 May 1476, in Sartori, 'Organs, Organ Builders, and Organists in Milan, 1450–1476', pp. 65–66.

[115] See Barblan, 'Vita musicale alla corte sforzesca', p. 811.

[116] Sartori, 'Organs, Organ Builders, and Organists in Milan', pp. 60–61.

Christoph Wolff, 'Paumann, Conrad', *The New Grove*, XIV, 308, writes that the famous organist Paumann was at Mantua in 1470 and turned down an invitation to visit Naples. However, the musician in whom Ferrante was interested at the time was one Johannes Orbo, who, like Paumann, was German, blind, and apparently in the service of Duke Albrecht IV of Bavaria. The confusion is first raised but then resolved in a series of three letters that Ferrante wrote to Ludovico III Gonzaga (all printed in Bertolotti, *Musici alla corte dei Gonzaga*, pp. 8–9):

It is unfortunate that the decade for which we have the least documentation about the chapel is the 1470s, for it is – to judge from the repertory in the extant music sources and from the documentation that does survive – during this decade and the next that music at the court reached its most brilliant heights; indeed, the 1470s and 1480s mark the high point of all cultural activities in Aragonese Naples. From the standpoint of the chapel, the crowning moment must be the arrival of Johannes Tinctoris sometime during the first half of the decade.[117] For the rest, the documentation for the early to mid-1470s consists of (1) the references to Dortenche and Cordier already cited, plus another for Dortenche (Filipocho di Borghonia) on 13 January 1473;[118] (2) three records of payment in 1473 to 'Giglietto di Pichardia chantore', the one for 13 April showing that he earned 3 ducats-4 tarì-4 grani 'per la provisione sua di gennaro e febraio';[119] (3) no fewer than eleven notices between July 1470 and July 1473 concerning the chapel master Pere Brusca;[120] (4) two to the tenor–scribe Fra Thomas from January 1473 and April 1474,[121] and another that shows that he prepared a missal for Ippolita Sforza for which he was paid 25 ducats on 17 February 1474 (see note 95); (5) the notice of Exarch's death in 1471; (6) four records of payment to Gonsalvo de Cordova in 1470–1471, in the last three of which he is referred to simply as 'musico del Re',[122] possibly an indication that he was now part of the secular music establishment; and (7) a papal document of 13 May 1473 that grants a benefice to the singer–chaplain Jacobus Villete of Cambrai, who may certainly be identified with the singer of the same name who had served at the court of Savoy from circa 1444 to circa 1466 and probably with the Jacobus Viletti who is represented in the Buxheim organ book.[123] Villette would appar-

20 May 1470 - Ferrante asks for the 'musico todisco ceco' whose name he does not know; 6 July 1470 – Ferrante has just heard from Joanne de Oriola (cousin of the singer–composer Pere Oriola: see Chap. III, n. 18 below), recently returned from Mantua, that the musician, cited as 'Orbo', has gone back to Germany; 21 July 1475 – Ferrante once again asks for the 'musico ceco tudisco, quale già altra volta fo qua'. Certainly, the blind German cannot be Paumann, who had been dead for two and a half years. These letters must be read in conjunction with certain Milanese–Mantuan correspondence of the same years, in which Galeazzo Maria Sforza also requested the service of 'Johannes Orbo the player from Munich'; on these letters, see Prizer, *Courtly Pastimes: The Frottole of Marchetto Cara*, pp. 3–4.

[117] Tinctoris's activities at Naples are discussed in Chap. III below.

[118] Galiano, 'Nuove fonti per la storia musicale napoletana', p. 4 and n. 32.

[119] *Ibid.*, p. 4 and nn. 32–33.

[120] ASN, TAF, Vol. Ia, fols. 93r, 96v, 99r, 101r, and 30r; De Marinis, *La biblioteca napoletana*, II, 255; Barone, 'Le cedole di tesoreria', IX, 232, 242, 245; Galiano, 'Nuove fonti per la storia musicale napoletana', pp. 3–4; Parenti, *Origini e vicende ecclesiastiche*, pp. 588–89.

[121] Galiano, *op. cit.*, p. 4 and nn. 32–33.

[122] ASN, TAF, Vol. Ia, fols. 98v, 99r, 100r, for July–December 1471, and Barone, 'Le cedole di tesoreria', IX, 229.

[123] Archivio Segreto Vaticano, MS Reg. Suppl., 690, fols. 76v–77r: 'Jacobus Villette, presbyter Cameracensis . . . in iure baccalaureus . . . cantor cappellanus . . . Ferdinand regis Sicilie . . .' I should like to thank Dr. Adalbert Roth for sharing with me this and many other products of his research in Roman archives that pertain to Naples. On Villette at Savoy, see Bouquet, 'La cappella musicale dei duchi di Savoia', pp. 250–51 and 285. His presence in Munich 352b is recorded by Southern, *The Buxheim Organ Book*, p. 44, who, however, calls the identification of the Buxheim composer and the Naples singer only 'remotely possible'; that identification was first proposed by Eitner, *Biographisch–bibliographisches Quellen-Lexikon*, 2nd ed., X, 87.

ently stay at Naples through the remainder of the decade, for he is among the singers named on the roster of 25 (?) October 1480; if, as seems perfectly possible, Tinctoris arrived at Naples before Cordier departed, the chapel enjoyed simultaneously the services of Tinctoris, Vincenet, Villette, Cordier, and Dortenche, a quintet of Franco–Netherlanders that was actually more distinguished than any that the papal chapel could boast of at the same time.[124] Finally, on 12 May 1473, a payment of 190 ducats-3 tarì-13½ grani was made 'per paghare a . . . chantori'; as Galiano notes, this might have been a payment to the singers of the chapel.[125]

From the second half of the decade there is documentation for three other singers of note. On 12 August 1476, 'Antonio Pons franzese' was paid six ducats.[126] This is surely the singer Antonio Ponzo, who would, then, have returned to Naples after his service at Milan. On 18 April 1478, Lorenzo de' Medici wrote to Francesco Nacci at Naples with the request that he should have 'Piavano cantore' come to Florence.[127] This would seem to refer to Jeronimo Milecto, dicto Piovano, who is recorded as a 'cantore della capella del S.R.' in 1480 (though not, as we shall see, on the roster of 25 (?) October) and 1481.[128] To risk further speculation: he may, as was already noted, also be identified with the Fra Geronimo whose name appeared on the roster of 8 November 1455; and if my identification of him as the 'Piovano cantore' in whom Lorenzo de' Medici was interested is correct, he could be the Piovano Girolamo who appears in off-and-on fashion at the SS Annunziata at Florence from January 1484 through December 1492.[129] If all these notices do refer to the same singer, his career at Naples and Florence spanned some three and a half decades. One last identification that can be made in connection with Jeronimo Milecto 'dicto Piovano' is that he is possibly the 'Molletto' to whom the poet Benedetto Gareth refers in lines 10 and 13–14 of his sonnet CLXXXIV: 'Quando parti di noi quel tuo Molletto . . . Et mischia il canto suo, dolce & perfetto/con la celeste, angelica harmonia'![130] Finally, it is in 1478 that the Catalan or Valencian composer–singer Bernardus Ycart is unequivocally recorded in the Neapolitan chapel for the first time, not in a document emanating from Naples, but in a papal provision of 27 October.[131]

---

[124] See the rosters for the early and mid-1470s in Haberl, 'Die römische "Schola cantorum" ', p. 231.

[125] 'Nuove fonti per la storia musicale napoletana', p. 5.

[126] Ibid., pp. 4–5.

[127] Del Piazzo, Protocolli del carteggio di Lorenzo il Magnifico, p. 218.

[128] Van der Straeten, La Musique aux Pays-Bas, IV, 31, who gives the name as 'Pianano'.

[129] D'Accone, 'The Singers of San Giovanni', p. 335.

[130] See Pèrcopo, Le rime di Benedetto Gareth, II, 222. If, as seems likely, Gareth is mourning over the singer's death, my identification of him as the singer in Florence may be weakened. On the other hand, he could have returned to Naples, or Gareth could have been lamenting his loss even though the singer had left Naples some years earlier. In all, the Jeronimo–Piovano identifications are tenuous.

[131] On Ycart's activities at Naples, see Chap. III (he may have been there since at least 1476: see p. 78 below). In his examination of papal documents of the period, Adalbert Roth has also ferreted out the names of a few other persons who make their first appearance in the chapel in the late 1470s: (1) Albertus, abbot of the monastery of St. Nicholas in [not legible = Bari?] 1477; (2) Blasius Loca, presbyter Asculanensis (Ascoli), 1478; (3) Petrus de Pineda, 1477–1480; and (4) Jacobus de Valentino, 1479, who may perhaps be identified with the Fra Jacobo da Valenza, who held the post of chapel master in 1492. All of

The final year of the decade brings what is perhaps the most frustrating document in the entire history of the chapel. It is a *motu proprio* issued by Sixtus IV and dated 1 September 1479. From it we learn that Sixtus had reserved benefices of up to 100 gold florins *de camera* for each of the forty (!) members of the chapel, who, unfortunately, are not named.[132] What is puzzling, of course, is that it describes a chapel that is about twice as large not only as any documented heretofore, but also as that which we find just one year later, in October 1480, when the chapel is known to have comprised twenty-one singers. Thus it raises the question of just what the chapel was, forces us to reconsider, perhaps, the meaning of the rosters of 1444, 1451, 1455, and 1480, and forms the basis of inquiry for the second section of this chapter, 'The Structure and Function of the Chapel'. (Or is it that Ferrante had simply 'padded' his request?)

Aside from the *motu proprio* of Sixtus, and the related document concerning the annates (see note 132), the only other important notice for 1479 refers to the chapel of Alfonso, Duke of Calabria, two of whose chaplains were Antonio and Nicola.[133] We can at least speculate about the identity of Antonio. Perhaps he is the Antonio Spagnuolo (in which case, Antoni if he was Catalan) who, on 15 June 1472, had been recommended to Ippolita Sforza, the duchess, by her brother Galeazzo Maria, in whose service he had previously been.[134] To push the speculation still further, perhaps the Spanish singer who went from Milan to Naples in 1472 is the singer whom Minieri Riccio lists as Antonio Ponte on the roster of 1451 and whose name I suggest may be Antoni Pont. Obviously, we can do little more than speculate in the case of so common a name, but the traffic in musical personnel between Naples and Milan was heavy, and we know – as in the case of Antonio Ponzo – that there was at least an occasional round trip.

On 25 (or 27) October 1480 a record was made of the expenses for the livery of Ferrante's singers. The document, headed 'Ad XXI canturi de la cappella del Signor Re infrascripti per loro vestiri. A ciascuno l'infrascripti panni a dì . . . dicto', provides us with our last roster of the chapel, or at least of that portion of it whose prime responsibility was musical. Since the types of cloth purchased and the cost of each item is for the moment irrelevant (the total cost was 172 ducats-2 tarì-19 grani), only the names and designations of positions as they appear in Van der Straeten are given:[135]

these men, for whom documentation exists only in papal documents concerning the granting of benefices, are cited only as 'capellanus capelle'; see Chap. IV for complete documentation.

[132] The document is in Rome, Biblioteca Apostolica Vaticana, MS Reg. Vat. 547, fols. 89ᵛ–96ʳ; I should like to thank Jeremy Noble for calling it to my attention. The number of chapel members is confirmed in Archivio Segreto Vaticano, MS Liber Annatarum 28, fol. 96ʳ, in which two of the chaplains, Petrus de Pineda and Jacobus de Valentino (see n. 131 above), obliged themselves to pay the annate on the benefices that they had apparently received. I am grateful to Adalbert Roth for this information. On the system of annates, see the discussion about Ycart in Chap. III.

[133] Van der Straeten, *La Musique aux Pays-Bas*, IV, 31.

[134] See Motta, 'Musici alla corte degli Sforza', p. 541.

[135] *La Musique aux Pays-Bas*, IV, 28–30; the document in its entirety also appears in Woodley, 'Iohannes Tinctoris: Documentary Biographical Evidence', pp. 244–45. On the final line, I have changed Van der Straeten's 'Monsieur Pasquale' to 'Monsser . . .', the form generally used by Pasquale Diaz Garlon, who made many of the entries in the account books during this period; see De Marinis, *La biblioteca napoletana, passim*.

> Joan de Ghianes
> messer Filippet Dortenche
> messer Guglielmo foro spul.
> Joan de Platea
> Joani Lothin
> messer Anselmo
> Salvatore Pinia
> Fra Alfonso Galeco
>
> Seguitano li canturi:
>
> Joan Brusca
> Baldassare Ospato
> Bernar Hicart
> Joan Tintoris
> Perot de Vertoya
> Iach Vilet cantore
> Cappellano maiore
> Luisot Patin cantore
> Abbate Iordi Marot
> Alon Aloth cantore
> Amatore cantore
> Fra Simon Ian. cantor

Per cautela di Monsser Pasquale 25 ottobre 1480

Valuable as it is, the account – at least the version offered by Van der Straeten – is riddled with ambiguities. First, Van der Straeten gives two different dates for it, the 27th at the beginning ('a di . . . dicto "[27 octobre 1480]" ') and the 25th at the end; perhaps the '27', which stands as an editorial insertion, is the error. Second, whereas the heading promises the names of twenty-one singers, the roster lists but twenty; Van der Straeten is of the mind that there is a name missing after that of Baldassare Ospato. Van der Straeten reasons that this is the case on the ground that Baldassare is 'l'object d'une quadruple gratification [four pieces of material], au rebours de la plupart de ses collègues, même de ceux appelés "messer" qui n'en ont reçu qu'une'. His reasoning does not entirely hold up, however, for Joan de Ghianes also received four pieces of material, and the term 'messer' seems to be used indiscriminately. In all it is just as possible that the error appears in the heading. And finally, though the heading mentions 'XXI Canturi de la cappella', the subheading 'Seguitano li canturi' is entered only after the eighth name, which therefore leaves only twelve names in the 'canturi' category, from which the singer Dortenche is excluded. Since some of these problems are better dealt with in the following section of the chapter, we may turn to some other aspects of the document.

First, the identity of Joan Brusca should be set straight. He is obviously not to be conflated with Pere Brusca, as has recently been done by Woodley (see note 73 above). Indeed, so far as I know this is the first appearance of Joan Brusca's name, and that he remained at Naples throughout the 1480s and was highly valued by

Ferrante is evident from his having been awarded 'l'ufficio di misuratore della dogana del sale della città di Napoli, sua vita durante' on 7 November 1488, no doubt a position that brought him a lucrative income.[136] Another member of the chapel who can be identified is Joani Lothin. He is the soprano ('supremus') Johannes de Lotinis Dinantinus to whom Tinctoris dedicated his *Expositio manus*.[137] Two other identifications may be risked, though they are admittedly tenuous: Joan de Ghianes could be the 'Domino Ghineto' (or Ghinet) who is recorded at Milan in 1474–1475,[138] while Perot de Vertoya might be the 'Perotto tenorista' who is active at Ferrara in 1473 and then at Milan in 1474–1475.[139] Finally, 'Iach Vilet cantore' is, as noted above, the Jacobus Villette who had arrived at Naples no later than May 1473 after a distinguished career at Savoy.

Another question about the wardrobe account concerns the unidentified 'cappellano maiore', who, significantly, is listed after the rubric 'Seguitano li canturi'. Perhaps it was Epo de Tropoya, who is listed as chapel master one year later, in 1481.[140]

Still another problem arises from two names that are not on the roster: Jeronimo Milecto, mentioned above, and the Catalan Luys Prats, both of whom are otherwise recorded as being in the chapel in 1480.[141] Either they were not among the singers at precisely the time the livery was purchased, or they were left off the list on the ground that they were not the recipients of new robes; the roster, after all, also fails to mention the chapel organists, one of whom may have been Fra Stefano del Paone of Salerno, who had been paid for building an organ for the king on 19 April 1474 and who would soon leave Naples for Rome, Florence, and the court of Matthias Corvinus and Beatrice d'Aragona at Buda.[142] The point, then, is that the number of singers may have been greater than either the twenty-one cited in the heading of the account or the twenty listed in its body.

---

[136] Jole Mazzoleni, *Regesto della cancelleria aragonese di Napoli*, pp. 181–82.

[137] See Albert Seay, *Johannis Tinctoris: Opera theoretica*, I, 14; Weinmann, *Johannes Tinctoris*, p. 33.

[138] See Sartori, 'Josquin Des Prés cantore del Duomo', pp. 64–66; the possibility of such an identification was raised by Motta, 'Musici alla corte degli Sforza', p. 526.

[139] Valdrighi, 'Cappelle, concerti e musiche di casa d'Este', p. 420; Sartori, *op. cit.*, pp. 64–66; Motta, *op. cit.*, pp. 383, 524.

[140] Van der Straeten, *La Musique aux Pays-Bas*, IV, 31.

[141] They are cited as singers in the chapel, *ibid.*

[142] On Stefano's payment of 19 April 1474, see Barone, 'Le cedole di tesoreria', IX, 399. There can be little doubt that it is this Stefano del Paone who is the Maestro Stefano da Napoli who was sent from Rome to Florence sometime before 8 October 1483 by the general of the Servite Order so that he might assist the chapel of the SS Annunziata and who, after being unfavorably received, was given three florins and ordered to leave. Confirmation of this – and a more precise fixing of the date – comes from two letters, one from Beatrice, the other from Matthias to Lorenzo de' Medici; the letters, dated 13 August and 20 August, ask Lorenzo to send 'frate Stephano Paone del Salerno nostro mastro d'organi', then at Florence, to Buda, where the royal couple wanted him to build an organ. That Stefano was still at Florence in late January 1484 is evident from yet a third letter to Lorenzo, dated 31 January, in which Beatrice again asks that Stefano be sent to Buda. (On Stefano and the Annunziata chapel, see D'Accone, 'The Singers of San Giovanni', p. 334. The letters from Buda to Florence are printed in Haraszti, 'Les Musiciens de Mathias Corvin et de Béatrice d'Aragon', pp. 46–47.) Finally, Stefano was present at Rome in 1499, when he worked on an organ in S. Maria del Popolo (see Galiano, 'Nuove fonti per la storia musicale napoletana', n. 13, and Romano, *L'arte organaria*, pp. 465ff).

For 1481 there is relatively little documentation; and from this point on, what notices have been recovered mention individual members of the chapel only. Epo de Tropoya is now the chapel master, and if we may hazard the speculation that 'Tropoya' could be a misreading by Van der Straeten (see note 140, above) for 'Tropeya' (= Tropea), a town on the Calabrian coast, it is possible that he is the first Italian to attain that position. Also in the chapel were Jeronimo Milecto and Alfonse Zamora,[143] who may, perhaps, be identified with the Alfonsus Sancij Zamorensis who sang in the papal chapel from 1434 to 1445 and then again in 1461.[144] And though 1481 is the last year in which we find reference to Gonsalvo de Cordova, whose career in the chapel had begun no later than November 1437, when he received 15 ducats for a horse, that he is again recorded as 'musico de la casa del S.R.'[145] – a designation first encountered in 1471 – seems to indicate that he had not returned to the chapel, but remained a member of the king's 'chamber music' (see Chap. V). In addition to the information on Ferrante's chapel, 1481 brings news about that of Alfonso, Duke of Calabria. The duke's first chaplain was the Olivetan Fra Jo. Franc. Miraballs, who held that position from at least November 1481 through December 1484.[146] That the head of Alfonso's chapel was an Olivetan is especially fitting in view of the duke's fondness for the church of Monteoliveto (Sant'Anna dei Lombardi), where he often dined and heard Mass.[147]

Documentation for the period 1482–1488 is exceptionally thin and consists mainly of notices about the concession of benefices and other prizes:[148] 21 February 1484: Pietro de Pineda, 'cappellano regio', received a benefice at the church of San Lorenzo di Picerno in the Abruzzi; 7 July 1484: a new member, Domenico Bartolo of Manfredonia, is admitted to the chapel; 1 October 1487: the abbot Luigi de Admiratis of Massafra is named archpriest of Palegiano; Alexander de Marra entered the chapel no later than January 1485; 8 February 1488: Luys Prats, with the chapel since at least 1480, is given a benefice at the church of Sant'Arcangelo de' Pedefumi in the Cilento (diocese of Salerno); he would receive another in the same area on 10 November 1490, this time at the church of San Nicola dei Campograssi; 2 August 1488: Giovanni Chirardo is awarded a 'cantorato' at Lucera, a position that carried a stipend of 72 ducats; 7 September 1488: Antonius Rocha was awarded a benefice in the diocese of Martorano (Cosenza); 16 September 1488: Esremus de Risis, 'clericus Neapolitanensis', is recorded as 'procurator regie capelle'; 7 November 1488: Joan Brusca took up his post as an official in the salt customs; and 11 December 1488: one Simplicianus de Abbate is recorded as a 'professor' (?) of the chapel. Finally, Juliano de Caiacza had been appointed chapel master by August 1488 at the latest.

[143] Van der Straeten, *La Musique aux Pays-Bas*, IV, 31.
[144] Schuler, 'Zur Geschichte der Kapelle Papst Martins V.', p. 45.
[145] Van der Straeten, *op. cit.*, IV, 31.
[146] ASN, TAF, Vol. Ia, fol. 50r; see also Barone, 'Le cedole di tesoreria', IX, 423. The master and almoner of the queen's private chapel was Joan Monelos, who is recorded in a papal document of 4 August 1480 as receiving a benefice at Taranzona; Archivio Segreto Vaticano, MS Reg. Lat., 796, fols. 253r–254v (information from Adalbert Roth).
[147] See Hersey, *Alfonso II and the Artistic Renewal of Naples*, p. 109.
[148] Documentation for all of these is given in Chap. IV below.

The most noteworthy document of those years, though, is the well-known letter of 15 October 1487 that Ferrante had Giovanni Pontano draw up for Tinctoris, in which the theorist is charged with the task of going north in order to recruit singers for the chapel.[149] Given his great renown – and, probably, equally widespread musical contacts in the north – it is not surprising that it was Tinctoris whom Ferrante chose for the mission. Nor is Ferrante's decision to seek singers in the north at all out of character by now; indeed, there were undoubtedly similar recruiting missions of which we have no record, since he had sent Dortenche across the Alps for the same reason some two decades earlier. What is interesting is Ferrante's admission that he could not find the kind of singers ('cantori della conditione a bucca vi havimo detto') that he wanted locally ('et non trovandoli in queste nostri parti de qua'), this because it is precisely at this time that Italians (mainly, if not exclusively, from the south), while not predominant in the chapel, seem to be joining it at a proportionally higher rate than ever before. If we consider the eleven chaplain–singers for whom there is extant documentation between 1482 and 1488 – I exclude Tinctoris himself – we see that eight of them are recorded for the first time: Domenico Bartolo of Manfredonia, Alexander de Marre, Juliano da Caiacza, Luigi de Admiratis of Massafra, Giovanni Chirardo, Antonius Rocha, Esremus de Risis of Naples, and Simplicianus. And at least six of these either definitely are or may be southern Italians: Domenico Bartolo, Juliano da Caiacza, Luigi de Admiratis, and Esremus de Risis are identified as such (Massafra is in Puglia, not far from Taranto), while there is nothing about the names of Antonius Rocha or Giovanni Chirardo that would necessarily suggest origins anywhere other than Italy. And this trend continues in the 1490s.[150] Singers, then, could be found locally. And Ferrante must therefore have been after singers of a very particular quality, perhaps singers with a certain range or 'star'-caliber singer–composers of the type that had recently arrived – or were just arriving – at Florence (Isaac) or Ferrara (Obrecht) or Rome (Josquin des Prez). If the latter is in fact what Ferrante hoped to attain, his ambitions remained unrealized; and when Ferrante came close to hiring Alexander Agricola in 1492–1493, the impending war with France spoiled his plans (see below).

The relative paucity of information for the 1480s is broken in 1489, though in a most frustrating manner. According to Riccardo Filangieri, there were forty-four people attached to the chapel that year.[151] Unfortunately, Filangieri provides neither documentation nor the names of the chaplains and singers. Who were some of the personnel? On the one hand, it is reasonable to presume that at least some of the singers who had just entered or had been in the chapel shortly before then were still active (Prats, as we have seen, is recorded in both 1488 and 1489); on the other hand, it may just as well be that some of the personnel for whom there is documentation only from the early 1490s had already joined the chapel by

---

[149] The letter has been printed three times: Volpicella, *Regis Ferdinandi Primi Instructionum liber*, p. 168; Van der Straeten, *La Musique aux Pays-Bas*, IV, 57; Woodley, 'Iohannes Tinctoris', p. 245.

[150] Lockwood, 'Strategies of Music Patronage in the Fifteenth Century: The *Cappella* of Ercole I d'Este', p. 238, notes a similar trend in Ferrara, where the proportion of Italians in the chapel went from one-fourth to one-third in the decade 1472–1481.

[151] *Castel Nuovo*, p. 242.

1489. The best year to look at is 1492, a year for which six members of the chapel are accounted for.

Still serving the chapel is Joan Brusca.[152] The new chapel master is once again a Spaniard, Fra Jacobo da Valenza, who was given ten ducats on 30 June to join Alfonso, Duke of Calabria, in the Terra di Otranto.[153] The man whom Jacobo had succeeded that very year was also present, Juliano de Caiacza, who is recorded for the first six months of the year without a specific title[154] after having been registered as chapel master and Bishop of Tropea for the period January–June 1491.[155] That Juliano de Caiacza – who had been chapel master from at least August 1488 and who had also taught at the Neapolitan *Studio* in 1487–1488[156] – was listed as chapel master in 1491 but not in 1492, when Jacobo da Valenza is so recorded, may indicate that the tradition of having two 'maestri' was no longer maintained during the period of Ferrante. In any event, that Juliano, an Italian, had served as first chaplain for no fewer than three years shows that the position was no longer reserved exclusively for Spaniards, if, indeed, that had not already been shown when Epo de Tropoya (Tropea?) held the post in 1481. Also new to the chapel was Nicolaus Volpe.[157] Finally, there are notices about two members of the chapel who also functioned as scribes. On 15 May Juliano Finero, 'cantore de la cappella', was given sixteen quinterns of 'paritatura' on which to notate 'canto figurato',[158] while on 19 December Juliano Ferrilla was paid for having copied 'certi misse de canto' and having made some entries 'in uno canczonero', both of which had been deposited in Ferrante's personal library the previous day.[159]

By far the most exciting event in the development of the chapel during the 1490s was Ferrante's attempt to hire Alexander Agricola after the composer had visited Naples in May–June 1492. As will be seen, Ferrante pursued the idea through the following winter, until his deteriorating political situation – war with France was becoming ever more imminent – caused him to abandon it.[160]

In February 1495, one month after the abdication of Alfonso II and the succession of his son, Ferrandino (Ferrante II), Charles VIII and his armies entered Naples. The occupation was short-lived, though, and Aragonese control of Naples was completely restored by November. Less than one year later, on 7 October 1496, Ferrandino died of natural causes and was succeeded by his uncle (the younger brother of Alfonso II), Federico. And it is with the few references to the chapel from the post-occupation period that our overview of its history ends.

---

[152] ASN, TAF, Vol. Ia, fol. 127ᵛ.
[153] Barone, 'Le cedole di tesoreria', X, 16–18.
[154] ASN, TAF, Vol. Ia, fol. 132ᵛ.
[155] ASN, TAF, Vol. Ia, fol. 114ᵛ; see also Barone, 'Le cedole di tesoreria', X, 9, for a reference to his having helped set – on 27 April 1491 – the rate of pay for Giovan Marco Cinico, one of the most active scribes at the court and a good friend of Tinctoris at Naples.
[156] See Cannavale, *Lo Studio di Napoli*, p. 52; the rosters of the *Studio* from 1488 to the end of the Aragonese reign had already been lost before Cannavale's research. Juliano was paid 80 ducats; his subject is not known.
[157] Archivio Segreto Vaticano, MS. Reg. Lat., 923, fols. 30ʳ–31ᵛ (my thanks to Adalbert Roth for this notice).
[158] De Marinis, *La biblioteca napoletana*, II, 297.
[159] Ibid., II, 304. To judge from their names, both men would appear to be Italians, thus showing that Italian singers were not only forming an increasingly large proportion of the chapel, but also taking on posts of musical responsibility.
[160] On Ferrante and Agricola, see Chap. III below.

The Royal Chapel

There are two notices for 1497, the first for a Marino della Falcuni, who is registered for the period January–June,[161] the second for Roberto de Credencijs, who is present from July through December.[162] Both men are simply designated 'cappellano del Re'. However, that the post-occupation chapel had not been reduced to a few ecclesiastics, but continued to perform a musical function, is attested by the diary of Silvestro Guarino, who notes that on 6 June 1500 the royal chapel sang at the funeral of Joanne Vasallo, Bishop of Aversa.[163] Finally, we may speculate about the presence in the chapel of two singers known to have been at Naples shortly before the demise of the kingdom, the basis of the speculation being the famous letter written to Ercole I d'Este on 2 September 1502 by his agent Gian. Although it is most often cited because of its references to Josquin and Isaac, the letter goes on to say that the soprano Coletta had just arrived at Ferrara from Naples, and that Ercole had sent to Naples for still another singer, Fra Felice da Nola.[164] Since both Coletta and Felice were intended for the flourishing Ferrarese chapel, perhaps they had been members of its Neapolitan counterpart.

The history of the chapel, then, spans the entire history of the dynasty. Indeed, the chapel was established – as an extension of that in Barcelona – even before the Aragonese Kingdom of Naples was a political reality. And though documentation for the chapel is often sparse or missing altogether, most unfortunately in the period of Ferrante – this, of course, owing to the devastating destruction of the 'cedole' in 1943 – there is never a hint that it was ever disbanded. In all, the history of the chapel may be roughly divided into three phases. The most clear-cut phase coincides precisely with the reign of Alfonso I, when the chapel reflected the predominantly Spanish ambiance of the court. Despite its having reached the rather sizeable force of more than twenty singers by the early 1450s, the chapel led a somewhat provincial life, isolated both from the Franco–Netherlandish mainstream and, for the most part, from the musical establishments at the other Italian courts.

Signs of change in this respect are first evident in the second half of the 1460s. With the political situation now stable following the defeat of the Angevins and their baronial allies, Ferrante soon entered the sometimes intense competition – and subterfuge – for the services of the prized ultramontanes, and by the first half of the 1470s he could count among the members of his chapel such Franco–Netherlandish composers as Tinctoris, Vincenet, and Villette, as well as the singers Johannes Cordier and Philippet Dortenche. A corollary of the rivalry for singers of this stature was an increase in the musical contacts with other Italian courts, at first primarily with Milan, but also with Ferrara (contacts with both of which owing also to royal marriages) and, when political conditions eventually permitted, Florence. Clearly, the chapel – and music at Naples in general – had entered its heyday.

---

[161] ASN, TAF, Vol. Ia, fol. 159r.

[162] ASN, TAF, Vol. Ia, fol. 164v.

[163] 'Diario fatto per Silvestro Guarino d'Aversa, delle cose a suo tempo accadute nel Regno di Napoli, e particolarmente nella Citta d'Aversa dall'anno 1492 insino all'anno 1507', published in Pelliccia, *Raccolta di varie croniche, diarj, ed altri opuscoli*, I, 238.

[164] The letter is printed in Van der Straeten, *La Musique aux Pays-Bas*, VI, 87–88; an English translation appears in Lockwood, 'Josquin at Ferrara: New Documents and Letters', pp. 132–33.

It is difficult to say just when this period ended and the next began. Tinctoris's 'official' presence in the chapel cannot be documented with certainty after 1487 (see Chap. III), nor is there any evidence that his mission to recruit singers in the North met with notable success. Indeed, so far as is known, almost five full years would pass before Naples is host to another musician of truly international stature: Agricola. It is in this light that Agricola's trip to Naples and Ferrante's futile attempt to hire him for the chapel are difficult to interpret. Was Agricola attracted to the court because its chapel was still a major musical force? Or does Ferrante's pursuit of him represent a last-ditch effort to turn around a chapel that was beginning to deteriorate or was even well along in that direction? Suffice it to say that the chapel must certainly have been affected by the political reversals that Naples began to experience in the early 1490s. And for the final decade of its – and the kingdom's – existence, there is no sign that the chapel was home to any musicians of great note.

One final question about the chapel may be posed here: how good a musical force was it? Though it is obviously impossible to measure its quality in an objective way, there is compelling evidence that shows that it was certainly highly regarded in its own day. The testimony comes not from Naples itself, but from Milan, Florence, perhaps Ferrara, and, most eloquently, early-sixteenth-century Rome. That the Milanese thought most highly of the chapel is attested first by their repeated raids on its personnel. We have seen that Francesco Sforza was happy to gain the services of the organist Joan Corbató in 1463, and that in 1469 Galeazzo Maria lured the singers Raynero and Antonio Ponzo from Naples. In the early 1470s, Galeazzo was even willing to risk Ferrante's diplomatic wrath in order to keep Johannes Cordier from returning to Naples. Indeed, on 6 November 1472 Galeazzo Maria, intent upon forming a chapel of renown, wrote to his ambassador at Naples, Francesco Maletta: 'mandamo in quelle parte [Naples] li presenti exhibitori per condurne certi ["cantorini"] alli nostri servitij . . . et li conforti ad venire alli nostri servitij . . .'[165] Thus, when Galeazzo needed singers, he often sought them in the Neapolitan chapel, something that attests to the high regard that he must have had for the personnel. Nor was Galeazzo content to obtain only singers from the Neapolitan chapel; he also wished to have some of its musical repertory. On 26 January 1473, Galeazzo wrote to Maletta again concerning the Neapolitan chapel. Now he instructed the ambassador to speak to the chapel master, then Pere Brusca, and to obtain from him copies of the psalms that the chapel sang to commemorate the military victories of Alfonso I.[166] Even some of the repertory of the chapel, then, was admired outside the confines of the court.

The evidence from Florence is quite different. No doubt Squarcialupi had heard

where it is precisely dated; a facsimile is in Die Musik in Geschichte und Gegenwart, VII, Tafel 10, opposite col. 194.

[165] Motta, 'Musici alla corte degli Sforza', p. 307.

[166] Ibid., pp. 307–8. Pirro, 'Un Manuscrit musical du XVe siècle au Mont-Cassin', p. 207, associates Oriola's setting of In exitu Israel de Egypto with these compositions; see also Pope and Kanazawa, The Musical Manuscript Montecassino 871, p. 33.

the chapel when he visited Naples in 1450, and it is difficult to imagine that the 'gran cose et magne' that he was going to describe to Giovanni de' Medici did not include a favorable review of Alfonso's chapel. In fact, just eight months later the Neapolitan chapel visited Florence. And though the visit was politically motivated, one can assume that Renaissance cultural exchanges, like those of the present day, tried to present the best that a society had to offer. In other words, it is unlikely that Alfonso would have used the chapel as a political tool had it not been up to the highest standards and bound to impress its Florentine hosts. Though there is no evidence to show that Florence sought singers from Naples to the extent that Milan did, it seems that Lorenzo de' Medici did entice Jeronomo Milecto 'dicto Piovano' to Florence sometime between 1480 and 1484.[167] Finally, there is, as we shall see, knowledgeable contemporary testimony that Lorenzo held the Neapolitan chapel in particularly high esteem.

The testimony from Ferrara is somewhat ambiguous, and we shall not belabor it. According to a Ferrarese chronicle of 1454, Leonello d'Este founded his chapel according to the 'more regio'.[168] Pirrotta has interpreted this as meaning that Leonello modeled his own chapel on that of Alfonso[169] – a perfectly reasonable assumption in view of the close political ties between Naples and Ferrara in the 1440s. However, as Lewis Lockwood has kindly pointed out to me, the phrase 'more regio' could just as well point to the chapel of the King of France as the source of Leonello's inspiration, especially since he recruited a large proportion of his singers from north of the Alps.[170]

If Leonello d'Este's regard for the Neapolitan chapel is open to question, that of Lorenzo de' Medici is not. After the force of singers at the Florentine baptistry had fallen upon hard times in the mid-1460s, it was Lorenzo who set about restoring it.[171] And it was to Naples that Lorenzo looked for a model. Evidence for this appears in Raffaele Brandolini's *Opusculum de musica et poetica*, written circa 1513 for Lorenzo's son, Pope Leo X:[172]

Ferdinand [Ferrante I] pursued musical science with such affection that not only did he cultivate it himself most frequently in his private leisure but also attracted from all over Europe by means of most excellent rewards men most learned in this discipline. . . . He had in fact . . . a most flourishing throng of singers selected from the French, British, Spanish, and German territories and charged only with the regular appointed praises and ceremonies of the church. In his chapel in Naples there are . . . two organs . . . as sweet as they are harmonious. . . . His emulator, Lorenzo de' Medici, lest anything surpass his native region in honor and distinction . . . embellished most beautifully the Church of San Giovanni . . . with a sweet concord of voices.

---

[167] As noted above, the identification is tenuous (see n. 130).
[168] Lockwood, 'Dufay at Ferrara', p. 18, n. 30.
[169] 'Two Anglo-Italian Pieces in the Manuscript Porto 714', p. 257.
[170] Lockwood, 'Dufay at Ferrara', p. 6.
[171] D'Accone, 'The Singers of San Giovanni', pp. 320–21.

[172] I quote the translation – only insofar as it refers directly to the chapel – in Perkins and Garey, *The Mellon Chansonnier*, I, 30; the Latin appears on p. 34. Excerpts from the treatise are also published in La Fage, *Essais de diptherographie musicale*, pp. 61ff; see also D'Accone, 'The Singers of San Giovanni', p. 327.

Brandolini's statement that Lorenzo drew on the Neapolitan chapel as his model can probably be trusted. First, since he was addressing his remarks to Leo X, he would have no obvious ulterior motive in saying that Lorenzo was beholden to Ferrante. Second, Raffaele (circa 1465–1517), the younger brother of the humanist Aurelio (see Chap. V), gained his acquaintance with Neapolitan musical life at first hand. The Brandolini family moved to Naples when Raffaele was an infant, and it was at the court that he was educated, eventually coming to frequent Pontano's academy. Just before the French invasion, Alfonso II appointed him tutor to his son Alfonso, Duke of Bisceglie. And even after his permanent move to Rome in 1496, Raffaele maintained contacts with the Neapolitan humanists.[173]

Thus, no less a patron of the arts than Lorenzo the Magnificent, when intent upon reviving the chapel of singers at the Florentine baptistry, looked to for inspiration, and chose to emulate, the chapel of the Aragonese court of Naples.

The Structure and Function of the Chapel

We have, up to this point, sidestepped two issues that pertain to the structure and the function of the chapel: that is, we have treated the chapel as though it were exclusively a musical organization, and no firm distinction has been drawn between 'cappellani' on the one hand and 'cantori' on the other. Yet to let the matters rest thus is to oversimplify – if not falsify – the situation, for the chapel was more than just an ensemble of singers, and not all 'chaplains' were necessarily 'singers', at least not of polyphonic music.

The case is well stated in general terms by Pirrotta:[174]

While some court chapels were already [in the 1430s] in the process of becoming the purely musical institutions we know from later times, they still retained a number of other features ... the *capella* of a prince combined the tasks of providing daily celebrations of private religious services with those of a 'cabinet', a body of competent assistants and advisors, working in close association with their masters.

And the profile of a chapel offered by Pirrotta appears to have obtained at Naples. First, in its descriptions of the posts of 'abat de santos creus' (read chapel master), 'monges', 'escola', 'almoyners', 'escola dela almoyna', 'servidor dela almoyna', and 'confessor', the fifteenth-century copy of that section of the Aragonese household ordinances drawn up by Pere the Ceremonious in 1344 that deals with the chapel fails to mention any musical duties for those who held the positions.[175] And though we have seen that Alfonso broke with the tradition of having the post of chapel master filled by the abbot of Santa Creus, it seems unlikely that he would have had the ordinances copied had their prescriptions no longer been relevant. In addition, Aragonese chapel rosters of 1417 and 1420 – that is, prior to Alfonso's

[173] See Quartana, 'Un umanista minore della corte di Leone X'.
[174] 'Music and Cultural Tendencies in 15th-Century Italy', p. 132.
[175] The *Ordinatio dela capella del Senyor Rey*, as the fifteenth-century copy is entitled, is housed at Paris, Bibliothèque nationale, f. esp. MS 64; see fols. 19r–26r.

arrival at Naples – are quite specific in their designations of singers on the one hand and monks, 'sacerdotes', 'escolans', and an 'ajudant' on the other.[176]

This profile of the chapel seems to have continued at least well into the reign of Ferrante I, as is evidenced by two documents that have already been cited: the *motu proprio* issued by Sixtus IV on 1 September 1479 and the chapel roster of 25 (?27) October 1480. Whereas the papal document set aside benefices for forty unnamed 'ecclesiastical persons, either secular or regular of whatsoever order, including friars currently performing the divine office in the chapel of the said king',[177] the roster of October 1480 refers only to 'XXI canturi de la cappella' and then offers the sub-heading 'Seguitano li canturi' between the eighth and ninth names. Since there is no reason to believe that the chapel forces were depleted by almost half during the fourteen months that separate the two documents – still less so since Naples was then at the height of its musical development – the two notices can only mean that the singers of polyphony (to whom the term 'canturi' must refer) constituted only about one-half of the chapel in its entirety. As for those who were not singers, their primary duties must have been ecclesiastical and administrative in nature, though their church backgrounds would surely have equipped them to take part in the performance of plainsong. In all, there was probably a continuum of sorts, with those whose primary duty was the singing of polyphony at one end (for instance, Dortenche, Vincenet, Cordier), those with a mainly liturgical–administrative function at the other (Albarells and others who held the post of chapel master), and any number of singer–chaplains spread across the middle (Cornago (chief almoner), Borbó (master of the boys) and perhaps Tinctoris).

This raises a question about the chapel rosters published by Minieri Riccio. What are we to understand when he reports that the chapel consisted of fifteen, twenty-one, and twenty-two persons in 1444, 1451, and 1455 respectively? Do these numbers represent the singers only, or do they account for the membership of the chapel in its entirety? Unfortunately, Minieri Riccio's 'commentary' sheds no light on the question, for he introduces the rosters as follows: 1444 – 'cappellani e diaconi della . . . cappella'; 1451 – 'stanno nella . . . corte messer Pirardo Taxamor e Taxmet di Santo Paolo cantanti tenori, messer Giacomo Borbo maestro di canto ed *i cantanti* [my emphasis] . . . [eighteen more names]'; 1455– 'Erano . . . al servizio della cappella . . . le seguenti persone'. If we take Minieri Riccio at his word in his description of the roster of 1451, it would seem that the twenty-one names cited are those of members of the chapel who functioned as singers. And I would conclude the same for the personnel listed on the other rosters – this despite Minieri Riccio's use of the appellations 'cappellani' and 'diaconi' at the head of the roll from 1444, since other documents leave no doubt about the musical function of a number of the 'chaplains–deacons' there listed (see above, pp. 29–30).

---

[176] See Anglés, 'La Música en la Corte Real de Aragón y de Nápoles', pp. 972–75.

[177] Fols. 89v–90r (see n. 132 above).

The same problem of function surrounds the post of chapel master: was it primarily a musical position, or did the man who filled the post serve mainly as an ecclesiastical administrator? In favor of the latter function was the long-standing Aragonese tradition that assigned the post of chapel master to whoever was the abbot of the Cistercian monastery of Santa Creus. And as we have mentioned, the ordinances of 1344 do not give that abbot a musical role to fulfill. Moreover, the information that we have on the two best-documented chapel masters – Domenic Exarch and Pere Brusca – fails to indicate a specifically musical function. All of the documents that pertain to them (see Chap. IV) describe duties that would fall to someone who was the administrator of an ecclesiastical organization and close confidant of the king; they made offerings on behalf of the king, took charge of liturgical books, oversaw the preparations for the liturgy, and so on. To this extent, then, the nature of the chapel master's role seems to be essentially non-musical, and the duties of the post resemble closely those at the court of Burgundy or among the papal singers.[178]

On the other hand, there are at least two pieces of evidence that may point to at least a semi-musical function for the chapel master. First, we have seen that Alfonso broke with the tradition of appointing the abbot of Santa Creus as the chapel master, and that after establishing his court at Naples he assigned the post to two persons. Surely, the most sensible reason for this joint assignment is that its co-holders divided the duties of the post, one carrying out a mainly musical function, the other an ecclesiastical–administrative one. Yet reasonable as such a conclusion appears to be, it is not strongly supported by the available documentation, for like the notices about Exarch, those that mention Jaume Albarells, the man with whom Exarch shared the post, do so only in connection with administrative tasks. We thus draw a blank. Finally, there is the evidence of the roster of October 1480. Here the unnamed chapel master is listed among the 'XXI canturi', where he is cited between the singers Jacobus Villette and Luisot Patin, surely a sign that he took part in the performance of polyphonic music. Does this signal a change in the character of the position? Perhaps; but once again there is no further evidence to support it. Indeed, the one specific piece of information that we have about the activities of a chapel master in the latter years of Ferrante's reign concerns Juliano da Caiacza, and shows that in August 1488 he carried out the quasi-administrative task of adding a postscript to a letter that Ferrante was sending to Francesco Gonzaga, Marquis of Mantua. Significantly, as a sign of the role that he played, Juliano's postscript dealt with matters of finance in connection with two pifferi from northern Italy, Bernardino of Mantua and Michele Todesco of Ferrara (see Chap. V). In all, perhaps the most balanced conclusion is that at least some of the chapel masters were perfectly capable of performing a truly musical function, but that their primary duties were ecclesiastical–administrative, charged as they were with supervising and maintaining all that was necessary for the smooth operation of the daily religious life of the court.

[178] See Wright, *Music at the Court of Burgundy*, pp. 75–76; Sherr, 'From the Diary of a 16th-Century Papal Singer', pp. 83ff.

The Royal Chapel

One final note about the duties of the chapel as a whole concerns the occasions – or at least the minimum number of them – on which the chapel was required to perform; the information reaches us in the fifteenth-century copy of the Aragonese household ordinances:[179]

Dels orguens sonar en los dies . . . En les festes qui s segueixen vol lo senyor Rey que los orguens sien sonats a les vespres e a la misa: primerament en la festa de Nadal. item de Ninou. Aparici. Pascha. Ascensió. Pentacosta e Trinitat. e Corpus Xristi. les IIII festes de la verge Maria, allistada la V.ª, so es [a] saber, la Conceptió. les II festes de Sancta Creu. Omnium Sanctorum, los Angeles, sent Johan Bautista. la festa de Apostol e vangelista item sent Marti. item sent Lorens. item sent Steva. item sent Iorgi. item ii dies apres Pascha. item los altres ii dies apres. item les quatre festes dels Doctors. Cinquagesma.

Two comments are in order. First, although the schedule is set forth in terms of when the organs are to be used, I would speculate that it also represents a list of feasts on which polyphony was used to underscore the solemnity of the occasion (which is not to say that polyphony was never sung on still other feasts);[180] and second, though we have seen that after Alfonso settled in Naples he broke with at least one important tradition of the chapel – the master was no longer the abbot of Santa Creus – this would seem to have been the type of tradition that was easily maintained, and if any changes were introduced, they would probably have been in the direction of increasing the uses of polyphony. The list, then, is likely to represent the minimum number of regular occasions on which the royal court celebrated the liturgy with polyphony accompanied by organs.

---

[179] MS Paris 64, fols.12ᵛ–13ʳ; the excerpt is published in Anglés, 'La Música en la Corte del Rey Don Alfonso V de Aragón', p. 365, and Gómez Muntané, *La Música en la Casa Real catalano-aragonesa*, I, 112.

[180] For a similar Florentine schedule of 1502, one that is set out in terms of a schedule for the performance of polyphony, see D'Accone, 'The Musical Chapels at the Florentine Cathedral and Baptistry During the First Half of the 16th Century', pp. 4–5.

CHAPTER III

The Composers in the Chapel and Other 'Illustrissimi' at Naples

If the sole criterion for judging the stature or quality of a late-fifteenth-century chapel were simply the number of first-rank composers that it had in its employ, especially at any given time, honors would have to go to the chapel assembled by Galeazzo Maria Sforza at Milan in the mid-1470s. On 15 July 1474, the duke enjoyed the services of Josquin, Compère, Agricola, Weerbecke, and Johannes Martini among his 'cantori de cappella [and] de camera'; and the first three of these spent at least eighteen months together at Milan, for they are recorded again on 30 March and 4 December 1475.[1] Among other chapels that would score high in this respect is that of Innocent VIII in the mid-1480s. Included among his singers in the Autumn of 1486, for instance, were Josquin, Weerbecke, Marbrianus de Orto, and Bertrand Vaqueras.[2] By the end of 1492, the singers at the Cathedral of Florence could count Isaac, Ghiselin, and such lesser lights as Pietrequin Bonnel, Arnulphus Giliardus, and Colinet de Lannoy among their number, while Agricola had been there earlier in the year.[3] North of the Alps, Charles the Bold had in 1468 – to choose one year from precisely the time that Ferrante began to recruit Franco–Netherlandish singers – Antoine Busnois, Hayne van Ghizeghem, Robert Morton, Adrien and Pierre Basin (at least one and possible both of whom composed),[4] Jehan le Caron (who might be the composer Caron),[5] and Gilles Joye in his employ.[6] Since the chapel personnel numbered twenty-seven at that time, it is possible that just about one-quarter of the singers were also composers. Finally, in 1486, Charles VIII could boast of having at least Ockeghem, Compère, Fresneau, and probably Agricola in his service.[7]

---

[1] Sartori, 'Josquin Des Prés cantore del Duomo', pp. 64–66. A fourth roster, undated but probably from 1473, already included the names of Josquin, Agricola, and Weerbecke; see Lowinsky, 'Ascanio Sforza's Life', p. 34, n. 12, and Barblan, 'Vita musicale alla corte sforzesca', p. 826.

[2] Haberl, 'Die römische "Schola cantorum"', pp. 243–44.

[3] D'Accone, 'The Singers of San Giovanni', pp. 345–46.

[4] See David Fallows, 'Basin, Adrien', *The New Grove*, II, 240.

[5] On the problem of which of several musicians named Caron is the composer, see Craig Wright, 'Dufay at Cambrai: Discoveries and Revisions', p. 205; Perkins and Garey, *The Mellon Chansonnier*, I, 9; and my review of the latter in *Journal of the American Musicological Society*, XXXIV (1981), 141–42.

[6] The names appear on the roster as published in Marix, *Histoire de la musique et des musiciens de la cour de Bourgogne*, p. 260.

[7] See the articles on these composers in *The New Grove*.

In contrast, the Neapolitan chapel is surprisingly poor in this respect. During the course of its sixty-year history, the membership of the chapel included only five men who may be considered composers of some stature: Oriola, Cornago, Vincenet, Tinctoris, and Ycart.[8] This paucity of first-rank composers admits of at least partial explanation. For the period of Alfonso I, the reason seems clear enough. As long as the king was content to have – or perhaps insisted upon having – a chapel that was thoroughly dominated by his fellow Spaniards, there was little room for the Franco–Netherlandish composers, whether of the first or somewhat lesser rank, who were already then monopolizing the field. Indeed, even had Alfonso sought to obtain such composers, there is the possibility that they would not have found the cultural ambience of his court very much to their liking. There is also the political factor. Although relations with Burgundy were cordial in Alfonso's day, they did not yet approach the degree of true alliance that would develop in the early 1470s. And France was certainly no ally with which to foster close cultural ties. Thus Alfonso's court was to a certain extent both culturally and politically removed from the very areas that were producing the great composers of the period. And whereas such chapels as those at Ferrara and Florence could very early on use their French connections to obtain the services of such composers as Johannes Fede (Ferrara) and Beltrame Feragut (Florence),[9] to cite just two examples, Alfonso could – or did – not.

The situation is different for the period of Ferrante, and I can do no more than offer some completely speculative explanations. First, I think it unlikely that the chapel had any truly major composers whose presence there in an 'official' capacity (see below) is completely unknown to us. If there were any such, documentation on them probably would have surfaced somewhere along the way. It is possible that by the early to mid-1470s Ferrante became temporarily complacent. With both Vincenet and Tinctoris (as well as such lesser lights as Villette and possibly Oriola) in the chapel, he might have felt that he had no need of other composers. It is also possible that the cast of composers assembled by Galeazzo Maria, for example, failed to impress Ferrante that much. After all, he may well have considered his own Tinctoris – singer, composer, theorist, teacher, and man of letters – to be far more eminent and worth much more than even a large group of composers who had yet to reach full artistic maturity. After all, in his *Liber de arte contrapuncti* of 1476, Tinctoris did not see fit to count any members of the Josquin generation among the leading composers of the day.[10] In addition, at the end of that decade Ferrante probably had access to the music of two composers who, though not officially in the chapel so far as is known, were nevertheless residing at Naples: Guillaume Guarnier and Gaffurius (see below).

[8] Obviously, there may have been others, composers whose works either do not come down to us, or do so without ascription. In addition, there may well have been other composers whose relationship with the court is now obscured. A prime group of candidates for this latter category are some of the composers whose names or initials appear in the Neapolitan manuscript Perugia 431 but who are otherwise unknown.

[9] See Lockwood, 'Dufay and Ferrara', p. 19, n. 31; D'Accone, 'The Singers of San Giovanni', pp. 310–12.

[10] See *The Art of Counterpoint*, ed. Seay, p. 15.

Likewise, the chapel could no doubt obtain additional repertory from a group of composers like those represented in the manuscript Perugia 431 – that is, composers who have no known connections with the court but who may have resided and worked at nearby monastic institutions that had close relationships with the royal household. Obviously, none of this is to say that Ferrante was averse to having new composers, for it is in the late 1470s that Ycart seems to have been hired.

Whatever the reasons might be for the absence at Naples in the 1470s of a group of composers comparable to those at the courts of Milan or Burgundy, the situation seems to have changed by the latter part of the 1480s. In October 1487, with Vincenet now dead for perhaps a decade, and with no extant documentation for Ycart since 1480, Ferrante, perhaps spurred on specifically by the arrival of Obrecht at Ferrara only two months earlier,[11] sent Tinctoris north to recruit singers. And, as I have already suggested, Ferrante's expressed desire to have a type of singer that could not be found locally may indicate that he wished to replenish his depleted corps of composers with one or more Franco–Netherlanders of the first rank. Indeed, perhaps Ferrante even then had his eye on Agricola, at that time presumably in the French royal chapel. Agricola, of course, would visit the Neapolitan court for a few weeks in May–June 1492, but Ferrante's plans to lure him from the French court – kept secret from Charles VIII, as was so often the custom in such matters – came to naught. The late 1480s, therefore, is a significant period for music at Naples; not only does it represent the last years during which Tinctoris can be documented as a member of the chapel, but whereas Ferrara, Florence, and Rome were just then strengthening their chapels, it is the last period in which there is a bona fide composer known to be in residence at the Neapolitan court.

Because they were so few in number, each of the five important composers who were associated with the chapel looms large not only in the development of that organization, but in the musical life of the court as a whole. What follows is an attempt at presenting the fullest possible picture of their activities at the court. And since the order in which they arrived at Naples is rather clear, they are treated chronologically.

Pere Oriola. Probably a native of Orihuela, a small town in the southwesternmost part of the region of Valencia (province of Alicante),[12] Oriola is recorded at Naples for the first time on 21 November 1441: 'Lo Senyor Rey en Santagata . . . Item a XXI doni a Pere Oriola, Phelipet, et Miguel Xandres del dit Senyor a cascu 1 ducat, en accoriment de lur quitacio . . . s. III duc'.[13] The same trio of singers is paid again

---

[11] Obrecht had been invited by Ercole d'Este, who had sent his singer Cornelio to Bruges in order to arrange for the composer's leave of absence in that city; see Murray, 'New Light on Jacob Obrecht's Development', pp. 510–15; Lockwood, 'Strategies of Music Patronage in the Fifteenth Century', p. 235.

[12] See Pope and Kanazawa, *The Musical Manuscript Montecassino 871*, p. 32. 'Orihuela' is the Castilian form of 'Oriola'.

[13] ASN, TAF, Vol. VI, fol. 47r; published in Jole Mazzoleni, *Fonti aragonesi*, I, 119. The singers Phelipet and Miguel are Phelip Romeu and Miguel Nadal.

less than one month later, on 17 December: 'Lo senyor Rey en Minyano... Item lo dit die doni a Pere Oriola, Phelip Romeu, Miguel Nadal, xandes de don Fferrando, per lur provisio a cascu 1 ducat... s. III duc'.[14] The notices are significant in that they document Oriola's presence at Naples some three years earlier than has been generally supposed.[15] As for Oriola and his companions being listed in the service of Ferrante, Duke of Calabria, on 17 December, the evidence of the entire series of notices for 1441 makes it clear that this was no more than a temporary arrangement (see above, p. 25). Finally, as I have already suggested, the one ducat that each singer received is likely to represent an adjusted rather than a full monthly salary, with Oriola's full wage perhaps being as much as three ducats per month (see above, p. 26).

Oriola is next recorded on the chapel roster of 26 October 1444,[16] and then again on that of 8 November 1455.[17] That he is not listed on the roster of 27 February 1451 may indicate that he had temporarily broken his service at the court; given the constant traffic between the Spanish and Italian parts of Alfonso's realm, a trip to Spain is one plausible explanation for his absence in February 1451. On the other hand, he might simply have left Naples temporarily on a short mission for the king.

After 1455, we must wait fifteen years for our next reference to the composer, for it is not until 1470, when – on the 3rd and 26th of October – Oriola addressed two letters to Ludovico III Gonzaga, Marquis of Mantua, that we hear of him again; the letters, which deal not with music, but with horses and money, were written at Naples and provide the last pieces of evidence for Oriola's activity there.[18] Finally,

[14] ASN, TAF, Vol. VI, fol. 50^v; Jole Mazzoleni, *Fonti aragonesi*, I, 124.

[15] See, for example, Pope, 'Oriola, Pietro', *The New Grove*, XIII, 822, or idem, 'La Musique espagnole à la cour de Naples dans la second moitié du XVe siècle', p. 42. Pope and Kanazawa, *The Musical Manuscript Montecassino 871*, pp. 32–33, mention the 1441 documents, graciously acknowledging my having called them to their attention. Anglés, 'La Música en la Corte Real de Aragón y de Nápoles', p. 1018, at least implies that Oriola may possibly be identified with the Pere Galiana, 'prevere' of Oriola, who carried out diplomatic missions for Alfonso at the Council of Constance. There is no evidence to support such an identification, and it is unlikely that someone already then mature enough in years to be entrusted with such missions would still be active as a singer – as was Oriola – in 1479–1480 (see below). In addition, there is no evidence that the singer Oriola was a priest ('prevere').

[16] Minieri Riccio, 'Alcuni fatti di Alfonso I', p. 246. Both Pirro, 'Un manuscrit musical', p. 207, and Anglés, 'La Música en la Corte Real de Aragón y de Nápoles', pp. 968, 1018, state that Oriola was at Naples in 1442. Although his presence there in November–December 1441 and October 1444 make this most probable, I know of no document from 1442 that confirms it.

[17] Minieri Riccio, 'Alcuni fatti di Alfonso I', p. 439.

[18] The letters, conserved at the Archivio di Stato, Mantua, Archivio Gonzaga, Busta 805, Nos. 306–7, were generously called to my attention by William Prizer. The date 1470 – missing in the letters – was supplied by a nineteenth-century archivist. And that the letters were in fact written in 1470 is attested by Oriola's references to a trip to Mantua made by his cousin Joanne earlier that year, the same trip to which Ferrante refers in his letter to Ludovico of 6 July 1470 in which he asks the Marchese to send the musician Orbo to Naples (see Chap. II, p. 43). It is clear from Ferrante's letter that Joanne had just returned from Mantua. An entry in the *Diccionario de la Música Labor*, II, 1685, lists a 'Juan' Oriola as a member of the Neapolitan chapel in 1472; the editors give no source. Perhaps both the date and the name represent slips of the pen, for the entry that follows goes on to describe Pere Oriola (though cousin Joanne may also have been a musician, given his report to Ferrante on matters musical).

Oriola – now recorded as Pedro Oriuela (the Castilian version of his name) – is listed as a singer in the service of Alfonso's nephew, Ferdinand the Catholic, in 1479–1480.[19] Thus Oriola's service at Naples spans some three decades, from at least 1441 to 1470. And though the possibility of one or more leaves of absence cannot be ruled out, his documented tenure at the court covers a period that is approximately twice as long as that of any other composer active there.

As a composer, Oriola is known through four extant works, two each in the Neapolitan manuscripts Montecassino 871 and Perugia 431. Thus it would seem that both his output and reputation were limited. The pieces in Montecassino consist of a setting of the psalm *In exitu Israel de Egypto* and *O vos homines qui transite*, the text of which is a parody of the antiphon sung on Holy Saturday.[20] The compositions in Perugia 431 are *Trista che spera morendo* – probably a setting of the same poem that Vincenet set and that appears in the manuscript New Haven 91, though words and music are not easily adjusted[21] – and the textless composition that appears in the edition of the present study (No. 11). Notwithstanding the lack of text, the piece exhibits none of the style characteristics that we generally associate with instrumental music of the time, and it is possible, especially given the two distinct sections, the two endings in the 'secunda pars', and Oriola's Spanish origins, that the music is a setting of a canción. Oriola appears as a competent craftsman with a penchant, in this piece, for imitation in the upper voices (measures 6, 11, 19, 25, and 32). This is probably the best of his four pieces.

Joan Cornago. The most important musician at the Aragonese court prior to the arrival of Tinctoris was undoubtedly the Spanish Franciscan Joan Cornago. The standard secondary literature lists three dates and gives the following information in connection with his biography: (1) 12 October 1455, when he is recorded at the court — not, as is often stated, on a diplomatic mission to Rome – with an annual salary of 300 ducats.[22] (2) 3 April 1466, when he is listed as Ferrante's chief

---

[19] See Anglés, *La Música en la Corte de los Reyes Católicos*, I, 116. It is difficult to understand why Stevenson, *Spanish Music in the Age of Columbus*, p. 183, n. 278, sees an irreconcilable conflict between the entry on Oriola in the *Diccionario de la Música Labor* (see n. 18 above) and the composer's service in Spain in 1479–1480.

[20] Both pieces are published in Pope and Kanazawa, *The Musical Manuscript Montecassino 871*, pp. 123–24, 188–89; on *In exitu*, see also Bradshaw, *The Falsobordone: A Study in Renaissance and Baroque Music*, pp. 24, 30.

[21] Perugia 431 gives only the text incipit. Vincenet's piece is published in Davis, *The Collected Works of Vincenet*, pp. 162–64, and Perkins and Garey, *The Mellon Chansonnier*, I, 149, II, 366–68.

[22] Minieri Riccio, 'Alcuni fatti di Alfonso I', p. 437. It is interesting to see how a number of musicologists have misinterpreted Minieri Riccio's admittedly elliptical style and mistakenly reported that Cornago was at Rome at that time. Minieri Riccio's *summary* of the 'cedole' for that day reads: 'Alfonso spedisce a Roma per missione affidatagli Don Giovanni Dixer [read: Juan or Joan d'Ixer] Signore della baronia di Ixer in Aragona, *che ora trovasi nella sua Corte, dove ancora sta* [my italics] Lazzaro de Andronico greco di Constantinopoli, maestro Luigi [read: Luys] Cardona, maestro in teologia con l'annua pensione di ducati 300; *e* [my italics] Fra Giovanni Cornago dell'ordine di S. Francesco con la pensione di ducati 300 annue.' For a sample of the twistings: Anglés, 'Cornago, Frater Johannes', *Die Musik in Geschichte und Gegenwart*, II (1952), col. 1680: 'dieser Konig [Alfonso] schichte ihn [Cornago] im Jahre 1455 nach Rom'; Stevenson, *Spanish Music in the Age of Columbus*, p. 121: '[Alfonso] sent an Aragonese noble residing at his Neapolitan court on a confi-

almoner ('elemosiniere maggiore') with the duty of dispensing royal charity; on that day he received 10 ducats-1 tareno for the cost of altering some garments from the royal wardrobe that were to be given to the poor of Naples and another 25 ducats that would be offered as alms on Good Friday during the ceremony of the Adoration of the Cross at Castelnuovo.[23] And (3) 1475, in which year he is recorded among the singers in the chapel of Ferdinand the Catholic.[24]

To the notices just cited can now be added three more. On 6 April 1453, Cornago received the following concession: 'Ioannis Cornago fratris, lictera concessionis provisionis annue unciarum L, taxata uncias duas, tarenos xv sed mandato Regio nichil'.[25] The document is significant for a number of reasons.

dential mission to Rome. The commissioning document refers to Johannes Cornago as a Franciscan residing in Rome'; or Pope, 'Cornago, Johannes', *The New Grove*, IV, 779: 'he [Cornago] was appointed a member of a confidential mission to Rome'. However, a close reading of Minieri Riccio shows that only d'Ixer was being sent to Rome; the others, including Cornago, are simply cited as being at the court. In addition, Stevenson is probably incorrect in stating that Cornago is mentioned in the same document as d'Ixer; a careful study of Minieri Riccio's article makes it evident that his entries for any given day consist of information drawn from a number of entries in the now-lost account books.

[23] Barone, 'Le cedole di tesoreria', IX, 209. Like so many other posts at the court, that of almoner was shared by two men. According to Ryder, *The Kingdom of Naples*, p. 86: 'The senior took charge of moneys destined for alms while the junior kept account of them. Both saw to the distribution among the poor of food left over from the tables of the dining hall and assisted the king in the ceremony of washing the feet of the poor on Maundy Thursday. In the chapel they alternated in saying mass before the king and assisted with other services.' Since Cornago is cited as 'elemosiniere maggiore', he must have been the senior of the pair.

[24] In *Riemann Musik Lexikon*, 12th ed., Personenteil A–K, p. 340, the date of service in Ferdinand's chapel is incorrectly given as 1473. Stevenson, *Spanish Music in the Age of Columbus*, p. 121, n. 43 (following a suggestion in Pirro, 'Un manuscrit musical', p. 206), questions Cornago's presence in Spain in 1475 on the grounds that he dates the composer's *Missa Ayo visto lo mapamundi* from 1480 at the earliest – when Ferrante commissioned the Neapolitan artist Giovanni di Gusto to draw a *mappamundi* on Holland linen (see Barone, 'Le cedole di tesoreria', IX, 46) – and that Trent 88, one of the two sources for the Mass (the other, Prague D.G. IV.47', should be added to the sources cited in Stevenson and *MGG*), contains an inscription that places Cornago at Naples at the time he composed the work. However, there is no reason to associate the Mass with the drawing of 1480. *Mappamundi* were quite popular in the fifteenth century, so much so that they constituted a genre of their own; see Kimble, *Geography in the Middle Ages*, pp. 181ff. At Naples, in addition to the drawing by di Gusto, there is a fine example in the manuscript Naples CF.III.4, which contains Ermolao Barbaro's commentary on Temestius's *Paraphrasis phisicae Aristotelis*; see Putaturo Murano, *Miniature napoletane*, pp. 72–73, tav. XXXVII. Moreover, Cornago may have been familiar with the well-known 'Catalan world map' of circa 1450 (see Bagrow, *History of Cartography*, pp. 71–72, Pl. XLVII), while the poem with which the cantus firmus of Cornago's Mass must have been associated, the 'siciliano' *Adxo visto lo mapamundi*, was known at Naples by 1460 at the latest, when it was entered into that part of the poetry anthology Barcelona 1 that was copied there (see below, Chap. VII, p. 145). Indeed, the poem and its melody seem far more likely to have been the catalyst of Cornago's Mass than any specific drawing. We may note that Snow, 'The Manuscript Prague, Strahov Monastery, D.G.IV.47', pp. 105ff, who dates the Mass from the 1460s on stylistic grounds, sees the ultimate origins of the poem, tune, and Mass in a *mappamundi* executed by Jan van Eyck circa 1430, the existence of which, at least, was known at Naples; see also Pope and Kanazawa, *The Musical Manuscript Montecassino 871*, p. 71. Finally, as Federhofer, 'Trienter Codices', *Die Musik in Geschichte und Gegenwart*, XIII (1966), cols. 667, 670, points out, Trent 88 was probably completed by circa 1475. Contrary to Stevenson's objections, then, there is no conflict between the Trent 88 redaction of the Mass and Cornago's having been in Spain in 1475.

[25] ASN, Miscellanae, no. 4, fol. 26ʳ; published in Bianca Mazzoleni, *Fonti aragonesi*, III, 35.

First, it pushes back Cornago's earliest known appearance at Naples by a full two and a half years. Second, if anyone might have doubted Minieri Riccio's report that Cornago had a yearly salary of 300 ducats, the concession gives sound confirmation of it, the 'oncia' being worth six ducats.[26] And third, if the notice marks Cornago's original appointment at the court, his salary of 300 ducats, together with the apparent waiving of the 'elagio' – in this case 5 percent[27] – shows that he must already have been a composer and cleric of some note. Unfortunately, nothing is known of his pre-Naples career in Spain.

The second new document, a surviving account from the 'cedole', dates from 15 September 1456 and simply shows that Cornago did in fact receive as high a salary as had been assigned: 'A frati Joan Carnago [sic] per la dicta paga de sua provisione – ducati CL'.[28] As the following notice will make clear, the 150 ducats must have been payment for the second half of the year.

The final document is perhaps the most interesting of all: 8 January 1457 – 'A frati Joan Cornago dela nostra cappella per la dicta paga de sua provisione de CCC ducati per anno havea supra lo sali per foculerj di terra di lavorj – ducati CL'.[29] Since Cornago had been paid half his yearly salary on the previous 15 September, that he is being paid the same amount again shows that the 150 ducats are now being allotted in advance for the first six months of 1457.[30] Most interesting, though, is the final phrase of the notice: 'havea supra lo sali per foculerj di terra di lavoro', which I take to mean that with his salary Cornago was given 'in addition, the salt for the hearth tax of the Terra di Lavoro'. The hearth tax, or 'ius focularium', which was instituted in 1443, levied a tax of ten carlini (one ducat) on all persons in the kingdom having their own 'patrimony or usufruct ... irrespective of whether [they] lived alone or in a family'.[31] In return, the crown had to distribute free of charge one 'tomolo' of salt to every household that paid the tax. However, each household had in addition to purchase another 'tomolo' of salt from the state monopoly. Finally, the Terra di Lavoro was one of the twelve provinces into which the kingdom was divided,[32] and as the province that included the city of Naples itself, together with such royal demesne towns as Gaeta, Aversa, Capua, and Terracina, the Terra di Lavoro was the most heavily populated of the provinces, one of the wealthiest in terms of commerce, and the one whose affairs were most closely regulated by the central government.[33]

What does this mean in terms of Cornago's compensation? Two interpretations seem possible. The more conservative is that perhaps Cornago was exempt both from the hearth tax and the required purchase of the extra 'tomolo' of salt. There are two problems with this: first, in terms of compensation the amount of money is virtually meaningless, since it would have saved Cornago a total of one and a half

---

[26] See the Note on Currency, p. x above.
[27] 2 oncie-15 tarì = 15 ducats.
[28] ASN, TAF, Vol. XVI, fol. 43ᵛ.
[29] ASN, TAF, Vol. XVI, fol. 2ᵛ.
[30] Unless one regards the payment of 15 September as being some two and a half months in arrears for the first half of the year, and the payment of 8 January as covering the second half of 1456.
[31] Ryder, *The Kingdom of Naples*, p. 210, n. 225; the information that follows is based on *ibid.*, pp. 210–13, 353–56.
[32] See the map on p. 65.
[33] Ryder, *The Kingdom of Naples*, pp. 320, 343.

The Kingdom of Naples (after Ryder, *The Kingdom of Naples under Alfonso the Magnanimous* (Oxford, 1976), p. 385)

ducats;[34] and second, I do not know if Cornago, a member of the chapel and therefore of the royal household, was subject to such taxes. The other possibility is more daring, perhaps, and involves a far greater amount of money. Under normal conditions the manufacture and sale of salt were state-controlled monopolies.[35] Exceptionally, however, licences were issued to private individuals for its private manufacture and sale – among those who received this privilege was Alfonso's mistress Lucrezia d'Alagno[36] – with such licences being reserved for special favorites of the king. Could Cornago have been so rewarded? Certainly, his position in the chapel, specifically his post of chief almoner, exemption from the 'elagio', and salary of 300 ducats show that he was in fact held in very high regard. To interpret the document in this way is therefore most tempting. And if Cornago did not actually have a hand in the manufacture of the salt, he may at least have been allotted a certain quantity that he could then dispose of as he saw fit.[37]

How good was Cornago's salary of 300 ducats per year? Before making some comparisons – both with musicians and with non-musicians, both at and outside Naples – we should recall three things already noted in our introductory Note on Currency: (1) the ducat referred to in Neapolitan documents had the same weight and value as the internationally esteemed ducat of Venice, and therefore no allowance need be made for differences in currency as long as the monetary unit in question is the ducat; (2) ducats paid in money of account were worth no more than 10 to 15 percent less than ducats paid in gold coin; and (3) since, in the comparisons to be made, none of the references to ducats can – unless otherwise stated – be definitely shown to involve either money of account or gold pieces, the sums may be compared at face value.[38]

Because of the destruction of the 'cedole', and because neither Minieri Riccio nor Barone included salaries in the chapel rosters that they published, the salaries that are known for the members of the chapel are precious few in number:[39] 1441 – Miguel Nadal, Phelip Romeu, and Gonsalvo de Cordova seem to earn three ducats per month, with Oriola perhaps earning the same; 1443 – the organist Perrinetto earns 120 ducats per year; 1448 – Fra Giordi and Fra Ruberto are each

[34] One ducat for the hearth tax and one-half ducat for the cost of the second 'tomolo' of salt; the cost of the latter is given by Borso d'Este in his 'Descrizione della città di Napoli . . . statistica del Reame nell'anno 1444' (written while Borso was residing at Naples', published in Foucard, 'Fonti di storia napoletana nell'Archivio di Stato di Modena', p. 753.

[35] I draw upon Ryder, *The Kingdom of Naples*, pp. 353–56.

[36] ASN, TAF, Vol. XVI, fol. 43v.

[37] For precedents for this at the court, see Ryder, *The Kingdom of Naples*, p. 197. We should recall that in 1488 Ferrante rewarded the singer Joan Brusca with an income-bearing post in the customs house. Alfonso was not the only Italian patron to offer such concessions. In 1476, Galeazzo Maria Sforza granted his chapel master, Antonio Guinati, the right to work certain mines in the duchy; see Motta, 'Musici alla corte degli Sforza', pp. 517–18, and Lowinsky, 'Ascanio Sforza's Life', p. 37. A rather similar situation also obtained at the court of Henry VIII in 1526, for example, when Philip Van Wilder, a member of the King's Musick, received a license to import an herbal plant called Toulouse wood and Gascon wine. A number of Henry's musicians were permitted to embark upon business ventures; see Bernstein, 'Philip Van Wilder and the Netherlandish Chanson in England', p. 58.

[38] See the Note on Currency, p. x above.

[39] The sources for the salaries that follow have already been cited in Chap. II.

paid six ducats per month; 1457 – the tenor Giovanni di Brusselle receives just over 14 ducats as one-third of his yearly salary; he thus earns slightly more than 43 ducats per year, or slightly more than three and a half ducats each month; and 1471 – Dortenche draws ten gold ducats per month. Thus, even if one allows for the possibility of Cornago's having been paid in money of account, his salary is still almost two and a half times that of Dortenche. Indeed, the Spanish composer's yearly compensation of 300 ducats is known to have been matched only by that offered to Agricola in 1492–1493.

To compare Cornago's salary with the earnings of a few composer–singers in chapels outside Naples, we turn first to the well-known Ferrarese document of 2 September 1502, which notes that Josquin was willing to come to Ferrara for 200 ducats per year, Isaac for 120. Cornago, then, earned a good deal more than two of the most famous composers of the period – at a time, moreover, when they had reached their full artistic maturity. And when Obrecht arrived at Ferrara in the Autumn of 1504, he settled for 100 ducats a year.[40] In July 1474, Gaspar van Weerbecke earned 144 ducats per year, while the highest-paid member of Galeazzo Maria's 'cantori de cappella', Antonio Guinati, earned 168.[41] In all, a check of available Italian chapel rosters and payrolls turns up no one who even approached the salary received by Cornago. Yet, as will be seen, the chapel salaries at Naples were by no means so generous across the board.

Cornago's salary may also be compared with the compensation offered to non-musical personnel at the court. In October 1455, 'mastro' Luys Cardona, teacher of theology at the *Studio*, also earned 300 ducats per year.[42] This is the same salary that was paid to Lorenzo Valla when he joined the court in 1437, and to the judges of the Vicaria.[43] It seems almost to have been a standard salary of sorts for moderately high-placed officials. To those who labored on the royal farm lands, Cornago's salary must have seemed magnificent. Full-time help were paid the following yearly wages: head cowman 24 ducats; mill hand 14 ducats-2 tarì; laborer 18 ducats. In addition, they received food and drink – as no doubt did Cornago, as a member of the royal household – which is estimated to have been worth four tarì a month.[44] But lest we think that composers, professors, and 'humanists' stood much higher on the economic scale than they do today, two sobering facts: one of Alfonso's most trusted aides, Eximen Perez de Corella, who was variously tutor to the children of the royal family, viceroy of the Terra di Lavoro, court chamberlain and 'mayordomen', and diplomat, drew an annual salary of 3,000 ducats, while in 1454 Alfonso granted Federigo da Montefeltro a yearly stipend of 6,000 ducats, not to fight for him, but simply to guarantee that he would not take up arms against him.[45]

[40] Lockwood, 'Josquin at Ferrara', p. 115, n. 38.
[41] Sartori, 'Josquin des Prés cantore del Duomo', p. 64.
[42] ASN, TAF, Vol. XVI, fol. 43ᵛ; see also n. 22 above. Not all professors were that well paid; Juliano de Caiacza, also a member of the chapel, received 80 ducats when he taught at the *Studio* in 1487–1488 (see above, p. 50).
[43] Minieri Riccio, 'Alcuni fatti di Alfonso I', p. 252; Ryder, *The Kingdom of Naples*, p. 151.
[44] Ryder, *op. cit.*, pp. 363–64.
[45] *Ibid.*, pp. 64–65, 264–65.

If the above comparisons give us an idea of the value of Cornago's salary in relation to the wages paid to well-known and high-ranking composer–singer–chaplains at other Italian courts, as well as to both chapel and other personnel at the court of Naples, two other documents show us the cost to Alfonso of the chapel as a whole. On 15 September 1456 and 8 January 1457, precisely the same days on which Cornago was paid semi-annual installments of his salary, entries were made for the semi-annual expenditures for the entire chapel: 15 September 1456 – 'A la nostra cappella per la dicta paga de sua assignatione — ducati d';[46] 8 January 1457 – 'A la nostra cappella per la dicta paga de sua assignationi di mille ducati per anno — ducati d'.[47] To the 1,000 ducats recorded in the register must be added at least 300 for Cornago (payments to whom were recorded separately), and perhaps the wages of the two organists, which, if Joan Corbató earned the same as Perrinetto, would come to an additional 240 ducats, for a total annual expenditure of either 1,300 ducats (including the organists in the 1,000) or 1,540 ducats (if the organists are separate) for a force that had numbered twenty-two singers and two organists just two years earlier. It is interesting to compare the annual cost of Alfonso's chapel with that of Galeazzo Maria Sforza's in the mid-1470s. If in 1474 Galeazzo paid salaries throughout the year as he did in July, his outlay just for the twenty-two 'cantori de cappella' would have come to 2,328 ducats; add to this the cost of the eighteen 'cantori de camera', and Galeazzo's total expenditure for his two chapels would have reached a substantial 4,560 ducats,[48] or approximately three times the larger of the two figures that Alfonso might have spent. Yet that Alfonso's budget for his chapel was by no means miserly is shown by the record of the chapel at the Florence Cathedral. On 27 July 1487, the overseers of the chapel fixed the cap on the budget at 240 florins;[49] with the florin being more or less equal in value to the ducat,[50] the Florentines, with a chapel about half the size of that in Naples, thus spent in real terms less than one-half of what Alfonso did.

Knowledge of the annual expenditures for the chapel also helps in obtaining an idea of the average salary of the chaplain–singers. Using the 1455 roster of twenty-two as a basis and the 1,000 ducats to pay only those twenty-two men (in other words, Cornago and the two organists are excluded), we get an average of approximately 45.5 ducats per man per year, or just under four ducats each month – that is, twice the monthly wage of Alfonso's head cowmen. If the 1,000 ducats had also to include the wages of the two organists, the average yearly income of the twenty-two chaplain–singers would fall to 34.5 ducats per year, for

[46] ASN, TAF, Vol. XVI, fol. 42v.
[47] ASN, TAF, Vol. XVI, fol. 4v. Since expenditure for such items as liturgical books, vestments, and other accessories of the chapel were listed separately and as they accrued, I take the 1,000 ducats listed here to represent the outlay for salaries only. Any other conclusion would be unreasonable with respect to the effect it would have on average salaries (see below).
[48] The figures are derived from the salaries listed in Sartori, 'Josquin des Prés cantore del Duomo', p. 64.
[49] See D'Accone, 'The Singers of San Giovanni', p. 340.
[50] See Gnecchi and Gnecchi, Le monete di Milano, p. liv. The 1:1 relationship between florin and ducat at Milan held also for Florence (I am grateful for this information to Dr. Alan Stahl of the American Numismatics Society, New York).

a monthly wage of about 2.8 ducats. In addition, since certain members of the chapel, Cornago aside, earned more than these averages – in 1448, for instance, Fra Giordi and Fra Ruberto had six ducats per month – some of the chaplains may well have earned as little as two ducats or even slightly less each month. While these salaries pale in comparison to those earned by the Milanese singers in 1474 – an average of 114 ducats per year or 9.5 per month – they are not at all low in relation to those paid to singers and chaplains of little note at other Italian courts. Thus, at the beginning of the sixteenth century in Ferrara, several of the chaplains had yearly incomes of only slightly more than 11 ducats a year – not including, of course, whatever supplementary benefices they may have had – while a number of others with lengthy records of service earned 45 ducats per year,[51] precisely the same as one of the possible figures for the average salary in Alfonso's chapel in 1457. Two other examples drawn at random: in the Spring of 1490, the composer–singer Pietrequin Bonnel was hired at the Cathedral of Florence for two florins a month;[52] while two or three ducats a month seems to have been about the normal salary for the singers of St. Peter's at Rome throughout the final quarter of the century. Thus except for the extraordinarily high salary paid to Cornago, wages at Naples seem to have been more or less on par with those paid elsewhere. And just as the average salary at Milan was 9.5 ducats a month in the mid-1470s, so Ferrante would pay Dortenche ten gold ducats per month in 1471. And like the other major patrons of the period, both Alfonso and Ferrante could and would reward their singers with benefices, tax exemptions, captaincies, and other lucrative posts.

One final question: how much did 1,300 or 1,540 ducats a year for the upkeep of the chapel mean to Alfonso? To put it briefly, not much. In 1444, Borso d'Este estimated that Alfonso spent approximately a thousand ducats a day to maintain his court, 1,500 per day when he was traveling outside Naples.[53] It is estimated that the cost of entertaining Frederick III for ten days in 1452 came to some 100,000 ducats, while a six-month campaign in the Marches in 1443 depleted the royal treasury by about 800,000 ducats.[54] The chapel, then, represented a very minor expense.

In the edition, Cornago is represented by his setting of *Yerra con poco saber*, a canción by the poet Pere Toroella (No. 9).

Vincenet.[55] Although the biography of Vincenet is beclouded not only by the vague nature of the known documents about him but also by the possibility of a 'Doppelmeister' problem, there are three documents that unequivocally attest to his presence at Naples during the reign of Ferrante I. The best known of these was published by Van der Straeten some one hundred years ago: 'Vannella, moglia del

---

[51] See Lockwood, 'Josquin at Ferrara', p. 115, n. 38. Ferrarese salaries are expressed in terms of lire-soldi-denari, with 3.2 lire being equal to one ducat.

[52] D'Accone, 'The Singers of San Giovanni', p. 342.

[53] Foucard, 'Fonti di storia napoletana', p. 753.

[54] Ryder, *The Kingdom of Naples*, p. 174.

[55] On the question of the composer's Christian name, which is never mentioned in the sources, see below.

quondam Vincenet, Cantor fo del *Senyor Rey*'.[56] Though the notice leaves many questions unanswered, it does tell us that Vincenet had presumably been a member of the royal chapel, that he died no later than 1479, and that his widow was still residing at Naples.

An earlier reference appears in a letter of 21 March 1469, written by Jachetto da Marvilla to Lorenzo de' Medici: 'I had advised Vincinet before he came to Florence that he ought to consider the commission I had had from your generous father and from Golino Martelli – that is, to find some fellows for your chapel'.[57] From the context of the letter as a whole, it seems clear that Vincenet was at Naples in 1469 – this is attested by the next document – and that he had not helped the Medici to obtain singers. It is also evident that Jachetto knew Vincenet rather well. Assuming that the friendship was formed – or resumed – at Naples, and knowing as we do that Jachetto had left Ferrante's employ by September 1466 at the latest, perhaps we can push the beginning of Vincenet's Neapolitan service back at least to the mid-1460s.[58] What Jachetto's letter fails to tell us, though, is the precise date and duration of Vincenet's Florentine sojourn or his purpose in visiting that city.

Finally, the most informative of the Vincenet documents is one that has hitherto escaped the notice of musicologists, although it was published some years ago by De Marinis: 19 August 1469 – 'A Vinxenet de Enaut xandre dela capella del Senyor Rey viii ducats los quals som per scrivere e notar de viii offices de cant d'orgue per la capella del dit senyor los quals offici ha consignats a mossen Pere Brusca.'[59] Thus we learn that Vincenet was a native of Hainault, that he was in fact a member of Ferrante's chapel, and that he was also active as a scribe. It is in this last respect that there is a tempting piece of speculation to be made: since (1) Vincenet was a scribe, (2) the manuscript New Haven 91 was written by a northerner, and (3) that manuscript transmits all four of Vincenet's known secular works, perhaps we may at least entertain the notion that it was Vincenet who copied the main part of that source.[60]

It is when we try to fill in an earlier phase of Vincenet's career that we encounter a 'Doppelmeister' problem. Can the Vincenet of Naples – whose Christian name is never mentioned, either in the music sources or the archival documents – be identified with the singer Johannes Vincinetti (Vincenot) who is recorded in the papal chapel from December 1425 through June 1429?[61] Though past opinion

---

[56] *La Musique aux Pays-Bas*, IV, 31; see also Davis, *The Collected Works of Vincenet*, p. ix; Perkins and Garey, *The Mellon Chansonnier*, I, 16.

[57] I cite the translation in D'Accone, 'The Singers of San Giovanni', p. 324; the original is given in Becherini, 'Relazione di musici fiamminghi con la corte dei Medici', p. 99; see also, Davis, *The Collected Works of Vincenet*, p. ix, and Perkins and Garey, *The Mellon Chansonnier*, I, 16.

[58] Using the same reasoning, Davis, *The Collected Works of Vincenet*, p. x, proposes that Vincenet may have come to Naples by 1458. However, that is the year by which we can only be sure that Jachetto was at Naples (see Chap. I, p. 37 above).

[59] *La biblioteca dei re d'Aragona*, II, 251.

[60] I have already expressed this idea in my review of Perkins and Garey, *The Mellon Chansonnier*, in *Journal of the American Musicological Society*, XXXIV (1981), 143, n. 15.

[61] The documents pertaining to the Vincenet of the papal chapel are most easily accessible and most clearly presented in Schuler, 'Zur Geschichte der Kapelle Papst Martins V.', p. 45; for a summary, see Davis, *The Collected Works of Vincenet*, pp. vii ff.

has been divided,⁶² the identification is most unlikely. As Schuler notes, the Vincenot of the papal chapel was a priest,⁶³ and would not therefore have married and left a widow.⁶⁴ Any lingering doubts about this are resolved by another point that has been overlooked. The papal documents of the 1420s refer to the singer–priest as being from Toul, which lies southwest of Nancy, whereas the Vincenet who worked at Naples was from Hainault. Thus the speculation that the two musicians were one and the same must be laid to rest.

One final reference may be considered. In the sixth stanza of his *Lettres missives de Verjus*, the poet Jean Molinet strings together a series of puns on the names of musicians with whom he was no doubt acquainted: Verjust (=Jean Corneul), Philippe (?) Verdelot, Jehan Maigret, and Vincenet; the poem itself is addressed to Nicolas Rembert, a singer at St. Peter's at Rome from 1475 to 1478 and later a member of the papal curia who will figure in a Tinctoris document from 1488.⁶⁵ To identify Molinet's Vincenet with the composer–singer active at Naples seems safe enough, since he hails from the same cultural milieu as the other figures concerned.

In the edition, Vincenet is represented by two pieces: the canción *La pena sin ser sabida* (No. 10), and a little-known intabulation of his most popular composition, *Fortune, par ta cruaulté* (No. 16).

Johannes Tinctoris. Despite a number of valuable discoveries by Tammaro De Marinis and the penetrating evaluation of the biographical documents by Leeman Perkins and more recently by Ronald Woodley, much about Tinctoris's career at Naples still remains unknown. To begin with, the date of his arrival at the court cannot be established precisely. Perkins has argued convincingly for fixing the *terminus ante quem* certainly before 15 September 1476, the date of Beatrice's marriage to Matthias Corvinus, and probably before the Summer of 1475, when she was officially betrothed to him.⁶⁶ These dates are based on Tinctoris's two dedicatory motets to Beatrice in the manuscript New Haven 91 – *O virgo, miserere mei* and *Virgo Dei throno digna* – as well as his three treatises that bear dedications to her – *Tractatus de regolari valore notarum*, *Complexus effectuum musices*, and the *Diffinitorium musicae* – all of which either refer specifically to her unmarried state

---

⁶² Bukofzer, 'An Unknown Chansonnier of the Fifteenth Century', p. 29, lacking evidence that has since come to light, maintained that the two men were the same; Davis, *The Collected Works of Vincenet*, p. ix, and Perkins and Garey, *The Mellon Chansonnier*, I, 16, both equivocate; Reese, *Music in the Renaissance*, p. 137, n. 188, and Schuler, 'Zur Geschichte der Kapelle Papst Martins V.', p. 45, argue against such an identification.

⁶³ Schuler, *op. cit.*, p. 45.

⁶⁴ The term 'priest' would not have been used had the papal singer done no more than taken minor orders, in which case he would not have been obliged to take the vow of celibacy.

⁶⁵ The passage reads: 'Verjus est parent a verdure / A Rosimbois, a vigue dure, / A Verdelot, quand l'yver dure, / A Vincenet, a Pinche Aigret / A Ripaupé, qui tout endure / Et a messire Jehan Maigret'. The poem is printed in Dupire, *Les Faictz et dictz de Jean Molinet*, II, 789; see also, Slim, *A Gift of Madrigals and Motets*, I, 44–45. On Rembert, see Noble, 'New Light on Josquin's Benefices', pp. 82–83.

⁶⁶ Perkins and Garey, *The Mellon Chansonnier*, I, 17; see also Reese, *Music in the Renaissance*, p. 139.

or at least fail to call her Queen of Hungary, a title that she was permitted to – and did – use from the time of her betrothal.

The problem, then, is: How long before the Summer of 1475 did Tinctoris arrive at Naples? The thinking here has been fuzzy at best. Apparently it was Reese who first suggested that Tinctoris must have come to the court no earlier than the Summer of 1473, when the Princess Eleanora left for Ferrara; this suggestion was based on the lack of any references to Eleanora in Tinctoris's works.[67] The argument is not convincing, however, for there seems little reason to insist upon Tinctoris's having to have mentioned Eleanora, much less to have dedicated a treatise or composition to her, simply because the two were at Naples at the same time. Indeed, among the members of the royal family only Beatrice and the king himself were favored with dedications, the latter being the dedicatee of the *Proportionale musices*, the *Liber de arte contrapuncti*, and the three-voice *Missa Sine nomine* that appears in the manuscript Verona 765.[68] Yet Tinctoris must certainly have had contacts with the other members of the family, and it seems unlikely that he could have failed to appreciate the cultural inclinations of so active a literary patron as Prince Federico. Moreover, even assuming that an initial lack of dedications to Eleanora did in fact result from her already having left Naples when Tinctoris arrived there, he must surely have met her when he visited Ferrara in May 1479;[69] yet she still fails to figure in any of his subsequent works. Finally, if Perkins is correct in suggesting that Tinctoris was in Beatrice's personal retinue before he obtained a position in Ferrante's chapel,[70] this would help explain the dedications to one sister and the lack of them to the other. Under such circumstances, it is even possible that dedications to members of the family other than Beatrice and the king would have been deemed out of place. In all, Eleanora's departure from Naples as a precise *terminus post quem*, while possible, cannot be sustained to the definite exclusion of some other date.

Another date recently favored is the more general 'circa 1472', proposed by Hüschen, Seay, and Woodley. This date is certainly possible, though there is something less than perfect about each argument for it. Hüschen postulates an arrival at Naples in 1472, with a break in service in 1474 in order to identify Tinctoris with the Iohannes Tectoris who is recorded as 'succentor' at St. Lambert at Liège on 23 September of that year.[71] However, as Woodley points out, the identification is untenable.[72] Seay simply begins with the *Liber de natura et proprietate*, completed on 6 November 1476, and, on the basis of the passage that

[67] *Op. cit.*, p. 139; the opinion is accepted in Perkins and Garey, *op. cit.*, I, 17.
[68] On the last dedication, see Feldman, *Johannes Tinctoris: Opera omnia*, I, p. ii; the new edition of Tinctoris's works (in the same series), Melin, *Johanni Tinctoris: Opera omnia*, fails to mention the dedication.
[69] See Lockwood, 'Pietrobono and the Instrumental Tradition at Ferrara in the Fifteenth Century', p. 128.
[70] Perkins and Garey, *The Mellon Chansonnier*, I, 18; however, Tinctoris refers to himself as one of Ferrante's chaplains in the *Proportionale musices*, which Seay, *Johannes Tinctoris: Opera theoretica*, I, 7, dates from as early as 1473.
[71] Hüschen, 'Tinctoris', *Die Musik in Geschichte und Gegenwart*, XIII (1966), col. 419; see also Schäfke, *Geschichte der Musikästhetik in Umrissen*, pp. 236–37; Weinmann, *Johannes Tinctoris*, p. 17; Seay, *Johannes Tinctoris: Opera theoretica*, I, 7.
[72] 'Iohannes Tinctoris', pp. 234–35.

states that a number of works – 'nonnulla opuscula' – had been completed, arrives at 1472 by assuming that Tinctoris wrote about a treatise a year.[73] Even Woodley, whose examination and consideration of the Tinctoris documents are as rigorous as any, becomes somewhat subjective here. Noting (1) that Ferrante was elected a Knight of the Order of the Golden Fleece on 8 May 1473, (2) that in July 1474 Antoine de Bourgogne was sent to Naples to administer the oath to the king, (3) that the investiture was confirmed by 20 April 1475, and (4) that paleographical analysis points towards Tinctoris's having translated and the scribe Cinico's having copied the statutes not long after they were acquired (1474–1475?), Woodley deduces that in order for Tinctoris to have gained enough fluency in Italian and to have commanded sufficient respect to have been commissioned for the task he would have to have been at the court for 'a good two or three years'.[74] Again, this is all quite possible, but at the same time somewhat impressionistic.

Equally difficult, if not impossible, to determine is the date at which Tinctoris ended his association with Naples. The latest known document that unequivocally attests both to Tinctoris's presence at Naples and to his definitely being a member of the chapel is the letter of 15 October 1487 in which the king instructed Tinctoris to go north in order to recruit new singers for the chapel. The letter reads in translation:[75]

Having need in our chapel, for the rendering of the divine service, of some singers of a certain type ['della conditione a bucca'] that we have described to you, and not finding them hereabouts, we want you to go across the mountains to France and to any other region, country, or place where you think you may find them, taking with you the letter of recommendation that we wrote for you to the Serene and Illustrious King of France and the King of the Romans; to exert and trouble yourself to find some good singer, of the type and register ['et che habbia la conditione et parte'] of which we told you: and, upon finding him, to bring him with you [that he may enter] our service and that of our chapel. And we shall honor quickly and to the letter any promises you make, concerning salary as well as to other matters, to the said singers whom you bring.

Take care, however, to use the expenses judiciously and in such a manner that we are content and satisfied, all of the above [having been entrusted to you] because you are so knowledgeable in that art of singing and so well aware of what we desire; and [this commission], to which we give great weight, will be easy since you perform in accordance with our wishes.

Tinctoris, then, was at Naples and participating in the affairs of the chapel in October 1487. After this time, though, the nature of his association with the court is difficult to pin down. That Tinctoris returned to Naples is evident from a notarial act that was drawn up in Tinctoris's behalf on 18 September 1488 by the Neapolitan notary Francisco Pappacoda.[76] And evidence that he either stayed in or occasionally returned to Naples during the next two and a half years may

---

[73] *Johannes Tinctoris: Opera theoretica*, I, 7.
[74] 'Iohannes Tinctoris', pp. 231–32.
[75] As already noted, the original Italian appears in Volpicella, *Regis Ferdinandi Primi Instructionum liber*, p. 168; Van der Straeten, *La Musique aux Pays-Bas*, IV, 157; Woodley,

'Iohannes Tinctoris', p. 245.
[76] The following is based on Woodley, *op. cit.*, pp. 236–7; see also Noble, 'New Light on Josquin's Benefices', p. 83. The document concerns a prebend at the church of St. Gertrude at Nivelles, and is discussed in full by Woodley.

possibly be derived from a marginal entry dated 27 February 1491 that was added to a document of 24 September 1488 from the papal curia that itself registered Pappacoda's notice of the previous week. The curial entry of 1491 reads:[77]

27th day of February 1490 [= 1491 new style] the abovementioned Nicolaus [Rembert], procurator for the person of Iohannis Trutoris [=Tinctoris], as it appears in the public instrument issued by the hand of Francisco Pappacoda, Neapolitan notary in Naples, where he, Iohannes, is delayed, in the year of our Lord 1488, indiction 7, the 18th day of the month of September of the pre-said fifth year [=1488], by the authority of the said instruments [which] obligated Iohannes for the said taxes.

The crucial phrase for us is, as Woodley points out, 'in Neapoli ubi ipse Iohannes moram habet', which has the force of saying that, at least for the person who made the entry, Tinctoris was no longer 'officially' residing at the court, but only lingering – or possibly, as Woodley notes, returned – there. Thus, Tinctoris must have ended his formal affiliation with Ferrante's chapel sometime between the latter part of 1488 at the earliest and the very beginning of 1491 at the latest; the available evidence does not permit a more precise date.

Two other dates remain to be discussed in connection with Tinctoris's Neapolitan period, one of them certain, the other conjectural. It is known that in May 1479 Tinctoris travelled to Ferrara, where, from the 7th of that month, he lodged for four evenings at the hostel of one Nichollo Matto, leaving on the morning of the 11th.[78] Although the purpose of the visit is not known, it coincides with the construction at Ferrara of the chapel of Santa Maria di Corte, and may, therefore, have had something to do with the Ferrarese musical establishment.[79]

The final date is one at which we can only guess. In the dedication of his *De inventione et usu musice*, Tinctoris writes that he once met the composer Johannes Stockem at Liège, and that after meeting him he then *returned* to Naples.[80] Since Stockem is last mentioned at Liège on 14 July 1481,[81] the meeting must have occurred before then, and Tinctoris had to have made an otherwise undocumented round-trip from Naples to the Low Countries and back. As Woodley suggests, the trip probably took place after 1476 – in the *Liber de natura et proprietate tonorum* of that year, Tinctoris laments that he has been away from home for quite a while – and may have coincided with the four-day stop at Ferrara in 1479.[82]

In all, the chronology of Tinctoris's Neapolitan period may be fixed approximately as follows: (1) arrival circa 1472–1473, with possible service in Beatrice's entourage before joining Ferrante's chapel; (2) a trip to Ferrara, possibly as part of

---

[77] The document was originally printed in Emile Brovette, *Les 'Libri annatarum' pour les pontificats d'Eugène IV à Alexandre VI*, IV, 68; it also appears in Woodley, *op cit.*, p. 246. The taxes to which the document refers were to be paid on the benefice at Nivelles. Both Noble, *op. cit.*, and Woodley accept the name 'Trutoris' as Tinctoris.

[78] The document is printed in Lockwood, 'Pietrobono and the Instrumental Tradition at Ferrara', p. 128, and Woodley, *op. cit.*, p. 243.

[79] See Woodley, *op. cit.*, p. 234.

[80] The passage reads: 'quod ab eo tempore quo abs te ex Leodio digressus: divino munere feliciter Neapolim regresses sum'; quoted after Weinmann, *Johannes Tinctoris*, p. 27.

[81] Quitin, 'Stokem', *The New Grove*, XVIII, 165.

[82] Woodley, 'Iohannes Tinctoris', pp. 237–38.

a longer journey to the North, in 1479; (3) definitely back at Naples in October 1480, when he is cited among the 'XXI Canturi' of the chapel; (4) presumably left Naples for France, Germany, and the Low Countries in October 1487; (5) apparently returned to Naples no later than September 1488; and (6) severed official association with the court by the end of 1490 or the beginning of 1491 at the latest.

No less sketchy than the chronology is our knowledge of the full range of Tinctoris's activities at the court. No doubt, his main task centered on his service in the chapel. And since there is no evidence that Tinctoris was a priest[83] or held a high position in the ecclesiastical hierarchy of that organization – as did Cornago, for example – his primary duties in the chapel were most likely musical rather than administrative. Whatever his precise responsibilities may have been, it is not probable, I think, that Tinctoris was ever the chapel master, a position attributed to him by his contemporary biographer, Johannes Trithemius, who in 1495 referred to him as 'regis ferdinandi neapolitani quondam archicapellanus et cantor'.[84] Not only is there no corroboration for Trithemius's statement, which I take as nothing more than the author's way of lauding Tinctoris, but there is at least some evidence – all of which, to be sure, is negative and circumstantial – that argues against it. First, Tinctoris himself never claims the title.[85] Second, he was certainly not the chapel master in 1472–1473, 1480, 1481, or, if he was still in Ferrante's service, from 1488 through June 1491, years or periods for which we know that the position was held by someone else.[86] Third, all the chapel masters for whom there is firm documentation – Exarch, Albarells, Cortes, Pere Brusca, Epo de Tropoya, Juliano de Caiacza, and Jacobo da Valenza – were priests, whereas Tinctoris, it seems, was not. And, finally, Woodley's admittedly cautious use of the letter of 15 October 1487 – 'it might seem reasonable to assume that the task of recruiting new singers should fall to the first chaplain' – will not work, and not just for the reasons that Woodley gives;[87] rather, neither Jaume Torres nor Philipet Dortenche, the only other members of the chapel whom we know to have been sent on recruiting missions, held the rank of chapel master.

Another question for which there is no definite answer concerns Tinctoris's activity as a composer: was he required to compose, and which of his works – apart from either those in the treatises or any others that might have served a purely

---

[83] On this point, see *ibid.*, p. 237 and n. 56.

[84] In *Catalogus illustrium virorum germaniam* ... (Mainz, n.d. [1495?]), fol. lxxii^v; the one-paragraph 'life' is reproduced in Woodley, *op. cit.*, p. 247.

[85] He does describe himself with the following titles: 'magister', 'regis Sicilie cappellanus', 'inter cantores minimus', 'inter musicae professores minimus', 'in legibus licentiatus', 'jurusconsultus', 'legum artiumque professor', and 'inter legum et artium mathematicarum professores minimus'; see Hüschen, 'Tinctoris, Johannes', *The New Grove*, XVIII, 838. Obviously, it is not impossible that Tinctoris assumed the position only after having completed his final treatise at Naples, in the introductions of which these designations appear, or that a reference to himself as chapel master appeared in one of the two treatises that are known to be lost.

[86] In 1472–1473 Pere Brusca; October 1480 unnamed, but not Tinctoris; 1481 Epo de Tropoya; 1488–1491 Juliano de Caiacza; see Chap. II.

[87] 'Iohannes Tinctoris', p. 233; 'the letter does not attach any descriptive tag to Tinctoris at all, and any argument *ex silentio* is clearly dangerous'.

didactic purpose[88] – were composed at Naples? Certainly, the three-voice Mass for Ferrante as well as the two motets for Beatrice must have been written there, as was probably the setting of the Italian poem *O invida fortuna*, which presumably dates from after his arrival in Italy and which, since it appears in the manuscript Florence 176, a Florentine source from circa 1480,[89] was composed before Tinctoris departed from Naples. In addition, we may assign to Naples the now-lost motet cited by Gaffurius and addressed 'ad regem Ungarie'; and whether the work honored Ferrante, who used that title, or his son-in-law, Matthias Corvinus, has no bearing on the case, since the treatise in which Gaffurius mentions the piece was completed by 1483.

On the other hand, the chanson *Vostre regart* probably antedates Tinctoris's Neapolitan sojourn, appearing as it does in the original layers of Dijon 517 and Washington L 25, both of which were compiled in the Franco–Burgundian territories, seemingly prior to the theorist's earliest supposed arrival at Naples.[90] Another pre-Naples work is the recently identified *Missa super Nos amis*, the Kyrie and Gloria of which appear in a fascicle of Trent 89 that dates from the 1460s.[91] And if these works date from before Tinctoris's arrival at Naples, perhaps so too do the chanson *Helas* and the now-lost Mass of the same name cited by Gaffurius (see below, p. 81). Finally, another work that no longer survives, the motet *Gaude Roma vetus*, was written in honor of Alexander VI in 1492, when Tinctoris was probably in Rome.[92] As for Tinctoris's other works, the evidence is not conclusive as to their provenance, and Melin's assertion that all of Tinctoris's known works date from his years at Naples[93] will not hold up. In all, that Tinctoris – whose compositional output is not voluminous in any case – may not have been especially active as a composer at Naples (or at least that this was not his main activity) may perhaps be adduced from his rather poor representation in the extant polyphonic sources known to have been written at Naples precisely during the years in which he was active there. For aside from the motets for Beatrice in New Haven 91, Tinctoris is otherwise represented only by the chansons *Vostre regart* and *Helas* (both of which may be pre-Naples works) in Seville 5-I-43/Paris 4379.

Still another shadowy aspect of Tinctoris's career at Naples concerns his role as a teacher. Although Pantaleone Melaguli – the contemporary biographer of Gaffurius – attests to Tinctoris's discussions with Gaffurius and Ycart on matters of music theory (see below, p. 80), and though Tinctoris may have served as music tutor to Beatrice,[94] claims that he founded a private music school[95] or taught

---

[88] On a piece by Tinctoris – *Difficiles alios* – that is obviously didactic in nature, but which does not appear in any of Tinctoris's own treatises, see Blackburn, 'A Lost Guide to Tinctoris's Teachings Recovered'.

[89] See my study *The Cappella Giulia Chansonnier*, I, 247–58.

[90] See my study *Robert Morton: The Collected Works*, p. xxiv.

[91] Strohm, 'Die Missa super "Nos amis" von Johannes Tinctoris', p. 43. The work, which is complete in the manuscript Prague D.G.IV. 47, is not included in the *Opera omnia*.

[92] See Lowinsky, 'Ascanio Sforza's Life', p. 47; Woodley, 'Iohannes Tinctoris', pp. 237–39.

[93] *Johanni Tinctoris: Opera omnia*, p. vii.

[94] See Perkins and Garey, *The Mellon Chansonnier*, I, 17ff; Woodley, 'Iohannes Tinctoris', p. 233.

[95] See, for example, Carpenter, *Music in the Medieval and Renaissance Universities*, p. 353. The idea that Tinctoris established a music school at Naples may have originated with Lichtenthal, *Dizionario e bibliografia della musica*, I, 359.

music at the Neapolitan *Studio* or held any formal teaching post outside the chapel or court cannot be substantiated.[96] At best, we may suppose that he sometimes held forth on music within the more informal context of Pontano's Academy or at similarly unofficial meetings of the cultural coterie that gathered about Prince Federico.

Finally, mention of the Academy calls forth yet another aspect of Tinctoris's career, one that was first brought to light by De Marinis and that has recently been reviewed by both Perkins and Woodley: his activity as a man of letters within the circle of Neapolitan humanists.[97] Thanks to De Marinis's research, it is known that Tinctoris translated – at the behest of Ferrante – the articles of Philip the Good's Order of the Golden Fleece from their original 'lingua de borgogna' into Italian.[98] No less interesting is the philosophical letter, laden with allusions to classical authors, that Tinctoris wrote to his friend the court calligrapher Giovan Marco Cinico.[99] The letter thus substantiates Trithemius's statement that Tinctoris wrote 'a good many letters in a very graceful style, dedicated to various persons'.[100] In many ways, then, Tinctoris was a Renaissance man of sorts during his two decades at Naples.

In the edition, Tinctoris is represented by the motet *O virgo, miserere mei* (No. 1).

Bernardus Ycart. That Ycart was active at Naples circa 1478–1480 has long been known on the basis of two documents: (1) he is listed among the twenty-one singers on the roster of 25 (27?) October 1480, which places his name just above that of Tinctoris and records that he received 'canna 5' – or approximately ten and one-half meters – of blue Florentine fabric for his choir robes;[101] and (2) he is mentioned by Pantaleone Melaguli, the contemporary biographer of Gaffurius, as

[96] The records of the Neapolitan *Studio* fail to mention either Tinctoris or a chair in music; see Cannavale, *Lo Studio di Napoli nel Rinascimento*, passim; Kristeller, *Studies in Renaissance Thought and Letters*, p. 457, note 26; Reese, *Music in the Renaissance*, p. 138.

[97] De Marinis, *La biblioteca napoletana*, I, 150ff, and II, 19, 138; Perkins and Garey, *The Mellon Chansonnier*, I, 21ff; Woodley, 'Iohannes Tinctoris', pp. 231–32.

[98] The translation appears in the manuscript Naples XIV.D.20; the incipit, fol. I^r, reads: 'Qua seguitana tutti li articuli et ordinatione dell'ordine del Toson d'oro: Del quale lo primo fundatore fu lo serenissimi Principe Philippo ducha de borgogna: Li quali articuli Johannis Tinctoris doctissimo et clarissimo musico per mandato dela Sacra Regia Maiesta ha traducti de lingua de borgogna in lingua Italiana.' Fol. 5^r bears the coat-of-arms of Ferrante. A detailed study of this manuscript has been announced by Woodley. Putaturo Murano, *Miniature napoletane*, p. 57, is incorrect in dating the source from as early as 1469.

[99] The letter is now bound as part of the manuscript Naples XII.F.50, fols. 11^r–14^r. The text of the letter is printed in De Marinis, *La biblioteca napoletana*, I, 80–81. However, De Marinis's conjecture (I, 44) – tentatively accepted by Perkins – that the letter is an autograph must be rejected. The letter is bound together in the manuscript with Giovanni Elisio's *Succinta insturatio di balnei totius campanie*, which was printed at Naples in 1519 and the paper of which was drawn from exactly the same stock as that of the letter. On Elisio, one of the court physicians, and his book, see Manzi, *La tipografia napoletana nel '500*, pp. 191–92.

[100] 'Epistolas ornatissimas complures dedit ad diversos'; cited after Woodley, 'Iohannes Tinctoris', p. 247.

[101] For the roster, see Van der Straeten, *La Musique aux Pays-Bas*, IV, 29, and Woodley, *op. cit.*, p. 244. At Naples, fabric was usually measured in terms of the 'canna', which was equal to eight 'palmi' or approximately 2.1 meters; on Neapolitan weights and measures, see the very useful study by Salvati, *Misure e pesi nella documentazione storica dell'Italia del Mezzogiorno*.

having discussed matters of music theory with the famous theorist at Naples in 1478–1480 (see below).

To these sources may now be added a third, a papal provision of 27 October 1478 in which Sixtus IV granted Ycart an abbacy 'in commendam' at the monastery of Santa Maria del Pendino in the diocese of Tricarico, a suffragan of Acerenza, in Basilicata, a position that brought him 50 gold cameral florins per year.[102] And that Ycart actually assumed the benefice is shown by his having paid the single-charge annate (tax) of one-half the yearly income from the benefice, payment of which was required to be made within six months of taking possession of it.[103]

The document in which Sixtus IV granted Ycart the benefice is valuable for another reason; it settles a long-standing dispute about the composer's nationality, one in which Van der Straeten and Hüschen claimed him for the Low Countries, while Anglés and Stevenson sought his origins in Spain.[104] The latter two were correct. Given the reference to Ycart as a 'clericus dertusensis' (see note 102) – that is, as someone from the diocese of Tortosa, on the east coast of Spain – his Spanish (more precisely, Catalan or Valencian) origins can hardly be doubted.

Finally, knowledge of Ycart's Spanish origins and, more precisely, his connections with Tortosa raise the possibility that there is yet another document – also only recently discovered – that places Ycart at Naples, one, in fact, that extends the Neapolitan phase of his career back at least two years earlier than hitherto suspected. Galiano has recently noted that an entry in the *Giornale Strozzi* for 17 April 1476 (Vol. 32, fol. 78ᵛ) contains a payment record of 58 ducats to Guillem Ribelles of Tortosa; of these, eight ducats were for the account of 'Bernardo Picchart per parte di maggior sonma'.[105] Surely, Galiano's conjecture that the Picchart mentioned might be the composer Ycart finds support in that 'Picchart' is

---

[102] Archivio Segreto Vaticano, Registri Lateranensi 797, fol 30ᵛ–31ᵛ: 'Sixtus etc.: Venerabilius fratribus Archiepiscopo Acheruntinensis . . . est providet oportuno cum itaque sicut accepimus Monasterium sancte Marie del Pendino Tricaricensis ordinis sancti Benedicti eui quondam Blasius eiusdem Monasterii Abbas dum viveret presidebat per obitum eiusdem Blasii qui extra Romana Curia diem clausit extremum vacaverit et vacet ad presentes Nos tam ipsi Monasterio de Gubernatore secundum cor nostrum utili et ydoneo per quem circumspecte regi et salubriter dirigi valeat quam dilecto filio Bernardo Ycart clerico dertusensis diocesis qui ut asserit Capelle Carissimi in Christo filii nostri Ferdinandi Regis Sicilie Illustris Cantor . . . Monasterium predictos cuius fructus redditus et proventus Quinquaginta florenos auri de Camera . . . Datum Rome apud Sanctum Petrum Anno Incarnationis domine Millesimoquadrigentesimo septuagesimo octavo Sexto kalendis Octobris anno Octavo.' Credit for the discovery of the document goes to Adalbert Roth, who was gracious enough to share its contents with me. To judge from its annual tax assessment of 300 florins, Tricarico was one of the better-off provincial dioceses; see Hay, *The Church in Italy in the Fifteenth Century*, pp. 112–16.

[103] The action was registered on 9 February 1480 (new style) in one of the registers of the cameral series Libri quittantiarum (annatarum): Archivio di Stato, Rome, Fondo camerale, I, Vol. 1133, fol. 208ᵛ: 'per manum Societati de Spannochis . . . pro annata Monasterii beate Marie de Pendino Tricaricensis'. Again, my thanks to Adalbert Roth for this information.

[104] Van der Straeten, *La Musique aux Pays-Bas*, IV, 27; Hüschen, 'Ycart', *Die Musik in Geschichte und Gegenwart*, XIV (1968), 931; Anglés, *La Música en la Corte de los Reyes Católicos*, I, 24; Stevenson, *Spanish Music in the Age of Columbus*, pp. 124–25.

[105] Galiano, 'Nuove fonti per la storia musicale napoletana', p. 7.

cited in the company of a fellow Tortosan. Ycart, then, may have been at Naples by 1476, a proposal that is not contradicted by any other evidence concerning the composer.

Although further comments about Ycart's life must be speculative, a number of pieces of evidence all seem to point in the same direction as regards at least one phase of his pre-Naples career. Given that (1) Ycart is cited in Johannes Hothby's *Dialogus . . . in arte musica*;[106] (2) Ycart and Hothby, who was active mainly at Lucca, are two of only four composers represented and named in the polyphonic section of the manuscript Faenza 117, which was added to the main body of the collection in 1473–1474 by Johannes Bonadies, possibly at the Ferrarese monastery of St. Paul (see Chap. VI); (3) Ycart is cited in the *Tractatus practicabilium proportionum* of Gaffurius (see below, p. 81), who had himself studied with Bonadies; and (4) Ycart uses in his *Magnificat sexti toni* – the work by which he is represented in this edition (No. 5, and see Chap. VII) – a technique that may be associated with northern Italian composers, perhaps we may hazard that Ycart was a member of a Hothby–Bonadies–Gaffurius circle in northern Italy sometime in the early 1470s. Indeed, if Seay is correct in identifying the 'discipulus' of Hothby's *Dialogus* as Bonadies himself,[107] then Ycart may well have been a student or friend of Bonadies, since the wording in the *Dialogus* is 'tuus Ycart'. At the very least, there must have been some kind of association between Ycart and the 'discipulus' and probably between Ycart and Hothby himself.

Finally, as there was for Tinctoris, there is the question of what Ycart may have composed during the years for which there is documentation for him at Naples. Of the seven works that can safely be attributed to him,[108] four – the three Magnificats and the fragmentary setting of the Ordinary (Kyrie–Gloria) – are clearly pre-Naples compositions, as they are included in the polyphonic portion of the manuscript Faenza 117, compiled at least a few years before Ycart makes his first appearance at Naples. The other three works, though, could, and probably do, come from Naples. The motet *O princeps Pilate* is an unicum in the Neapolitan manuscript Montecassino 871.[109] The large-scale setting of the *Lamentations* in Petrucci 1506[1] accords well with the lavish role that music played in the celebration of Holy Week at the court.[110] As for the chanson *Non toches a moy*, it is unique to the Florentine manuscript Paris 15123, a source that is rather certain to have drawn a good deal of its repertory from the Neapolitan tradition in the early 1480s.[111] Three other pieces – *Pover me mischin dolente, Se io te o dato l'anima e'l core*, and a textless composition – are problematical on the ground that the manuscript to which they are unique, the Neapolitan Perugia 431, ascribes them

---

[106] See Seay, 'The *Dialogus Johannis Ottobi Anglici in arte musica*', p. 92; idem, *Johannis Octobi: Tres tractatuli contra Bartholomeum Ramum*, pp. 13, 65.

[107] Seay, *Johannis Octobi: Tres tractatuli*, pp. 13–14.

[108] The entry '3 motets' in the work list of my article on Ycart in *The New Grove*, XX, 573, should be emended to read '2 motets'.

[109] Edited in Pope and Kanazawa, *The Musical Manuscript Montecassino 871*, pp. 105–7.

[110] The work is edited in Massenkeil, *Mehrstimmige Lamentationen aus der ersten Hälfte des 16. Jahrhunderts*, pp. 1–13.

[111] See Atlas, *The Cappella Giulia Chansonnier*, I, 255, and Perkins and Garey, *The Mellon Chansonnier*, II, *passim*.

only to a 'M. Ic̃'. Although both Martin Staehelin and I have quite independently of one another suggested that the initials are far more likely to stand for 'magister Icart' than they are to have any connection with Isaac, as Johannes Wolf believed,[112] the three works are stylistically unlike any other pieces by Ycart.[113] Thus, the best that can be said is that if the compositions are by Ycart, then on the basis of their status as unica in a source that was compiled at Naples soon after Ycart was known to have been active there, they are as likely to date from his Neapolitan period as from any other time in his career. In the edition, Ycart is represented by a *Magnificat* (No. 5).

In addition to the composers who served in the chapel, a number of other distinguished composers and theorists either made Naples their temporary residence or at least paid short-term visits to city and court.

Franchinus Gaffurius. When, in November 1478, the Doge of Genoa, Prospero Adorno, sought and received political asylum at the Aragonese court, he was accompanied to Naples by Gaffurius, who had come to Genoa during the previous year, after having served at Lodi, Mantua, and Verona.[114] Short though it was – from late 1478 to late 1480 – and though there seems not to have been an official position at the court,[115] Gaffurius's Neapolitan sojourn was both productive and stimulating. According to his contemporary biographer, Pantaleone Melaguli, Gaffurius, 'being well versed in musical studies . . . distinguished himself so much that he did not hesitate to discuss music very sagaciously . . . with Johannes Tinctoris, Guglielmus Guarnerius, Bernard Ycart, and many other distinguished musicians'.[116] It was at Naples that Gaffurius completed and saw through the press his first major theoretical work, the *Theoricum opus musicae disciplinae*, published by Francesco di Dino in October 1480, and distinguished for being the first Neapolitan print to contain woodcuts;[117] and it was there that he may have added the glosses – one of which refers to Ycart – to two earlier treatises, the

---

[112] Staehelin, 'Isaac, Heinrich', *The New Grove*, IX, 336; Atlas, 'On the Neapolitan Provenance of the Manuscript Perugia, Biblioteca Comunale Augusta, 431 (G20)', pp. 65–66; Wolf, *Heinrich Isaac: Weltliche Werke*, p. 201.

[113] A thorough analysis that led to this conclusion was carried out by Dr. Scott Freuhwald of the City University of New York.

[114] For a capsule biography, see Miller, 'Gaffurius, Franchinus', *The New Grove*, VII, 77–79; see also Caretta et al., *Franchino Gafori*.

[115] According to a little-noted passage in a treatise by the Neapolitan poet–musician Giovan Tomaso Cimello, Gaffurius held the position of chapel master at the church of the SS Annunziata at Naples; see the excerpts from Cimello's *Della perfettione delle 4 note maggiori* . . . in Gaspari, *Catalogo della Biblioteca del Liceo Musicale di Bologna*, I, 204–5, and the reference in Cesari,

'Musica e musicisti alla corte sforzesca', p. 23. On Cimello, one of the early composers of the *villanella alla napoletana*, see Cardamone, 'Cimello, Tomaso', *The New Grove*, IV, 403–4, and idem, 'The Debut of the "*Canzone villanesca alla napoletana*"', pp. 85ff.

[116] Melaguli's biography appears as an appendix to Gaffurius's *De harmonica musicorum instrumentorum opus*, the earliest known manuscript copy of which dates from 1500; a facsimile of the Milanese print of 1518 appears in the series *Biblioteca musica bononiensis*, II/7. The above translation is from Miller, *Franchinus Gaffurius: De harmonia musicorum instrumentorum opus*, pp. 212–13, who follows the text of the 1518 print.

[117] The *Theoricum* was later reprinted at Milan in 1492, the text having been revised and expanded and the title having been altered to *Theorica musicae*.

Extractus parvus musice and the *Tractatus brevis cantus planis*,[118] and must certainly have conceived the *Tractatus practicabilium proportionum* (completed between 1481 and 1483), which was later incorporated as Book IV of the *Practica musicae* and which, with its discussion of proportions and mensurations, probably shows the influence of his discussions with Tinctoris.[119]

Two of the three Gaffurius treatises just mentioned – the *Extractus* and the *Tractatus practicabilium proportionum* – are also valuable as sources of information on composers who were active at Naples, since they contain references to compositions by Tinctoris, Ycart, and Guillelmus Guarnerius that either have not come down to us or at least cannot be identified.[120] Thus it is Gaffurius who tells us that Tinctoris, with whom he was apparently very close,[121] composed a *Missa Helas* and a motet 'ad regem Ungarie', a work that, as we have noted, could have been intended either for Ferrante I or for his son-in-law, Matthias Corvinus. Ycart was the author of two Masses: *De amor tu dormi* and *Voltate in qua* (see Chap. VII, p. 134). And finally, Guarnerius is credited with a *Missa Moro perche non dai fede*, now lost (see below).

With respect to Gaffurius's compositional activities at Naples, we are somewhat in the dark. Perhaps it was there that he wrote the motet *Nunc eat et veteres*, a work that he refers to in the *Tractatus practicabilium proportionum* as being addressed 'ad Ioannem Tinctoris' and demonstrating the use of proportions.[122] Among his other

---

[118] Both the *Extractus* and the *Tractatus* survive in a manuscript copy, Parma 1158, a Gaffurius autograph that also contains polyphonic compositions by the theorist and other composers. The *Extractus* is edited in Gallo, *Franchini Gafurii: Extractus parvus musice*, pp. 150–52, and discussed in Miller, 'Early Gaffuriana: New Answers to Old Questions', p. 387. It is Miller (pp. 372–73) who asserts that Gaffurius added the glosses to the *Extractus* at Naples, this on the ground that one of them refers to Ycart. (The glosses are actually excerpts from an otherwise unknown treatise by Dufay, which Gaffurius cites as *Musica* and to which, Miller believes, Gaffurius added the Ycart citation.) There are, perhaps, two arguments that can be mustered against the proposition that the glosses were written at Naples. First, Gallo, 'Citazioni da un trattato di Dufay', believes that the Ycart reference was not added by Gaffurius at all, but was part of the original Dufay *Musica*. Miller counters by noting that Ycart probably belonged to a later generation than did Dufay and that it would be unlikely that the older composer would cite the younger one. Second, we should recall that Gaffurius might well have encountered Ycart's music – if not Ycart himself – before coming to Naples, specifically when Gaffurius studied with Bonadies, whose own familiarity with Ycart's music is evidenced by his having copied some of the composer's works into the manuscript Faenza 117 (see above, p. 79). On the other hand, Miller's argument may possibly be bolstered by the fact that among the pieces that Gaffurius copied into Parma 1158 is Robert Morton's *Que pourroit plus faire une dame*, which otherwise reaches us only in the Neapolitan source Seville 5-I-43/Paris 4379 and which was thus known at Naples; in fact, Morton's music was extremely popular with compilers of Neapolitan sources (see Atlas, *Robert Morton: The Collected Works*, pp. xxvi–xxvii, xxxii), and it is possible that it was at Naples that Gaffurius came across the Morton chanson. If this is so, it would indicate that Gaffurius had the Parma 1158 copy of the *Extractus* with him at Naples and that the glosses could have been entered there. In all, Miller's suggestion seems convincing.

[119] Miller, 'Early Gaffuriana', p. 385; this *Tractatus* also survives only in manuscript, Bologna A 69.

[120] The following is based on Miller, 'Early Gaffuriana', pp. 373, 377–79, 387.

[121] According to Cimello (see n. 115 above), Gaffurius was Tinctoris's 'carissimo amico'; see Gaspari, *Catalogo della Biblioteca del Liceo Musicale di Bologna*, I, 26–27, 204–5.

[122] See Miller, 'Early Gaffuriana', p. 377, who notes that Gaffurius and Tinctoris exchanged pedogogical motets.

82 *Music at the Aragonese Court of Naples*

works only two can be safely assigned to Naples, the hymns *Hostis Herodis impie* and *Christe Redemptor omnium, Ex Patre Patris*, both of which are unique to the Neapolitan manuscript Montecassino 871 and are the only hymn settings by Gaffurius that use chants of the Roman, rather than of the Ambrosian, rite.[123]

In the edition, Gaffurius is represented by *Christe Redemptor omnium* (No. 7).

Guillelmus Guarnerius. One of the more shadowy figures of the late fifteenth century, Guarnerius – singer, teacher,[124] and, according to Gaffurius, composer – was at Naples from mid-1476 at the earliest to the spring of 1479 at the latest.[125] Although Melaguli records that Guarnerius engaged in conversations concerning music theory with Tinctoris, Gaffurius, and Ycart, and though it may have been at Naples that Guarnerius composed his now-lost *Missa Moro perche non dai fede* (attributed to him by Gaffurius), which was no doubt based on pre-existent material from Cornago's secular work of that name, Guarnerius's association with the court is probably best remembered for his having instructed Serafino dall'Aquila in music. That Guarnerius must certainly have impressed Gaffurius at Naples is attested by the famous theorist's reference to him as both being an 'optimus contrapunctista' and standing among the 'peretissimi' of the science of music.[126]

Serafino dall'Aquila. Although the court was host to a number of famous poet–improvisators – among them Benedetto Gareth and Aurelio Brandolini – none came to enjoy such widespread fame as did Serafino de' Ciminelli dall'Aquila.[127] Born on 6 January 1466, Serafino first came to Naples in 1478, when he entered the service of Antonio de Guevara, Count of Potenza, as a page.[128] There the twelve-year-old boy studied music with 'Guglielmo fiammengo ... musico famosissimo' (who is generally identified as Guillelmus Guarnerius), learning to

[123] See Pope and Kanazawa, *The Musical Manuscript Montecassino 871*, 31–32.

[124] Aside from his having instructed the poet Serafino dall'Aquila in music (see below), Guarnerius taught at the Collegio degli Innocenti, the school for choirboys that was attached to the ducal chapel at the court of Savoy, from at least 1 February to 19 June 1473; see Bouquet, 'La cappella musicale dei duchi di Savoia', p. 266.

[125] His sojourn at Naples is framed by periods of service in the papal chapel. He is recorded at Rome from September 1474 through April 1476, at which time there is a break in the Roman records, and then again from sometime in the first half of 1479 through March 1483; see Haberl, 'Die römische "Schola cantorum"', pp. 231–41.

[126] In the *Tractatus practicabilium proportionum* (Bologna A 69, fol. 20ᵛ); see Miller, 'Early Gaffuriana', pp. 378–79.

[127] On Serafino's importance as a poet for the early frottola, see Rubsamen, *Literary Sources of Secular Music in Italy (ca. 1500)*, pp. 12–19; Giazotto, 'Onde musicali nella corrente poetica di Serafino dall'Aquila', pp. 3ff. On his association with Josquin, see Helmuth Osthoff, *Josquin Desprez*, II, 32ff; Lowinsky, 'Ascanio Sforza's Life', pp. 51ff.

[128] The main source of biographical information on Serafino is the contemporary account by Vincenzo Collo ('il Calmeta'). The biography, which is entitled *Vita del facondo poeta vulgare Serafino Aquilano*, was first printed at Bologna in 1504 and subsequently appeared in various editions of Serafino's works. For a modern edition, see Grayson, *Vincenzo Calmeta: Prose e lettere edite e inedite*, pp. xxx, 60–63; Menghini, *Le rime di Serafino de' Ciminelli dall'Aquila*, pp. 1–15. A thorough biography appears in Bauer-Formiconi, *Die Strambotti des Serafino dall'Aquila*, pp. 11ff.

sing and play the lute. Although his studies with Guarnerius could not have lasted very long – the Flemish musician was back at the papal chapel by the Spring of 1479 at the latest (see note 125) – Calmeta tells us that he made such remarkable progress that 'a ciascuno altro musico italiano nel componere canti tolse la palma'. Serafino remained at Naples until 1481, when, upon the death of his father, he returned to Aquila. A second encounter with Neapolitan culture began in 1487, when Serafino accompanied his patron, Ascanio Sforza, to Milan.[129] There he joined the circle of Isabella d'Aragona, wife of Gian Galeazzo Sforza, and met the Neapolitan courtier Andrea Cossa, who, according to Calmeta, introduced Serafino to the strambotti of Benedetto Gareth.[130] Finally, Serafino made a second journey to Naples at the end of 1491. He stayed there for three years, playing an active role in Pontano's academy and leaving the city only in mid-1494, when he traveled north with Ferrandino, who was preparing to meet the approaching forces of Charles VIII.[131] In compliance with a request from Elizabeth Gonzaga, Ferrandino left the poet at Urbino, from whence he proceeded to Mantua. Though Serafino was invited to return to Naples upon the restoration of the Aragonese late in 1495,[132] he never did return to the city whose cultural ambience so markedly influenced him.

Obviously, the inclusion of Serafino in the present survey of composers and theorists presupposes that Serafino was indeed a composer, and not merely a poet–improvisator. Quite aside from the difficulty of drawing a line between improviser on the one hand and composer on the other, that Serafino may have composed in the traditional sense of the term is suggested not only by his studies with Guarnerius, but also by a letter recently discovered by Lowinsky. The letter, from a Frater Christophorus to an official in the Sforza chancery, is dated 4 November 1490 and begins: 'Si Seraphino poeta havera ancora facto cosa nova usaro omne diligentia per haverla notata et le parole . . .'[133] Though Serafino may have lacked the compositional skills necessary to have written the polyphonic *Credo* attributed to a Seraphinus in the manuscript Perugia 431 (No. 4 in our edition), he probably could have composed the entire polyphonic fabric that sets his strambotto *Sufferir so disposto*, the poem – and presumably the music – by which he is represented in our edition (No. 14).[134]

Florentius de Faxolis and Josquin des Prez (?). In 1480, as a result of some poorly conceived political machinations, Ascanio Sforza was sent into exile from Milan.

[129] Bauer-Formiconi, *op. cit.*, p. 13, gives the date as 1489; for the correction, see Lowinsky, 'Ascanio Sforza's Life', p. 51.

[130] It seems unlikely, however, that this was Serafino's first meeting with Gareth's work. The Spanish poet had arrived at the court of Naples in 1467 or 1468, and there can be little doubt that Serafino came to know his poetry during his stay at Naples in 1478–1480. Even a literal reading of Calmeta – that is, that it was at Milan that Serafino first came to know Gareth's strambotti

in particular – does not seem likely.

[131] As Lowinsky, 'Ascanio Sforza's Life', pp. 51–52, points out, Josquin scholarship has long erred in placing Serafino in Ascanio's retinue in 1491–1493.

[132] See Bauer-Formiconi, *Die Strambotti des Serafino dall'Aquila*, p. 21.

[133] Lowinsky, 'Ascanio Sforza's Life', pp. 52–53.

[134] On Serafino's musical accomplishments, see *ibid.*, p. 53.

After pausing first at Ferrara, he continued on to Naples where he spent all of 1481 and most of 1482. Among those who followed Ascanio to Naples were the poet–physician Pietro Giannetti, the music theorist Florentius de Faxolis, and – perhaps – Josquin des Prez.[135] There is proof of Florentius's presence at Naples, for the 'Prooemium' of his *Liber musices*, written expressly for Ascanio, contains the following statement: 'ac fueram cum Neapoli Romaeque tecum una essemus'.[136] The theorist, then, had accompanied his patron to Naples and Rome. Although Florentius did not write the *Liber musices* at Naples, the treatise may contain an interesting Neapolitan connection, one that might possibly not have appeared had Florentius not visited the city. Among the 'moderniores' upon whom Florentius draws – and Tinctoris is conspicuously absent – there is an obscure 'Abbas populeti sive Magister Blasius'. Who is this abbot? In the marginal notes made at the beginning of the manuscript by the eighteenth-century bibliophile Carlo Trivulzi,[137] who purchased the treatise in 1775, he is identified as Blasio Romero, abbot of the monastery of Santa Maria del Popolo at Naples during the latter part of the fifteenth century.[138] Now, though we can do no more than speculate, perhaps the abbot can be identified as the Blas Romero who is recorded as a singer in Alfonso's chapel on 27 February 1451. If both Trivulzio's identification and our speculation are correct, it seems likely that Florentius came to know the obscure abbot's views on music while he was at Naples with Ascanio.

The case for Josquin's presence at Naples is completely speculative, and there is in fact no hard documentary evidence for such a sojourn. Nor does Lowinsky insist that Josquin was part of Ascanio's retinue there; rather, he writes: 'If a poet–physician like Giannetti and a modest and obscure musician–priest like Florentius were then in Ascanio's train, the likelihood of Josquin's being with him looms larger.'[139] To this I can add but a single piece of information that has hitherto been overlooked. Indeed, it was not until Lowinsky even raised the possibility of Josquin's having followed Ascanio to Naples that its possible relevance for Josquin became apparent. There is in the Neapolitan manuscript Bologna Q 16 an unicum whose text incipit reads *Je ne demano de vos* (No. 17 in our edition). What is interesting is that this is the only piece in the manuscript for which the scribe entered an ascription: 'J.P.' Until now, the only composers with matching initials whose possible claims to the piece have been considered are Jehan Pullois and Johannes Prioris, but a stylistic analysis of the work shows that authorship by Pullois is well-nigh impossible, while ascription to Prioris is unlikely on the basis of the pattern in which all his other secular works were disseminated.[140] Thus it is

---

[135] *Ibid.*, pp. 43, 47–48, 51.

[136] The most thorough study of the treatise is Seay, 'The "Liber Musices" of Florentius de Faxolis' (the quotation appears on pp. 74 and 77); see also Lowinsky, 'Ascanio Sforza's Life', pp. 47–50, where Seay's dating of the treatise is revised and the work dated from between 1484 and 1492.

[137] After whom the Biblioteca Trivulziana at Milan is named; the manuscript is now housed at the library under the signature 2146.

[138] See Seay, 'The "Liber Musices"', p. 80 and n. 15. Since 1519 the monastery has been the Ospedale di Santa Maria del Popolo degli Incurabili.

[139] 'Ascanio Sforza's Life', p. 51.

[140] This has been shown rather convincingly in an unpublished seminar paper by Mr. E. Terry Ford, a doctoral candidate at the City University of New York. With respect to Prioris, Mr. Ford's

time to throw still another name into the ring: Josquin des Prez (the initials perhaps standing for Jodocus Pratensis). And though the piece clearly lacks the stamp of Josquin's customary genius, there is nothing – notwithstanding its dullness – that definitely rules out his having composed it, especially as the work would probably date from the hypothetical sojourn at Naples in the early 1480s (the main section of Bologna Q 16 was completed by 1487)[141] and does not seem to have been written for any very special event. We have, then, the following circumstances: Ascanio's presence at Naples; the inclusion of the musician Florentius in his retinue; the appearance of a work that bears an attribution to a 'J.P.' and that is unique to a source compiled at Naples not more than a few years after Ascanio was in that city (as the only ascription in the source, it may well have had special significance); the possibility that Josquin was in Ascanio's service; and no documentation that places the composer elsewhere in 1481–1482. To be sure, the evidence is clearly insufficient to make a case either for Josquin's having been at Naples or for his having composed *Je ne demano*, but neither should those conjectures be altogether forsaken.[142]

Alexander Agricola. As I have shown in detail elsewhere,[143] Agricola's presence at Naples in May–June 1492 and Ferrante's unsuccessful attempt to hire him – behind the back of Charles VIII – at an annual salary of 300 ducats are attested by a series of six letters: (1) 13 May 1492, Piero de' Medici to Niccolò Michelozzi at Naples – Agricola is at Naples and should return to Florence in order that he may continue on to France, where Charles VIII is waiting for him; (2) 13 June 1492, Ferrante to Charles VIII – having been at Naples, where the court admired his talent, Agricola is now on his way back to France, and Ferrante asks Charles to consider permitting him to return to Naples; (3) 11 February 1493, Ferrante to Giovanni Battista Coppola, Neapolitan ambassador to the French court – Coppola should speak to Agricola and convey to him Ferrante's offer of 300 ducats per year if he is willing to serve the Aragonese court; (4–6) 12 June, 12 August, and 4 September 1493, all Ferrante to Coppola – Ferrante has changed his mind owing

conclusion finds a second in Wexler, 'Prioris, Johannes', *The New Grove*, XV, 276, where, however, it is noted that Prioris is supposed to have composed a now lost – or at least unidentifiable – *Missa Je ne demande*, something that might ordinarily strengthen his claim to the piece. Fuller, 'Additional Notes on the 15th-Century Chansonnier Bologna Q 16', p. 81, n. 2, claims that Pullois and Prioris are 'likely candidates'. Another composer who can certainly be ruled out on chronological–stylistic grounds is the 'J.P.' whose initials appear above two virelais in the manuscript Oxford 213; Cattin, 'Johannes de Quadris', *The New Grove*, IX, 667, interprets the initials as '? Johannes Presbyter'. The latter 'J.P.' has also been interpreted as a reference to Johannes de Quadris himself (Cattin, without taking a firm stance in the *New Grove* work list, did omit the two works from his edition of the composer).

[141] See Chap. VI, p. 121.

[142] One other possibility is that the letters 'JP' are not initials, but rather an abbreviation of sorts of a single name. In that event, perhaps the ascription refers to Johannes 'Japart', who, on the basis of the style of the piece, is a more likely candidate to have written it than is Josquin.

[143] 'Alexander Agricola and Ferrante I of Naples', where excerpts of the letters cited are given in the original Italian and in English translation. The five letters from Naples are printed in their entirety in Trinchera, *Codice aragonese o sia lettere regie, ordinamenti ed altri atti governati de' sovrani aragonesi in Napoli*, II, Nos. 137, 315, 430, 541, 567.

to the 'occurrentie de Italia' and tells Coppola to inform Agricola that he is no longer needed at Naples. The 'occurrentie' to which Ferrante refers in his letter of 12 August must certainly have been the anti-Naples political alliances that had taken hold earlier that year with the signing of the Pact of San Marco, an act that left Naples politically isolated. In addition, it was becoming ever more clear that war with France was imminent. In all, there could hardly be a better example of the way in which matters of politics and foreign affairs influenced royal decisions about artistic concerns.

CHAPTER IV

The Singers and Chaplains: An Inventory

The inventory that follows presents as complete a list as possible of the singers and chaplains who served in the royal chapel from the early 1440s to the end of the dynasty in 1503. Although I had originally intended to keep the rosters of polyphonic singers and those listed only as chaplains separate from one another, it proved impossible to do so for the reasons cited in the second part of Chap. II. And the risk of consigning to the list of chaplains someone who may have been a singer of polyphony seemed to outweigh whatever benefits the two-part division may have had. There is, then, a single alphabetical list.

Although the format of the inventory is self-explanatory, a few words about its contents are necessary:

Column 1: As in Chap. II, I have attempted to restore to their native form those Spanish names that I suspect were italianized by Minieri Riccio.[1] Where the evidence for Spanish origins was beyond doubt – whether from other documents, a reference in the name to a Spanish place name, or Anglés's suggested hispanizations based on his obvious knowledge of the names of his native Catalonia and neighboring Valencia – the change has been effected silently. When the evidence was not as strong, the version offered by Minieri Riccio is also given (in column 6).

Column 2: All dates are given in 'new' style.

Column 3: If the individual's function in the chapel – that is, singer, chaplain, or some other special position – can be determined from either an extant document or a trustworthy transcription of one that is now lost, that designation is given in quotation marks after the document or publication from which it is taken. When an individual's position can only be deduced or is reported only in summary fashion, the designation is recorded in English. In those cases in which a person's precise function is not clear, this column is left blank. Other information given in this column may include notices about salary, special services rendered, benefices received, function as a scribe, or any other events that may shed light on the individual's activities. If there is no entry in this column, we know only that the person in question was at Naples and was serving in the chapel on that particular date or during the period indicated.

---

[1] See Chap. II, nn. 21, 35, 50.

Column 4: For a primary archival source to be cited, two conditions had to have been met: (1) the source must be extant; and (2) I must either have consulted it myself or worked from a reliable transcription or summary of it.[2] Thus, there are no references to either the destroyed Neapolitan 'cedole' or the documents in the Barcelona archives, the latter of which, though extant, I had no opportunity to consult. Information from these documents is referred to through secondary sources (column 5).

Column 5: Although a reference to a singer or chaplain may often appear in a number of secondary sources, only one such source is generally cited: the earliest and the one on which the others obviously depend. The sources and their sigla are:[3]

AngM	Anglés, *La Música en la Corte de los Reyes Católicos* (1960)
AngMC	———, 'La Música en la Corte del Rey Don Alfonso V' (1940)
AngR	———, 'La Música en la Corte Real de Aragón y de Nápoles' (1961)
BarbV	Barblan, 'Vita musicale alla corte sforzesca' (1961)
BarC	Barone, 'Le cedole di tesoreria' (1884–85) (references are to vol. IX unless noted)
BertM	Bertolotti, *Musici alla corte dei Gonzaga* (1890)
CannS	Cannavale, *Lo Studio di Napoli nel Rinascimento* (1895)
D'AccS	D'Accone, 'The Singers of San Giovanni' (1961)
DelPP	Del Piazzo, *Protocolli del carteggio di Lorenzo il Magnifico* (1956)
DeMarB	De Marinis, *La biblioteca napoletana* (1952)
FerrF	Ferrante, *Fonti aragonesi*, VIII (1971)
FilD	G. Filangieri, *Documenti . . . delle provincie napoletane* (1883–91)
GalN	Galiano, 'Nuove fonti per la storia musicale napoletana' (1983)
GómM	Gómez Muntané, *La Música en la Casa Real catalano-aragonesa* (1977)
GregM	Gregori i Cifré, 'Mateu Ferrer' (1983)
HabR	Haberl, 'Die römische "schola cantorum"' (1887)
LockJ	Lockwood, 'Josquin at Ferrara' (1976)
MazzB	B. Mazzoleni, *Fonti aragonesi*, III (1963)
MazzF	J. Mazzoleni, *Fonti aragonesi*, I (1957)
MazzIC	———, *Il 'Codice Chigi'* (1965)
MazzR	———, *Regesto della cancelleria aragonese di Napoli* (1951)
MinA	Minieri Riccio, 'Alcuni fatti di Alfonso I. di Aragona' (1881)
MottM	Motta, 'Musici alla corte degli Sforza' (1887)
ParO	Parente, *Origini e vicende ecclesiastiche . . . Aversa* (1858)
PrizB	Prizer, 'Bernardino Piffaro' (1981)
RydK	Ryder, *The Kingdom of Naples* (1976)
SanD	Sanchis i Sivera, *Dietari del capellá d'Anfos el Magnànim* (1932)
VdS	Van der Straeten, *La Musique aux Pays-Bas*, IV (1878)
WalM	Walsh, 'Music and Quattrocento Diplomacy' (1978)
WoodT	Woodley, 'Iohannes Tinctoris' (1981)

Column 6: This column, headed 'Comments', is a miscellany of sorts and contains information that would not have fit comfortably in column 3.

---

[2] All references to documents in the Vatican archives were taken from transcriptions and summaries supplied me by Adalbert Roth.

[3] I cite only author's surname, short title, and date; see the Bibliography for more complete bibliographical information.

The Singers and Chaplains

Name	Date	Citation/activity	Primary source	Literature	Comments
Admiratis, Luigi de	1 Oct 1487	'cappellano'; named archpriest of Palagiano	BBN, MS X.B.58, f. 47ᵛ	MazzR, 161	he is from Massafra
Adroner, Luys	8 Nov 1455			MinA, 439	
Adzemar, Lambert	Oct 1444	singer		MinA, 245	his service with Alfonso extends back to 1431 at Barcelona; he accompanied Alfonso to Messina in 1432 and to Ischia in 1433; see GómM, I, 108; see AngR, 1013
	8 Nov 1455			MinA, 439	
	27 Apr 1457	a 'libro di canta' for the chapel consigned to him		MinA, 456	
Albarells, Jaume	Oct 1444			MinA, 245	a Cistercian
	7 June 1447	with Alfonso at Tivoli		RydK, 85–86	
	1447–1448	with Alfonso on Tuscan campaigns; 'cappellanus major'		RydK, 85–86	
	Nov 1451			MinA, 413	
	3 Nov 1453	at Gaeta, had presided over ceremonies for All Saints' Day		MinA, 426	
	1454	conducted a visitation of royal churches and chapels in Calabria		RydK, 85–86	
Albertus	29 Mar 1477	receives benefice at Capaccio (Salerno)	ASV, Reg. Suppl. 749, f. 182ʳ		cited as 'Albertus Abbas Monasterii Sancti Nicolai de . . . [?]'
Alegre, Gabriele	Oct 1444			MinA, 246	
Alfonso Galeco	25(?) Oct 1480	one of 'XXI Canturi'		VdS, IV, 29	
Alos, Francisco	8 Nov 1455			MinA, 439	
Aloth, Alon	25(?) Oct 1480	one of 'XXI Canturi'		VdS, IV, 29	
Amatore	25(?) Oct 1480	one of 'XXI Canturi'		VdS, IV, 29	
Andrea	1 Nov 1482	'cappellano'	ASF, MAP, Filza cxxxviii, No. 174		
Angerran, Ffilion	8 Nov 1455	singer		MinA, 439	with Alfonso at Messina in 1432; see AngR, 1013
Anselmo	25(?) Oct 1480	one of 'XXI Canturi'		VdS, IV, 29	
Antonio	Oct 1444			MinA, 245	could be Antonio de Lenti or Antoni Pont (= Antonio Ponzo? = 'Antonio Pons franzese'?)
Bartoli, Domenico	7 July 1484	'cappellano'	ASN, Priv. II, f. 172ᵛ	MazzR, 48	he is from Manfredonia
Borbó, Jaume	2(?) Oct 1444	master of the boys		MinA, 245	
	26 Oct 1444	received 95 ducats to buy 6 horses for himself and 5 boys		MinA, 245	precise date in FilD, V, 62–63
	27 Aug 1450	acting as chapel master		FilD, V, 44	
	27 Feb 1451	master of the boys		MinA, 411	
Borbó, Joan	27 Feb 1451	singer		MinA, 412	related to Jaume Borbó (?)
Botells, Jaume	8 Nov 1455			MinA, 439	MinA gives the name as Giacomo Botella
Brandano, Matteo	8 Nov 1455			MinA, 439	identical with Matteo de Capua (?)
Brusca, Joan	25(?) Oct 1480	one of 'XXI Canturi'		VdS, IV, 29	
	7 Nov 1488	received position of 'misuratore della dogana del sale'	BNN, MS X.B.58, f. 225ʳ	MazzR, 181–2	the appointment was for the duration of his life
	July–Dec 1492		ASN, TAF, Iᵃ, f. 127ᵛ		
Brusca, Pere	15 Apr 1454	master of the boys		MinA, 429	MinA and AngM, I, 22, give the name incorrectly as Brusia; AngM, I, 146, and WoodT, 233, confuse him with Joan Brusca
	Aug–Dec 1465	'cappellano maggiore' (until stated otherwise)	ASN, TAF, Iᵃ, f. 73ʳ		
	13 Dec 1465	a book of 'canto d'organo' consigned to him		BarC, 34	

Name	Date	Citation/activity	Primary source	Literature	Comments
	2 Feb 1466	made an offering on behalf of Ferrante		BarC, 206	
	11 Apr 1466	reimbursed for offerings for the king		BarC, 209	
	7 May 1466	received a book of 'cant d'orgue'		DeMarB, II, 247	
	4 June 1466	paid for offerings for Ferrante		BarC, 211–12	
	24 June 1466	reimbursed for offerings		BarC, 213	
	13 Jan 1467	reimbursed for offerings		BarC, 215	
	23 Feb 1468	given a chant book		BarC, 222	notated by Oddo Quarto
	27 Feb 1468	given a book of 'cant d'orgue'		DeMarB, II, 249	
	9 June 1468	a gradual consigned to him		DeMarB, II, 249	
	23 Mar 1469	an antiphonary given to him		DeMarB, II, 250	
	24 Mar 1469	given 4 ducats for expenses for 'rappresentazione' for Holy Thursday		BarC, 222	
	29 Apr 1469	reimbursed for further expenses and given charge of 6 pairs of white sheepskins		BarC, 223	
	19 Aug 1469	given charge of 'viii offices de cant d'orgue'		DeMarB, II, 251	notated by Vincenet
	July–Dec 1470		ASN, TAF, I^a, f. 93^r		
	1471	made Bishop of Aversa		ParO, II, 588–89 GalN, 10, n. 29	
	Jan–July 1471		ASN, TAF, I^a, f. 96^v		
	26 Mar 1471	reimbursed for offerings for Ferrante		BarC, 232	
	28 May 1471	an illuminated missal given to him		DeMarB, II, 255	
	July–Dec 1471		ASN, TAF, I^a, f. 99^r		
	Jan–June 1472		ASN, TAF, I^a, f. 101^r		
	13 Apr 1472	18 sheepskins given to him for the 'representations' on Good Friday		BarC, 242	
	12 May 1472	reimbursed for offerings		BarC, 245	
	5 March 1473	cited as Bishop of Aversa		GalN, 4	
	12 Apr 1473			GalN, 4	
	17 Apr 1473			GalN, 4	
	7 May 1473			GalN, 4	
	11 June 1473	made an offering for the king		GalN, 4	
	July 1473	cited as Bishop of Aversa	ASN, TAF, I^a, f. 30^r		
	2 Jan 1474	died		ParO, 588–89; GalN, 4	
Camtins, Genis	27 Feb 1451	singer		MinA, 412	MinA gives name as 'Camptius'
Campi, Giovanni	23 Feb 1465	singer; notated a book of polyphony		BarC, 34	
Casanova, Giuliano	9 Dec 1452	named a 'cappellano'	ASN, Priv. I, f. 47^v	MazzR, 12	he is a Carmelite
Chirardo, Giovanni	2 Aug 1488	'cantore'; given a 'cantorato' at Lucera	ASN, Priv. IV, f. 31^r	MazzR, 71	the 'cantorato', which had the value of 72 ducats, was vacated by Biagio Locha (see below)
Cini, Bernardo	2 Sept 1493	'cappellano'	ASF, MAP, Filza cxxxvii, No. 298;		in the service of the Duke of Calabria

The Singers and Chaplains

Name	Date	Citation/activity	Primary source	Literature	Comments
Citroli, Angelus Antonius	2 May 1489	'capellanus'; received a benefice at Salerno	ASV, Reg. Lat. 879, f. 296^r–297^v		he is from Salerno
Coletta	before 2 Sept 1502	'soprano'		LockJ, 123, 133	his presence in the chapel can only be presumed; see Chap. II, p. 51
Cordier, Johannes	between July 1471 and July 1474			BarbV, 843–44; HabR, 230–31; WalM, 439ff	on the dates, see Chap. II, p. 41
Cornago, Joan					see Chap. III, pp. 62–69
Cortes, Martin	Sept 1455			DeMarB, II, 238	he is a Cistercian
	7 Nov 1455	'locumtenens'		MinA, 439	
	8 Nov 1455	acting as chapel master		MinA, 439	
	16 May 1457	'locumtenens'; made an offering for Alfonso		MinA, 456	
	18 May 1457	another offering for Alfonso		MinA, 457	
	30 May 1457	an offering for Alfonso		MinA, 457	
Credencijs, Alberto de	Jan–June 1469	'cappellano'	ASN, TAF, I^a, f. 87^r		
Credencijs, Roberto de	July–Dec 1497	'cappellano'	ASN, TAF, I^a, f. 164^v		listed as 'Abbate'; despite the 28 years that separate them, could the names have been confused ('Al-' and 'Ro-' '-berto') and could they be the same?
Dornis, Antoni	27 Feb 1451	singer		MinA, 412	
Dortenche, Filippet	7 May 1466	singer; paid for a book of 'cant d'orgue'		DeMarB, II, 247	cited on this date as 'Ffelippo de Burgunya'; that he is Dortenche is my assumption; see Chap. II, p. 40
	24 July 1470	'regii cantoris'	ASN, Misc. I, 4, f. 85^v	MazzB, 124	
	27 May 1471	just returned from recruiting mission		D'AccS, 325	
	13 Jan 1473 25(?) Oct 1480	one of 'XXI Canturi'	ASF, Strozzi, 27	GalN, 4, n. 32 VdS, IV, 28, 31	
Dragonexo, Johanne	April 1443	'scolà'; given 25 ducats to buy a breviary		DeMarB, II, 227	
Egidio di Martello	1 Feb 1470	singer; in debt to two merchants for 50 ducats worth of material		FilD, V, 128–29	cited as 'francese'
Epo de Tropoya	1481	'cappellano maior'		VdS, IV, 31	Tropoya = Tropea (?), town on Calabrian coast
Exarch, Domingo	20 May 1439	'locumtenens'		MinA, 21	
	17 Jan 1441	4 tari 'per fer dir certes misses'	ASN, TAF, VI, f. 56^r	MazzF, 130	
	13 Nov 1441	received 4 ducats-1 tareno-2 grani for saying Masses	ASN, TAF, VI, f. 46^v	MazzF, 118–19	
	21 Nov 1441	3 tari-10 grani for 7 Masses	ASN, TAF, VI, f. 47^r	MazzF, 119	
	3 Dec 1441	included in his payment: 7 carlini for 7 Masses	ASN, TAF, VI, f. 48^r	MazzF, 120	1 carlino = 10 grani; the last two payments show that he was usually paid $\frac{1}{15}$ of a ducat for saying Mass
	12 Dec 1441	received 1 ducat to give to the poor	ASN, TAF, VI, f. 50^v	MazzF, 124	
	1441	'loctinent del cappellano maggior'	ASN, TAF, I^a, f. 7^v		
	June 1442	given two chaplaincies attached to the royal chapel of San Ludovico at the Duomo		RydK, 88	
	Oct 1442–July 1443	'cappellano maggiore'	ASN, TAF, I^a, f. 20^v		

Music at the Aragonese Court of Naples

Name	Date	Citation/activity	Primary source	Literature	Comments
	14 May 1443	countersigned privileges for the appointment of royal chaplains		RydK, 86	
	26 Mar 1444	Alfonso tries to have him made almoner of the monastery at Ripoll		RydK, 85	
	Oct 1444	cited as 'loctinent' again		MinA, 246; DeMarB, II, 229	
	4 Apr 1445	Alfonso uses his 'jusparonatum to give him an abbacy		RydK, 85	
	19 June 1445	chapel master		RydK, 85	
	Oct 1446	'locumtenent de capellan maior'		DeMarB, II, 229	
	6 Jan 1447	resigned chaplaincies at Duomo		RydK, 85	
	Nov 1451	chapel master		MinR, 413	
	1451	becomes Bishop of Agrigento		RydK, 85	
	5 June 1452	living at Santa Maria Incoronata		MazzIC, 331–32	
	1471	dies		RydK, 85	
Felice da Nola	before 2 Sept 1502			LockJ, 133	as with Coletta, his presence in the chapel can only be assumed; see Chap. II, p. 51
Fenice, Giovanni	Oct 1444			MinA, 246	
Ferrero, Giovanni	8 Nov 1455			MinA, 439	possibly Spanish: Joan Ferrer
Ferrero, Matteo	27 Feb 1451	singer		MinA, 412	possibly Spanish: Mateu Ferrer, and if so, possibly identical with the tenor (and later chapel master) Mateu Ferrer recorded at Barcelona in the period 1475–1498; see GregM, 12ff
Ferrilla, Juliano	19 Dec 1492	singer; notated 'certi misse de canto'		DeMarB, II, 304	
Figueras, Bartolome	Oct 1444			MinA, 246	
Finero, Juliano	15 May 1492	'cantore'; received 16 quinterns ruled for music in which he was to notate polyphony		DeMarB, II, 297	
Furtado, Pietro	8 Nov 1455			MinA, 439	possibly Spanish: Pedro Hurtado
Garitxo, Gonsalvo (= Gonsalvo de Cordova)	8 Nov 1437	'cantador'; received 15 ducats to buy a horse	ASN, TAF, II, f. 1ʳ	MazzF, 83	he was with Alfonso at Barcelona in 1430; see GómM, 108
	27 Dec 1441	received 3 ducats	ASN, TAF, VI, f. 54ʳ	MazzF, 128	
	Oct 1444			MinA, 245	MinA gives the name as 'Garzia'
	8 Nov 1455			MinA, 439	MinA gives the name as 'Garisso'
	1469	reimbursed for expenses in connection with the feast of St. John the Baptist		GalN, 5	

Name	Date	Citation/activity	Primary source	Literature	Comments
	5 June 1470	reimbursed for expenses from the preceding year		BarC, 229	there are further notices on him, July–Dec 1471 (ASN, TAF, I^a, f. 98^v–100^r), 29 Feb 1476 (ASF, Strozzi, 32, f. 41^r; GalN, 5), 25 March 1473 (ASF, Strozzi, 32 f. 149^r; GalN, 5), and 1481 (VdS, IV, 31), but always as a 'musico del Re', a term used not for members of the chapel, but for secular entertainers
Garzia, Sancio	Oct 1444			MinA, 245–46	
	8 Nov 1455			MinA, 439	
Gerardo de Cimiterio	20 Sept 1452	singer; received a benefice at the church of San Vito, diocese of Sessa	ASN, Priv. I, 31^r	MazzR, 5	cited as 'prete'
	9 Nov 1452	'cantoris Regii'	ASN, Misc. I, 4, f. 15^r	MazzB, 21	
	8 Nov 1455			MinA, 439	
Geronimo	8 Nov 1455			MinA, 439	perhaps he is to be identified with Jeronimo Milecto
Giacomo di Capua	27 Feb 1451	singer		MinA, 412	
Giglietto	13 Jan 1473		ASF, Strozzi, 27, f. 12^v	GalN, 4, n. 32	
	13 Apr 1473	'chantore'; paid 3 ducats-4 tari-4 grani for Jan–Feb	ASF, Strozzi, 27, f. 111^v	GalN, 4	cited as being from 'Pichardia'
	21 Apr 1474	received 4 ducats	ASF, Strozzi, 27	GalN, 4, n. 32	probably the Ghilet who sang in the Milanese chapel in 1475
Giordi	13 Dec 1448	received salary of 6 ducats for Nov	ASN, TAF, XIII, f. 12^r		cited as 'Fra Giordi'; possibly the Jordi Marot listed in 1480
Giovanni di Brusselle	27 Apr 1457	'tenore'; received 14 ducats-2 tari as one-third of annual salary		MinA, 455–56	
Giovanni di Sant' Angelo	15 Dec 1452	named a 'cappellano'	ASN, Priv. I, f. 48^r	MazzR, 13	a Carmelite
Guglielmo	25(?) Oct 1480	one of 'XXI Canturi'		VdS, IV, 28	
Jacobo da Valenza	30 June 1492	'cappellano maggiore'; received 10 ducats for travelling to the Terra di Otranto		BarC, 16–17	
	23 July 1492	'appraised' a number of books		BarC, 17–18	
Jachetto de Marvilla	arrived no later than June 1458; left by Sept 1466	singer		D'AccS, 321; BertM, 10–11	on the dates, see Chap. II, pp. 37–38
Jeronimo Milecto 'dicto Piovano'	18 Apr 1478	cited as 'Piovano cantore' in letter from Lorenzo de' Medici		DelPP, 218	the identification is an assumption, as are those with the Fra Geronimo listed in 1455 and Piovano Girolamo who sang at Florence from 1484 (see Chap. II, p. 44); the Jo. Mileti in the papal chapel in 1432 (HabR, 221) is certainly not the same
	1480	'cantore' (but not on roster of 25[?] Oct)		VdS, IV, 31	
	1481			VdS, IV, 31	
Joan de Ghianes	25(?) Oct 1480	one of 'XXI Canturi'		VdS, IV, 28	perhaps the 'Domino Ghineto' at Milan in 1474–1475 (MottM, 526)

Name	Date	Citation/activity	Primary source	Literature	Comments
Joan de Platea	25(?) Oct 1480	one of 'XXI Canturi'		VdS, IV, 29	
Johannes de Aragonia	19 Jan 1491	'cappellanus'; received benefice at Caiazzo	ASV, Reg. Lat. 880, f. 229^v–230^r		
Johannes de Lotinis	25(?) Oct 1480	one of 'XXI Canturi'		VdS, IV, 29	dedicatee of Tinctoris's *Expositio manus*; soprano
Juan de Epila	8 Nov 1455			MinA, 439	MinA gives name as 'Giovanni', but Épila is in Aragon
Juliano de Caiacza	1487–1488	taught at the Studio; received 80 ducats		CannS, 82	
	18 Aug 1488	'maior cappellanus'		PrizB, 180	adds a postscript to letter by Ferrante cited as bishop of Tropea
	Jan–June 1491	'cappellano maggiore'	ASN, TAF, I^a, f. 114^v		
	27 Apr 1491	helped determine wages for the scribe Cinico		BarC, 9	
	Jan–June 1492		ASN, TAF, I^a, f. 132^v		no longer listed as chapel master; see Jacobo da Valenza
Lenti, Antonio de	8 Nov 1455			MinA, 439	could be the Antonio of 1444
Leonardo Egizio	8 Nov 1455			MinA, 439	
Locha, Blasius	25 Feb 1479	'capellanus'; received a benefice at Troja	ASV, Reg. Lat. 785, f. 56^r–57^v		he is a priest from Ascoli
	2 Aug 1488	vacated the 'cantorato' at Lucera in favor of Giovanni Chirardo	ASN, Priv. IV, f. 31^r	MazzR, 71	
Loret, Joan	27 Feb 1451	singer		MinA, 412	
Marino della Falcuni (?)	Jan–June 1497	'cappellano'	ASN, TAF, I, f. 159^r		listed as 'Reverendo Abbate'
Marot, Jordi	25(?) Oct 1480	one of 'XXI Canturi'		VdS, IV, 29	possibly the Fra Giordi listed in 1448
Marra, Alexander de	5 Jan 1486	'cappellanus'; received a benefice at Benevento	ASV, Reg. Lat. 843, f. 217^r–219^r		
Marrotta, Giorgio	Jan–June 1469	'cappellano'	ASN, TAF, I^a, f. 87^r		
Marti, Pere	27 Feb 1451	singer		MinA, 411	
Matteo di Capua	27 Feb 1451	singer		MinA, 412	FilD, V, 94, 204, incorrectly conflates him with Matteo Ferrero
Miró, Benet	27 Feb 1451	singer		MinA, 412	
Nadal, Miguel	10 Jan 1441	'xandre'; received 3 ducats	ASN, TAF, VI, f. 56^r	MazzF, 130	
	21 Nov 1441	received 1 ducat	ASN, TAF, VI, f. 47^r	MazzF, 119	
	17 Dec 1441	received 1 ducat	ASN, TAF, VI, f. 50^v	MazzF, 124	in the service of Ferrante
	27 Dec 1441	received 1 ducat	ASN, TAF, VI, f. 54^r	MazzF, 128	in Alfonso's service again
Nardello de Composta	4 Jan 1453	named a 'cappellano'	ASN, Priv. I, f. 48^r	MazzR, 14	a Carmelite
Navarro, Luis	27 Feb 1451	singer		MinA, 412	
Nicola de Rinaldo	22 Sept 1452	began service as a 'cappellano'	ASN, Priv. I, f. I^v	MazzR, 5	he is from Carife
Oriola, Pere					see Chap. III, pp. 60–62
Ospato, Baldessare	25(?) Oct 1480	one of 'XXI Canturi'		VdS, IV, 29	
Pando, Tancredus de	20 May 1466	'capellanus'	ASV, Reg. Suppl. 595, f. 54^v–55^r		
Pascale	Oct 1444			MinA, 246	
Patin, Luisot	25(?) Oct 1480	one of 'XXI Canturi'		VdS, IV, 29	
Perez, Berthomeo	29 Dec 1448	'scolà'; reimbursed 4 ducats-2 tari for offerings made on behalf of Alfonso	ASN, TAF, XIII, f. 4^r		
Perez, Jaime	8 Nov 1455			MinA, 439	
Perot de Vertoya	25(?) Oct 1480	one of 'XXI Canturi'		VdS, IV, 29	perhaps the Perot active at Ferrara and Milan, 1473–1475; see MottM, 383, 524

The Singers and Chaplains

Name	Date	Citation/activity	Primary source	Literature	Comments
Petrus de Pineda	27 Mar 1477	'cappellano'; received a benefice, diocese of Teramo	ASV, Reg. Suppl. 749, f. 182^r–182^v		
	10 Nov 1477	benefice in Naples	ASV, Reg. Lat. 784, f. 70^v–71^r		
	9 Oct 1479	benefice in diocese of Teramo	ASV, Reg. Lat. 787, f. 40^v		
	11 Oct 1479	obliged himself to pay the annate on a benefice	ASV, Lib. Annat. 28, f. 96^r		
	16 Mar 1480	benefice at Sarno	ASV, Reg. Lat. 799, f. 181^v–183^r		
	Apr 1480	concerns annate on benefice at Sarno	ASV, Lib. Annat. 28, f. 176^v		
	21 Feb 1484	receives benefice at San Lorenzo di Picerno (Abruzzo)	ASN, Priv. II, f. 79^v	MazzR, 39	cited as abbot
Pinia, Salvatore	25(?) Oct 1480	one of 'XXI Canturi'		VdS, IV, 29	
Pont, Antoni	27 Feb 1451	singer		MinA, 412	MinA gives the name as 'Antonio Ponte'; could be the 'Antonio' of 1444 or the Ponzo–Pons franzese
Ponzo, Antonio	25 Mar 1469	singer; writes to Duke of Milan and accepts invitation to go there		BarbV, 820	apparently returned to Naples briefly in 1470 to pick up his wife
	12 Aug 1476	received 6 ducats	ASF, Strozzi, 32, f. 193^v	GalN, 4–5	he had apparently returned to Naples again; cited as 'Antonio Pons franzese' (the Antonio (Antoni) Pont–Ponzo–Pons situation cannot be settled decisively)
Porcello, Felippo	Jan–June 1469	'cappellano'	ASN, TAF, I^a, f. 87^r		
Prats, Luis	1480			VdS, IV, 31	not on roster of 25(?) Oct
	8 Feb 1488	'cappellano'; received benefice at Sant' Arcangelo dei Pedefumi (in the Cilento)	BNN, MS. X. B. 58, f. 102^r		
	10 Nov 1490	benefice at San Nicola dei Campograssi (Cilento)	ASN, Priv. IV, f. 226^v	MazzR, 94	although the Marturiano Prats in the papal chapel 1491, 1501, may be related, Prats is a common Valencian name
Rabaça, Joanet	27 Feb 1451	singer		MinA, 412	
Raynero	25 Mar 1469	singer; with Antonio Ponzo writes to Duke of Milan and accepts invitation to go there		BarbV, 820	
Recellani, Angelo	15 Dec 1452	named a 'cappellano'	ASN, Priv. I, f. 48^r	MazzR, 13	a member of the order of Eremiti; he is from Buccino
Regades, Pere	27 Feb 1451	singer		MinA, 412	
Risis, Esremus de	16 Sept 1488	'procurator . . . capelle'	ASV, Lib. Resig. 4, fragment		he is from Naples
Roberto, Francesco	8 Nov 1455			MinA, 439	possibly the Fra Ruberto recorded in 1448
Rocha, Antonius	7 Sept 1488	'capellanus'; received benefice at Martorano	ASV, Reg. Lat. 879, f. 199^r–200^r		
Romero, Blasius	27 Feb 1451	singer		MinA, 412	possibly one of the authorities cited by Florentius de Faxolis; see Chap. III, p. 84

Name	Date	Citation/activity	Primary source	Literature	Comments
Ruberto	13 Dec 1448	received a salary of 6 ducats for the preceding Nov	ASN, TAF, XIII, f. 12^r		possibly the Francesco Roberto recorded in 1455; could also be the Bernart Rubert who is 'cappella maior e dispenser de la casa del don Ferrando' in 1441 (see FerrF, 32–33)
Romeu, Phelip	10 Jan 1441	'xandre'; received 3 ducats	ASN, TAF, VI, f. 56^r	MazzF, 130	
	21 Nov 1441	received 1 ducat	ASN, TAF, VI, f. 47^r	MazzF, 119	
	17 Dec 1441	received 1 ducat	ASN, TAF, VI, f. 50^v	MazzF, 124	listed as being in the service of Ferrante
	27 Dec 1441	received 1 ducat	ASN, TAF, VI, f. 54^r	MazzF, 128	he must be the 'Philipeto Romeo nostro cantorino' in the employ of the Sforza in 1469 (MottM, 298)
Salvatore de Capua	27 Feb 1451	singer		MinA, 412	
Santa, Jaime/Jaume	Oct 1444			MinA, 246	
Santillo	30 Jan 1461	reimbursed for offerings made for Ferrante		BarC, 16	cited as 'Abate' Santillo
Sanya, Jaime/ Jaume	Oct 1444			MinA, 246	
	8 Nov 1455			MinA, 439	
Simon, Jan.	25(?) Oct 1480	one of 'XXI Canturi'		VdS, IV, 30	
Simplicianus	11 Dec 1488	'professor [?] . . . in capella'; received benefice at Oppido	ASV, Reg. Lat. 869, f. 171^v–172^v		cited as 'Simplicianus de Abbate'; formerly at Milan (?)
Soler, Joan	27 Feb 1451	singer		MinA, 412	
Steve, Joan	27 Feb 1451	singer		MinA, 412	
	8 Nov 1455			MinA, 439	
Suval, Fferrando	17 Jan 1441	'xandre'; received 4 tarì to rent a horse in order to accompany Alfonso	ASN, TAF, VI, f. 57^r	MazzF, 131	
	Oct 1444			MinA, 245	
Tabaria, Mateu	9 Nov 1437	'cantador'; received 15 ducats to buy a horse	ASN, TAF, II/1, f. 1^r		
	27 Dec 1441	received 2 ducats for trousers	ASN, TAF, VI, f. 51^r	MazzF, 124	
	Oct 1442–July 1443		ASN, TAF, I^a, f. 17^v		
Tassinot	8 Nov 1455			MinA, 439	
Taxamor, Pirardo	27 Feb 1451	'tenor'		MinA, 411	
Taxmet de Sancto Paolo	27 Feb 1451	'tenor'		MinA, 411	
	4 Aug 1451	received 30 ducats to buy a 'libre de cant' for the chapel		DeMarB, II, 231	
Thomas de Alamanya	30 Apr 1466	'tenorista'; given paper to copy a psalter, collectional, and antiphonal for the chapel		DeMarB, II, 247	
	4 Nov 1468	notated a 'Dominical'		DeMarB, II, 249	
	13 Jan 1473	received a share of 20 ducats	ASF, Strozzi, 27, f. 12^v	GalN, 4, n. 32	
	17 Feb 1474	received 25 ducats for a missal for the chapel of the duchess		DeMar B, II, 262	cited as 'frare Thomas del Cayre del orde de Sanct Domingo'
	21 Apr 1474	received 6 ducats	ASF, Strozzi, 27	GalN, 4, n. 32	
Tinctoris, Johannes					see Chap. III, pp. 71–77
Torres, Jaime	12 Sept 1446	sent to Spain to recruit singers		SanD, xvii	cited as 'ajudant de . . . cambra'; AngMC, 372, claims that he was chapel master
Trirades, Joan	27 Feb 1451	singer		MinA, 412	
Tuppo, Francesco	15 Apr 1454	among the boy singers		MinA, 429	see Chap. II, p. 35
Valentino, Jacobus de	11 Oct 1479	obliged himself to pay the annate on a benefice	ASV, Lib. Annat. 28, f. 96^r		

Name	Date	Citation/activity	Primary source	Literature	Comments
Villette, Jacobus	13 May 1473	'cantor capellanus'; received benefice at Bari	ASV, Reg. Suppl. 690, f. 76^v–77^r		cited as 'presbyter cameracensis . . . in iure baccalaureus'
	25(?) Oct 1480	one of 'XXI Canturi'		VdS, IV, 29	
Vincenet					see Chap. III, pp. 69–71
Volpe(?), Nicolaus	5 June 1492	'capellanus'; received benefice at Naples	ASV, Reg. Lat. 923, f. 30^r–31^r		
Ycart, Bernardus					see Chap. III, pp. 77–80
Ynnya, Jaume	10 Nov 1451	received 15 ducats to buy a breviary		DeMarB, II, 232	
Zamora, Alfonse	1481	singer		VdS, IV, 31	probably the Alfonso Sancij de Moya (Zamorencis) in papal chapel from 1434 through 1445 (see HabR, 221–24)

CHAPTER V

Music for Secular Entertainment

As impressive as were the achievements of the royal chapel and the tradition of liturgical music at Naples in general, their brilliance was matched by the court's accomplishments in the area of secular music. From the grand public ceremonies that marked the coronations of the kings to the intimate evenings of song at Poggioreale, music was a constant partner to the activities of the court. And it is the various roles that secular music filled as well as the musicians and ensembles that participated in them that form the subject matter of the present chapter.[1]

The grandest of the public ceremonies for which there is ample documentation about the participation of musicians was Alfonso I's spectacular triumphal procession into Naples on 23 February 1443. In addition to the customary trumpeters – on 2 March, payments were made to twelve trumpeters who had been stationed on a 'carro trionfale'[2] – there were numerous music-filled *carri* or floats that lined the streets of the city. Among them was one described by Panormita; it held a tower in which four singers, dressed as the allegorical figures Magnanimity, Constancy, Clemency, and Liberality, 'cantantes suam quaeque compositis versibus cantionem'.[3] In another part of the city, in the Largo del Mercato, atop a gilded wooden arch, there sat 'sei giovani cantando come angeli vestite alle ninfale con ali',[4] while throughout the city, in each of the *seggi*, richly costumed women danced to the music of the *ministres*.[5]

Similarly, we have eyewitness accounts of the music that accompanied the coronation of Alfonso II on 8 May 1494: 'alle 12. hore lo re Alfonso insiò dallo castiello nuovo con tanto trionfo, et con tante manere de instrumenti'; while after Mass, 'se sono viste de tutte maniere de musica, che era una maraviglia a sentire, pensati che tutti li canturi d'Italia erano qua'; finally, in the procession that

---

[1] Again, discussion of the music itself is reserved for Chap. VII, 'The Repertory'.
[2] Minieri Riccio, 'Alcuni fatti di Alfonso I', p. 232.
[3] See Francesco Torraca, *Studi di storia letteraria napoletana* p. 14. The float is also described in the chronicle of Angelo Tummulillo, who took over verbatim Panormita's description of the procession; see Corvisieri, *Notabilia temporum di Angelo Tummulillis de Sant'Elia*, p. 48. In the musicological literature the passage is cited in Pope, 'La Musique espagnole à la cour de Naples', p. 38, and Hucke, 'Neapel', *Die Musik in Geschichte und Gegenwart*, IX (1961), col. 1313.
[4] Torraca, *Racconti di storia napoletana*, p. 479, and Hersey, *The Aragonese Arch at Naples*, p. 15.
[5] See the letter of 28 February 1443 from Antonio Vinyes to the *Conselleres* of Barcelona; printed in Madurell Marimón, *Mensajeros barcelonenses en la corte de Nápoles de Alfonso V de Aragón, 1435–1458*, No. 164; Riccardo Filangieri, *Rassegna critica delle fonti per la storia di Castel Nuovo*, pp. 330–32; Hersey, *op. cit.*, p. 63.

wended its way through the city, 'cosi è cavalcato [Alfonso] per Napoli, et ha portato con seco tanti suoni, e trombette che non basta a dirle'.⁶ In this instance, we can even get an idea of the approximate number of musicians that participated in the cavalcade, for as another, semi-anonymous chronicler – he was a member of one of a number of Neapolitan Ferraiolo families – tells us, and as the somewhat crude but detailed illustrations that accompany his narrative show, there were:

> in primis innante de tutta le giente andavano trombette schiate numaro XXXXVI, et ditte trombette protavano ippune vestute de divisa de inborchato et villuto carmosino, et tamborrine numaro XII, et bifare numaro X, et liute badose et arpe et tremmune senza numaro de tutte quiste sune, et tamburre grusse a piede numaro IIII, et sey tamburre grusse sopre a tre mule che le sonavano tre schiave nigre . . .⁷

And even allowing for some exaggeration in the numbers given and for the fact that not all the instruments mentioned would have played together, it is evident that the band must have been a large one.⁸

Obviously, such processions of massed musical forces were not limited only to such august events as coronations. As in all other major courts and cities of the time, the arrival or departure or celebration of any important personage gave reason for a parade. Thus for the investiture of Filippo Maria Sforza as Duke of Bari on 22 September 1465, an anonymous chronicler records the presence of no fewer than 'trombette 82., et alcuni bifari'.⁹ Likewise, '62. trombette, pifari, e tamburini assaissimi' played at the welcoming ceremonies for Queen Joanna d'Aragona on 11 September 1477.¹⁰

Given their importance in the civic and ceremonial life of the court, the royal trumpeters warrant a short digression. Like most of the personnel in the early

⁶ See the untitled chronicle of Giuliano Passero, published as *Storia in forma di giornale*, pp. 60–61.

⁷ The chronicle – preserved in New York, Pierpont Morgan Library, MS 801, fols 88ʳ–150ʳ – is edited in its entirety, including all 117 of its illustrations, in Riccardo Filangieri, *Una cronaca napoletana figurata del Quattrocento*; the passage cited appears on p. 93. The illustrations constitute a rich source of iconographical evidence for the use of music in processions, military campaigns, proclamations, public executions, and wedding festivities at Naples.

⁸ Just how inflated the numbers might be is difficult to say. Consider the following entry – typical of many – from the Mantuan chronicle of Andrea Schivegnola, who reports on the arrival at Mantua of Margaret of Bavaria on 7 June 1463: '107 trombi, pifari, tromboni, 26 tamburij, pive . . . et altri instrumenti . . . paria che tutto el mondo sonasse' (quoted after Prizer, 'Bernardino Piffaro e i pifferi e tromboni di Mantova', p. 165). When Isabella d'Este arrived at Mantua for her marriage with the Marchese Francesco II, she made her entry to the fanfare of 'doxento sonatori tra pifari e trombeti' (Prizer, p. 164). Schivegnola ends by saying that it appeared that 'all the world played', and Giuliano Passero stated, in his description of the procession for Alfonso II, that it seemed as if 'all the singers of Italy were here' and that the wind-players were 'beyond description': indications that many of these accounts suffer from 'chronicler's jargon'. In addition, the illustration in the manuscript New York 801 that accompanies the notice about forty-six *trombette* and ten *bifare* depicts but three players of each instrument. Yet we might note that during the course of 1491 the court had no fewer than thirteen different trumpeters on its payroll (see below and n. 13), and to these could always be (and often were) added the trumpeters of various members of the Neapolitan nobility; thus at various times the royal household made payments to the trumpeters of the Duke of Bari (ASN, TAF, VI, fol. 39ʳ), the Duke of Cessa (ASN, TAF, VI, fol. 53ᵛ), the Count of Lorano (ASN, TAF, VI, vol. 53ʳ), and others. In all, it may well be that for truly special occasions the court could raise an ensemble of a few dozen trumpeters.

⁹ 'Diario anonimo dell'anno MCXCIII sino al MCCCCLXXXVII: Diverso dagli Annali del Raymo', in Pelliccia, *Raccolta di varie croniche, diarj ed altre opuscoli*, I, 130–1.

¹⁰ Passero, *Storia in forma di giornale*, p. 52.

days of the court, the trumpeters tended to be Spaniards, some having arrived with Alfonso during the 1430s. Thus on 21 November 1437, Alfonso had three trumpeters with him – Andreu Bonsenyore, Johan Lombart, and Jordi Avinyo[11] – while the number had grown to six by 18 February 1441, when payments were made to the same three trumpeters plus Johan de Saragoza, Perrinetto, and Romanello (and two trumpeters of the Duke of Bari), all of whom had followed the king to Benevento.[12] The largest single roster of which I know that names the trumpeters dates from 15 May 1491, when Ferrante ordered payments of 28 ducats (reduced to 25 ducats-3 tarì-16 grani after the 'elagio' was deducted) to each of seven trumpeters – Donato da Tarj, Bernardino d'Ascholi, Andrea d'Ascholi, Jacomo d'Ascholi, Giorgio Meo calabrese, Pericho Spagnolo, and Clarino Trombetta (= Rafaele Genovese Clarino) – in order to cover in advance one-third of their annual salaries (May through August).[13] And though their salaries exceed those of many of the members of the royal chapel, they seem in line with trumpeters' wages elsewhere. Thus the leading trumpet-player at the court of Ferrara, one Raganello, earned 252 lire (= about 78 ducats) in 1503, more than any singer at the court except Josquin.[14]

Finally, the generous salaries that the trumpeters received underscore the multi-faceted – generally non-artistic – services that they rendered, the latter point often emphasized by their payments being listed together with those for the condottieri and other men-at-arms. Aside from their participation in the grand processions, the trumpeters announced royal proclamations, played signals at public executions, and served as messengers; for example: 11 January 1493 – Rizzardo and Cola each received one tareno to publicize a ban on carts that were not specifically intended for use in Naples;[15] 9 August 1495 – an unidentified trumpeter, his instrument bearing a pennant with the royal arms, signaled the execution of Leonardo de Bianco;[16] 31 December 1493 – Berardino Trombecto left for Piombino with a letter from Ferrante instructing Joan de Itro to return to Naples;[17] or, finally, the poor trumpeter (unnamed) who on 28 January 1503 made two complete round-trips between Barletta and Ruvo (in Puglia), and thus logged approximately 120 kilometers as he relayed messages between contingents of Italian and French soldiers.[18]

Although it was the massive ensembles of the great public processions that most

---

[11] ASN, TAF, II¹, fol. 2ᵛ. The first two had accompanied Alfonso on his Naples expedition of 1432; see Anglés, *La Música en la Corte de los Reyes Católicos*, I, 20.

[12] ASN, TAF, VI, fols. 38ᵛ–39ʳ.

[13] ASN, TAF, XXIX, fol. 55ʳ. At least six other trumpeters are on the payroll at various other times during the year: Socio de Montecatondo, Martino nigro, Giorgio de Vesi, Belardino venitiano, Rugieri, and Carlo de Rugieri (ASN, TAF, XXIX, fols. 30ʳ, 31ʳ, 33ᵛ, 67ᵛ, 75ᵛ).

[14] Lockwood, 'Josquin at Ferrara', p. 115, n. 38.

[15] Barone, 'Le cedole di tesoreria', X, 21.

[16] Riccardo Filangieri, *Una cronaca napoletana*, Plate LIX and pp. 166–67. On the concern for the appearance of the pennants, we have Ferrante's letter of 2 June 1467 to Johanne Olzina: 'Inteso che a quilli nostri trombecti quale andarono con le prime gente so male fornite de bandare per le trombette havemo deliberato mandareve doe de seta: et le mandamo coperte de uno panno incerato dentro uno morzapane de ligno et le dirizamo a vui fate che receputele li donati a detti trombecti' (Trinchera, *Codice aragonese*, I, 185).

[17] Trinchera, *op. cit.*, II, 380.

[18] Passero, *Storia in forma di giornale*, pp. 131ff.

often caught the attention of the chroniclers, it was through its cultivation of a far more intimate genre – the art song – that Naples became a center of the first rank in the field of secular music. If, as Isabel Pope suggests, it was Cornago who 'developed the distinctive Spanish style of the polyphonic courtly love song',[19] then Naples, as much as any place in Spain, deserves to be designated as the birthplace of Spanish secular polyphony.[20] Later, during the reign of Ferrante, the court became an important center for the production of the early frottola as well as for the art of the improvisators, while the entire Aragonese period witnessed a lively tradition of instrumental music, both as chamber music and as music for the dance.

In the main, secular music-making took place at the various royal residences, two of which – Castelnuovo and Castel Capuano – had rooms that were specifically designated as 'cambre della musica' and were outfitted with organs and other instruments.[21] Castelnuovo, moreover, had on the east wall of its 'Sala dei Baroni' (also called 'Sala dei Trionfi' and 'Gran Sala') two balconies, one above the other, where musicians were stationed for the celebrations that were held in that richly tapestried room; still another room in which music was performed was the 'camera delle reggiole', or dining room, which was also furnished with its own organ.[22] And known to have furnished organs for these rooms were: Rigo de Borgogna (1453),[23] Gerardo di Olanda (1456),[24] Fra Stefano del Paone of Salerno (1474), who was also an organist at the chapel,[25] Giovanni Donadio di Mormanno,[26] and Fra Tommaso Angelo, who in 1493 completed an organ in the 'camera delle reggiole' that had been begun by Giovanni Donadio.[27]

Occasionally a chronicler gives us a glimpse – though seldom a very informative one – of the musical mornings, afternoons, and evenings at the royal households. Typical of the entries that appear are the following three from the *Effemeridi* of Joanpiero Leostello, whose diary reports on the daily life of Alfonso, Duke of Calabria, in particular and the Aragonese court in general from 1485 to 1491:[28]

---

[19] 'Cornago', *The New Grove*, IV, 779.

[20] On this point, Anglés, 'Cornago', *Die Musik in Geschichte und Gegenwart*, II (1952), col. 1683, writes: 'Die Vorläufer des mehrstimmigen Liebesliedes mit kastilianischen Text sind am neapolitanischen Hofe . . . zu suchen.' On the general importance of Naples in the development of Spanish literature prior to the unification of Spain – it provided a central meeting ground for writers of different regions – see Croce, *La Spagna nella vita italiana durante la Rinascenza*, p. 45.

[21] Riccardo Filangieri, *Rassegna critica delle fonti per la storia di Castel Nuovo*, III, 64; Pane, 'Le Effemeridi di Joanpiero Leostello', p. 82; and see below, p. 105.

[22] Riccardo Filangieri, *op. cit.*, III, 45, 56–57.

[23] Riccardo Filangieri, *Castel Nuovo*, p. 242.

[24] Minieri Riccio, 'Alcuni fatti di Alfonso I', p. 442. He is to be identified with the organ-builder of the same name who was active at Ferrara in 1476, and was probably the father of the organist Giorgio di Gerardo di Olanda who was at Milan in 1475 and Lucca in 1483; see Motta, 'Musici alla corte degli Sforza', pp. 290–92.

[25] Riccardo Filangieri, *Rassegna critica delle fonti per la storia di Castel Nuovo*, III, 64; on Stefano see Chap. II above, p. 47 and n. 142.

[26] See Chap. II, n. 47, and Ceci, 'Maestri organari a Napoli', p. 5.

[27] Riccardo Filangieri, *Rassegna critica delle fonti per la storia di Castel Nuovo*, III, 56–57. Fra Tommaso completed another organ for the court in 1497, and another instrument for the Neapolitan church of Santa Maria Maddalena in 1503; see Gaetano Filangieri, *Documenti*, V, 15, 19.

[28] Leostello's chronicle, entitled 'Effemeridi delle cose fatte par il Duca di Calabria', is printed in Gaetano Filangieri, *Documenti*, I; the passages cited appear on pp. 181–82, 223, and 230; the entry for 2 June 1489 is also in Hersey, *Alfonso II and the Artistic Renewal of Naples*, p. 62. On Leostello, see Pane, 'Le Effemeridi di Joanpiero Leostello', pp. 77–85.

14 December 1488: Ante lucem fu in pede lo prefato I.S. . . . et innanzi facesse collatione . . . fu visitate da tucti trombecti et altri sonatori del S. Duca da Milano . . . con belle sonate.

2 June 1489: . . . venne lo prefato S. Re al poggioreale: dove riposato aliquantulum tucto quello jorno se prese piacere de soni et canti.[29]

21 June 1489: Sua I.S. . . . cavalco al S. Re in Castello novo et trovò che sua maesta volea cavalcare in castello de l'ovo che la facea lo convito a la S. Regina et a li imbasciatori che se trovavano a Napoli . . . Finito convivio tutto quello jorno stetteno in festa cum danza et soni et ad ore xxj imbarchoreno et circundoreno intorno napoli cum canti et soni . . .

Or, on the occasion of the visit to Naples of Frederick III during Holy Week of 1452, dinner at the richly draped Castelnuovo was followed by 'moltes maneres de sons, menistres, xantres e moltes maneres de festes que no se escrivir ni dir'.[30]

Although the chroniclers never mention specific kinds of 'canti' (much less composers or compositions), we can, as the next chapters will show, gain a fairly good idea of the character of the song repertory. During the reign of Alfonso I, there must certainly have been a strong preference for settings of Spanish lyrical verse, with the canciones of such composers as Cornago and Oriola taking pride of place. With the succession of Ferrante, and probably under the influence of Prince Federico, it was settings of Italian lyrics that came to the fore, first – if the chronology of the sources reflects that of styles – in the form of the ballata, then the strambotto.[31] In addition, the vast number of Franco–Netherlandish chansons in the Neapolitan music sources – from the later works of the Dufay generation through those of the Busnois–Ockeghem generation and the early songs of the Josquin period – testifies to the popularity of that genre at the court. Finally, there was the music of the unwritten tradition, the performances of the poet–improvisators whose skills were so highly prized by the Italian humanists. Most renowned among them was the young Serafino Aquilano (see Chap. III), while other major figures were Benedetto Gareth, 'il Chariteo', who is reported to have sung the verses of Vergil;[32] Andrea Coscia, of whom Serafino's biographer Calmeta wrote that he 'molto soavamente cantava nel liuto' and that he influenced Serafino when the latter heard him perform at Milan;[33] and the humanist Aurelio Brandolini, sometimes called the 'Christian Orpheus', the brother of the Raffaele who so wholeheartedly praised the musical life of Naples.[34] Indeed, Naples played a leading role in the development of this style of improvised performance.[35]

One of the favorite pastimes of the court, and one in which members of the royal family participated, was the dance. And as we learn from a lengthy poem in honor of Alfonso I, the preferred dances during his reign were of Spanish origin:

---

[29] This entry refers to the housewarming for the duke's villa; see Hersey, *Alfonso II and the Artistic Renewal of Naples*, p. 62.

[30] Sanchis i Sivera, *Dietari del capellá d'Anfos el Magnànim*, pp. 173–74; Anglés, *La Música en la Corte de los Reyes Católicos*, I, 21; Hucke, 'Neapel', col. 1313.

[31] See Chap. VII, p. 146.

[32] According to Paolo Cortese, *De cardinalatu* (1510); see Pirrotta, 'Music and Cultural Tendencies', p. 154.

[33] Grayson, *Vincenzo Calmeta*, p. 60.

[34] On Aurelio Brandolini, who was at Naples from 1466 to 1480 and who wrote poems in praise of both Pietrobono and Squarcialupi, see Mayer, 'Un umanista fiorentino alla corte di Mattia Corvino'; see also Haraszti, 'Les Musiciens de Mathias Corvin et de Béatrice d'Aragon', p. 54.

[35] See Pirrotta, 'Novelty and Renewal in Italy', p. 58.

> li balli maravigliusi,
> tratti di catalani;
> li loro mumi giusi,
> tan zentili e sopranni.[36]

The poet then proceeds to list some of the popular dances at the court: the *cascarda*, the *palonella*, the *moresca*, the *momos*, and the *basce e l'alta*, a set of paired dances that constituted the Spanish version of the basse dance and saltarello.[37] For at least one of these dances, the *momos*, a type of costumed dance, there is a reference of unknown date – it must be after March 1444[38] – that shows that the music was supplied by the alta cappella of the court and that a harpist named Diego de Soto also participated.[39]

By the mid-1460s, tastes in dance had begun to change, as they had in almost all cultural activities at the court. When Ippolita Sforza arrived at Naples in 1465, she was accompanied by her dancing-master Giovanni Ambrosio da Pesaro, who is now generally identified as Guglielmo Ebreo da Pesaro, the two names being found interchanged in various manuscript copies of Guglielmo's treatise *De pratica seu arte tripudii*.[40] That Giovanni Ambrosio–Guglielmo Ebreo taught the art of dancing at the court, and that he introduced, or at least helped further, a new, Italian style is evident from a letter – signed 'Johanne Ambrosio da Pesaro ballarino' – that he sent from Naples to Bona Sforza (wife of Galeazzo Maria) at Milan on 15 July 1466, in which he states that he is engaged in teaching the princesses Eleonora and Beatrice how to dance in the 'Lombard' style ('alo ballare lombardo').[41] His most talented pupil, though, may have been the Duchess of Calabria herself, for in the same letter he goes on to write that Ippolita 'ave facto duy balli novj supra duy canzuni francese de sua fantasia che la Maesta de Re non ave altro piacere ne altro paradiso non pare che trova se non quando la vede danzare e anche canthare'. Still later in the letter, the dancing-master continues that although he would like to return to Milan, neither the king nor the Princess Eleonora are disposed to let him go; and he was to stay at Naples until 1468,[42]

---

[36] The poem appears in the manuscript Paris 1069 (fols. 61r–63r), compiled at Naples in the mid fifteenth century, but later decorated with the royal arms of France. A modern edition appears in Mandalari, *Rimatori napoletani del Quattrocento*, pp. 183–84; see also Croce, *La Spagna nella vita italiana durante la Rinascenza*, p. 43, and Anglés, *La Música en la Corte de los Reyes Católicos*, I, 21.

[37] On the *bassa–alta* pair, see Dolmetsch, *Dances of Spain and Italy from 1400 to 1600*, pp. 1, 34–39; Heartz, 'Hoftanz and Basse Dance', p. 18.

[38] At which time some of the musicians who participated were still in Spain (see below).

[39] See Anglés, 'La Música en la Corte Real de Aragón y de Nápoles', p. 1021.

[40] On the identification, see Kinkeldey, 'Dance Tunes of the Fifteenth Century', p. 8; Michel, 'The Earliest Dance Manuals'; Reese, *Music in the Renaissance*, p. 176; Gallo, 'Il "ballare lombardo" (circa 1435–1475)', p. 67; and Brainard, 'Guglielmo Ebreo da Pesaro', *The New Grove*, VII, 798. For a dissenting opinion that holds that Giovanni Ambrosio and Guglielmo were not one and the same, see Inglehearn, 'A Little-Known Fifteenth-Century Dance Treatise', pp. 176–77.

[41] The letter is printed in Motta, 'Musici alla corte degli Sforza', pp. 61–62; see also Barblan, 'Vita musicale alla corte sforzesca', p. 814. The year in which the letter was written is not signed; however, it dates from the fourteenth indiction ('Ex Neapolij die XV mensis Julij, xiiiia Indictione'), which in Ferrante's reign occurred in 1466 and 1481, with 1466 being the year in which Ippolita, her dancing-master, Eleonora, and Beatrice were all in Naples together.

[42] Brainard, 'Guglielmo Ebreo da Pesaro', p. 798.

coaching the royal family in the art of the dance. No doubt it was during his Neapolitan sojourn that – assuming the identification, of course – he wrote the arrangement *a 2* of the *La Spagna* melody that bears an ascription to 'M[agister] Gulielmus' in the manuscript Perugia 431 (see No. 18 in the edition). And the likelihood of Neapolitan provenance for the piece is strengthened by the sole concordance for the work, the Neapolitan manuscript Bologna Q 16.

Finally, as it did at all the great Italian courts, music played an important role in theatrical productions. Of these, the best documented insofar as music is concerned are the two well-known pieces that were staged in honor of the Spanish victory over the Moors at Granada in 1492 (the kings of Naples and Spain were, after all, cousins). The first, *La presa di granata*, a *farsa* attributed to Sannazaro, was performed at Castelnuovo on 4 March. The play concluded with 'Letizia cantando, accompagnata da tre altre Ninfe, de la quale l'una sonava una suavissima cornamusa, l'altra una violetta ad arco e la terza uno flauto, e con dolce armonia se accordavano con la voce e con la viola che sonava.'[43] After Gaiety concluded her song, Prince Federico, dressed as the King of Castille, took the center of the floor together with others in the audience and, to the music of the pifferi, danced the *bassa e l'alta*.[44] Two days later, on 6 March, Sannazaro's *Il triunfo de la Fama* was performed in Federico's apartments. Now it was Apollo who, following a long recitation, 'prese subito una viola e suavissimamente cantò certi versi in laude di tal vittoria'.[45]

From the time that it was established in the early 1440s to its demise in 1501 the court supported an impressive array of singers and instrumentalists whose primary function was to provide the music for its secular entertainments. And some idea – imprecise though it turns out to be – of the number of secular musicians who were employed at the court at a given time may be gained from what appears to be our only integral roster of such musicians, one that dates from 1499, just two years before Federico was deposed:

Nell'anno 1499
 Soldi, et Provisioni marittime . . .

Musichi
 Joan Orosco lxxij
 Hyeronimo de Manzo lxxij
 Petro d'Alano cc
 Antonio de Lagona cxx
 Altobello xxxij
 Fra Joan Musico [blank]

---

[43] See Mauro, *Iacobo Sannazaro: Opere volgare*, p. 282; Croce, *I teatri di Napoli, secolo XV–XVIII*, pp. 13–14. Einstein, *The Italian Madrigal*, I, 35–37, attempts to identify Gaiety's song with the barzelletta *Viva el Gran Rey Don Fernando* (that is, Ferdinand the Catholic), which was included in a drama written by Carlo Verardi and performed at Rome in honor of the same event. See, however, the comments of Wolfgang Osthoff, *Theatergesang und darstellende Musik*, I, 15ff. The barzelletta is conveniently edited in Einstein, *op. cit.*, I, 36–37, and Stevenson, *Spanish Music in the Age of Columbus*, p. 248.

[44] Mauro, *Iacobo Sannazaro: Opere volgare*, p. 285; Croce, *I teatri di Napoli*, p. 14.

[45] Mauro, *op. cit.*, p. 294; Croce, *op. cit.*, pp. 14–16; Einstein, *The Italian Madrigal*, I, 38.

Madamma Anna	cl
Galderi de Madamma Anna	xxxiiij
Fra Pietro d'Evoli	xxij
Bartolomeo de Pistoja governava la camera de la Musica al Castello de Capuana	lxxij
Joan della Musica governava la camera della Musica al Castello novo	xxxvj

Ministeri et Trombetti
[blank]

Trombetti
[blank][46]

Quite aside from the information that it provides regarding personnel, the roster is particularly significant in that it offers confirmation of the existence of a royal 'camera della musica' that had its own 'governor'. This agrees with the description given by Raffaele Brandolini in his *Opusculum de musica et poetica*,[47] where, in discussing music at the court during the period of Ferrante I, he writes that the king 'had not far from his own chambers a certain hall most elegantly furnished with paintings and sculptures to which he could quickly come and in which no instrument that might be sounded with hand, plectrum, or mouth was wanting'.[48] Complementing the 'music chambers' was the royal 'chamber music', an ensemble whose members – consisting of singers, players of string instruments (both plucked and bowed), and keyboard-players – are referred to by Brandolini as 'cubicularios musicos'.[49] No doubt it is the personnel of this ensemble that appears on the roster of 1499. And since a few of the musicians listed can be identified, as can members of the group from earlier periods, a discussion of some of the chamber musicians is called for.

The best-known name among those serving Federico in 1499 is that of the singer Madama Anna, who may be identified with the 'Madama Anna Inglese' who is recorded at Naples as 'musica del S.R.' first in 1471 and then again in 1476, in 1480, and during an unspecified year later in the 1480s.[50] And though

---

[46] Naples, Biblioteca Oratoriana dei Filippini, MS S.M. XXVIII.4.22 part 5, fols. 150ᵛ–151ʳ. The document from which the roster is drawn bears the title 'Copia d'un libretto dove si notano gli offitii, et servituri della casa delli Serenissimi Re di Napoli con le provisioni che se li deva'; it was copied early in the nineteenth century by Agostino Gervasio, who in turn drew upon a seventeenth-century manuscript that had passed through the libraries of a number of distinguished Neapolitan families – the Petrone, the Prince of Cimitile, and the Duke of Cassano – before it ended up in London, where Gervasio bought it. I am extremely grateful to Keith Larson, who discovered the document in the Library of the Filippini and was kind enough to communicate its contents and history to me in a letter of 15 April 1983. According to Galiano, 'Nuove fonti per la storia musicale napoletana', n. 43, the roster is also preserved in Naples, Biblioteca della Società Napoletana di Storia Patria, MS XXI.C.22, where it precedes the 'Diarii di Silvestro Guarino d'Aversa'. I have not been able to consult this manuscript, and my own references to Guarino's diary are to the edition by Pelliccia (see Chap. II above, n. 163).

[47] See Chap. II above, p. 53 and n. 172.

[48] Again, I draw on the translation in Perkins and Garey, *The Mellon Chansonnier*, I, 30.

[49] 'In addition to numerous persons in his service whom he called "chamber musicians" from the comfort and solace of voices and strings given in private . . .'; see *ibid.*, I, 30 and 34.

[50] Galiano, 'Nuove fonti per la storia musicale napoletana', p. 5; Van der Straeten, *La Musique aux Pays-Bas*, IV, 131; Pope and Kanazawa, *The Musical Manuscript Montecassino 871*, p. 69, n. 3; Pèrcopo, *Barzellette napoletane*, p. 11.

Anna, who had come to Naples between 1468 and 1471 via Monferrato and Milan,[51] is the only woman on the roster, Naples must have been host to other women musicians, enough so as to prompt the construction of special lodgings for them; and from 1499, they were housed near Castelnuovo, in newly built apartments above the 'casa grande dell'Artiglieria'.[52] Anna apparently was not the only member of her family in the ensemble; it seems safe to conclude that Galderi de Madamma Anna was the singer's son. Another musician about whom we have definite information from an earlier period is Joan Orosco, who is recorded as in Ferrante's employ in 1479–1481[53] and in February–March 1476 and July–December 1471 before that,[54] and whose career in the service of the royal family can be traced back to at least May 1444.[55] His career thus spanned almost the entire life of the Aragonese dynasty at Naples. Although we do not know the identity of the Joan who governed the 'camera della Musica' of Castelnuovo in 1499 (but see note 64 below), we do have information about an earlier head of the chamber music, the organist and organ-builder Giovanni da Gaeta. In 1470, Giovanni was receiving a salary of 36 ducats per year, an amount that was probably augmented through his work as a builder of organs – one of which he built for the chapel that year – and other instruments.[56] By 1476, however, he had left Naples and arrived at Rome with the intent of securing a position at Milan, and it was to that end that the Cardinal of Pavia wrote to Galeazzo Maria Sforza on 14 February and 4 May of that year. The first letter mentions that Giovanni had constructed an organ for Ferrante, and then goes on to say that the organist 'havere havuta cura della camera della musica della prefata maesta gia anni xxv'.[57] Finally, the Bartolomeo de Pistoja who headed the 'camera' at Castel Capuano was already in Ferrante's service in May 1476, when on the 27th of that month he received 36 ducats in payment for six months' salary.[58] He was still earning the same wages twenty-three years later.

There were among the chamber musicians a fair number of more than ordinary talent and renown, while others, though their reputations may not have gone beyond the confines of the court, enjoyed exceptional careers for other reasons. Most important among the latter group is Gonsalvo de Cordova, who, after having served in the chapel between 1437 and 1470, is recorded as a 'musico del Re' in

---

[51] See Barblan, 'Vita musicale alla corte sforzesca', p. 819; Anna had been sent to Milan by Duke Guglielmo of Monferrato in 1468 on the occasion of the wedding of Galeazzo Maria Sforza and Bona of Savoy.

[52] Riccardo Filangieri, *Rassegna critica delle fonti per la storia di Castel Nuovo*, III, 24.

[53] Van der Straeten, *La Musique aux Pays-Bas*, IV, 31.

[54] For 1476, see Galiano, 'Nuove fonti per la storia musicale napoletana', p. 5; for 1471, ASN, TAF, Vol. Ia, fol. 99r.

[55] Baldelló, 'La Música en la Casa de los Reyes de Aragón', p. 51.

[56] Gaetano Filangieri, *Documenti*, V, 2; Riccardo Filangieri, *Rassegna critica delle fonti per la storia di Castel Nuovo*, III, 7.

[57] The letter is published in Motta, 'Musici alla corte degli Sforza', p. 292; both letters are given in English translation – they say essentially the same thing – in Sartori, 'Organs, Organ-Builders, and Organists in Milan, 1450–1476', pp. 65–66. Obviously, the reference to twenty-five years must, if it is even close to being accurate, refer to service at the court in general, not just the years in Ferrante's employ, unless, of course, Giovanni had served Ferrante while the latter was still Duke of Calabria.

[58] Galiano, 'Nuove fonti per la storia musicale napoletana', pp. 5–6.

July–December 1471,[59] in February–March 1473,[60] and again in 1481.[61] One can only wonder whether other members of the chapel were likewise 'retired' to the royal chamber music in their later years.

Three of the more prominent (or at least potentially so in two cases) chamber musicians may be taken up in the order in which they make their first known appearance at the court. Certainly, we may speculate that the Tommaso Damiano (Tomás Damia according to Anglés) listed as a wind-player in 1456 may be the composer Damianus who is represented by settings of *Ave maris stella* and *Christus factus est* in the manuscript Montecassino 871.[62] Even more conjectural has been my suggestion that the singer Alessandro Alemanno who was also at the court in 1456 might be the very young Alexander Agricola.[63] Finally, there is the Laurenczecto, 'musico de casa del S.R.', who is listed in 1479, and who had already been recorded at Naples on 24 May 1476, when he received 96 ducats in salary.[64] This is no doubt the musician whom Ferrante introduces to Lorenzo de' Medici in a letter of 9 March 1484: 'venerabile et dilecto nostro Messer Laurenzo de Cordova, abbate de Santa Cruce de Venafro . . . è peritissimo in musica'.[65] Given the knowledge of his place of origin, we may now identify Ferrante's Laurenczecto as the famous Laurentius of Cordova whom the humanist Paolo Cortese cites as the most renowned player of the 'gravecordium' (clavichord): 'in quo quidem genera maxime est Laurentii Cordubensis facilitas interpuncta nota'.[66]

The royal chamber musicians also included players of plucked-string instruments, namely harpists and lutenists. On 17 [?March] 1437 Messer Pere del arpa was given 18 ducats to buy a horse in order that he could follow Alfonso.[67] Later that year, the harpist Pietro di Gaeta had also joined Alfonso's court.[68] In 1443, the resident harpist was Pietro d'Alemagna, who received a salary of 120 ducats

---

[59] ASN, TAF, Vol. Ia, fols. 98ᵛ, 99ʳ, 100ʳ.

[60] Galiano, *op cit.*, p. 5, n. 42.

[61] Van der Straeten, *La Musique aux Pays-Bas*, IV, 31.

[62] See Minieri Riccio, 'Alcuni fatti di Alfonso I', p. 444; Anglés, 'La Música en la Corte Real de Aragón y de Nápoles', p. 1024; Pope and Kanazawa, *The Musical Manuscript Montecassino 871*, p. 34.

[63] See my article 'Alexander Agricola and Ferrante I of Naples', p. 319, n. 23.

[64] For 1479: Van der Straeten, *La Musique aux Pays-Bas*, IV, 31; for 1476: Galiano, 'Nuove fonti per la storia musicale napoletana', p. 5. Thanks to Van der Straeten's notice, we are fairly well informed about the musicians who served Ferrante in 1479–1481. In addition to the keyboard-player just mentioned, and the musicians Joan Orosco and Anna Inglese cited above, the ensemble included Antonello Ascolano, Jeronomi Dormatja, Jacomo Eximenez (at Naples by 29 February 1476 (Galiano, p. 5)), Joan de Stefano, Joan Sagarra (already at Naples by July 1471 (ASN, TAF, Vol. Ia, fol. 98ᵛ), and recorded again on 1 and 29 February 1479 (Galiano, p. 5)), and Vincent Sallit. Perhaps Joan de Stefano and Joan Sagarra are the two imprecisely identified musicians named Joan on the roster of 1499.

[65] The letter is preserved in ASF, MAP, Filza XLV, No. 100; it is printed in its entirety in Pontieri, 'La dinastia aragonese di Napoli e la casa de' Medici di Firenze', p. 333. Ferrante had given Laurenzo permission to go to Florence for twenty-five days.

[66] Cortese, *De Cardinalatu* (1510), Bk. II, fol. 73ʳ. The passage is given in Pirrotta, 'Music and Cultural Tendencies in 15th-Century Italy', pp. 149 and 153, who, however, was unable to identify him (p. 157); nor is he identified in Galiano, 'Nuove fonti'.

[67] ASN, TAF, Vol. IV, fol. 2ʳ. The month is not designated; however, the next month that is recorded in the fragment is April.

[68] By 22 October; see Gaetano Filangieri, *Documenti*, V, 240.

per year,[69] while an Antonio da Venezia had joined the court by February 1456.[70] Finally, Aniello Palumbo is recorded as a 'suonatore di arpa' in 1486.[71]

References to specific lutenists at the court of Naples are almost non-existent (though some of the harpists may well have doubled on the lute). They are lacking completely in the secondary literature, and I can furnish only one notice from the material drawn from the archives. On the same day that the harpist Messer Pere received 18 ducats to buy a horse, another Pere, one Pere Puig, 'luytador', was given 25 ducats for the same purpose.[72] Thus even while he was waging war against the Angevins, Alfonso was accompanied by at least a small staff of musicians who played for his enjoyment as he moved from one camp to another.[73]

Despite the paucity of documentation, neither the court nor Naples as a whole was without its share of lutenists. Not only do the extant Neapolitan lute sources of the period – with their unique 'tabulatura alla Napoletana'[74] – bear witness to a local tradition of lute-playing, but there is also the occasional letter that served as a purchase order for lute strings. Thus on 1 October 1493, Ferrante wrote to Carlo de Rogeriis, his ambassador to Venice:

Noi havimo recipiuto uno maze de corde de liuto: le quale non hanno valuto niente: et in dì passati ne mandastevo un altro mazo multo peio: del quale ve ne mandamo due nerfule che non servono ad niente: et perchè sonno grosse, et negre, che ve le mandamo ad fine le vedate: et cognosciate che non valeno niente: et ve ne mandamo un altra nerfula per mostra, secundo la quale vorriamo ne facessevo cercare, et celi mandassevo, che si non fossero bone, non le vorriamo.[75]

Yet regardless of who the court lutenists might have been, it is doubtful that any of them enjoyed the reputation of a non-resident player of the lute, one who was but a short-term visitor to the court: Pietrobono de Burzellis of Ferrara. Pietrobono, who was also a singer, visited Naples in 1473 as part of the Ferrarese delegation that came to Naples with Sigismondo d'Este in order to escort the Princess Eleonora back to Ferrara as the bride of Ercole d'Este.[76] And that Pietrobono's playing made a powerful impression upon the court is attested by a letter of 16 April 1476 from Diomede Carafa to Ercole: 'La M. de lo S. Re averia multo piacere la S.V. li lassase per questa state Pierbono vostro sonatore de liuto.'[77] Obviously, Ferrante wished to borrow Pietrobono for a few months during the coming summer. However, given the underhanded way in which the poten-

---

[69] Ibid., V, 7.
[70] Minieri Riccio, 'Alcuni fatti di Alfonso I', p. 445.
[71] Gaetano Filangieri, Documenti, V, 243.
[72] ASN, TAF, Vol. IV, fol. 2ʳ. Also recorded on that same day is the trumpeter Jordi Avinyo.
[73] On the instrumentalists who accompanied Alfonso on his early Italian expeditions, see Anglés, 'La Música en la Corte Real de Aragón y de Nápoles', pp. 971ff.
[74] On the manuscripts Pesaro 1144 and Bologna 596 H.H.2⁴, see Chap. VI below, pp. 123–24.

[75] Trinchera, Codice aragonese, II, 258. The word 'nerfula' is a strange one, and was perhaps coined by Pontano, who signed the letter. In any event, its derivation from the Latin root 'nerv-', meaning string or wire, and the diminutive '-ula' seems evident. The use of 'f' for 'v' could reflect local pronunciation.
[76] See Lockwood, 'Pietrobono and the Instrumental Tradition at Ferrara', p. 117; Barblan, 'Vita musicale alla corte sforzesca', p. 801, n. 1.
[77] The letter is printed in its entirety in Moores, 'New Light on Diomede Carafa and his "Perfect Loyalty" to Ferrante of Aragon', pp. 18–19.

tates of fifteenth-century Italy often recruited their musical talent, it is no less likely that Ferrante had a much more permanent arrangement in mind. In any event, we do not know if Pietrobono ever did return to Naples.

Pietrobono was not the only musician in the Ferrarese delegation that visited Naples in 1473. The entourage included Pietrobono's 'tenorista', seven trombetti, two pifferi, two tromboni, an organist, and, according to the 'Lista de la cometiva che va a Napuli per la Ill.ma Madona Duchessa de Ferrara', three 'sonadurij de viola': Andrea, Zampolo, and Rainaldo, all three of whom hailed from Parma.[78] To a certain extent, then, the Ferrarese visitors constituted nothing less than a musical goodwill mission of sorts, like the journey of the Neapolitan royal chapel to Florence in 1451. And together with such gifts as the beautifully illuminated music manuscripts that one court occasionally bestowed upon another, such trips serve as a reminder of the value that Renaissance diplomacy could place on both music and musicians.

Still another performer whose role in the secular music of the Aragonese court must be mentioned is Antoni Tallender, known to his contemporaries as 'Mossen Borra' (1360–1443). Diplomat, jester, and according to Giovanni Pontano a favorite of the Emperor Sigismund, who showered him with silver in appreciation of his talents when he served the Imperial court in 1416–1418,[79] Tallender was almost a permanent fixture at the Aragonese court – mainly at Barcelona, but also at Naples in his final years – from the end of the fourteenth century. Tallender's advanced age when he arrived at Naples circa 1440 (he was still at Barcelona in 1438) probably means that he was more honored than active as a performer, and that his role at Naples may have been purely administrative; nonetheless, a document of 1413 in which he is listed as 'mestre de ministres de boca de casa del senyor rey'[80] makes it clear that he had in the past performed a true musical function (which has heretofore been disputed).[81] He cannot, however, be credited either with the chanson *Se Dedalus* that appears in the manuscript Chantilly 564 or with a three-voice *Credo* that reaches us in Apt 16 and other sources. The latter work is by Pierre Tailhandier, the former by either Pierre or Leonardus Tailhandier, who is variously described as Antoni's brother or son.[82]

The designation of Mossen Borra as master of the 'ministres de boca' raises the question of just what kind of minstrels he had been in charge of at Barcelona. Baldelló interprets the term as a reference to an instrumentalist, a wind-player,

---

[78] Lockwood, 'Pietrobono and the Instrumental Tradition at Ferrara', p. 117, n. 7; Barblan, 'Vita musicale alla corte sforzesca', p. 805.

[79] Pontano, *De liberalite*, XVII; see the edition by Tateo, *Giovanni Pontano: I trattati delle virtù sociali*, pp. 31 and 185. On Tallender's service with Sigismund, see Schuler, 'Die Musik in Konstanz während des Konzils, 1414–1418', p. 164. Tallender also performed before John the Fearless in 1418; see Craig Wright, *Music at the Court of Burgundy*, p. 102, n. 101.

[80] Baldelló, 'La Música en la Casa de los Reyes de Aragón', p. 42.

[81] See, for example, Günther, 'Tailhandier, Pierre', *The New Grove*, XVIII, 527.

[82] On the attribution of these pieces and on the somewhat muddled relationships among the three musicians, see Günther, 'Tailhandier', p. 527; Gómez Muntané, *La Música en la Casa Real Catalano-Aragonesa*, p. 102; Anglés, *Historia de la Musica en Navarra*, p. 300; Stäblein-Harder, *Fourteenth-Century Mass Music in France: Critical Text*, p. 62.

obviously seeing it as being parallel to a designation such as 'ministrer de corda' for a lutenist or harpist,[83] an opinion that concurs with that set forth some fifty years ago by Yvonne Rokseth.[84] However, Craig Wright has recently shown that Burgundian references to 'menestrels de bouche' go on to describe a minstrel who had 'dist' or 'chanté', and that they must, therefore, pertain not to instrumentalists in general or wind-players specifically, but to minstrels who were singers.[85] And this, I believe, is also the correct interpretation for the reference to Mossen Borra. For, while the term 'ministrer' must be taken as pertaining to an instrumentalist when it appears in Aragonese documents without further qualification, those same documents will often provide a specific reference to the precise instrument – such as 'ministrer de xalamia' – when they name a player of a wind instrument. No musician who is definitely known to have been a wind-player is referred to as a minstrel 'de boca'. Mossen Borra, then, was in charge of a group of singers. All of this serves to show that the Neapolitan practice of having a *group* of singers whose main task was to perform secular music can be traced back to the traditions that had developed at Barcelona.

In addition to the royal chamber players, the court had another ensemble whose duties centered mainly on music for secular entertainment: the 'alta cappella'. Consisting of three shawms (both discant and the lower-pitched bombard) and, after circa 1450, a trombone (earlier in the century a slide trumpet would have been used),[86] the ensemble performed at a variety of functions, these being spelled out by Tinctoris in his *De inventione et usu musicae*. They played at weddings, banquets, *trionfi*, public and civic ceremonies, and even at the battlefield and in the church;[87] and always they provided music for the dance. Just how important a role they played in the social life of the court may be appreciated from the negotiations involving two members of the ensemble who are actually better known for their successful careers at two of the foremost courts of northern Italy, the pifferi Bernardino of Mantua and Michele Tedesco of Ferrara. The negotiations may have begun as early as 1477, when, in a letter of 1 August from Federico I Gonzaga to his father, Ludovico, we learn that Bernardino, together with some of the other Mantuan pifferi, had asked permission to go to Naples – a request that Ludovico refused.[88] It is hard not to suspect that it was Ferrante who had planted the idea of a Neapolitan sojourn in the minds of the Mantuan musicians. We do not know what kind of dialogue took place next between the court of Naples and the northern Italian pifferi, but from a letter that Ferrante wrote to Francesco Gonzaga a decade later, on 18 August 1488, it is clear that Michele Tedesco had joined the

[83] Baldelló, 'La Música en la Casa de los Reyes de Aragón', p. 38.

[84] *La Musique d'orgue au XVe siècle et au début du XVIe*, p. 24.

[85] *Music at the Court of Burgundy*, p. 27 and n. 36.

[86] A fine summary of much of the earlier research on the instruments that made up the ensemble is Prizer, 'Bernardino Piffaro', pp. 158ff.

[87] Weinmann, *Johannes Tinctoris*, p. 39.

[88] Prizer, 'Bernardino Piffaro', pp. 154–55 and p. 178, where the letter is printed in full. The discussion that follows is based on Prizer, pp. 154–55 and 179–81, where all the letters are printed. I should like to thank Prof. Prizer for having shared this information with me prior to its publication.

Music for Secular Entertainment 111

Neapolitan alta cappella by circa 1485 ('Sonno tre anni che essendo a li nostri servicij Michel Todesco bifaro'). The same letter also provides the following information: (1) Michele had returned home to collect his family, and knowing that one of Ferrante's pifferi had recently died, he recruited Bernardino for the vacant position; (2) the two musicians had returned to Naples only a few days earlier; (3) Bernardino agreed to serve at Naples for a salary of ten gold ducats per month; and (4) the two musicians had suddenly departed Naples without permission and, Ferrante believes, had gone home. Thus Michele and Bernardino had been at the court together for perhaps no more than a few days. For the remainder of the letter, Ferrante implores Francesco Gonzaga to instruct Bernardino to return to Naples, for not only will he be happy there, but it is the honest thing to do. Ferrante had good reason to want Bernardino back. He had, after all, advanced the two musicians 148 ducats.[89] But even more important, perhaps, the flight of the two musicians had obviously depleted the alta cappella, and this in turn hurt the social life of the royal family itself. As Ferrante puts it: 'Movene ad recondure qua dicto Bernardino la causa del continuare de le feste che se fanno in Napoli, in le quale multo spesso è necessario che danze la serenissima Regina, nostra consorte, insieme con la Illustrissimi Infanta, nostra et sua figlia.' Thus the alta cappella was one of the vital keys to the secular entertainments of the court.

Finally, though it is clearly tangential to the subject matter at hand, I should like to conclude the present chapter with a few remarks on music education in and around Naples, a topic on which there is too little information to warrant a chapter of its own and one that seems less jarringly out of place here than elsewhere. As we have noted in Chap. II, one of the functions of the royal chapel itself was that of a teaching institution, and it is known that both Jaume Borbó and Pere Brusca were masters of the boys at various times, while Guillaume Guarnier may also have filled that role (assuming, of course, that he was a member of the chapel during his Neapolitan sojourn), especially since he had performed a similar service at the Savoyard court and then instructed the young Serafino Aquilano at Naples.[90]

The big question mark in this respect is Tinctoris. As mentioned in the sketch of his activities at Naples, there is no evidence of his ever having held a formal teaching position, whether at the court, the *Studio*, or the mythical music school that some have claimed he founded. Yet the close rapport that he apparently enjoyed with Beatrice may well speak for a teacher–student relationship between musician and princess. But what form could the instruction have taken, and what if anything does it say about Beatrice's musical inclinations or aptitude? That she must have displayed more than the common degree of sensitivity to or appreciation of music that was expected of someone of her station would seem to be indicated by the fact that she was made gifts of the manuscripts New Haven 91

---

[89] This is noted in a postscript to the letter by 'Ju. Episcopus maior cappellanus', who may be identified as the Juliano de Caiacza, Bishop of Tropea, who is otherwise recorded as chapel master in 1491 (see Chap. IV above, p. 94).

[90] See the biographical sketches in Chap. III, pp. 82–83.

and Naples VI.E.40 (see Chap. VI). And even if the presentation of such manuscripts was impelled by political motives (the Naples manuscript a gift from the court of Burgundy?) or personal ones (New Haven 91 an act of homage on the part of Tinctoris?), the cost and effort involved in preparing such royal presents would hardly have been expended on someone altogether lacking in musical interests. On the other hand, it seems doubtful that Beatrice would have been particularly interested in what Tinctoris had to say about sesquialteral proportions or other intricacies of mensural notation, or that she could have found her way through the theorist's *Difficiles alios*, a task that she would no doubt have found fitting only for the professional musician. Perhaps, if her voice was tolerable, she would sing one of his chansons or play a tune on harp or lute in the intimate company of the royal family, thus entertaining her relatives musically as Ippolita had with her dancing. In all, though, there seems to be no way that we may judge either the level at which Tinctoris may have tutored the princess or the skill at music that his presumed student may have attained.

We may also wonder about the musicality of the other members of the royal family. Although Alfonso I was an avid collector of artists, literary figures, and musicians, it is difficult to escape the impression that his personal involvement with music was superficial at best. Granted that he constantly combed his Valencian and Catalan territories for musicians and presented his favorites among them with handsome rewards, and granted also that he pulled his singers and instrumentalists from one encampment to another during the war years of the 1430s and early 1440s, Alfonso's true passions were for political intrigue and territorial expansion. Indeed, that it took so long for his musical establishment to begin to shed its provincialism may even indicate a certain unawareness, on Alfonso's part, of what really constituted the best that contemporary music had to offer. He seems in general to have been much more the *Liebhaber* than the *Kenner*. Ferrante's musical credentials are perhaps even less impressive. While Raffaele Brandolini writes that the king had a magnificent collection of instruments just an arm's length away, it seems significant that he does not tell us that he ever picked one of them up, as he no doubt would have done had Ferrante been able to perform on them. Moreover, Ferrante's correspondence concerning musicians is always rather cold, dispassionate, and businesslike, and his parting shot in the instructions to Tinctoris of 1487 is basically a warning not to squander his money. In all, the rather negative picture that one gets of Ferrante's aesthetic sensibilities in general and with respect to music in particular is one that is probably to be expected from the person who ordered the painting-over of the Giotto frescoes in Castelnuovo. Regarding the other kings – Alfonso II, Ferrandino, himself a poet, and Federico, around whom a number of local poets gathered – there is simply no basis for judgment.[91]

[91] The passage in Giuliano Passero's chronicle that describes the coronation Mass for Alfonso II (8 May 1494) and then goes on to report: 'lo Re Alfonso cantai l'evangelio . . . et dopo che fu detta la messa lo Re se spogliai, *et* untai avanti de tutti . . . *et* dopoi cantai lo Evangelio' probably indicates nothing more than that Alfonso read from the scriptures, with the use of the verb 'cantare' not having any musical significance; see *Storia in forma di Giornale*, p. 60.

No one, then, among the members of the royal family shows any particular talent for music; there is no counterpart of the composer–Pope Leo X or of the truly informed patronage of an Isabella d'Este. Rather, one senses a patronage undertaken for the sake of duty and tradition, or, insofar as Ferrante's recruitment of well-known Franco–Netherlanders for the chapel is concerned, out of the desire for royal prestige and self-glorification. Perhaps it was this lack of personal musical involvement on the part of the royal family that led so many of the musicians – Giovanni da Gaeta, Phelip Remeu, Antonio Ponzo, Raynero, Jachetto da Marvilla, Cordier, Philipet Dortenche, *et al.* – to seek and often find employment elsewhere.

To return to musical pedagogy, we may cite a number of examples of instruction on a non-royal level in and around Naples. On 28 October 1474, the pifferi Tommaso Ferrillo di Giuliano and Menichello Menaro agreed to form a fifteen-year partnership in which they would teach various wind instruments and split the earnings.[92] On 12 December 1474, Giovanni de Lautis di Sicilia agreed to teach both chant and polyphony to a number of priests and clerics of Maiori (on the Amalfi coast). He was, however, disappointed and angry when, upon arriving for the first class, he found only two students.[93] And in another example from outside the capital, Giovanni de Angelo da Bari set up school in Cava dei Tirreni on 27 August 1472 and undertook to instruct Coluccio de Angrisano in 'canto fermo, contraponto colle melodie perfette, et passare a canto figurato'.[94] Finally, at least some Neapolitans could not resist the lure of an out-of-town music education. In 1473, the Count of Altavilla, wishing to have his son study organ and other instruments, decided to send him to Florence, where he could work with the renowned Antonio Squarcialupi; on 5 February, Ferrante sent the following letter of introduction to Lorenzo de' Medici:

nostro Comte de Altavilla per ordination nostra have mandato loco in Fiorenza uno figliolino . . . nominato Angelo per fareli imparar de sonare organi et altri instrumenti de musica, et lo have donato ad Maestro Antonio . . . haverimo grandissimo piacere che dicto figliolo venga ad perfectione de la opera quale impara, et sapemo dicto Mastro Antonio essere tucto cosa vostra ve pregamo et stringemo che ve piaccia strecta et caldamente recomandarceli dicto figlolo, in modo che se habia de sforzare in havere cura et diligentia allo insegnarlo lo piu che sia possibile, che lo averimo ad piacere singularissimo.[95]

[92] Gaetano Filangieri, *Documenti*, V, 206.
[93] *Ibid.*, VI, 55.
[94] *Ibid.*, V, 19.
[95] ASF, MAP, Filza XLV, No. 82; the letter is printed in its entirety in Pontieri, 'La dinastia aragonese di Napoli e la casa de' Medici di Firenze', p. 300.

CHAPTER VI

The Music Sources

Thanks to Tammaro De Marinis's monumental study on the library of the Aragonese kings of Naples,[1] we are reasonably well informed about those activities of the court that concerned the compilation or purchase of both music and other liturgical books for use in the chapel. And that such books were both as numerous[2] and as varied in type as they were (see the table that follows) provides yet another indication of the value that the Aragonese kings placed on the royal chapel.

Manuscripts Compiled or Purchased for the Royal Chapel[3]

Date	Activity	Scribe	Illuminator	Citation in De Marinis	Comments
4 Aug 1451	purchased one 'libre de cant'			II, 231, No. 5b	the purchase was made by the tenor Taxmet de Santo Paulo
24 Apr 1457	purchased a 'libro di canto'				cited in Minieri Riccio, 456; the book was consigned to the singer Lambert Adzemar
23 Feb 1465	'libro di canto d'organo . . . notato diversi ufficii . . .'	Giovanni Campi			cited in Barone, 34; Campi was a member of the chapel; 'cant d'orgue' is the standard term in the documents for polyphony; see also note 26 below
30 Apr 1466	psalter and antiphonary	frate Thomas de Alamanya		II, 247, No. 222	the scribe is a tenor in the chapel

[1] *La biblioteca napoletana dei re d'Aragona.*

[2] According to Prof. Jole Mazzoleni (in a conversation of June 1976), De Marinis's study – the archival research for which was done before the 'cedole' were destroyed in 1943 – accounted for all the notices that concerned the compilation and purchase of books both at and for the court (971 documents in all). However, see the entries in the table for 23 April 1457 and 23 February 1465.

[3] Notes to the table: Under the heading 'Activity', I give only as much information as is necessary to make clear what took place. Where the type of book involved is unambiguous, it is cited by name; where that is not clear, the wording of the document itself is given. Books that were purchased are cited as such; books copied at the court itself receive no special indication. Citations in De Marinis are given by volume, page, and serial number of the document.

The Music Sources

Date	Activity	Scribe	Illuminator	Citation in De Marinis	Comments
30 Apr 1466	collectar	frate Thomas		II, 247, Nos. 224–25	
7 May 1466	'libre de cant d'orgue . . . notats diversos officis'	Ffelippo de Burgunya		II, 247, No. 226	Ffelippo may be the singer Dortenche; see Ch. II, p. 40. consigned to Pere Brusca
12 June 1466	vesperale and hymnal	Dominico de Modo		II, 248, No. 231	on the scribe, see De Marinis, I, 69
14 July 1467	'per lo scrivre del offici de nadall'	Minico de Croffo		II, 248, No. 234	on the scribe, see De Marinis, I, 69
31 July 1467	antiphonary	Domingo de Croffo		II, 248, No. 235	
9 Sept 1467	missal	Oddo Quarto		II, 248, No. 236	on the scribe, see De Marinis, I, 51
25 Sept 1467	antiphonary		Cola Rabicano	II, 248, No. 237	possibly the book written by Croffo earlier that year
5 Dec 1467	missal	Oddo Quarto			probably continuing work on the missal noted for 9 Sept
24 Dec 1467	'antiffinari que son l'offici de nadal e dela setmana santa'	Domingo de Modo	Cola Rabicano	II, 248, Nos. 242–43	
27 Feb 1468	purchased a 'libre de cant d'orgue'			II, 249, No. 249	consigned to Pere Brusca
30 Mar 1468	dominical	Oddo de Alamanya		II, 249, No. 252	the scribe is Oddo Quarto
31 May 1468	antiphonary			II, 249, No. 255	
9 June 1468	gradual		Cola Rabicano	II, 249, No. 256	consigned to Pere Brusca
2 Aug 1468	antiphonary			II, 249, No. 257	
4 Nov 1468	dominical and sanctoral	fra Thomas		II, 249, No. 258	
11 Feb 1469	sanctoral	Oddo Quarto		II, 249, No. 262	
23 Mar 1469	antiphonary	Oddo Quarto	Cola Rabicano	II, 250, No. 268	consigned to Pere Brusca
12 Aug 1469	a 'libre . . . scrits e notats'	Oddo Quarto		II, 250, No. 274	
19 Aug 1469	'VIII officis de cant d'orgue'	Vinxinet de Enaut			the scribe is the composer–singer Vincenet; consigned to Pere Brusca
14 Oct 1469	antiphonary	Oddo de Alamanya		II, 251, No. 284	
31 Oct 1469	'un libre per la capella . . . del ordens de la Eglesia'	Matteo de Lauro		II, 251, No. 286	
14 Mar 1470	gradual	Oddo de Alamanya	Cola Rabicano	II, 251, Nos. 301–2	
26 Apr 1470	antiphonary	Oddo Quarto		II, 252, No. 305	
16 May 1471	antiphonary	Ell Matex		II, 254, No. 369	
20 May 1471	antiphonary			II, 255, Nos. 372–74	
25 May 1471	purchased a missal			II, 255, No. 376–77	consigned to Pere Brusca on 28 May

Date	Activity	Scribe	Illuminator	Citation in De Marinis	Comments
17 Feb 1474	missal	frate Thomas			for the chapel of the Duchess of Calabria
12 Apr 1482	purchased a missal	Lancilao Boemio		II, 283, No. 656	purchased from the monastery of San Pietro Martire; the scribe was paid for correcting and enlarging it
Dec 1488	missal			II, 290, No. 738	for the chapel of the duchess
9 Apr 1491	vesperale		Christofano Mayorana	II, 292, No. 770	
15 May 1492	'per la paritatura di 16 quinterni . . . per servitio de notare canto figurato'			II, 297, No. 819	the quinterns were consigned to the singer Juliano Finero, presumably for him to notate
7 Dec 1492	missal			II, 304, No. 884	
19 Dec 1492	'sey quinterny . . . in li quale a notati certi misse de canto'	Juliano Ferrilla		II, 304, No. 887	the scribe was a member of the chapel; it is not completely clear whether these quinterns were consigned to the chapel or (together with a 'canczonero') to the king's private library

In addition to the music books intended for and consigned to the chapel, it is known that the court had a number of other books either with or about music that were housed in the private collections of one or another of the members of the royal family. There was the sumptuous Tinctoris manuscript – now at the University Library at Valencia (MS 835, *olim* 844) – that was decorated with the royal arms and prepared in part by Cristoforo Majorana and Matteo Felice (or their workshops), two of the most active illuminators at Naples; the manuscript, probably compiled for Ferrante,[4] contains nine of Tinctoris's twelve treatises and may have constituted an *opera omnia* of his then completed works. At least two music manuscripts were intended for the princess Beatrice: the Mellon Chansonnier (New Haven 91), prepared for her at the court (see below), and the manuscript Naples VI.E.40, which contains a cycle of six *L'homme armé* Masses (possibly by Caron); this manuscript appears to have been a gift from the court of Burgundy, and probably came to Naples only when Beatrice returned there (from Buda) in 1501.[5] Still other books for which there is documentation can no longer be identified. On 22 November 1468, Cola Rabicano was paid five ducats for having decorated a 'libre de cant' with the royal arms; the book was consigned to

---

[4] See De Marinis, *La biblioteca napoletana dei re d'Aragona*, I, 150–55; Perkins and Garey, *The Mellon Chansonnier*, I, 22.

[5] On this manuscript, see Cohen, *The Six Anonymous L'Homme armé Masses in Naples, Biblioteca Nazionale, MS VI E 40*, pp. 62ff, and *Census-Catalogue of Manuscript Sources of Polyphonic Music 1400–1550*, II, 247–48. The Masses are assigned to Caron by Gillers, 'The Naples L'Homme armé Masses and Caron'.

the 'guardaroba'.⁶ And that the royal library was indeed well stocked with books pertaining to music is evident from a gift of royal manuscripts presented to Lorenzo de' Medici. Among the items sent to Florence were five volumes either with or about music: *Musica Boetij, Musica Isadori, Musica Tinctoris, Liber diversarum cantionum* and *Musica Lippi*.⁷ How we should like to know the contents of the 'song book'! Was it a chansonnier, and could it have been one of the channels through which such a manuscript as the Florentine chansonnier Paris 15123 received its Neapolitan-influenced readings?

Useful as the above information about the chapel and private collections might be from a purely quantitative point of view – for example, there were at least eight books of polyphony – it also underscores certain other aspects of music at the court. First, the documentation shows that by far the greatest amount of activity in connection with the compilation and acquisition of music and other liturgical books for the chapel occurred during the second half of the 1460s – that is, at precisely the time that Ferrante was beginning to alter the character of the chapel and enhance its prestige by turning his recruitment efforts toward the Franco–Netherlanders of international repute. Thus the acquisition of music books, especially those containing polyphony, went hand in hand with the arrival of the northern singers, and it is reasonable to conclude that the change in the character of the personnel was accompanied by a similar change in – and enlargement of – the repertory.

Second, we see that scribal duties were often undertaken by the singer–chaplains themselves. Of the ten scribes named in the table, five – Giovanni Campi, Fra Thomas, Dortenche (= Ffelippo de Burgunya?), Vincenet, and Juliano Ferrilla – are known to have been members of the chapel. And in each instance, they were awarded extra compensation for their work as scribes. In addition, of the four books of polyphony that were prepared for the chapel at the court itself,⁸ the names of the scribes are known for three; and each time the scribe was one of the chapel singers. Chant sources, on the other hand, though they might be written by one of the singers – see the references in the table to the tenor Fra Thomas – could just as well be copied by scribes who are not known to have been singers. Perhaps they were like the scribe Donato di Andri and held positions as 'scriptori de li libri per la capella'. Finally, in the few instances in which the documents tell us

---

⁶ De Marinis, *La biblioteca napoletana dei rei d'Aragona*, II, 249, No. 260.

⁷ De Marinis, *La biblioteca napoletana*, II, 194; see also Perkins and Garey, *The Mellon Chansonnier*, I, 30. The date of the gift is unknown, but Perkins is probably correct in assuming that it was made in the 1480s (perhaps the early years of that decade being the most likely period). The donation is documented in Rome, Biblioteca Apostolica Vaticana, Vat. lat., MS 7134, a collection of library inventories (and copies of inventories) that dates from circa 1508–1515 (De Marinis, II, 193). The gift to Lorenzo is recorded on fols. 255ʳ–259ʳ under the heading: 'Index regalium codicum Alfonsi Regis ad Laurentium Medicem . . .' The reference to Alfonso as king must be incorrect. Alfonso I is obviously too early, while Alfonso II did not attain the throne until after Lorenzo's death. The gift must have been sent either by Ferrante or by Alfonso while he was still Duke of Calabria.

⁸ See the entries for 23 Feb 1465, 7 May 1466, 19 Aug 1469, and 15 May 1492; a fifth book of polyphony was purchased rather than compiled at the court (27 Feb 1468).

that the books prepared or purchased for the chapel were consigned to someone other than the chapel master, it was to one of the singers that they were entrusted. In all, then, it was often to the singers themselves that the responsibility fell of notating, maintaining, and presumably gathering the repertory of the chapel.

There is one respect, though, in which the documents fail us. Not once in the documentation that concerns the polyphonic holdings of either the chapel or private collections is a description of a book sufficiently detailed to permit us to glean even the slightest idea of its contents. Yet the character and contents of a surprisingly large number of Neapolitan manuscripts can be assessed, for in addition to the previously cited manuscript New Haven 91, there are, I believe, no fewer than seven other extant sources of polyphony and two surviving tablatures for plucked string instruments whose origins can be traced back to Naples[9] and whose contents provide us with a comprehensive record of the richness and diversity of Neapolitan musical life.[10]

The polyphonic sources fall conveniently into one of three groups depending upon the decade – 1460s, 1470s, or 1480s[11] – in which they or their main sections were written.

1460s: Of the two manuscripts – Escorial IV.a.24 and Berlin 78.C.28 – that have been dated from about the middle of this decade, it is Escorial IV.a.24 that begins to show signs of a recognizably home-grown repertory.[12] Alongside its

---

[9] The claim that a manuscript is from Naples always raises the following question: does 'Naples' mean the royal court, another institution or family in the city, or even somewhere else in the kingdom? Except in connection with two sources – Montecassino 871 and New Haven 91 (see below) – the question cannot be answered with certainty. Yet given the degree to which cultural affairs – no less than governmental – were centralized at the court and in the capital, one must probably assume, unless there is strong evidence to the contrary (as there seems to be for Montecassino 871), that polyphonic music manuscripts were far more likely to have been written at, or at least close to, the court than in the less culturally developed provinces. For the same point in connection with the Neapolitan literary tradition, see Tateo, *I centri culturali dell'umanesimo*, p. 130. In addition to the sources of polyphony accounted for in the present chapter, two more manuscripts must probably now be added to the Neapolitan camp; see Chap. VII, n. 2.

[10] For notices on a number of Neapolitan chant sources of the period (from both the city and the provinces, but not from the court, see Arnese, *I codici notati della Biblioteca Nazionale di Napoli*, passim.

[11] I know of no extant polyphonic sources from the reign of Alfonso I.

[12] For an edition of the manuscript and a discussion of its provenance and contents, see Hanen, *The Chansonnier El Escorial IV.a.24*; the Neapolitan provenance is also discussed in Jeppesen, *La frottola*, II, 18–19. Cf. also the inventory that appears in Southern, 'El Escorial, Monastery Library, MS IV.a.24', pp. 58–77, while the same scholar has recently published *Anonymous Pieces in the MS El Escorial IV.a.24*. We should note that Pirrotta, 'Su alcuni testi italiani di composizioni polifoniche quattrocentesche', p. 136, questions Jeppesen's suggestion that the manuscript was compiled at Naples and suggests northern Italy as the more likely place of origin. Pirrotta's view is accepted without question by Donato, 'Contributo alla storia delle siciliane', p. 188, and (though with some discussion) by Southern, *Anonymous Pieces*, pp. xi–xiv, who, however, dates the MS too late, but still comes to the conclusion that the manuscript was brought to Naples by the 'late 1470s' (p. xiv). A suggestion that the manuscript might be of Milanese origin was long ago put forth by Thibault, 'Du rôle de l'ornamentation dans la musique profane au Moyen-Age', p. 456, n. 86. Actually, Hanen (I, 40–42) – whose dissertation Pirrotta could not have known when he wrote his own article (Southern, *Anonymous Pieces*, cites the dissertation, but simply ignores the conclusions about the provenance) – dis-

predominantly Franco–Burgundian repertory, it contains two pieces by Cornago – one of which, *Yerra con poco saber*, is included in the present edition (No. 9) – and two other compositions, *Hora may che fora son* (No. 12 in the edition) and *Fate darera* (=*Fatti inderier*), that are referred to respectively as a 'napoletana' and 'chanzone chalavrese' in various poetry anthologies of the period and that no doubt originated at Naples.[13]

The provenance of Berlin 78.C.28 is admittedly problematical. Because it contains the coats-of-arms of the Florentine Niccolini and Castellani families, as well as illuminations that were executed in the Florentine workshop of Gherardo and Monte di Giovanni, Reidemeister concluded that the manuscript was written at Florence.[14] However, as I have argued elsewhere, Berlin 78.C.28 also contains compelling evidence that points to Naples as its place of origin.[15] And as if the manuscript were intended to cause problems for present-day musicologists, its one composition that, to judge from the text with which it appears in Montecassino 871, seems obviously to be associated with Naples – *Viva, viva rey Ferranddo* – is transmitted without text or text incipits in Berlin 78.C.28, but with capital initials that imply that the Spanish poem may well be a contrafactum (see the commentary in Chap. VII, p. 149; No. 2 in the edition). Given both the controversy that surrounds its origins and its completely international repertory, therefore, Berlin 78.C.28 has not been used as either the principal or unique source for any of the pieces in the edition.

1470s: Only one manuscript in its entirety can be assigned to this decade, New Haven 91 (the Mellon Chansonnier), which Perkins dates from circa 1475 and which he associates specifically with Tinctoris and his patroness, the Princess Beatrice.[16] Indeed, New Haven 91 is the only manuscript among the extant

cusses the possibility of Milanese origins, but after weighing the evidence assigns the source to Naples. The Naples–Milan ambiguity is not especially surprising in view of the fact that the manuscript was probably written about the middle to latter part of the decade – that is, at a time that witnessed a lively musical exchange between the two courts as a result of the marriage of Alfonso, Duke of Calabria, and Ippolita Sforza. Three arguments seem to be used to support the contention that the manuscript originated in northern Italy: (1) the presence in the Italian compositions of northern Italian linguistic elements; (2) the ascription of a number of the poems to Leonardo Giustinian and the request made in the 1470s by Galeazzo Maria Sforza to have that poet's works sent to him from Venice; and (3) the appearance in the manuscript of *Hè Robinet – O rosa bella* and the request made by the same duke in 1472 that he be sent a copy of the same piece from the court of Savoy. With respect to the second and third of these arguments, we may note not only that many of the ascriptions to Giustinian are quite uncertain, but also that the duke's request for the pieces in question came some years after the manuscript was already compiled. As for the northern Italian linguistic elements, they may well indicate that a repertory of Italian compositions was sent to Naples from the north of Italy. This would be perfectly in keeping with the Milanese–Neapolitan contacts of the period. In all, I find Hanen's arguments in favor of Naples (and against Milan) as the place of origin totally convincing.

[13] See Bronzini, 'Poesia popolare del periodo aragonese', pp. 260, 269–70, and the discussion of *Ora may* in Chap. VII, pp. 144–46 below.

[14] Reidemeister, *Die Handschrift 78C28 des Berliner Kupferstichkabinetts*, pp. 14–15. The study contains an inventory, which is not entirely accurate, together with a partial transcription and facsimile of the manuscript.

[15] Atlas, 'La provenienza del manoscritto Berlin 78.C.28', pp. 10–29.

[16] Perkins and Garey, *The Mellon Chansonnier*, I, 28–32. The study contains both modern and facsimile editions of the manuscript, together with an exhaustive commentary on its origins and contents. It supersedes Bukofzer, 'An Unknown Chansonnier of the 15th Century', who

Neapolitan sources of polyphony whose origins at the royal court can be established beyond doubt. Though the repertory is still overwhelmingly Franco–Burgundian, the Neapolitan character of the manuscript emerges through its works by Tinctoris and Vincenet. Tinctoris is represented by two compositions with Latin texts – *O virgo, miserere mei* (No. 1 in the edition) and *Virgo Dei throno digna* – both of which are addressed to Beatrice.[17] Vincenet's presence is recorded by all four of his known secular works, which in addition to pieces based on French and Italian poems includes a setting of the Castilian *La pena sin ser sabida* (No. 10 in the edition).

1480s: The four manuscripts that were written either entirely or mainly during this decade – Montecassino 871, Perugia 431, Seville 5-I-43/Paris 4379, and Bologna Q 16[18] – constitute what may be called the 'central' corpus of Neapolitan sources, for it is here that a local repertory, both sacred and secular, truly comes to the fore. And though the manuscripts display the kind of interrelationships that one would expect from sources that belong to the same tightly knit tradition, each of them retains a distinct profile of its own.

The two manuscripts with the most clearly pronounced Neapolitan characters are Montecassino 871 and Perugia 431. The first of these may have been copied at the Benedictine monastery of Sant'Angelo at Gaeta, at which it at least came to reside by the early sixteenth century.[19] The precise place at which Perugia 431

claimed (pp. 16–17) that the manuscript originated within the Burgundian realm. Two important reviews of the Perkins and Garey edition are my own in the *Journal of the American Musicological Society*, XXXIV (1981), 132–43, and David Fallows, 'Three Neapolitan Repertories 1460–90: Three Recent Editions', where Tinctoris's involvement with the compilation of the manuscript is questioned (p. 498); on this point, see also Woodley, 'Iohannes Tinctoris', p. 232, n. 35, where it is claimed that Tinctoris 'was in fact the musical scribe of the manuscript (though not of the literary text), but that his function as . . . "compiler" of the collection is more obscure'. I do not know if Woodley has actually managed to identify Tinctoris's hand in the manuscript. Perhaps such northern musician–scribes as Vincenet – who is especially well represented in the manuscript (see below) – or Dortenche should also be considered as candidates.

[17] On the allusion to Beatrice in *Virgo Dei throno digna*, see Perkins and Garey, *The Mellon Chansonnier*, I, 19, and II, 425; on *O virgo miserere mei*, see Chap. VII, pp. 148–49.

[18] Though it is possible that various sections of these sources date from the latter part of the 1470s or the beginning of the 1490s, I believe that we can safely assign all of Perugia 431 (except for the later-sixteenth-century additions and marginalia) and the greater parts of Montecassino 871 and Seville 5-I-43/Paris 4379 to the 1480s; on Bologna Q 16, see below.

[19] See Pope and Kanazawa, *The Musical Manuscript Montecassino 871*, pp. 2–3, 19–21; the publication contains an edition and inventory of the manuscript and a commentary on its contents. The proposed origin at Gaeta has been questioned by Ward, 'The Polyphonic Office Hymn and the Liturgy of Fifteenth-Century Italy', pp. 179–80; Giulio Cattin, 'Canti polifonici del repertorio benedettino', pp. 492ff, suggests that the manuscript may have been compiled at the Benedictine monastery of SS Severino e Sossio in Naples and then removed to the monastery at Gaeta. Pope and Kanazawa (p. 19) show conclusively that the source could not have been completed before Gaffurius's sojourn at Naples in 1478–1480. However, their suggestion that the manuscript was copied over a lengthy period of time, ('perhaps ten years, or even twenty') and that 'one may cite the last two decades of the fifteenth century as the most probable date of the manuscript' seems to allow far too much leeway. That the manuscript contains none of the more modern repertory that appears in the Florentine sources of the 1490s or even in the later section of the Neapolitan manuscript Bologna Q 16 probably points to the 1480s as the decade by which the source was completed. On the question of the date, see also my review of Pope and Kanazawa in *Notes*, XXXVII (1980), 45–47.

was written is not so easily pinned down; however, since it displays so extraordinarily close a relationship with Montecassino 871, it too would appear to be monastic in origins, perhaps having been compiled at a Benedictine monastery or (as Giulio Cattin has recently suggested) at a Franciscan institution.[20] Both manuscripts transmit mixed repertories of secular and sacred music – whereas in Montecassino 871 the emphasis in the sacred repertory is on the small-scale forms for the Hours, Perugia 431 contains a large selection of music for the Mass[21] – and reflect the wide range of the musical activities and tastes at the Aragonese court and its musical–cultural dependents. Among the better-known composers who are represented in the two sources and who are known to have worked at Naples are Cornago (No. 10), and Ycart (No. 5). Alongside them is a group of otherwise unknown composers whose presence at Naples can probably be assumed on the ground that their music appears in no other sources: Damianus, Seraphinus (No. 4), Fra M. di Ortona, Aedvardus di Ortona, Petrus Caritatus, and a number of composers who are identified in Perugia 431 by their initials only.[22] Finally, with their many strambotti – most of them with the so-called 'sicilian' rhyme scheme (Nos. 13–14 in the edition) – and barzellette (No. 12), Montecassino 871 and Perugia 431 afford us our first truly large-scale glimpse at the early development of the frottola.

Of the four sources that belong to the Neapolitan tradition of the 1480s, only one can be dated precisely: Bologna Q 16, the original layer of which was completed in 1487, with additions probably having been made in the early 1490s, perhaps – given the ties of these additions with Florentine manuscripts – after Alexander Agricola's journey from Florence to Naples in May–June 1492.[23]

[20] On the origins of Perugia 431, see Atlas, 'On the Neapolitan Provenance of Perugia 431', 45–105, where there is also an inventory and short description of the contents of the manuscript. It was on the basis of its close ties with Montecassino 871 that I suggested (in the article cited) that Perugia 431 may have been compiled at a Benedictine house, singling out the monastery of SS Severino e Sossio because of its proximity to the court and the favors that it received from the royal family. Recently, however, Cattin has pointed out that the manuscript contains two pieces – a setting of the hymn *Decus morum dux minorum* and another of the *Benedicamus Domino* prosa *Qui nos fecit ex nichilo* – that have Franciscan associations, and that it might therefore have been written at a Franciscan institution. Cattin's conclusions appear in his paper 'Il repertorio polifonico sacro nelle fonti napoletane del Quattrocento' (I am grateful to Prof. Cattin for sharing his findings with me prior to their publication). For an edition of the pieces with Italian texts, see Michael Hernon, 'Perugia MS 431 (G 20): A Study of the Secular Italian Pieces'.

[21] The sacred repertory of the two manuscripts is now most fully discussed in Pope and Kanazawa, *The Musical Manuscript Montecassino 871*, pp. 29–46, and Cattin, 'Il repertorio polifonico sacro'.

[22] On the question of whether the Damianus represented in Montecassino 871 may be identified with the wind-player of that name who is recorded at Naples in 1456, see Pope and Kanazawa, *The Musical Manuscript Montecassino 871*, p. 34. As already noted in the preceding chapter (p. 107), Minieri Riccio, 'Alcuni fatti di Alfonso I', p. 444, lists him as 'Tommaso Damiano'; Anglés, 'La Música en la Corte Real de Aragón y de Nápoles', p. 1022, regards him as 'Tomás Damia', thus making him a Spaniard. In an earlier study, Anglés, *La Música en la Corte de los Reyes Católicos*, I, 149, had cited him as 'Damiano Guterrit', thereby confusing him with another instrumentalist at the court, Gilet Guterrit. On the two composers from Ortona, see Atlas, 'On the Neapolitan Provenance of Perugia 431', pp. 54–55, and my forthcoming edition of an untitled Mass by Aedvardus (to be published by Antico Edition).

[23] On the Neapolitan origins of the manuscript, see Atlas, *The Cappella Giulia Chansonnier*, I, 235–36, and idem, 'On the Neapolitan Provenance of

Although the lack of complete texts and the presence of but two attributions – to 'Dux Burgensis' (Charles the Bold?) and the uncertain 'J.P.' (Josquin des Prez? – see Chap. III, p. 84 above, and No. 17 in the edition) – complicate the task of identifying the Neapolitan portion of the repertory, a number of pieces or groups of compositions can probably be singled out as local products. Certainly, the strambotto siciliano *Sera nel core mio doglia*, which appears in each of the other three Neapolitan sources of this decade, must have originated within the artistic circle of the court. Also prime candidates for Neapolitan origin are three entire complexes of compositions. First, there are the four pieces notated with gamma clef; that this clef is otherwise unknown in the secular music of the period, and that all four works are unique to Bologna Q 16, may well point to a local style trait, a conclusion that is reinforced by the association of this clef with Tinctoris. Second, the original layer of Bologna Q 16 contains at least five – and possibly seven – settings of Castilian texts, all but one of which are unica;[24] given the Aragonese court's long poetic tradition in this language and the settings of Castilian poems by Cornago and even the non-Spanish Vincenet, a local repertory must be suspected. Yet a third group of unique pieces, these having such epigrammatic titles as *La taurina*, *Per la goula*, and *La rocca de fermesa*, may also have local connotations that await discovery.[25] Finally, two other pieces can probably be assigned to Naples with a fair degree of certainty: the large-scale *Missa L'homme armé* (No. 3 in the edition), which is unique to Bologna Q 16, and the arrangement *a 2* of the well-known *La Spagna* melody, a setting that also appears in Perugia 431, where it bears an ascription to the dancing-master Guglielmus Ebreo (No. 18 in the edition), who was present at Naples in the late 1460s. Thus, although the specific connections between Bologna Q 16 and Naples may not be as immediately obvious as are those between Naples and either Montecassino 871 or Perugia 431, the 'specialized' – that is, non-Franco–Burgundian – part of the Bologna Q 16 repertory is definitely meridional in character.

The fourth manuscript of the 1480s tradition is Seville 5-I-43/Paris 4379, which eventually found its way to Rome, where it was purchased by Ferdinand Columbus in September 1515.[26] In addition to Cornago's *Moro, perche non da fede*,

Perugia 431', p. 46, n. 5; see also Fuller, 'Additional Notes on the 15th-Century Chansonnier Bologna Q 16', p. 86; Haberkamp, *Die weltliche Volkmusik in Spanien um 1500*, p. 66; Jeppesen, *La frottola*, II, 11. The assertion by Anglés, 'El "Chansonnier français" de la Colombina de Sevilla', p. 1391, that the manuscript was compiled in Spain must be disregarded. For a list of the contents of the source, see Pease, 'A Report on Codex Q 16', where, unfortunately, music and text incipits are given separately and concordances are omitted; for a list of the composers represented and a partial concordance, see Fuller, *op. cit.*, pp. 81–82, 101–3, and Jeppesen, *La frottola*, II, 110. For an edition of thirty-one pieces from the manuscript, see Benton, *Fifteenth Century Anonymous Chansons*.

[24] Fuller, 'Additional Notes on the 15th-Century Chansonnier Bologna Q 16', p. 85, n. 13. Urrede's popular *Nunca fue pena maior* is among the later additions to the manuscript.

[25] See Fuller, *op. cit.*, p. 97.

[26] For a discussion and inventory of the source, see Plamenac, 'A Reconstruction of the French Chansonnier in the Biblioteca Colombina, Seville'. A facsimile edition appears in idem, *Facsimile Reproduction of the Manuscripts Sevilla 5-I-43 and Paris N.A.Fr. 4379 (Pt.I)*. The manuscript is transcribed, though not entirely accurately (this is especially true of the poetic texts) in Moerk, 'The Seville Chansonnier'. On the provenance of the manuscript, see Atlas, *The Cappella Giulia Chansonnier*, I, 257. An attempt to date the source more precisely appears in

Tinctoris's *Helas* and *Vostre regart* – which, however, probably date from before his Neapolitan period[27] – and Vincenet's popular *Fortune, par ta cruaulté* (see No. 17 in the edition), the Neapolitan repertory consists of a large number of Italian pieces, including a group of strambotti siciliani, some of which also appear in Montecassino 871, Perugia 431, and Bologna Q 16. And from among these works, two – *La morte che spavento de felice* (No. 13) and the forward-looking, villanella-like *Cavalcha Sinisbaldo tula la note* (No. 15) – are included in the edition.

In all, the four 'central' Neapolitan sources of the 1480s provide a detailed picture of the musical life of Aragonese Naples, at least as it flourished mainly during the reign of Ferrante I. The manuscripts transmit music by such major figures at Naples as Tinctoris and Cornago as well as compositions by minor, local composers who are otherwise unknown. The contents range from complete settings of the Ordinary of the Mass to the small-scale barzellette and strambotti that set the dialectal texts of the Neapolitan court poets. Finally, the sources continue to attest to the great popularity at Naples of the Franco–Netherlandish chanson of the Busnois–Ockeghem generation. And it is with good reason, then, that these are the manuscripts most often drawn upon in our edition.

The final polyphonic manuscript of Neapolitan origin is the small fragment housed at the Biblioteca Comunale of Foligno, which, however, can be dated only from the late 1470s or 1480s. That its origins are to be traced to Naples is evident not only from the very close relationship between its reading for *A, ladri, perche robbate le fatige* and that in Perugia 431, but also from its use of southern dialect, from its inclusion of a strambotto siciliano, and from the fact that it was in the possession of a Neapolitan in the sixteenth century.[28]

In addition to the above sources of polyphonic music, Aragonese Naples has, I believe, bequeathed to us our two earliest extant tablatures of Italian provenance

Schavran, 'The Manuscript Pavia, Biblioteca Universitaria, Codice Aldini 362', pp. 53–58, who claims that part of the manuscript probably dates from the 1470s. Finally, Boorman, 'Limitations and Extensions of Filiation Technique', pp. 335–39, argues that part of the manuscript – those layers copied by Scribe I – may have originated at a center other than Naples, and he at least implies that some consideration should be given to Rome. Despite his skillful marshaling of the evidence, I cannot agree with his conclusions. What Boorman shows, I think, is (1) that the Neapolitan 'tradition' – that is, its readings for the Franco-Netherlandish chanson repertory – is not absolutely homogeneous (I address this conclusion, with which I concur, in a forthcoming essay entitled 'Some Strambotti Siciliani and the Reconstruction of a Neapolitan Fascicle-Manuscript'), and (2) that the readings for some chansons are shared by the sources of both the Neapolitan and Florentine traditions (another conclusion with which I agree, as witness my remarks in *The Cappella Giulia Chansonnier*, I,

258). Columbus described his purchase as a 'Cancionero de canto d'organo ... viejo y mutilado'; see Plamenac, 'A Reconstruction of the French Chansonnier in the Biblioteca Colombina', pp. 504–5, and idem, 'Excerpta Colombiniana: Items of Musical Interest in Fernando Colon's "Regestrum"', II, 678.

[27] See Chap. III, p. 76.

[28] I discuss the provenance of the manuscript more fully in my article 'The Foligno Fragment: Another Source from Fifteenth-Century Naples'. Further descriptions of the manuscript appear in Rubsamen, 'The Earliest French Lute Tablature', p. 294; Jeppesen, *La frottola*, II, 61–62, and Plates XXV–XXVII, which constitute a facsimile edition of the polyphonic portion of the fragment; and *Census-Catalogue of Manuscript Sources of Polyphonic Music, 1400–1550*, I, 247, which, however, partially confuses the source with an earlier manuscript that is housed at the Archivio di Stato, Foligno; see n. 1 in my article 'The Foligno Fragment'.

for plucked-string instruments. The more extensive of the two sources is the heart-shaped lute manuscript Pesaro 1144, the proposed pre-1500 date of which has engendered some debate. In part, the controversy resulted from a somewhat misleading description of the source by Rubsamen, who, in dating Pesaro 1144 from before 1500, failed to explain the presence of the fifteenth-century lute pieces – and watermarks – in the context in which they appear, that is, within a poetry anthology compiled by Tempesta Biondi in the late sixteenth century.[29] Obviously, what is at issue is not the date of Pesaro 1144 as a whole, but simply that of its original layers of lute music on fols. 1r–32v, 78r–81v, and possibly 33r–40v. Hopefully, the question has been settled by David Fallows, who, having subjected the manuscript to an intensive paleographical examination, concludes that the original layers most probably date from the end of the fifteenth century.[30] What has not been pointed out, however, is that the original sections of Pesaro 1144 were most likely written at Naples: (1) on fols. 39v–40v, the scribe employed the so-called 'tabulatura alla napoletana', a system not known to have been used in any source that can be shown to have been compiled outside Naples; (2) the watermark, a 'balance', though not restricted to Naples, is frequently found on paper used in the Neapolitan chancery during the 1470s and 1480s;[31] and (3) one of the pieces in Pesaro 1144, *A, ladri, perche robbate le fatige*, survives in its original polyphonic version only in the Neapolitan manuscripts Perugia 431 and Foligno. While no single piece of evidence is conclusive by itself, the three strands of evidence taken together point more strongly to Naples than to any other musical center in late-fifteenth-century Italy.

The second tablature source is Bologna 596 H.H.2[4], a small three-leaf fragment that transmits intabulations of Vincenet's *Fortune, par ta cruaulté* – the piece is here entitled *Fortuna vincinecta*, as it is also only in Perugia 431 – and Juan de León's *Ay, que non se rremediarme*, which also reaches us in Bologna Q 16. Again, the intabulator used the tablature 'alla napoletana', and the Neapolitan provenance of the source seems beyond question.[32] The Bologna fragment is represented in the edition by its arrangement of Vincenet's well-known chanson (No. 16).

Finally, for the purposes of the edition I have drawn upon one non-Neapolitan manuscript, the polyphonic segment of Faenza 117. Though primarily a source of keyboard music, it was augmented with polyphonic compositions in 1473–1474

---

[29] Rubsamen, *op. cit.* For the objection to Rubsamen's date, see Heartz, 'Mary Magadalen, Lutenist'; see also Saviotti, 'Di un codice musicale del secolo XVI'.

[30] Fallows, '15th-Century Tablatures for Plucked Instruments', pp. 10–18; the pre-1500 date is also accepted by Brown, *Sixteenth-Century Instrumentation: The Music for the Florentine Intermedii*, p. 41.

[31] The watermark is reproduced in Rubsamen, 'The Earliest French Tablature', pp. 289–90. On its use in Neapolitan documents, see Barone, 'Le filigrane delle antiche cartiere nei documenti dell'Archivio di Stato in Napoli', pp. 83 and 94, No. 62.

[32] Fallows, '15th-Century Tablatures for Plucked Instruments', pp. 18–28. The manuscript was first described in a paper by Hans T. David, 'An Italian Tablature Lesson of the Renaissance', at the annual meeting of the American Musicological Society at Boston in 1958; it will be published in a forthcoming posthumous collection of Prof. David's essays.

by Johannes Bonadies.³³ And alongside pieces by John Hothby, Erfordia, and Bonadies himself, there are four liturgical works by Bernardus Ycart, one of which, a setting of the *Magnificat*, is included in the edition (No. 5). Indeed, that as many as four of Ycart's compositions are transmitted together with those by Hothby and Bonadies may, as was already noted (Chap. III, p. 79), shed light on at least one period of Ycart's pre-Naples activity.

³³ Plamenac, 'Faenza, Codex 117', *Die Musik in Geschichte und Gegenwart*, III (1954), cols 1709–10.

CHAPTER VII

The Repertory

Our survey of the repertory at Naples takes the form of a commentary on the eighteen pieces included in the edition, these being representative of all segments of that repertory except the imported Franco–Netherlandish chanson in its original polyphonic form; however, there is a reminder of that genre in the arrangement for solo voice and lute (or vihuela) of Vincenet's *Fortune, par ta cruaulté*.

It is virtually certain that all the pieces save one – Ycart's *Magnificat* – come either from the royal court itself or from institutions (generally monastic) that must have had a musical alliance with it. The works by Oriola, Cornago, Vincenet, Tinctoris, and Ycart are all by composers affiliated with the court, while Gaffurius seems to have worked just around the corner. The compositions by Tinctoris and Gaffurius definitely date from their periods at Naples. The arrangement of Vincenet's chanson is unique to a Neapolitan manuscript, and Serafino dall'Aquila's *Sufferir so disposto* was written and composed before his sojourns in northern Italy. Only Ycart is represented by a pre-Neapolitan work, one that I have included because of the interesting historical questions that it raises.

The provenance of other compositions can be assigned to Naples for a variety of reasons: the work may (1) be unique to a Neapolitan source, (2) set a poetic form that was favored at the court, (3) contain touches of southern dialect, (4) refer to a member of the royal family, or (5) display certain stylistic characteristics that appear frequently in other works thought to be of local origin. Only the Neapolitan provenance of the *Je ne demande* ascribed to 'J.P.' is tenuous.

Finally, although Tinctoris's *O virgo, miserere mei*, and the anonymous *Viva, viva, rey Ferranddo* occupy first and second place in the edition, they are discussed fairly late in the commentary, within the discussion of secular music at the court, under the sub-heading 'Pieces for the Royal Family'. The pieces in the edition, then, are taken up in the following order:

Liturgical Music	
Music for the Ordinary of the Mass	Nos. 3, 4, 4a
Music for Vespers and the Good Friday Liturgy	5, 6, 7, 8
Secular Music	
Settings of Spanish Texts	9, 10, 11
Settings of Italian Texts	12, 13, 14, 15

Pieces for the Royal Family	1, 2
A French Chanson for Solo Voice and Lute (*Vihuela da mano*)	16
Pieces for Instrumental Ensemble	17, 18

Liturgical Music

Music for the Ordinary of the Mass

Despite their wide-ranging repertory, there is one important body of compositions about which the Neapolitan sources are (with one exception – see note 2 below) problematically silent: the large-scale Masses of the Franco–Netherlandish masters, works that are known to have circulated at such other Italian musical centers as Rome, Ferrara, Milan, and (at least by the beginning of the sixteenth century) Venice.[1] Yet circumstantial evidence at least suggests that these Masses were also known at Naples: (1) beginning in the mid-1460s, the royal chapel was home to a number of distinguished Franco–Netherlanders who could well have brought their northern Mass repertory with them; (2) in his *Liber de arte contrapuncti* and *Proportionale musices*, both of which were written at Naples, Tinctoris makes a number of quite specific references to notational problems in Masses by Franco–Netherlanders, problems of a type that must surely have required his having the music before him;[2] and (3) Naples was, as we shall see, well acquainted with the Franco–Netherlandish *L'homme armé* tradition, and must certainly have known at least some of the Masses based on that famous tune.

Reference to the *L'homme armé* tradition brings us to the first work in our survey, the anonymous *L'homme armé* Mass that appears as an unicum in the

---

[1] As witness the contents of such sources as Rome B.80 and a number of the Cappella Sistina manuscripts (Rome); Modena α.M.1.2, Modena α.M.l.13, and Modena AS (Ferrara); Milan 1, 2, 3, and 4 (Milan); and the Petrucci prints devoted to this genre (Venice).

[2] Seay, *Johannes Tinctoris (c. 1435–1511): The Art of Counterpoint*, passim; idem, 'The *Proportionale musices* of Johannes Tinctoris'. The composers cited are Barbingnant, Busnois, Jean Cousin, Dufay, Faugues, Le Rouge, Ockeghem, Pasquin, Pullois, and Regis. Though one could argue that Tinctoris was working from notes about these pieces that he had brought with him, that these Masses had made their way to Italy is attested by the appearance of six of them in the manuscript Rome 14. This close connection between the references in Tinctoris and Rome 14 has led Seay to speculate that Tinctoris 'may well have worked with the codex' (*Johannis Tinctoris: Opera theoretica*, I, 25; see also Blackburn, 'A Lost Guide to Tinctoris's Teachings Recovered', p. 44, n. 34), a channel of transmission that seemed unlikely until now if Seay intended by his suggestion that Tinctoris actually became acquainted with these works through the Roman source. (Or was the Tinctoris–Rome 14 connection a hint to look elsewhere for the provenance of that manuscript?)

This problem is resolved in the recent dissertation by Adalbert Roth, 'Studien zum frühen Repertoire der päpstlichen Kapelle unter dem Pontifikat Sixtus IV. (1471–1484). Die Chorbücher 14 und 51 des Fondo Cappella Sistina der Biblioteca Apostolica Vaticana', Ph.D. dissertation, Johann Wolfgang Goethe-Universität (1982), a partial copy of which I obtained (thanks to Richard Sherr) only after the present study had been written. Roth claims Neapolitan provenance for two early Cappella Sistina sources, Rome 14 and 51, thus substantiating (what I could only speculate about) that the Franco-Flemish Mass repertory was indeed known at the Neapolitan court of Ferrante I. (A publication by Roth on these matters is forthcoming.)

manuscript Bologna Q 16 (No. 3 in the edition). As Lewis Lockwood has noted, the three Italian musical centers at which the *L'homme armé* tradition was strongest were Naples, Ferrara, and Rome.[3] At Naples the vogue is attested by (1) the quodlibet *O rosa bella–L'homme armé* in Tinctoris's *Proportionale musices*;[4] (2) the same theorist–composer's *Missa L'homme armé*, which if not actually composed at Naples may at least be presumed to have been known there;[5] (3) the inclusion in New Haven 91 of the three-voice combinative chanson *Il sera pour vous–L'homme armé*, a four-voice version of which appears in the Ferrarese manuscript Rome 2856 with an ascription to Robert Morton;[6] (4) the cycle of six *L'homme armé* Masses (by Caron?) in the manuscript Naples VI.E.40, which was seemingly a gift to Beatrice d'Aragona from the court of Burgundy[7] (and even if the manuscript itself came to Naples only when Beatrice returned there in 1501, copies of the music itself could easily have reached the court decades before that); and (5) the present, relatively little-known *L'homme armé* Mass in Bologna Q 16.[8]

The Mass in Bologna Q 16 is of special interest in that it is the only known *L'homme armé* Mass for three voices.[9] Indeed, at a time when the four-voice Mass had already established itself as the norm, composers at Naples continued to show a certain predilection for Masses *a 3*. This is evident not only from the present work, but also from Tinctoris's Mass for Ferrante; perhaps – if it was composed at Naples – the same composer's *Missa Sine nomine II*;[10] Cornago's *Missa Ayo visto lo mapamundi*; and the numerous settings of the Ordinary in Perugia 431 (see below and Nos. 4–4a in the edition). Perhaps the use of a three-voice texture is a sign of a certain Neapolitan provincialism, a verdict that is in keeping with various stylistic aspects of both the *Missa L'homme armé* in Bologna Q 16 and much of the Mass music in Perugia 431.

Although the present Mass has already been edited by Feininger, a new edition is warranted on the grounds that Feininger's leaves much to be desired, quite apart from his use of original clefs and time values, which makes his edition rather unwieldy for purposes of performance. First, there is his treatment of the Agnus

[3] 'Aspects of the "L'homme armé" Tradition', p. 110.

[4] See Seay, *Johannis Tinctoris: Opera theoretica*, IIa, 51, and 'The *Proportionale musices* of Johannes Tinctoris', 70–71; Coussemaker, *Scriptorum de musica medii aevi*, IV, 173.

[5] The unique source for the work is Rome 35, a manuscript compiled at Rome principally during the reign of Innocent VIII; on the date of the manuscript, see Lockwood, 'Aspects of the "L'homme armé" Tradition', p. 110; an edition appears in Melin, *Johanni Tinctoris: Opera omnia*, pp. 74–114.

[6] An edition and facsimile of the version *a 3* appear in Perkins and Garey, *The Mellon Chansonnier*, I, 124–25; both versions are included in Atlas, *Robert Morton: The Collected Works*, pp. 7–10, which also includes a discussion of the problem of authenticity (pp. xxxiii–iv).

[7] See Chap. VI, p. 116 and n. 5.

[8] The work is not included in the lists of *L'homme armé* Masses given either by Cohen, *The Six Anonymous L'homme armé Masses*, p. 72–74, or by Gombosi, *Jacob Obrecht: Eine stilkritische Studie*, pp. 47–48; nor is it among the Masses discussed by Lockwood, 'Aspects of the "L'homme armé" Tradition', pp. 97ff, or by Reese, *Music in the Renaissance, passim*.

[9] This was noted both by Feininger, in his edition of the Mass, *Documenta majora polyphoniae liturgicae sanctae ecclesiae romanae*: No. 1, and by Lowinsky, 'Laurence Feininger (1909–1976): Life, Work, Legacy', p. 343.

[10] The work is so designated in Melin, *Johanni Tinctoris: Opera omnia*, p. 33; Tinctoris's *Missa super Nos amis* is also *a 3*; but as we have noted (Chap. III, p. 76) it was composed before his arrival in Naples.

Dei. Bologna Q 16 contains two sections of music for this movement: the first has the superimposed mensuration signs ○/₵, the text 'Angnus [*sic*] dei qui tollis miserere nobis' beneath the superius, and a final cadence on G, the 'tonic' of the Mass as a whole; the second section has the successive mensuration signs ₵ and ₵3: no more text than the incipit 'Angnus dei qui tollis', and a final cadence on the triad *d-a-f'*. In his edition, Feininger completed the tex of this latter section with the words 'dona nobis pacem', thus making it the final section of the movement and producing an A A' B form and a final cadence on the 'dominant' for the Mass as a whole. This solution is certainly incorrect. Rather, the text incipit of the second section should be completed with a second statement of 'miserere nobis' and then followed by a return to the first section, now sung with the words 'dona nobis pacem'. This brings about an A B A' structure for the Agnus Dei and a final cadence on G, which agrees with the closing cadences of the first four movements.[11]

A second problem concerns Feininger's approach to musica ficta, which is, as Lowinsky has noted, rather arbitrary.[12] And here it is not a matter of quibbling over this or that editorial accidental, but rather of Feininger's having altered the entire modal framework of the Mass. Although Bologna Q 16 transmits the piece without flats in any voice, Feininger has flatted almost every *B* – including those in the cantus firmus – thus changing the mode from mixolydian to transposed dorian. My own approach has been to walk a tightrope, as it were, between *B*-natural and *B*-flat, flatting the *B*s only where the 'rules' of musica ficta seem to demand them.

A third problem in Feininger's edition concerns the text underlay. Feininger followed Bologna Q 16 in placing text only beneath the superius in all movements except the Kyrie, where he adjusted the text to all three voices. Quite apart from not texting the same number of voices throughout the Mass, Feininger's general practice of texting only the upper voice goes against what now seems to be the consensus of scholarly opinion about the manner in which liturgical music was customarily performed in this period, that is, *a cappella*, with the possible accompaniment of the organ (however, see the discussion of Ycart's *Magnificat* below).[13] I have, therefore, placed text beneath each of the voices, though sometimes in a way that calls for comment. In both the Gloria and the Credo, the cantus-firmus tenor, which moves in long, sustained values with frequent ligatures and rests, does not have enough notes to accommodate the lengthy texts of those movements. At times, therefore, I have not only omitted sections of the text (deletions are indicated by means of ellipses),[14] but have even broken up individual words,

---

[11] The tempo markings in this and the other movements that juxtapose the mensuration signs ○ and ₵ are, of course, approximations.

[12] 'Laurence Feininger', pp. 343 and 365, n. 29.

[13] See, for example, D'Accone, 'The Performance of Sacred Music in Italy during Josquin's Time', pp. 614–18; Wright, 'Dufay at Cambrai: Discoveries and Revisions', pp. 199–202; idem, 'Performance Practices at the Cathedral of Cambrai, 1475–1550', pp. 322–23; Polk, 'Ensemble Performance in Dufay's Time', p. 66.

[14] In the Credo, the composer seems intentionally to have omitted the phrases 'Et resurrexit tertia die, secundum Scripturas' and from 'Et in Spiritum Sanctum' through 'Confiteor unum

assigning to a given note or ligated group of notes a single syllable of one word and then continuing with another word or syllable on the following note or ligature. Thus, when the tenor enters at measure 19 of the Gloria, the superius and contratenor are about to begin the phrase 'Gratias agimus tibi propter magnam gloriam tuam', which they sing over a passage of eight measures before coming to a cadence on the syllable '-am' at measure 25. Against this, the tenor first has a two-note ligature that spans four measures and then a three-note ligature that covers five measures. Since even the splitting of ligatures and sustained notes would not give the tenor room enough to sing more than a fragment of the seventeen-syllable text, I have assigned it the syllable 'Gra-' on the first ligature and the syllable '-am' on the second, a solution that at least achieves a sense of euphony of vowels at the beginning and end of the phrase. (When such isolated syllables occur, they are printed with ellipses and capital letters.) The only alternatives to such shredding of the text would be a vocalized – but untexted – performance of the tenor or instrumental execution of the part (again, see the discussion of Ycart's *Magnificat*).

Finally, we may hazard a guess as to what event – if indeed there was a specific one – may have occasioned the composition of the Mass. Whatever other connotations the *L'homme armé* tune may have had for the composers and educated listeners of the fifteenth century, one of its associations had to do with the ever-present threat of the Turks.[15] And that this 'meaning' of the tune was known at Naples is evident from the appearance in New Haven 91 of a double chanson by Robert Morton that combines the *L'homme armé* tune with the rondeau *Il sera pour vous conbatu*, which jokingly urges the musician Symon le Breton to do battle with the 'doubté Turcq'. Now, assuming that the *L'homme armé* Mass was composed at Naples – and its three-voice texture and its status as an unicum in Bologna Q 16 together speak strongly for such origins – and that it too may partake of the anti-Turk meaning of the tune – this of course is speculation – then the single event that would most likely have inspired its composition was surely the Battle of Otranto, at which Alfonso, Duke of Calabria, led the Neapolitan army to victory over the Turkish occupation forces in September, 1481. Perhaps, then, the present Mass celebrates that victory, and perhaps the person to whom the Mass is addressed is the duke himself, whose own reputation as a military leader would have made him a fitting dedicatee.[16]

Very different from the *L'homme armé* Mass with respect to both structure and

baptisma in remissionem peccatorum'. On the problem of textual deletions in the Credo, see Hannas, 'Concerning Deletions in the Polyphonic Mass Credo'; Chew, 'The Early Cyclic Mass as an Expression of Royal and Papal Supremacy'; see also Bent and Bent, 'Dufay, Dunstable, Plummer – A New Source', pp. 413–14; Kenney, *Walter Frye and the Contenance Angloise*, pp. 52–53; and the communications by Jeremy Noble and W. K. Ford in *Journal of the American Musicological Society*, VI (1953), 91–92, and VII (1954), 170–72, respectively.

[15] See Hannas, *op. cit.*, pp. 168–69; Chew, *op. cit.*, pp. 266–67.

[16] The association of the Mass with the Battle of Otranto also fits well with the date of the original layer of Bologna Q 16, which was copied in 1487. For speculation that the dedicatee of one or another of the *L'homme armé* Masses by northern composers might have been Charles the Bold, Duke of Burgundy, see Lockwood, 'Aspects of the "L'homme armé" Tradition', p. 109, n. 34.

general style is the *Credo* attributed to Seraphinus in Perugia 431 (No. 4 in the edition). About the identity of the composer we can only speculate, but perhaps he may be identified with the Seraphinus Baldesaris who is represented by a lauda in Petrucci's *Laude libro II* of 1508.[17] Certainly, this Seraphinus is a more likely contender than either of the other two musicians of that name who have been proposed: (1) the famous poet–improvisator Serafino dall'Aquila,[18] who, despite his having studied music with Guillaume Guarnier at Naples (see Chap. III above, pp. 82–83) is unlikely to have composed any large-scale polyphony, and (2) Franciscus Seraphinus,[19] who, on the basis of his being represented by a motet in Giunta's *Fior de motetti e canzoni* of circa 1526 and having taken part in the well-known musical correspondence with Giovanni del Lago,[20] would have been too young to have been included in a manuscript compiled during the 1480s; indeed, Franciscus Seraphinus did not die before 1541.[21]

Seraphinus has set the lengthy Credo text in a rather unusual way. He composed four sections of three-voice polyphony, beneath the superius parts of which the lines of the text are disposed as follows:

Section A:	[2.]	Patrem omnipotentem . . .
	[9.]	Crucifixus etiam pro nobis . . .
	[16.]	Confiteor unum baptisma . . .
Section B:	[4,]	Et ex Patre . . .
	[11.]	Et ascendit in caelum . . .
	[18.]	Et vitam venturi seculi. Amen.
Section C:	[6.]	Genitum, non factum . . .
	[13.]	Et in Spritum Sanctum . . .
Section D:	[8.]	Et incarnatus est . . .

Presumably, the lines of text that are not accounted for would have been sung in plainsong, performed on the organ, or (as we shall see presently) filled in with polyphonic fragments probably composed by someone else. Thus the movement could have been performed in *alternatim* fashion: chant ('Credo in unum Deum') – A – chant – B – chant – C – chant – D – etc. This simple pattern of alternation is

---

[17] I have already offered this identification in 'On the Neapolitan Provenance of Perugia 431', pp. 64–65; his name is also suggested, though in connection with a *Magnificat* in Perugia 431, as one of two possibilities in Kirsch, *Die Quellen der mehrstimmigen Magnificat- und Te Deum-Vertonungen bis zur Mitte des 16. Jahrhunderts*, p. 557, n. 519. This identification is not accepted by Cattin, 'Il repertorio polifonico sacro nelle fonti napoletane del Quattrocento', on the ground that Petrucci's two lauda collections are far removed from the Neapolitan orbit; he prefers simply to group Seraphinus with a number of other unidentifiable composers who are represented in Perugia 431.

[18] Seraphinus is so identified in Hernon, 'Perugia MS 431 (G 20)', pp. 104–5.

[19] He is the other composer named by Kirsch, *Die Quellen der mehrstimmigen Magnificat- und Te Deum-Vertonungen*, p. 557, n. 519; he is also suggested as the possible composer by Jeppesen, *Italia musica sacra*, I, xiv.

[20] See Jeppesen, 'Eine musiktheoretische Korrespondence des früheren Cinquecento'; Harrán, 'The Theorist Giovanni del Lago: A New View of his Music and his Writings'.

[21] An entry in the *Giornale Strozzi* for 8 January 1473 (Vol. 27, fol. 8; see Galiano, 'Nuove fonti per la storia musicale napoletana', n. 57) mentions a 'frate Seraphinus', but without stating whether or not he was directly associated with the court or if he was a musician. Could he be our elusive composer? In any event, Leone, *Il Giornale del banco Strozzi di Napoli*, p. 564, n. 229, is certainly incorrect in identifying 'frate Seraphinus' as the poet Serafino dall'Aquila.

interrupted twice. After the first statement of section D (= 8. 'Et incarnatus est . . .'), the singers must forgo the expected plainchant and return immediately to section A for a polyphonic statement of line 9, 'Crucifixus etiam pro nobis'. After this, the alternation begins anew, now with the polyphonic sections serving for the odd-numbered lines of text instead of the even-numbered ones as they had the first time through.

The second interruption once again involves the return from section D to section A. Line 14 of the text, 'Qui cum Patre et Filio', is sung to plainchant (following section C), while line 16, 'Confiteor unum baptisma', appears beneath the polyphonic section A. The problem, then, is whether line 15, 'Et unam sanctum', should be sung in plainsong (which would give us two such sections in succession) or set editorially to the polyphony of section D. I have chosen the second alternative on the ground that there is no other instance of two successive lines of text being sung in plainsong, whereas we have already seen that back-to-back performance of the polyphonic sections D and A is specifically called for in conjunction with lines 8–9 of the text.[22]

Finally, although Seraphinus begins section A by closely paraphrasing the melody of Credo I (*Liber usualis*, 64–66) in the superius, he proceeds rather freely thereafter, recalling the plainchant only intermittently. Yet the cadences on G at the end of each polyphonic section correspond with those in the chant except for that at the end of line 18, 'Et vitam venturi seculi. Amen'. And because this line must be sung to the polyphony of section B, which had already served for lines 4 and 11, the piece as a whole closes on the 'wrong' final, as it were, G instead of E.

The Seraphinus *Credo* occupies fols. 22v–26r in Perugia 431. The three preceding openings, fols. 19v–22r, also transmit a *Credo*, this one in the form of six polyphonic sections that appear without an attribution (No. 4a in the edition). What is particularly noteworthy about the composition is that except for its lack of music for line 17 of the Credo text, 'Et exspecto resurrectionem mortuorum', it otherwise provides polyphonic settings for precisely those lines of the text that Seraphinus had left unset.[23] Thus it seems apparent that the six anonymous sections, which agree with Seraphinus's composition with respect to number of voices, approximate range (the superius parts are exactly the same in this respect), mode, and occasionally even melodic material, were intended to complement the Seraphinus *Credo* and interlock with it in *alternatim* fashion. And when Seraphinus's setting is performed with the anonymous 'fillers', line 17 of the text, for which there is no polyphony in either setting, must be omitted – as it frequently was.[24]

The relationship between the two settings calls forth an obvious question: could

---

[22] It is, of course, possible that the phrase 'Et unam sanctam', which was frequently deleted in settings of the Credo, should be omitted altogether. However, as Table III in Hannas, 'Concerning Deletions in the Polyphonic Mass Credo', pp. 183–85, makes clear, that phrase was almost always omitted not by itself but together with the two phrases that precede it. In addition, the phrase 'Et unam sanctam' is among those that are set polyphonically in No. 4a (see below).

[23] I should like to thank Prof. Martin Staehelin for calling my attention to the relationship between the two settings.

[24] See Hannas, *op. cit.*, pp. 184–85.

the complementary sections also have been composed by Seraphinus? It seems unlikely because of the stylistic differences between the anonymous sections and those that appear beneath Seraphinus's name. With their almost unrelieved chordal texture and persistent use of root-position triads, the anonymous sections seem to represent little more than an improvisatory style, one that recalls the technique of late-fifteenth-century *falsobordone*,[25] a genre that, as Pere Oriola's setting of *In exitu Israel* in Montecassino 871 demonstrates, was certainly known at Naples.

One feature of the edition of No. 4a calls for comment, the use of occasional three-four or five-four measures (see measures 11, 27, and 45) that are caused by phrases with an odd number of minims. Although such rhythmic patterns are not characteristic of the period, I have retained them on the grounds that (1) there is no authority to support an emendation; (2) they appear often enough for us to conclude that they are intentional; (3) to emend them means charging the scribe with no fewer than nine errors – one in each voice part in each of the three instances – even though all the parts fit together; and (4) they may represent a vestige of a rhythmically free improvisatory style.[26]

The two compositions for the Ordinary of the Mass, then, represent the two polyphonic Mass traditions that were cultivated at Naples. The anonymous *Missa L'homme armé*, whether written by a Franco–Netherlander active at Naples or by a native Italian, represents the northern, mainstream tradition of Mass composition. The joint Seraphinus–anonymous *Credo*, on the other hand, with its far less ambitious – at times even crude – polyphony, must derive from a local tradition, one that was prevalent at various monastic institutions in the area (to judge from the appearance of the style in both Perugia 431 and Montecassino 871) and at the royal court itself. Together the two compositions illustrate the wide range of polyphony that must have been available to the chapel for the celebration of the Mass.

Music for Vespers and the Good Friday Liturgy

Although a number of Ycart's compositions can be associated with his stay at Naples (see Chap. III above, pp. 79–80), I have chosen to represent him in the edition (No. 5) with a work that antedates his Neapolitan period, the previously unpublished *Magnificat sexti toni*, an unicum in Faenza 117 that raises a number of interesting questions.

First, Ycart shaped the piece as a whole with a combination of the so-called 'strophic' and 'alternation' techniques; to set the six even-numbered verses of the

---

[25] Technically, pieces designated as *falsobordone* were for four voices and drew their texts mainly from the psalms sung at Sunday Vespers; see Bradshaw, *The Falsobordone*, pp. 19–39.

[26] In his *Liber de arte contrapuncti*, Tinctoris writes that singing *super librum*, that is, improvisation upon a plain-chant, may be done 'without measure'; see Seay, *Johannis Tinctoris (c. 1435–1511): The Art of Counterpoint*, p. 110.

canticle, he wrote only three sections of polyphony: section I = verses 2 and 8, section II = verses 4 and 10, section III = verses 6 and 12, a plan that Kirsch associates specifically with such northern Italian composers as Gaffurius and Antonius de Janua.[27] And that the structural plan carries with it such an association offers at least some support to our speculation that Ycart himself may have had contacts with a Bonadies–Hothby–Gaffurius circle in northern Italy before he came to Naples.[28]

What is particularly interesting about Ycart's structural plan is that the composer rejects the customary device of paraphrasing the Magnificat tone in the superius and uses instead a cantus-firmus tenor of the kind that is more closely associated with the composition of Masses. Ycart uses the same twenty-six-note cantus firmus in each of the three polyphonic sections, with not a single note changed. And although Stevenson has claimed that the cantus firmus is drawn from the responsory verse *Et misericordia ejus*, a chant that is sung on the Feast of the Assumption (*Liber responsorialis*, 257),[29] the relationship between Ycart's cantus firmus and the Assumption chant seems tenuous at best.[30] Indeed, just how weak his identification is becomes apparent from his discussion of another of Ycart's pieces in Faenza 117, the *Kyrie–Gloria* that appears on fols. 8v–11r. Stevenson notes that the cantus firmus of this piece bears some resemblance to the melody of Kyrie XIV (*Liber usualis*, 54) – which it does not after the first few notes – but transposed down one step from G to F.[31] Yet what Stevenson failed to notice is that the cantus firmus of the *Magnificat* is precisely the same - note for note – as that of the *Kyrie–Gloria*.

Unfortunately, my own attempts to identify the cantus firmus have been equally unsuccessful, but I should like to offer some speculation about the matter. First, there can be no doubt that the *Kyrie–Gloria* movements represent only a fragment of a complete cyclic cantus-firmus Mass, for not only was the practice of writing only paired movements long out of fashion, but the two movements in question did not constitute one of the normal pairs. Second, we know from comments in Gaffurius's *Extractus parvus musice* and *Tractatus practicabilium proportionum* that Ycart was the author of two now-lost Masses: *De amor tu dormi* and *Voltate in qua*.[32] Could the *Kyrie–Gloria* be the remains of one of those Masses? Although the *Missa Voltate in qua* can probably be ruled out as the parent work on the ground that the cantus firmus bears no resemblance to the basse-danse melody *Voltate in ça, Rosina*,[33] on which the lost Mass was presumably based, *Dę amor tu dormi* certainly remains a possibility, especially if those words represent

[27] Kirsch, *Die Quellen der mehrstimmigen Magnificat- und Te Deum-Vertonungen*, p. 48; see also Lerner, 'The Polyphonic Magnificat in 15th-Century Italy', pp. 50–52.

[28] See Chap. III, p. 79.

[29] Stevenson, *Spanish Music in the Age of Columbus*, p. 125, n. 61.

[30] In fairness, Stevenson cites the chant after a Spanish Hieronymite processional of 1526; I have been able to check the melody only as it appears in modern chant books.

[31] Stevenson, *Spanish Music in the Age of Columbus*, p. 125, n. 62.

[32] Miller, 'Early Gaffuriana', pp. 373, 379.

[33] The melody appears in the treatise of Giovanni Ambrosio–Guglielmo Ebreo in the version transmitted in the manuscript Paris 476. For its subsequent use in the frottola repertory, see Jeppesen, *La frottola*, III, pp. 32–35.

the beginning of a contemporary strambotto, since the twenty-six notes of the cantus firmus would, when stripped of their ligatures, be well suited for a largely declamatory statement of the two hendecasyllabic lines that form a single complete couplet of a strambotto.

The relationship between the *Magnificat* and the *Kyrie–Gloria* goes beyond their shared cantus firmus; occasionally the two works are quite similar throughout their respective polyphonic fabrics, and there can be no doubt that Ycart was engaging in conscious self-borrowing. And since chronological priority must certainly be accorded to the *Kyrie–Gloria* on the ground that the cantus-firmus technique displayed in the two works was customary in settings of the Ordinary while it was not in the Magnificat (but see below), the *Magnificat sexti toni* must be considered an extremely early forerunner of the 'parody' Magnificat, which on the Continent would take hold only with Lassus in the final decades of the sixteenth century, though it appears earlier in that century in England in the Magnificats of Fayrfax and Ludford. Finally, that Ycart chose for the model of his *Magnificat* a work that itself contained a clear-cut cantus firmus may supply still further evidence for a link between Ycart and Hothby, since the use of a voice with a cantus-firmus function was yet another characteristic of English Magnificats.[34]

The polyphonic sections of the *Magnificat* and the whole of the related *Kyrie–Gloria* also present a problem in connection with performance practice. Although we have already noted in connection with the *L'homme armé* Mass of Bologna Q 16 that the fifteenth century seems generally to have adhered to an *a cappella* tradition – with the possible accompaniment of the organ – in the performance of liturgical music, all attempts to fit the Magnificat text – or that of the Kyrie or Gloria – to any voice other than the superius, which is the only voice part texted in Faenza 117, meet with failure. Perhaps the other three voices were performed on the organ, a method of performance that would have presented little difficulty for the Aragonese chapel, which regularly employed two organists and which normally used the organ at Vespers of major feast days (see Chap. II above, p. 57). Perhaps the lower voices were vocalized without text. Or perhaps the superius was accompanied by instruments other than, or together with, the organ. That voices and instruments at least sometimes joined together on liturgical occasions is at least thrice documented in late-fifteenth-century Italy, with the choir each time being accompanied by wind instruments: (1) the wedding of Constantine Sforza and Camilla d'Aragona in 1475; (2) the marriage of Bianca Maria Sforza and Maximilian I in the Cathedral of Milan in December 1473; and (3) the Mass performed on Assumption Day, August 1495, in honor of Francesco Gonzaga's designation as Captain General of the Venetian armies.[35] In addition, we should

---

[34] Kirsch, 'Magnificat', *The New Grove*, XI, 497.
[35] See D'Accone, 'The Performance of Sacred Music in Italy during Josquin's Time', p. 615; Kinkeldey, *Orgel und Klavier in der Musik des 16. Jahrunderts*, p. 166; Polk, 'Ensemble Performance in Dufay's Time', p. 67; Prizer, 'Bernardino Piffaro', pp. 174–76. On the use of wind instruments in liturgical music outside Italy, see (among others) Bouquet, 'La cappella musicale dei duchi di Savoia', pp. 250–51; Clement Miller, 'Erasmus on Music', pp. 339–41; Pietzsch, 'Die Beschreibungen deutscher Fürstenhochzeiten von der Mitte des 15. bis zum Beginn des 17. Jahrhunderts', p. 34; Schuler, 'Die Musik in

remember that the court of Savoy often retained the services of one or two *tromba*-players as part of the regular personnel of its chapel.³⁶

Finally, there are two strands of evidence that may well point to the use of wind instruments as at least occasional participants in the performances of sacred music at Naples. First, in listing the duties of the *alta cappella* in his *De inventione et usu musicae*, Tinctoris writes that the instrumentalists of that ensemble played in the 'temple', and that they performed 'omnis generis et sacros et prophanos cantus'.³⁷ Surely this sounds as if the wind-players took some kind of role in the performance of liturgical music, and Tinctoris must just as certainly have had in mind his very own wind-player colleagues at Naples. More intriguing still are the implications of a letter of 24 August 1420 written by Alfonso I at Alghero (Sardinia) to the Valencian organ-builder Jacme Gil. In it Alfonso asks Gil to build an organ for his chapel in Barcelona that 'sien intonats ab los ministres, ab cinch tirants'.³⁸ Thus Alfonso wanted a chapel organ that could be used together with a group of wind instruments, a request that makes sense only if the wind-players were sometimes employed in the performance of a sacred polyphony. And since at least some of the traditions of the Barcelona chapel were transplanted to Naples, as was eventually Jacme Gil himself, it seems safe to hazard that the Neapolitan court, too, at least occasionally used instruments other than the organ in its liturgical ceremonies, and that a modern-day performance of Ycart's *Magnificat* with the lower three voices performed by wind instruments and one or two organs would be in keeping with the traditions of Aragonese performance practice.³⁹

The repertory for Vespers is rounded out in the edition by two hymns, a genre that appears in both Montecassino 871 and Perugia 431, though not without rather distinct differences in character. Unlike its closely related companion Montecassino 871, which, with its thirty-seven hymns partially arranged in order of the liturgical year, constitutes one of the major hymn sources of the fifteenth century,⁴⁰ Perugia 431 transmits but a small number of hymns, these being scattered throughout the manuscript with little care as to systematic ordering.⁴¹

Konstanz während des Konzils, 1414–1418', p. 165; Wright, 'Performance Practices at the Cathedral of Cambrai', pp 323–24, and the references listed there; see also Planchart, 'Fifteenth-Century Masses: Notes on Performances and Chronology', pp. 6ff.

³⁶ Bouquet, 'La cappella musicale dei duchi di Savoia', pp. 237, 250–52.

³⁷ See Weinmann, *Johannes Tinctoris*, p. 39; Prizer, 'Bernardino Piffaro', p. 164.

³⁸ Anglés, 'La Música en la Corte del Rey Don Alfonso V de Aragón', p. 956.

³⁹ It may well be that the consensus for the *a cappella* tradition has gained just a bit too much ground, and that fifteenth-century performance practice was more varied and localized than we are ready to admit. A fresh look at the problem has recently appeared in Planchart, 'Fifteenth-Century Masses', pp. 3ff. Given the probable transplantation of certain Spanish performance traditions to Naples, the use of instruments in the performance of liturgical music at Naples makes especially good sense, since Spain was among the first places in which instruments joined with voices in sacred music; see Stevenson, *Spanish Cathedral Music in the Golden Age*, pp. 251ff, and Planchart, *op. cit.*, p. 4.

⁴⁰ On the hymns of Montecassino 871, see Pope and Kanazawa, *The Musical Manuscript Montecassino 871*, pp. 36–44; Gerber, 'Die Hymnen der Handschrift Monte Cassino 871'; Ward, 'The Polyphonic Office Hymn and the Liturgy of Fifteenth-Century Italy', pp. 166ff.

⁴¹ The hymns are listed in Atlas, 'On the Neapolitan Provenance of Perugia 431', pp. 78ff. It is possible that the manuscript originally contained as many as eight additional hymns. Of the original opening gathering, a sextern, all that remains

The two manuscripts also differ with respect to the origins of their hymn repertories: whereas Montecassino 871 contains hymns by Dufay, Gaffurius, and such minor but still relatively well-known composers as Johannis de Quadris and Antonius de Janua, the hymns in Perugia 431 appear to be mainly, if not entirely, local products, being ascribed to such now-unidentified – almost certainly local – composers as F. M. di Ortona, 'F.M.', 'M', and 'P'.[42]

Perhaps the most attractive of the hymns in Perugia 431, none of which has heretofore appeared in a modern edition,[43] is the anonymous setting of the hymn *Pange lingua gloriosi*, sung at Vespers on the feast of Corpus Christi (No. 6 in the edition). In contrast with such famous settings of the melody as those by Dufay and Josquin, in which the phrygian version of the chant is used, the composition in Perugia 431 is based upon the dorian version of the plainsong (see *Liber usualis*, 950–51; *Antiphonale monasticum*, 547, where the melody appears a fifth higher and contains variants), which for the greater part of the piece is lightly paraphrased in the superius. However, the composer abandons his adherence to the chant on two occasions. At measure 13, the cadence for the third phrase should come on G; instead, our setting cadences on A, which then necessitates a further departure from the chant at the beginning of the next phrase. The second and more noteworthy digression appears at measures 17–22, where the superius sings the words 'Fructus ventris generosi' to what is apparently a freely composed melody until the very end of the phrase, where the cadence on G once again matches that called for in the chant. Particularly notable are the sense of metric instability and the numerous instances in which diminished triads in root position cannot be avoided. Both of these stylistic characteristics occur frequently in the 'local' sacred repertory.[44]

The second hymn is Gaffurius's setting of *Christe Redemptor omnium, ex Patre Patris* (No. 7 in the edition), the Vespers hymn for the feast of the Nativity (*Antiphonale monasticum*, 238). Together with his setting of *Hostis Herodis impie*, it is one of the two hymns that can safely be assigned to Gaffurius's Neapolitan period on the grounds that it is unique to Montecassino 871 and employs a chant of the Roman, rather than the Ambrosian, rite.[45] Gaffurius follows the customary fifteenth-century procedures for the genre; he sets only the odd-numbered verses polyphonically and paraphrases the chant in the superius, permitting it to permeate the tenor by means of imitation. As Pope and Kanazawa have noted, its use of a four-voice texture, imitation, and metrical regularity make *Christe*

---

is the center bifolio, fols. 6ʳ–7ᵛ, which contains one complete hymn and fragments of two others. Perhaps the entire gathering was devoted to this genre.

[42] On F. M. di Ortona and the possible identities of the composers represented by their initials, see Atlas, 'On the Neapolitan Provenance of Perugia 431', p. 65, and Cattin, 'Il repertorio polifonico sacro nelle fonti napoletane del Quattrocento'.

[43] Nor have the hymns in Perugia 431 received much attention in the literature on the genre. For

a discussion of one of them, a fauxbordon setting of *Christe Redemptor omnium*, see Ward, 'The Polyphonic Office Hymn from the Late Fourteenth Century until the Early Sixteenth Century', p. 283; see also Cattin, *op. cit.*

[44] On the diminished triads in root position in this repertory, see my forthcoming edition, *Aedvardus of Ortona: Missa Sine nomine*, to be published by Antico Edition, Newton Abbott.

[45] See Chap. III above, p. 82.

redemptor one of the more progressive hymn settings within the combined Montecassino 871–Perugia 431 repertory of hymns.[46]

The final sacred composition in the edition is an anonymous setting of *Adoramus te, Christe* (No. 8), a text that appears on three different occasions during the course of the liturgical year: (1) as an antiphon during the service of the Adoration of the Cross on Good Friday (*Liber usualis*, 746); (2) as the first part of the tract in the votive Mass for the Invention of the Holy Cross when that Mass happens to be said after Septuagesima Sunday (*Graduale romanum*, 104–5); and (3) as a short responsory during Sext of the Office for the Invention of the Holy Cross on 3 May (*Liber usualis*, 1458). If the present setting of the text, an unicum in Perugia 431, was intended for liturgical duty, we may reasonably suppose that it served in the ceremony of the Adoration of the Cross, the most solemn of the three feasts and one that was celebrated with particular solemnity at Naples.[47] On the other hand, it may just as well have served in the lavish paraliturgical processions and *sacre rappresentazioni* that the court had mounted each Good Friday during the reigns of both Alfonso I and Ferrante I.[48] In any event, the composition underscores the extremely important role that polyphony played in the Neapolitan celebration of Holy Week, a role that is most clearly hinted at by the many Passiontide compositions in Montecassino 871.[49] And that the royal singers were kept especially busy during this season is attested by the previously cited response of the singers Raynero and Antonio Ponzo to Galeazzo Maria Sforza in a letter of 25 March 1469; though they were eager to take up service at Milan, their departure from Naples would have to wait until they had fulfilled their duties for the 'settimana santa'.[50]

A comparison of the text of the setting in Perugia 431 with that in the *Liber usualis* (p. 746) discloses two discrepancies. The text in the chant book omits the word 'sanctam' in the phrase 'quia per sanctam Crucem tuam' (measures 16ff) and ends with the words 'redemisti mundum', thus leaving out the tag 'miserere nobis' that appears in Perugia 431 (measures 29ff).[51] Yet the version in Perugia 431 seems to have been commonplace in fifteenth- and early-sixteenth-century settings of the text; the 'miserere nobis' tag also appears in the setting by Jacopo Fogliano (see note 47), while that same piece together with the anonymous settings in Florence 2356 (fols. 16v–17r), Capetown 3.b.12 (fols. 29v–31r), and Montecassino 871 (fol. 3r) all transmit the 'sanctam' interpolation.[52]

---

[46] *The Musical Manuscript Montecassino 871*, p. 41.

[47] Pope and Kanazawa, *ibid.*, pp. 36, 556, tentatively assign the unique *Adoramus te, Christe*, in Montecassino 871 to the same service. On the other hand, Jeppesen, *Italia sacra musica*, I, xvii, associates Jacopo Fogliano's setting of the text in the *prima pars* of a motet with the short responsory text.

[48] Pope and Kanazawa, *op. cit.*, pp. 45–46; see also, Corbin, *La Déposition liturgique du Christ au Vendredi Saint*, pp. 117, 257–58, where there is presented a number of documents drawn from Minieri Riccio and Barone.

[49] See Pope and Kanazawa, *op. cit.*, pp. 45–46.

[50] See Chap. II above, pp. 40–41.

[51] Although the words 'miserere' and 'nobis' appear in the verse of the tract for the votive Mass for the Invention of the Holy Cross, they do not follow directly after 'redemisti mundum' and are themselves widely separated. Thus, the inclusion of 'miserere nobis' is not likely to signal a connection with the tract.

[52] For an edition of the setting in Capetown 3.b.12, see Cattin, *Italian Laude and Latin Unica in MS Capetown, Grey 3.b.12*, pp. 4–5. The opening

In all, Naples knew two distinct styles of sacred music. If the mainstream Franco–Netherlandish tradition had not already arrived at Naples by at least the latter part of the reign of Alfonso I, it would certainly have been introduced and then cultivated there by the likes of Vincenet and Tinctoris. And that not all Italian composers were immune to the style is attested by the imitative texture of Gaffurius's hymn settings and the cantus-firmus technique of the *L'homme armé* Mass, the Italian origin of which at least seems likely.

The other style was a local, rather provincial one, smaller in scale, less ambitious polyphonically, and sometimes even crude (one can attribute just so much to scribal error).[53] One puzzling aspect of much of this latter repertory concerns the precise place of its origin, or at least the milieu in which it was for the most part cultivated. At least three pieces of evidence point to a monastic provenance: (1) the two manuscripts that transmit the repertory, Montecassino 871 and Perugia 431, were seemingly compiled at Benedictine and Franciscan (?) institutions respectively; (2) certain of the pieces within the repertory are clearly associated with the two orders;[54] and (3) the composers that Perugia 431 names in connection with its portion of the repertory – for instance, Seraphinus, Aedvardus of Ortona, 'Fr. M.' of Ortona, *et al.* – cannot be associated directly with the court. Yet these same two manuscripts transmit a sizeable number of compositions that were indeed composed at the court. And in addition to the many settings of secular Italian and Spanish texts, there are liturgical–devotional works by Cornago, Oriola, Ycart, and Damianus, all of whom – if we assume that the Damianus represented in Montecassino 871 is one and the same with the musician who is documented in 1456 – served at the royal court. Thus the channels of musical communication between court and monastry were open, and musical repertory must no doubt have flowed from one to the other. Moreover, the falsobordone technique of Oriola's *In exitu Israel* and the awkward voice-leading of Damianus's *Ave maris stella*[55] show that the composers of the royal court sometimes wrote in much the same style that characterizes those pieces in Perugia 431 that seem to represent a monastic tradition. In all, to distinguish between the courtly and monastic segments of this local sacred repertory seems impossible in all but the few obvious cases in which either a text or an ascription points more strongly in one direction than the other. Indeed, the very idea that a clear stylistic distinction exists between them may well be illusory.

---

phrase of the text in Montecassino 871 inserts the words 'domine, Jesu' so that it reads 'Adoramus te, domine, Jesu Christe', and then reads 'benedicamus' instead of 'benedicimus'; see Pope and Kanazawa, *The Musical Manuscript Montecassino 871*, p. 556, where neither the 'sanctam' interpolation nor the use of 'benedicamus' is noted.

[53] See the transcriptions in Pope and Kanazawa, *op. cit.*

[54] On the pieces in Perugia 431 that are associated with the Franciscans, see Chap. VI, n. 20. For the Benedictine provenance of three hymns – the most important of which is *Phebus astris*, in honor of St. Giustina – in Montecassino 871, see Pope and Kanazawa, *op. cit.*, pp. 20–21.

[55] The pieces are edited in Pope and Kanazawa, *op. cit.*, pp. 123–24, 520–22.

Secular Music

Settings of Spanish Texts

During the reign of Alfonso I, the chief lyric language at the court was Castilian. A vivid reminder of this is the fact that no group of Italian sources includes as many pieces with Castilian texts as are found in the Neapolitan music manuscripts, especially in the 'central' sources of the 1480s: one piece in Escorial IV.a.24,[56] one in New Haven 91,[57] nine in Montecassino 871 (plus one in Catalan),[58] two in Perugia 431,[59] and eight (possibly ten) in Bologna Q 16.[60] In addition, the manuscript Bologna 596 H.H.2⁴ contains an intabulation of Juan de Leon's *Ay, que non se rremediarme*, one of the Spanish pieces transmitted in Bologna Q 16.[61]

The composer who contributed most prominently to the Spanish repertory at the court was, of course, Joan Cornago. In the edition, Cornago is represented by his setting of *Yerra con poco saber* (No. 9), a canción by the Catalan poet Pere Torroella,[62] who was himself at Naples circa 1456–1458 – that is, at the same time as Cornago – residing there in the company of Juan of Aragon, nephew of Alfonso I.[63] It was no doubt while they were both at the court that Cornago and Torroella collaborated on the work.

The structure of Torroella's poem conforms to the rhyme scheme and metrical pattern that were characteristic in the fifteenth-century canción. In order of popularity, the three most commonly used rhyme schemes – Torroella uses the first – were:[64]

---

[56] No. 91 in the inventory by Southern, 'El Escorial, Monastery Library, Ms. IV.a.24', p. 70, where Cornago's *Morte merçe gentil aquila* is listed incorrectly as a Spanish canción. Although the form of the poem is somewhat irregular, it is in Italian.

[57] No. 44; see Perkins and Garey, *The Mellon Chansonnier*, II, 368.

[58] Nos. 10, 16, 19, 27, 84, 102, 103, 104, and 111, and No. 127 in Catalan; see Pope and Kanazawa, *The Musical Manuscript Montecassino 871*, p. 86, where No. 104 is omitted. The manuscript contained at least eight (and possibly nine) more Castilian texts that are now lost (*ibid.*, p. 86, n. 1).

[59] Nos. 40 and 54; see Atlas, 'On the Neapolitan Provenance of Perugia 431', pp. 86, 90; the text of No. 40, Robert Morton's *Pues serviçio*, must certainly be a contrafactum, the original poem having probably been a bergerette.

[60] Nos. 66, 70, 81, 87, 99, 116, 121, and 125 (the texts of Nos. 9 and 19 are too short to allow identification as Spanish or Italian); see Fuller, 'Additional Notes on the 15th-century Chansonnier Bologna Q 16', p. 85 and n. 13.

[61] For a fine general treatment of the Spanish repertory at the court, see Pope and Kanazawa, *The Musical Manuscript Montecassino 871*, pp. 86–99, and Pope, 'La Musique espagnole à la cour de Naples', pp. 35ff.

[62] The poem is attributed to him in both the manuscript London 10431 and the *Cancionero general* of 1511; it is ascribed to Juan de Mena in Modena XI.B.10. The poem is accepted as Torroella's in Bach y Rita, *The Works of Pere Torroella*, p. 270. On London 10431, see Rennart, 'Der spanische Cancionero des British Museums'; on Modena XI.B.10, see Bertoni, 'Catalogo dei codici spagnuoli della Biblioteca Estense in Modena', p. 321.

[63] Mele, 'Qualche nuovo dato sulla vita di Mossèn Pere Torroella e suoi rapporti con Giovanni Pontano', pp. 83ff.

[64] See Navarro, *Repertorio de estrofas españolas*, p. 63.

	copla	
estribillo	mudanza	vuelta
a b a b a	*c d c d*	*a b a b a*
a b b a b	*c d c d*	*a b b a b*
a b a a b	*c d c d*	*a b a a b*

In addition, Torroella employs the often-found device of casting the octosyllabic lines of the estribillo in alternating 'agudo' and 'llano' verses, that is, alternating lines of seven separately pronounced syllables, with the last one receiving an accent (and thus counting as two), and lines of eight separate syllables. No less conventional is Cornago's musical setting: A B B A, with the estribillo and vuelta being sung to the outer sections, the two couplets of the mudanza to the two B sections, each of which has its own ending.

The various redactions of the piece raise a question with respect to the music–text relationship. The scribes of both Montecassino 871 and Escorial IV.a.24 placed what fragments of text they entered beneath the tenor voice (labeled the contratenor in Escorial IV.a.24),[65] which led Haberkamp and Pope and Kanazawa to text only that voice in their editions of the piece.[66] Indeed, Pope and Kanazawa claim to see almost what amounts to word-painting of a sort in the relationship between the poem and the melody of the tenor. Yet despite the evidence of the sources, I have placed the poem in the superius, certainly the more customary position in a performance in which only one part is sung.[67]

Another example of the canción is Vincenet's *La pena sin ser sabida* (No. 10 in the edition). The piece is notable for two reasons, for unless we are dealing with a contrafactum it shows that Spanish poetry was still being set well into Ferrante's reign and that the language held some appeal even for non-Spanish composers. As was the case in Torroella's poem, the anonymous poet wrote an estribillo of five lines ('quintilla')[68] with the rhyme scheme *a b a b a*. Where the two poems differ is in the vuelta, where the author of *La pena sin ser sabida* not only reproduces the rhyme scheme of the estribillo, but actually restates its final three lines, so that they have the effect of a refrain.[69] In fact, it is the lack of a true refrain in the canción – the estribillo is not repeated after the vuelta – that is one of the distinguishing features between the Spanish form on the one hand and its French and Italian equivalents – the bergerette and the ballata – on the other.[70]

The main musical problem in the piece occurs at the repeat sign that signals the first and second endings in the mudanza. Here the superius and contra altus each have a blackened breve superimposed above the normal void breve – e' over c' in

---

[65] According to Hanen, *The Chansonnier El Escorial IV.a.24*, I, 185, the text in Escorial IV.a.24 was entered by a later hand, not by the main scribe.

[66] See the Critical Notes.

[67] It is the superius that is texted in the version in Trent 89, where, however, the piece appears with a Latin contrafactum, *Ex ore tuo*.

[68] The four-line type is called a 'redondilla'.

[69] On this feature of the canción, see Pope and Kanazawa, *The Musical Manuscript Montecassino 871*, p. 91 and n. 25.

[70] For an instructive tabular comparison of the three types, see Perkins and Garey, *The Mellon Chansonnier*, II, 95.

142 *Music at the Aragonese Court of Naples*

the superius; *g'* over *e'* in the contra altus – just before the repeat sign, after which all four voices break into a sesquialteral proportion denoted by coloration.[71] Three different editions each transcribe the passage in a different way (I give the superius only): Ex. 1.

Ex. 1a (Davis, *The Collected Works of Vincenet*, p. 161)

Ex. 1b (Perkins and Garey, *The Mellon Chansonnier*, I, 153)[72]

Ex. 1c (the present edition: see p. 215 below)

Of the three, Davis's solution seems least desirable in that it calls for precisely the same cadence to be performed twice, in effect dispensing with alternative endings. In addition, the two breves are not written as a ligature, as Davis's edition would lead one to believe. Perkins's interpretation is certainly possible. My own transcription interprets the blackened *e'* as a sign to leap to the same blackened pitch at the beginning of the coloration section, a skip that maintains the rhythmic momentum and the pace of the harmonic rhythm by avoiding the *e'* breve at the beginning of the second ending. In other words, my transcription has only one breve in the passage that leads to the second ending (the *d'*), while Perkins has two and Davis three.

[71] See the facsimile in *ibid.*, I, 152.
[72] I have doubled the values of Perkins's 4:1 reduction in order to facilitate comparison.

Although the single piece by which Pere Oriola is represented in the edition (No. 11) reaches us as a textless unicum in Perugia 431, the structure of the piece – two sections, the first of which can accommodate five verses of poetry, while the second is shorter and has first and second endings – and Oriola's Spanish origins make it likely that we have still another setting of a canción. And despite the lack of text, a few observations can be offered about the probable nature of the now-lost poem: (1) the estribillo was of the 'quintilla' (five-line) type (see note 68), with the following music–verse relationship: measures 1–5 = line 1; measures 6–11:2 = line 2; measures 11:3–14 = line 3; measures 15:3–19 = line 4; measures 20–24 = line 5; (2) the third verse must have been a 'verso agudo' on the ground that the superius at measures 11:3–14 seems capable of carrying comfortably no more than seven separately pronounced syllables; and (3) if the latter point is true, verses one and five may also have been 'agudos', since my own reading of a large selection of canciones has failed to turn up an example in which only a single line was so treated. Indeed, frequently used combinations of 'llano–agudo' alternation in a five-line estribillo seem to be 7* 8 7* 8 7*, 8 7* 8 8 7*, and 8 7* 8 7* 8 (7* = the 'verso agudo'). Finally, if the piece is less than inspired, Oriola at least comes off as a competent craftsman who shows a somewhat surprising penchant for imitation (see measures 6, 11, 19, 25, and 32).

Unfortunately, there are no polyphonic sources from Alfonso's period, so that any statements about the nature of the secular music repertory at his court remain conjectural. Yet given the strong Spanish character of the court, the virtual monopoly by Spaniards in the fields of music and poetry, and, finally, the arrival of Cornago, there can be no doubt that settings of Spanish lyrics constituted a major portion of the repertory, possibly sharing the spotlight with the chansons imported from the Franco–Burgundian domains.[73] What is somewhat surprising, though, is the apparent tenacity with which the Spanish repertory held fast during the reign of Ferrante, a period in which Spanish influence at the court generally declined. Not only did the Franco–Netherlander Vincenet feel drawn to the repertory (assuming that the Spanish verse is not a contrafactum, which would itself say something about the continuing vogue that the tradition enjoyed), but almost 20 percent of the secular compositions in the *Tabula* of Montecassino 871 (that is, the manuscript in its original state) were settings of Spanish verse. And from where else would that monastic collection have derived its Spanish repertory if not from the court itself? No doubt it was, among other things, the continued presence of such composers as Cornago and Oriola, the arrival of the Spaniard Ycart, and the lingering of the Spanish heritage in general that kept the Spanish

---

[73] That the chansons by the Dufay–Binchois generation were known at Naples during the period of Alfonso may be attested by the sizeable stock of these pieces that were available to the compilers of Escorial IV.a.24 and Berlin 78.C.28, both of which were probably compiled less than a decade after Alfonso's death and, significantly, only shortly after Ferrante had restored peace to the kingdom after seven years of struggles against the Angevins and their allies. I prefer to speculate that the repertory – or part of it at least – had already found a home at Naples during the reign of Alfonso, who, as we have noted, appreciated the art of the North, than to posit that it arrived *en masse* just prior to the compilation of the two chansonniers.

musical tradition alive for some time after the musical–literary establishment of the court had turned in other directions.

Settings of Italian Texts

In the field of lyric verse the turn was toward italianization; and by the mid- to late 1460s, a group of Neapolitan poets – some of the first rank, like de Jennaro, Galeotta, Caracciolo, and de Petruciis, others of the 'Sunday poet' variety – was cultivating a native lyric tradition, often popular in tone and frequently shot through with dialect.[74] A fine example of both of these currents is the anonymous barzelletta *Ora may, que ffora·n ço* (No. 12 in the edition), one of the few secular songs of the period for which there is precise documentation concerning a performance. On 29 June 1465, the Sienese chronicler Allegretto Allegretti made the following entry in his *Diario . . . delle cose sanesi*:

Per le Arti alla Duchessa fu ordinato un bellissimo Apparato e Ballo, a piei al Palazzo de' Signori, e furono convitate quanto Giovane da bene, e Fanciulla aveva Siena, le quali andarono molto bene ornate di veste, e Gioje; e giovani da danzare; e facesi una Lupa grande tutta d'orata, della quale usci una Moresca di 12 Persone molto bene e ricamente ornate, e una vestita a Monaca, e ballavano a una Canzone, che dice: *Non vogl'essere più Monaca; arsa le sia la Tonica, chi se la veste piu . . .*[75]

The event that occasioned these festivities was the stopover in Siena of Ippolita Sforza, who was on her way to Naples to take up residence as the Duchess of Calabria. And the canzona to which the young merrymakers danced must have been the melody – if not the entire polyphonic fabric – of the four-voice barzelletta that appears in Escorial IV.a.24 with the text *Hora may che fora son, non vo' io essere più moniche*.[76] That the tune and its poem – which deals with the nun who wishes to flee the convent – enjoyed widespread popularity is attested both by the many lauda texts that were sung to the melody[77] and by the five extant poetry anthologies in which the poem is found, sometimes with the designation 'canzona napoletana' – which, since the poem exhibits no unusual generic or structural features, has been interpreted as an indication of its provenance.[78]

---

[74] A useful anthology is Altamura, *La lirica napoletana del Quattrocento*. For a concise summary of the tradition and its relation to music, see Pope and Kanazawa, *The Musical Manuscript Montecassino 871*, pp. 71ff.

[75] The diary is printed in Muratori, *Rerum italicarum scriptores*, XXIII; the passage cited is in col. 772.

[76] Apparently the identification was first made in Pirro, *Histoire de la musique de la fin du XIVe siècle à la fin du XVIe*, p. 156. The extremely awkward altus part may well be a later addition to the piece.

[77] On the laude by Feo Belcari, Piero di Mariano Muzi, and Francesco degli Albizzi, see Cattin, 'Le poesie del Savonarola nelle fonti musicale', pp. 272–81, which includes a facsimile and transcription of Belcari's *Hora mai sono in età* – text and melody – after Milan S.P.II.5, a manuscript written by Savonarola; Jeppesen, 'Laude', *Die Musik in Geschichte und Gegenwart*, VIII, col. 319, gives a partial transcription of a two-voice setting of Belcari's text after Paris 16664; see also D'Ancona, *La poesia popolare italiana*, pp. 488–89.

[78] The poem is so designated in the manuscripts Florence 3 and Milan C 35 sup; on the Neapolitan origins of the text, see Bronzini, 'Poesia popolare del periodo aragonese' p. 260, n. 8. The theme of the regretful nun who wishes to flee the convent in order to marry was popular with both poets and musicians; see D'Ancona, *op. cit.*, p. 147, and Wendland, '"Madre non mi far Monica": The Biography of a Renaissance Folksong'.

The most intriguing redaction of the poem – and the one used in the present edition (the unique source for the music, Escorial IV.a.24, gives only the opening fragment of the text) – is the version in the manuscript Barcelona 1, a collection of 229 Catalan (and two Italian) poems[79] that was compiled at least in part at Naples, circa 1460, either for or perhaps by the Catalan poet–notary Joan Fogassot.[80]

As it stands in Barcelona 1, the poem is a fine example of what Altamura calls the 'Neapolitan *koine*', that is, a linguistic style that is neither wholly Tuscan Italian nor Neapolitan dialect, but rather a mixture of the two that came to characterize much of the poetry written at the Aragonese court.[81] And in this particular case the Neapolitan character is further highlighted by the consistent use of Catalan orthography, a strong reminder of the prestige that that language enjoyed at the court of Naples under Alfonso I. Among the linguistic characteristics that justify the designation 'canzona napoletana' are the following:[82] stanza 1 line 5: the word 'suta' is short for 'isciuta' or 'issuta', the Neapolitan form of 'uscita'; stanza 3 lines 3 and 6: the forms 'nx' and 'nxe', which represent the Catalan version of the Neapolitan–Calabrian 'nce', are used instead of 'ce'; stanza 4 line 3: 'dotxa' is the Catalan spelling of the Neapolitan 'doce', which is used in place of 'dolce'; stanza 7 lines 2, 4–5: the final words of these lines, 'potesse–misse–scrisse', constitute the so-called Neapolitan or Sicilian rhyme in which '-esse' is pronounced in precisely the same way as '-isse', the difference in written vowels notwithstanding.

In order to set the text of Barcelona 1 to the music of Escorial IV.a.24, it has been necessary to emend three lines in order to rid the verse of hypermeter – normal elision of syllables was not possible – and thus achieve a better relationship between poetry and music: stanza 1 line 1: the 'E' of 'Estava' (certainly a sign of the scribe's Spanish origin) has been dropped, an emendation supported by many sources, including Escorial IV.a.24; stanza 3 line 8: the nine syllables of 'Abra-me, que frate Petro so' have been reduced to seven in 'Abra, que fra Petro so', this change being supported by Paris 1069, which offers the Tuscanized 'Apri, che fra Piero son'; stanza 6 line 6: the opening word, 'Que', which is probably nothing more than a scribal error, has been omitted entirely.

Two points remain to be made about the music. Both music and text follow the standard scheme of the barzelletta:

	ripresa	piedi		volta	(ripresa)
		strophe			
verse	a b b a	c d	c d	d b b a	(a b b a)
music	A	B	B	A	(A)

A glance through the volte of the eight strophes, though, shows that the final three

---

[79] The other Italian poem is the 'siciliano' *Adxo visto lo mapamundi*, on whose melody Cornago based his *Mappamundi* Mass (see Chap. III, p. 63).

[80] On the manuscript Barcelona 1, see Aramon i Serra, 'Dues cancons populars italianes'.

[81] Altamura, *La lirica napoletana del Quattrocento*, pp. 9–11.

[82] The discussion is based on Aramon i Serra, 'Dues cancons populars italianes', pp. 180–85, which contains a detailed discussion of the poem, and Rohlfs, *Grammatica storica della lingua italiana e dei suoi dialetti*, III, 255–56.

lines of five of them (1–2, 5–7) actually repeat the corresponding verses of the ripresa. Thus the ripresa becomes superfluous after these strophes and should be omitted.[83]

Finally, it has been necessary to emend the reading that Escorial IV.a.24 transmits for the first two notes of the superius at measure 2. The reading calls for Ex. 2a. However, as the transcription makes clear, the a' on the downbeat of

Ex. 2a

measure 2 results in a stylistically unacceptable dissonance against the three supporting voices. And that it is the superius that is at fault is demonstrated by the two-part lauda setting that appears in Paris 16664 (the tenor part is the same in both works): Ex. 2b,[84] where the g' on the downbeat resolves the problem. My own

Ex. 2b

emendation is a compromise of sorts, retaining the whole of measure 1 in Escorial IV.a.24, but following the melodic suggestion of Paris 16664 (with the rhythmic–ornamental pattern of Escorial IV.a.24) at the beginning of measure 2: Ex. 2c.[85]

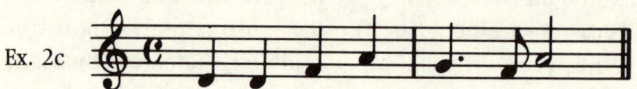

Ex. 2c

As popular as the barzelletta and the structurally related ballata might have been, the appeal that they held for composers and compiler–editors of manuscripts at Naples was soon superseded by that of the strambotto, the form that comes strongly to the fore in the 'central' sources of the 1480s.[86] And particularly popular was the so-called *strambotto siciliano*, which, with its rhyme scheme of *a b a b a b a b* – in contrast to the *a b a b a b c c* of the more widely circulated Tuscan strambotto[87] – came to be the preferred form at the Neapolitan court. Thus all the strambotti of Francesco Galeota, for example, are of the 'Sicilian' type,[88] as are all

---

[83] On this practice, see Pope and Kanazawa, *The Musical Manuscript Montecassino 871*, p. 78 and n. 39.

[84] Jeppesen, 'Laude', col. 390.

[85] My emendation causes octaves between superius and altus, but the latter voice may have been added later, and octaves are common in these works.

[86] Just how dramatic the shift in taste was can be seen from the following statistics:

	ballata	barzelletta	strambotto
Escorial IV.a.24 (1460s)	15	1	0
New Haven 91 (1470s)	0	1	0
Montecassino 871 (1480s)	3	3	16
Perugia 431 (1480s)	1	6	18

[87] Other rhyme schemes, less commonly used, were *a b a b c c d d* in the *strambotto romagnolo* and *a a b b c c d d* in the so-called *rispetto toscano*.

[88] Flamini, 'F. Galeota e il suo inedite

eight of the strambotti in Montecassino 871 that survive with complete texts[89] and the majority of those in Paris 1035, the canzoniere compiled for Giovanni Cantelmo in the 1460s.

The strambotto tradition is represented in the edition by three pieces, perhaps the most typical of which is the anonymous *La morte che spavento de felice* (No. 13), which reaches us in both Seville 5-1-43/Paris 4379 and Perugia 431. Musically, the setting of the poem, a *strambotto siciliano* with such dialectal touches as the use of 'seria' for 'sarebbe' and 'oru' for 'oro'[90] (the latter in Perugia 431 only), is simplicity itself. The composer wrote two phrases of music, one for each verse of the first couplet. The same two phrases then serve for the three succeeding couplets, though we may suppose that they were embellished and varied in performance. As for the texture, the main melodic interest appears in the superius, with the lower voices providing a simple accompaniment that often has the tenor moving in the same rhythm as the superius. No doubt, the style as a whole is an outgrowth – perhaps even a written representation – of the extempore performances of the poet–improvisators who found such favor at Naples and throughout the rest of Italy in the fifteenth century.

The most renowned of the Neapolitan poet–improvisators was Serafino Aquilano, who is represented in the edition by the *ottava rima* (and its musical setting?)[91] *Sufferir so disposto* (No. 14). It is interesting to compare the version of the poem in Perugia 431 – the principal source for our edition – with that of Giunta's 1516 edition of Serafino's works, for it demonstrates the risks run by literary scholars when they base their editions of poets whose works were set to music on apparently authoritative poetry anthologies and fail to consult the music sources of the period. Aside from such minor alterations as Giunta's use of 'viver' for 'esser' (line 3), 'tengo' for 'porto' (line 4), 'cor' for 'petto' (line 5), and the Tuscan 'ascoso' for the meridional 'ascuso' (line 4), the print of 1516 offers the following reading for the final couplet: 'Doglioso viver che di morir consento/ Consento di morir da poi ch'io sento', whereas Perugia 431 reads: 'Doglioso vivo et del mio male consento/Contento de morir, o Gloriüso'.[92] Thus the version in Giunta alters the 'Sicilian' rhyme scheme of Perugia 431 ('-ento' and '-uso'/'-oso') and comes up instead with a somewhat irregular Tuscan scheme: *a b a b a b a a*, which nevertheless emphasizes the distinctness of the final couplet. And that it is Perugia 431 that offers the earlier – if not the original – version seems evident from

canzoniere', pp. 30ff. On the other hand, such poets as Serafino Aquilano and Benedetto Gareth – that is, those who most completely succumbed to the Petrarchism imported from Tuscany – used the form sparingly. On Serafino's use of the *strambotto siciliano*, more presently.

[89] Pope and Kanazawa, *The Musical Manuscript Montecassino 871*, p. 76, list only seven of the eight strambotti with complete texts as being of the 'Sicilian' type. However, the text of the strambotto *Correno multi cani* (No. 140 in Montecassino 871) is complete in Perugia 431, and the work can be added to the 'Sicilian' list.

[90] See Grandgent, *From Latin to Italian*, pp. 6–7, 21, 147.

[91] On the question of whether Serafino might have composed the music, see Chap. III, p. 83.

[92] Line 7 of both versions contains an extra syllable. I have emended the reading in Perugia 431 by using the shortened 'mal' instead of 'male'. We may note that later music sources for the piece (Florence 121, Florence 27, and Paris 676) agree with the version printed by Giunta – as does the poetry anthology Rome 5170.

several considerations: (1) Perugia 431, probably compiled by the mid-1480s, antedates by two to three decades both Giunta's print and any of the manuscript sources that agree with it; (2) Serafino had been active at Naples only shortly before Perugia 431 was compiled, so that that manuscript would seem to have added authority; and (3) sixteenth-century editors and publishers – Giunta included – frequently tampered with the texts that they printed.[93] Thus *Sufferir so disposto* should be added to the list of Serafino's *strambotti siciliani*, thus bringing the number of his poems in that form from five to six.[94]

Finally, we come to *Cavalcha Sinisbaldo tuta la note* (No. 15 in the edition), an anonymous unicum in Seville 5-I-43/Paris 4379. Although classified as a strambotto by Cardamone,[95] the poem contains a number of features that set it apart from the other strambotti: (1) there is a recurring refrain, 'Pan e paneda . . .', that returns after each couplet, thus imparting to the piece one of the main characteristics of the *villanesca alla napoletana*, which was itself a strambotto blown up by the insertion of a refrain;[96] (2) the number of couplets has been increased from four to five; and (3) the rhyme scheme does not conform to any of the standard patterns. *Cavalcha Sinisbaldo* also differs from most of the strambotti in the Neapolitan sources with respect to its musical style. Instead of the usually lyrical superius above a thin and ever-so-slightly contrapuntal support, the main melody is here in the tenor, being stated twice within each couplet. And given that the two statements are thoroughly syllabic and identical, it is likely that the composition is a setting of a pre-existent tune,[97] one that was almost certainly popular in origin.

Pieces for the Royal Family

To wade through the Neapolitan music manuscripts in search of compositions written for members of the royal family is a somewhat disappointing experience. Out of a total of 783 works transmitted by the eight polyphonic sources that I have assigned to Naples,[98] only three short pieces display associations with the ruling family: Tinctoris's two song-motets for Beatrice – *O Virgo, miserere mei* (No. 1 in the edition) and *Virgo Dei throno digna* – both of which appear (the first as an unicum) in New Haven 91, and the problematical *Viva, viva, rey Ferranddo* (No. 2), which reaches us in both Berlin 78.C.28 and Montecassino 871.[99]

---

[93] On this point, see Bauer-Formiconi, *Die strambotti des Serafino dall'Aquila*, p. 167; Migliorini, *Storia della lingua italiana*, p. 282.

[94] The other examples of Serafino's 'Sicilian' strambotti are listed in Bauer-Formiconi, *op. cit.*, p. 54, n. 76.

[95] Cardamone, 'Forme musicali e metriche della canzone villanesca e della villanella alla napolitana, p. 37.

[96] Cardamone, 'The Debut of the "*Canzone villanesca alla napolitana*"', p. 93.

[97] The tenor alone is transcribed in Pirrotta, *Li due Orfei*, p. 120 (idem, *Music and Theatre*, p. 88).

[98] The number includes multiple redactions of the same piece. By manuscript, the figures break down as follows: Escorial IV.a.24, 118; Berlin 78.C.28, 42; New Haven 91, 57; Montecassino 871, 141; Perugia 431, 122; Bologna Q 16, 131; Seville 5-I-43/Paris 4379, 167; Foligno, 6.

[99] My speculation that the *L'homme armé* Mass in Bologna Q 16 may be associated with Alfonso, Duke of Calabria (see above, p. 130), is nothing more than that. Tinctoris's *Missa a trium vocum* appears only in the manuscript Verona 755, which is not of Neapolitan provenance.

The association between *O Virgo, miserere mei* and Beatrice is made explicit by the inscription that accompanies the piece: 'Beatissime virgini domini Beatrici de Aragonia'.[100] Although Perkins's contention that the motet was originally intended to serve as the opening composition in New Haven 91 remains hypothetical,[101] the inscription does establish a *terminus ante quem* for both the composition and its entry into the manuscript, Summer 1475, when Beatrice was officially betrothed to Matthias Corvinus, after which time the reference to Beatrice as a 'maiden' would have been inappropriate.[102]

The association between Beatrice and the motet extends beyond the inscription, for, as Jaap van Benthem has recently shown, Tinctoris 'personalized' the motet by imbuing it with number symbolism on a number of levels. Thus, to cite but two of his examples: there are 133 notes in the superius, that number – using simple gematria applied to the Latin alphabet – being the numerical equivalent of 'Beatrice de Aragonia'; there are twenty-one notes that form a rhythmically distinct (almost irrational) passage at measures 16–18, with the ciphers '2 1' probably standing for the initials 'BA', those of the dedicatee herself.[103]

Finally, a word is in order about the relationship between music and text in the motet. Perhaps it is a result of the constraints imposed by the use of number symbolism and the necessity of shaping the lengths of phrases to serve that purpose, but there is a sense of 'abstractness' about the music that causes difficulties with respect to text underlay, difficulties that are certainly not helped by the scribe's placement of the text in New Haven 91. More so than in most pieces, therefore, the solution to the problem of text underlay must be regarded as even more tenuous than usual, and those who wish to perform the piece would do well to compare it with those offered by Perkins and by Melin.[104]

Less certain is the association between the anonymous *Viva, viva, rey Ferranddo* and Ferrante I. What seems at first to be a clear case of an occasional composition in honor of the king in Montecassino 871 is complicated by a concordance in Berlin 78.C.28, where the piece was entered without text or text incipit, but with the capital letters 'S' and 'D' at the beginning of its two sections. On the ground that Berlin 78.C.28 is the earlier of the two manuscripts, Reidemeister contends that the now-lost text of Berlin 78.C.28 – perhaps a bergerette – must have been the original one and that the Spanish poem that lauds Ferrante is a contrafactum.[105] He supports this conclusion by noting two small but important rhythmic alterations at the beginning of the superius of Montecassino 871, changes that he claims were made in order to accommodate the new text:

---

[100] Although no such similar inscription accompanies *Virgo Dei throno digna*, Perkins and Garey are convincing in viewing this work as a companion piece to *O Virgo* (*The Mellon Chansonnier*, I, 19; II, 425).

[101] *Ibid.*, I, 20.

[102] I cannot, however, agree with the use to which Perkins puts the inscription as evidence – in conjunction with other pieces of evidence – for pre- and post-betrothal stages in the compilation of the manuscript (*The Mellon Chansonnier*, I, 32).

My objections are noted in my review of the edition (see p. 120 above, n. 16), p. 138, n. 8.

[103] Van Benthem, 'Concerning Johannes Tinctoris and the Preparation of the Princess's Chansonnier'.

[104] *The Mellon Chansonnier*, I, 85; *Johanni Tinctoris: Opera omnia*, p. 123, where the word 'meorum' is read incorrectly as 'in corum'.

[105] Reidemeister, *Die Handschrift 78C28 des Berliner Kupferstichkabinetts*, pp. 28 and 104–5.

Berlin 78.C.28:

[Vi - va, vi - va, rey . . .]

Montecassino 871:

[Vi - va, vi - va, rey Fer-ran - . . . .]

Further evidence in support of Reidemeister's conclusion may be found in the lopsided relationship between the music and the Spanish text, which calls for either inordinately long melismas (which, given the many rests and generally square rhythm of the superius, tend to sound rather labored), instrumental interludes, or extensive repetition of text – the last being the solution offered in the present edition.[106] On the other hand, the poor music–text relationship at the beginning of the superius of Berlin 78.C.28 is a common enough fault in late-fifteenth-century chansonniers, especially those from Italy, and the type of alteration that occurs in Montecassino 871 (the splitting of breves into semibreves) is one that scribes introduced frequently, even when not dealing with contrafacta. Thus, while Reidemeister's argument is compelling – the rhythmic alteration in Montecassino 871 does seem well calculated – the possibility that the scribe of Berlin 78.C.28 may simply have entered the wrong initials cannot be altogether excluded.

Also problematical is the event that occasioned the composition of the piece or – if the Spanish text is a contrafactum – its union with the poem in honor of Ferrante. Unfortunately, not only does the text of the canción lack any allusions to a specific historical event – nor is it likely that any such clue appeared in the now-missing vuelta of the poem[107] – but after its initial reference to the king it turns away from Ferrante's exploits and dwells on the victory of love. It seems, then, that past proposals that the piece celebrates either Ferrante's coronation or his victory over Jean of Anjou and the pro-Angevin barons remain somewhat unconvincing.[108]

A French Chanson for Solo Voice and Lute (or Vihuela de mano)

That the secular works of Vincenet were appreciated at the royal court is attested by the inclusion of all four of his known settings of vernacular lyric poetry in New Haven 91. And by far the most popular of these songs was *Fortune, par ta cruaulté*, which appears in at least thirteen polyphonic sources, among them all the

---

[106] Text-repetition, though far less extensive, is also employed in Pope and Kanazawa, *The Musical Manuscript Montecassino 871*, p. 442–48; Haberkamp, *Die weltliche Vokalmusik in Spanien um 1500*, pp. 284–87, uses melismas, in many of which the syllables of individual words are separated by lengthy rests; Reidemeister, *op. cit*, No. 34, offers a transcription without text.

[107] Pope and Kanazawa, *op. cit.*, p. 91, speculate that there may never have been a vuelta and that it might have been replaced by the initial refrain.

[108] Reidemeister, *Die Handschrift 78C28 des Berliner Kupferstichkabinetts*, p. 28; Pope and Kanazawa, *op. cit.*, p. 642.

Neapolitan manuscripts that date from after the mid-1470s except Montecassino 871. Indeed, in terms of the number of extant sources in which it survives, Vincenet's chanson may be said to have enjoyed the widest circulation of any piece either composed at Naples or written by a composer who was active there. In addition, its popularity is further attested by two instrumental arrangements, one for solo lute in Francesco Spinacino's *Intabolatura de liuto, libro II* (Venice, 1507), and the other, the present version for solo voice and lute accompaniment, in the manuscript fragment Bologna 596 H.H.2⁴ (No. 16 in the edition).

After transposing the entire piece up one whole step, from C to D, so that it fits an instrument tuned to A, the intabulator retained Vincenet's superius without change – there are no important variants between the superius in the present version and that in New Haven 91, the most authoritative source for the polyphonic model – and arranged the tenor and contratenor parts for the lute or vihuela de mano. These voices, however, are treated more freely. While the tenor part of the intabulation is slightly embellished near the very end (measures 47ff), the contra is simplified throughout, often sustaining a tone or even resting when its polyphonic prototype had been very much on the move (measures 10–12, 27–33, 44–51).[109] At times, the contra part of the intabulation is so skeletal as to raise problems in the transcription (see below).

The differences between the polyphonic and intabulated contratenor parts raise the question of what the intabulator had before him as a model. Unfortunately, a comparison of the instrumental arrangement with various redactions of the polyphonic original leads to no firm conclusions. However, that the intabulation shares with the Neapolitan manuscript Perugia 431 not only the small detail of a passing-note g in the contratenor on the final eighth-note of measure 7, but also the unusual entry of a combined attribution–title – *Fortuna vincinecta* – that appears in no other source points to a possible relationship with the reading of Perugia 431. Yet that Perugia 431 itself could not have served as the direct source for the intabulation is evident from the many corrupt passages in its own contra part: measures 14–30:1 are lacking, while measures 38:1–44:3 are written a third too low.

A notable feature of the intabulation is its use of the so-called tablature 'alla napoletana'. Like the customary Italian tablature, the Neapolitan system uses numbers to signify the frets; yet contrary to normal Italian practice, it uses the numeral '1' – rather than '0' – to designate the open string. Even at Naples, however, this procedure apparently failed to gain widespread acceptance, and besides its appearance in Bologna 596 H.H.2⁴ it is otherwise known from its use in only three other sources: (1) Pesaro 1144, where it is found on fols. 39ᵛ–40ᵛ; (2) a Neapolitan edition of Francesco da Milano that was published in 1536 with the title *Libro secondo de la Fortuna*; and (3) Michele Carrara's *Intavolatura di liuto* of 1585, where it is expressly designated as 'Modo de intavolare alla Napoletana'.[110]

---

[109] The relationship between the intabulation and the lower parts of the original chanson has already been noted by Fallows, '15th-century Tablatures for Plucked Instruments', p. 25.
[110] *Ibid.*, pp. 22, 25.

The transcription of the lute or vihuela part is not without its problems and has required three important emendations. On the final beat of measure 13, the intabulator calls for an *e* in the contra, thus producing consecutive octaves with the superius (measures 13:4–14:1). I have followed the voice-leading of all the polyphonic sources and substituted the note *a*. The other two emendations are more problematical, for it is difficult to say whether we are dealing with scribal errors or whether the troublesome places represent the intabulator's intentions. Should we, on the first two beats of the tenor at measure 4, continue to hear the *f'* of the previous measure, or should there be a rest, or was an *e'* omitted? Similarly, at measure 16, should the *b/d'* on the third beat have been sounded on the first beat of the measure, or did the scribe simply omit the *g/d'*? In both instances, the transcription follows the voice-leading of the polyphonic model. A final remark about the transcription of the music concerns the barring in Bologna H.H.2⁴. Although the scribe used bar lines, they appear at irregular intervals and in what seems to be a thoroughly capricious manner. Moreover, the bar lines for the voice part do not always coincide with those of the accompaniment, despite the scribe's belated effort to remedy the situation with bar lines that sometimes resemble the letter 's'. In the edition, I have resorted to regularly recurring bar lines.

Pieces for Instrumental Ensemble

The two instrumental pieces in the edition are representative of two kinds of works that would have made up the repertory of the instrumental ensembles at the court: the 'free' instrumental chanson and music for the dance.

Although it is sometimes difficult to distinguish between a 'chanson' that was conceived from the outset as a piece for an instrumental ensemble – a Renaissance 'song without words', as the genre has recently been called[111] – and a true *forme-fixe* setting that has merely been shorn of its text,[112] *Je ne demande de vous* (No. 17 in the edition; in Bologna Q 16, the unique source for the composition, the incipit reads *Je ne demano de vos*) clearly belongs to the former group, as demonstrated by (1) alternation between two- and three-part writing that seems quite divorced from references to words; (2) the rhythmic parallelism between the parts in the duo sections;[113] (3) the use of a short, incisive motive – again seemingly conceived without regard for text – that is stated sequentially (measures 12–17); and (4) a phrase structure that will not easily accommodate either the *quatrain* or *cinquain* type of rondeau.[114]

---

[111] By Edwards, 'Songs Without Words by Josquin and his Contemporaries', p. 91.

[112] For the repertory of the late fifteenth century, the problem has recently been discussed at length by Edwards, *op. cit.*, and by Litterick, 'On Italian Instrumental Ensemble Music in the Late Fifteenth Century'; see also Litterick, 'Performing Franco-Netherlandish Secular Music of the Late 15th Century', pp. 482–83.

[113] As already noted by Fuller, 'Additional Notes on the 15th-century Chansonnier Bologna Q 16', p. 89, n. 19, who also accepts the piece as being for instruments.

[114] The piece is not related to either of two chansons by Busnois, *Je ne demande liaulté* or *Je ne demande autre a me degré*.

The chief question about the piece, however, centers upon the identity of its composer: 'J.P.' Could it be Josquin des Prez (Jodocus Pratensis, Jodocus a Prato)? Though a firm conclusion cannot be offered, I should – at the risk of repeating some points already noted in Chap. III[115] – like to make the following observations: (1) the style of the piece virtually precludes its having been composed by Jehan Pullois or the 'J.P.' of Oxford 213; (2) its very presence in a Neapolitan source of the 1480s runs counter to the known pattern of dissemination of the works of Johannes Prioris; (3) the ascription to 'J.P.' is one of only two attributions in Bologna Q 16,[116] and must therefore have had some special significance for the scribe or compiler of the manuscript; (4) there is nothing in the piece that would definitely rule out the possibility of Josquin's having composed it (though it is certainly less than Josquin at his best); and (5) there is a short passage of two-part imitation at the close time interval of a minim (measures 36–38) – a technique that, while not exclusive to Josquin, would be handled brilliantly in later works by the composer.[117]

In all, then, the best that can be said is that *Je ne demande* could be by Josquin (though the style also admits the possibility that it was written by Japart – another resolution of '.J.p:'?), and if it is, it lends at least some support to Lowinsky's notion that the composer might have been part of the entourage that accompanied Ascanio Sforza to Naples. And if that is true, to push the hypothesis one step further, the unicum status of *Je ne demande* in Bologna Q 16 could indicate that the piece was composed there, in which case it might well represent the sole surviving legacy of Josquin's very hypothetical Neapolitan sojourn.

Finally, music for the dance is represented in the edition by the well-known arrangement *a 2* of the popular basse-danse melody *La Spagna* (No. 18).[118] The 'M. Gulielmus' to whom the work is ascribed in Perugia 431, where it appears with the title *Falla con misuras* – the piece appears in Bologna Q 16 without an attribution and with the title *La bassa castiglya* – has been identified as the famous dancing-master Gulielmus Ebreo da Pesaro,[119] who may be the same as Giovanni Ambrosio da Pesaro.[120] To the literature that has already grown up about this arrangement[121] may be added two further observations, both of which concern

[115] See p. 84 and n. 140.

[116] In No. 126 in that manuscript, the place normally reserved for the text incipit bears the entry 'Dux Carlus'; whether this should be understood as a title or an attribution – to Charles the Bold – is not clear. The same piece reaches us with the incipit *Madame, helas* and an ascription to Josquin in the Bologna copy of the *Odhecaton* (removed in subsequent editions) and in the manuscript Zwickau 78, which no doubt took its attribution from Petrucci's print. (See Noble, 'Josquin Desprez; [work list]', *The New Grove*, IX, 736.)

[117] The redaction in Bologna Q 16 seems to contain at least a few scribal errors; these are recorded in the Critical Notes.

[118] For a list of *La Spagna* settings, see Gombosi, *Compositione di messer Vicenzo Capirola*, pp. lxii–lxiii.

[119] See Bukofzer, *Studies in Medieval and Renaissance Music*, p 196.

[120] See Chap. V above, p. 103.

[121] See, among others, Bukofzer, *Studies in Medieval and Renaissance Music*, pp. 196ff; Gombosi's review of Bukofzer in *Journal of the American Musicological Society*, IV (1955), 144–45; Heartz, 'Hoftanz and Basse Dance', pp. 18–19; Anthony Baines, *Brass Instruments*, p. 102. Both Gombosi and Heartz note that Gulielmus's setting is more properly classified as a saltarello than a basse danse, on the ground that the tenor moves in perfect breves (when the semibreves of

154 *Music at the Aragonese Court of Naples*

Bukofzer's reading of the version in Perugia 431, with one of them having some effect on the consequent application of editorial accidentals. First, the upper voice is notated with the mensuration sign ⌽, not ¢, as appears in Bukofzer's diplomatic facsimile of the incipit.[122] And second, although Bukofzer states that the manuscript lacks any notated accidentals in its redaction of the piece,[123] there is in fact a flat before the *e'* at measure 21 of the superius, one that Bukofzer may have overlooked not only because of its extreme faintness in photographic reproductions of the manuscript, but because the flat appears as the very last notational symbol on its staff, while the *e'* to which it applies follows as the first note on the next staff. At the very least, the presence of the flattened *e'* at measure 21 causes the *b* on the second minim of measure 22 to be flatted and perhaps also the *b* and *e'* in the somewhat analogous passage at measure 10, where these notes are once again pivot notes of a sort and the sustained tone in the tenor is once again *g*. In the edition, I have flatted all the notes in question, using parentheses for those at measure 10 in order to underscore the uncertainty about them. For those notes the performer will have to make his own choice, just as Ferrante's own royal pifferi must have done some five hundred years ago.

the notation are augmented under the mensuration sign ⌽) rather than the imperfect longs required by the basse danse. Gombosi alone asserts that the cantus part of the duo is stylized to the point of not reflecting the improvisational practice of the time; his opinion seems unfounded. Finally, Baines discusses a matter of orchestration–transposition, noting that the lowest pitch of the cantus voice, *g*, was beyond the reach of the treble shawm, and that if that instrument were used in a performance of the piece an upward transposition of a fifth would have been necessary.

[122] *Studies in Medieval and Renaissance Music*, p. 199, and again in the description of the piece on p. 200.

[123] *Ibid.*, p. 200.

Postlude

If the course of music at the Aragonese court of Naples were to be characterized by a single predominating theme, perhaps it is a sense of contradiction, one whose axes are both chronological and synchronic. First, there is the obvious contrast not only between the styles of musical patronage fostered by Alfonso I and Ferrante I but also, within Alfonso's reign itself, between the patronage of music and that of the other arts. Though impractical in his grandiose dreams of territorial expansion, and though willing to lavish funds on the finest paintings and tapestries of northern Europe, to say nothing of refurbishing Castelnuovo, constructing the Triumphal Arch, and collecting jewels, precious metals, manuscripts, and exotica, Alfonso was, in comparison, strangely 'quiet' in his patronage of music. Indeed, insofar as they remained faithful to his roots in Spain, Alfonso's activities as a patron of music may even be termed 'sentimental', with the music and musicians with which he surrounded himself forming a strong cultural link to his homeland. Willing to forgo the new trends of the Franco-Flemish mainstream, or perhaps unable to recognize them, Alfonso preferred musicians with whom he shared a cultural bond. And because of this one-sided Spanish orientation, Alfonso's court was, as we have noted, always marked by a certain provincialism, though perhaps some signs of change began to appear toward the very end of his reign.

With Ferrante, the picture changes, a result not only of his personality – more pragmatic, less sensitive – but also of changing attitudes toward music throughout Italy. When, beginning in the 1470s, the court *cappella* became an ever-increasing symbol of power and cultural prestige, Ferrante would not be outdone by his Italian rivals, and he vied vigorously with them for the services of the ultramontane singers, at times to the point of losing all perspective, as when he played political brinkmanship with Milan over their claim to Johannes Cordier. In all, where Alfonso's style was subdued and marked by a sense of self-contentment, Ferrante's was aggressive, often boorish, and sometimes downright deceitful.

A second axis that displays a sense of contradiction is the degree to which the court made a truly meaningful contribution in the fields of sacred and secular music. Though Naples knew the large-scale Masses of the Franco–Netherlanders at least as they extend through the Ockeghem–Busnois generation, and though Cornago's *Mapamundi* Mass is a fairly early example of a cyclic Ordinary based on a secular cantus firmus, Aragonese Naples failed, in the end, to play a leading role in the development of sacred polyphony. One searches in vain for a parallel at Naples to the forging of a new 'classical' style by Josquin and Compère at Milan or the cultivation of a polychoral tradition by Martini at Ferrara. And even the more modest, often intimate, chordal style that characterizes many of the 'local' pieces in the manuscripts Montecassino 871 and Perugia 431 may well represent a pan-Italian monastic tradition rather than one that was indigenous to the court or even to its nearby monastic satellites. Perhaps the one sacred stylistic feature with which Naples early on stood in the forefront was the falsobordone (witness Oriola's setting of *In exitu Israel*), and it may have been the identification of this style with Alfonso's court that led Galeazzo Maria Sforza to request copies of the psalms that were sung to celebrate Alfonso's victories.

The situation is dramatically different in the field of secular music, where Naples was a leader for half a century. Already during the reign of Alfonso, Naples established itself as the cradle of fifteenth-century Spanish polyphonic song. Still more central, however, was the important role that Ferrante's court played in the rebirth of Italian secular polyphony. The dozens of barzellette and strambotti in the 'central' sources of the 1480s attest strongly to Naples' leadership in the development of the frottola, while the presence at the court of Serafino, Il Chariteo and Aurelio Brandolini shows that Naples was completely attuned to the unwritten tradition so much favored by the humanists. To be sure, the focal point of Italian secular music would, by the last years of the century, pass to such northern courts as Mantua, Ferrara, and Urbino, and one can only wonder about the extent to which the history of Italian secular music might have differed had the Aragonese court of Naples not suffered its political reversals and, as a consequence, had its very life snuffed out.

Finally, to return to the matter of sacred polyphony, there is still another contradiction to be pointed out, one that is possibly based more on present-day perception (only my own, perhaps?) than it is on fifteenth-century evidence, and that is the contradiction between what Naples might have accomplished and what it actually did produce, or (to put it another way) the opposition between a certain superficial glitter and an emptiness at the core. In part, the problem centers on the following question: why, with such stellar personnel in the chapel, did Naples not contribute more than it did? Clearly, the answer has to do in part with its having been unable to obtain the services of a top-notch composer of the Josquin generation – one who was looking forward instead of, at best, sideways – as did every other important Italian musical center by the mid-1480s. Thus, Naples stalled just as others shifted into high gear. But why? Could the problem have been Tinctoris himself? Is it possible, as I have suggested, that the very presence at the court of the famed theorist made Ferrante complacent? Or is it possible that Tinctoris took too little note of his younger contemporaries, none of whom figures in the list of composers that he praises, had their works cited by him, or had their styles emulated in his own rather small compositional output? Or does the answer lie with the patron? Was there something about Ferrante's brand of patronage – he was not known for his sensitivity to the arts, or anything else for that matter – that not only kept the great composers away, but also caused one musician after another either to quit Naples or at least to express a desire to do so? And when Ferrante finally set his mind firmly on hiring Agricola in 1492–1493 (is it just coincidence that the call went out only shortly after Tinctoris had severed relations with Naples?) it was too late, as music had to take a back seat to the impending political disaster. In the end, then, there remains a picture of a development laden with contradictions: between Alfonso and Ferrante, sacred and secular, internationalism and provincialism, promise and accomplishment. And perhaps we should not be surprised by this. For what else was the Aragonese court of Naples itself if not a contradiction in the grandest of terms: a dynasty of kings in search of a country?

THE EDITION

Editorial Methods

Although the editorial methods used in the present edition generally agree with those that are more or less standard in editions of fifteenth-century music, a few procedures warrant explanation. With respect to the reduction of note values, I have permitted myself the inconsistency of using either a 2:1 or a 4:1 reduction depending upon the character of the piece and the tempo that the reduction would suggest to the modern performer. While such inconsistency might be less than desirable in an edition of a single composer, manuscript, or genre, it does not seem out of place in an anthology such as the present one.

Regularly recurring bar lines have been used throughout the edition except in a few instances in which their retention would grossly distort the rhythmic sense of the music. Thus I have sometimes inserted one or more measures of triple meter in a duple-meter framework or vice versa. Shifting meters are especially prevalent in Nos. 4 and 4a, where the meter often seems ambiguous.

As in any edition of fifteenth-century music, the most troublesome problems occur in connection with musica ficta and text underlay, and my solutions for these certainly represent no more than one possibility. With respect to musica ficta, I have tried to follow the guidelines set forth by the theorists of the late fifteenth and early sixteenth centuries. However, I have not shied away from using and sometimes even creating diminished triads in root position. Not only does Tinctoris remark on their use by composers of his time – in the *Liber de arte contrapuncti*, Bk. II, Chap. xxxiii – but to avoid them often results in even more difficult problems. Thus, given the choice of lowering a *B* or raising a *G* when those notes sound above an *E* in a cadential passage, I have sometimes lowered the *B* on the grounds that it gives preference to musica recta over musica ficta and that it frequently makes better sense in the overall musical context.

The problem of text underlay is perhaps even more frustrating, for here there is surely no single, definitive solution, especially in those obviously non-syllabic passages in which a few syllables of text must be stretched over a lengthy expanse of music. Although the suggestions of the theorists once again provided the basic guidelines, I have occasionally broken even the most fundamental of their rules. Thus, I have sometimes assigned more than one syllable to a ligature or to what was notated – perhaps arbitrarily – as a single sustained tone simply in order that the text could fit the music. Especially problematic in this respect is the tenor part in the Gloria and Credo of the *Missa L'homme armé*, and the solution resorted to is discussed in the commentary on the piece (p. 130 above). Throughout the edition, I have felt free to resort to text repetition, taking care, though, that the repeated portions of text make syntactical sense. Repetitions are indicated by means of square brackets. In presenting the texts, I have retained the original spellings but have consistently added apostrophes, accent marks, and punctuation. For capitalization I have followed a double standard; the original orthography has been retained in the prose texts of the Mass settings, while a capital letter has been used at the beginning of each line in those texts that are in verse. In most cases the texts of the liturgical compositions were incomplete and appeared in only one voice part; I have completed them after the versions that appear in modern chant books, using brackets to enclose those portions of text that were so added. Throughout the edition, scribal abbreviations have been expanded silently.

Finally, errors in the musical manuscripts have been emended, with the emendations being indicated by means of brackets. The original readings are listed in the Critical Notes, as are variants in concordant sources. Variants in the poetic texts, on the other hand, have not been listed unless they are substantial or in some other way noteworthy; on the few occasions when this occurs, the variants are discussed in the commentary on the individual piece.

1. O virgo, miserere mei
Johannes Tinctoris

2. Viva, viva, rey Ferranddo

Anon.

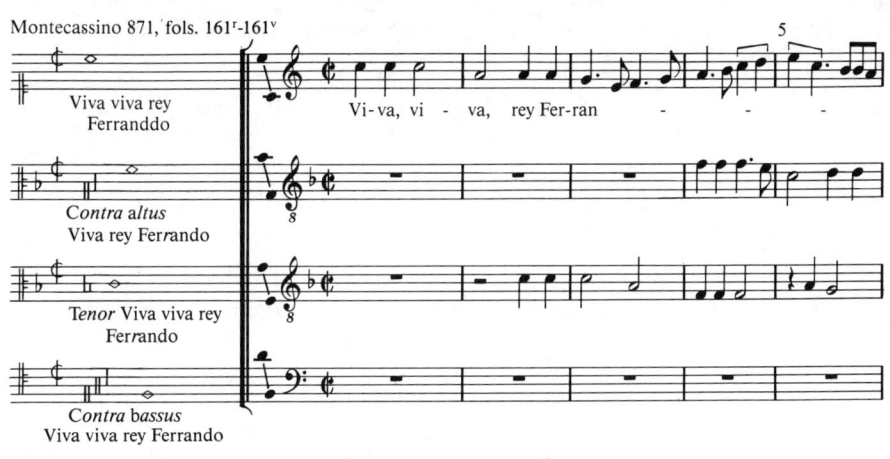

3. Missa L'homme armé

Anon.

Gloria

172

Credo

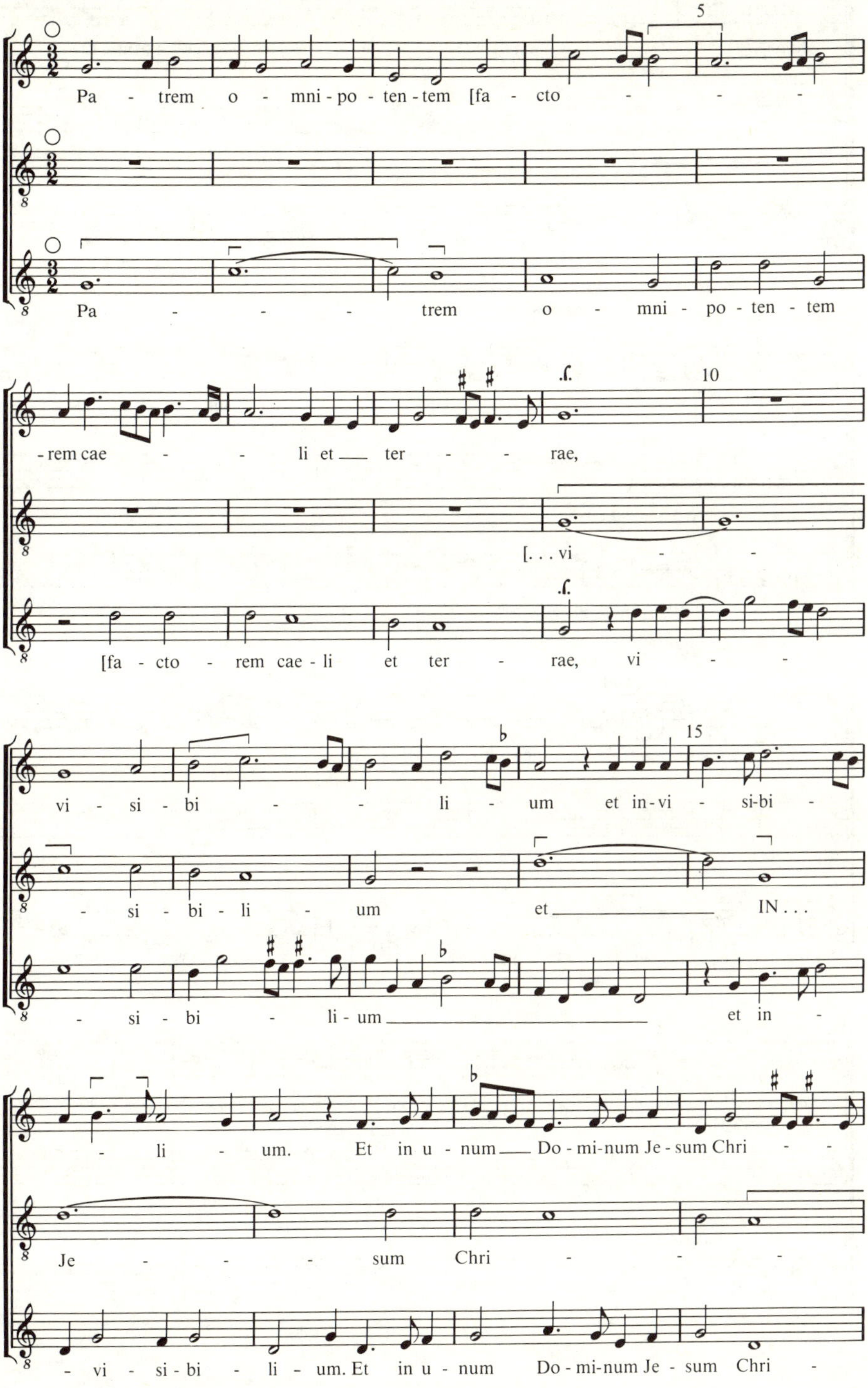
5
Pa - trem o - mni - po - ten - tem [fa - cto - - -
Pa - - - trem o - mni - po - ten - tem
- rem cae - - li et ter - - rae,
10
[. . . vi - -
[fa - cto - rem cae - li et ter - rae, vi - -
15
vi - si - bi - - li - um et in - vi - si-bi -
- si - bi - li - um et IN . . .
- si - bi - li - um et in -
- li - um. Et in u - num Do - mi - num Je - sum Chri - -
Je - - - sum Chri - - -
- vi - si - bi - li - um. Et in u - num Do - mi - num Je - sum Chri -

182

Sanctus

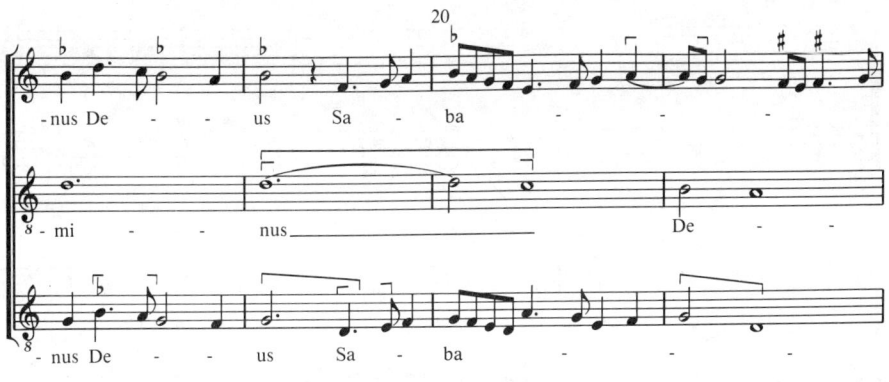

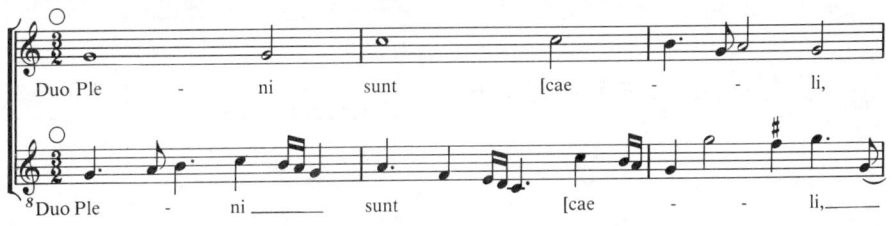

Agnus Dei

[1.] A - - - ngnus De - i
[3.] A - - - ngnus De - i
[1.] A - - - ngnus De - i
[3.] A - - - ngnus De - i
5
qui tol - lis pec - ca - ta mun - -
qui tol - lis pec - ca - ta mun - -
[1. . . .
[3. . . .
[qui tol - lis pec-ca-ta mun - -
qui tol - lis pec-ca-ta mun - -
10
- di mi - se - re - re no -
- di: do - na no - bis pa -
mi - se - re - re no - - bis,
do - na no - bis pa - - cem,
- di mi - - se - re - - re no - -
- di: do - - na no - - bis pa - -
15
- - bis [mi - se - re - - re no - -
- - cem, do - na no - - bis pa - -
no - - bis,
pa - - cem,
- - - bis, mi - se - re - re no -
- - - cem, do - na no - bis pa -

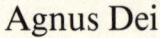

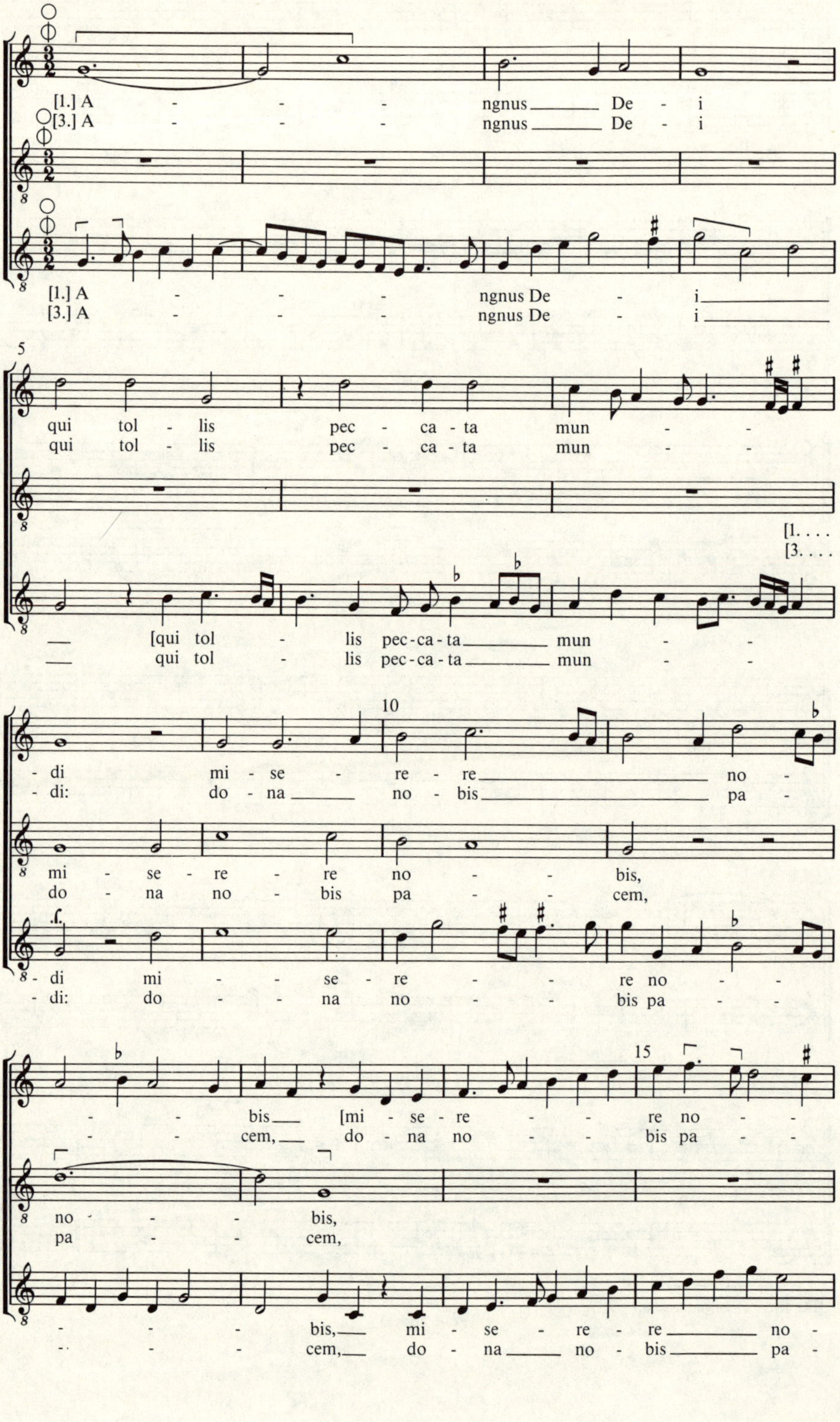

[Da capo Agnus 3; $o = 60 \rightarrow d. = 72+$]

4. Credo

Seraphinus

4a. Credo

Anon.

[To No. 4, B/4, 'Et ex Patre']

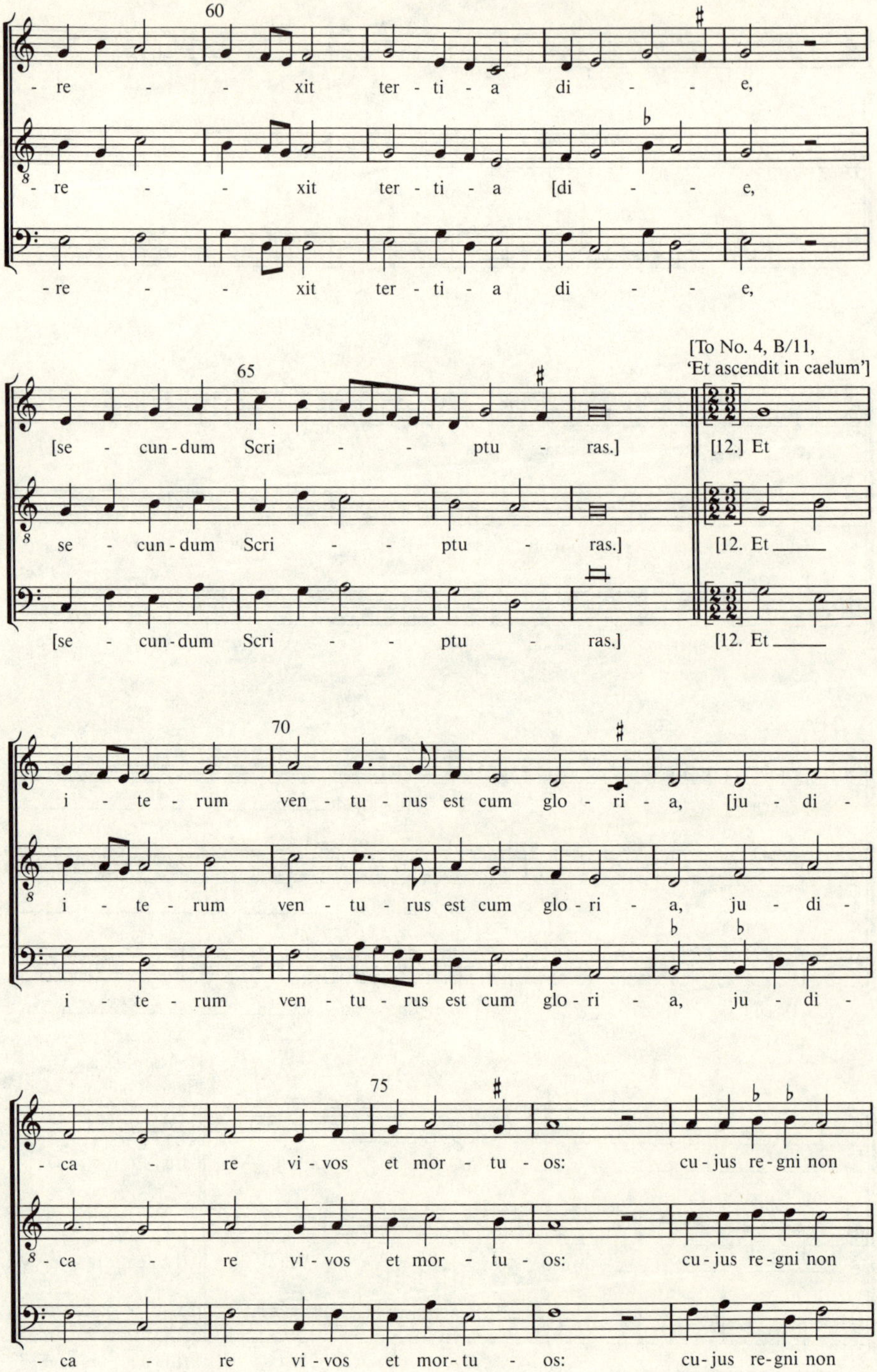
60
- re - - xit ter - ti - a di - - e,
- re - - xit ter - ti - a [di - - - e,
- re - - xit ter - ti - a di - - - e,
65
[To No. 4, B/11, 'Et ascendit in caelum']
[se - cun - dum Scri - - - ptu - ras.]
[12.] Et
se - cun - dum Scri - - - ptu - ras.]
[12. Et
[se - cun - dum Scri - - - ptu - ras.]
[12. Et
70
i - te - rum ven - tu - rus est cum glo - ri - a, [ju - di -
i - te - rum ven - tu - rus est cum glo - ri - a, ju - di -
i - te - rum ven - tu - rus est cum glo - ri - a, ju - di -
75
- ca - re vi - vos et mor - tu - os: cu - jus re - gni non
- ca - re vi - vos et mor - tu - os: cu - jus re - gni non
- ca - re vi - vos et mor - tu - os: cu - jus re - gni non

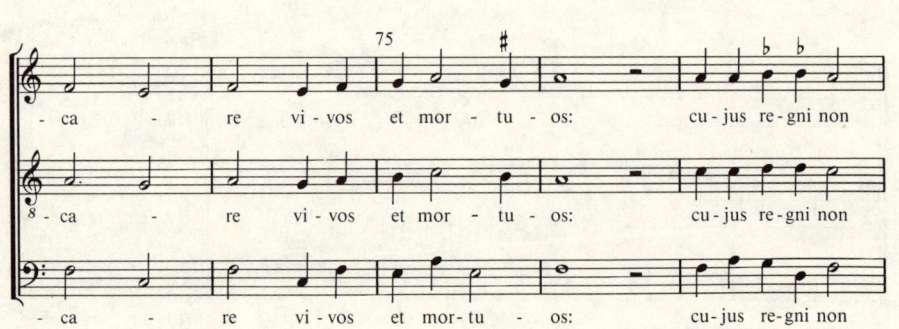

[To No. 4, C/13, 'Et in Spiritum Sanctum']

[To No. 4, D/15, 'Et unam sanctam']

5. Magnificat [6th tone]

Bernardus Ycart

Faenza 117, fols. 6ᵛ-7ʳ

202

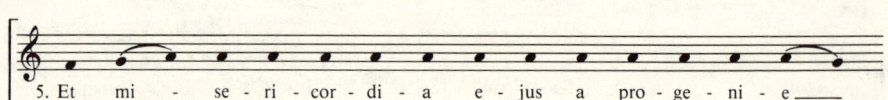
5. Et mi - se - ri - cor - di - a e - jus a pro - ge - ni - e

in pro - ge - ni - es ti - men - ti - bus e - um.

11. Glo - ri - a Pa - tri et Fi - li - o, et Spi - ri - tu - i San - cto.

6. Adoramus te, Christe

Anon.

Perugia 431, fols. 168ᵛ-169ʳ

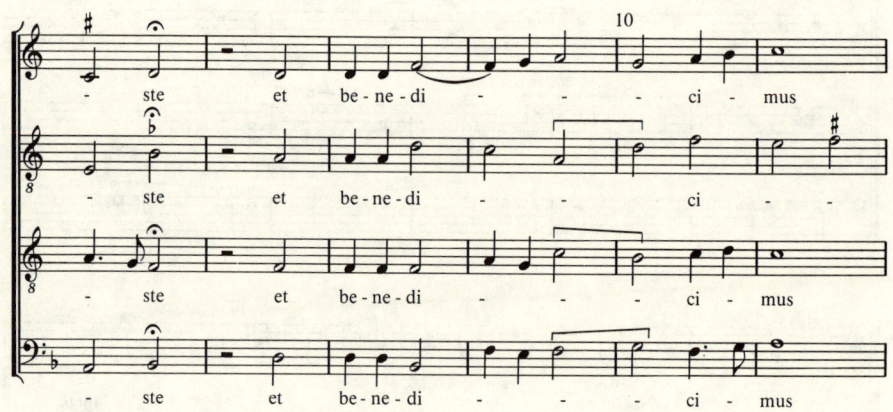

7. Christe Redemptor Omnium, Ex Patre Patris

Franchinus Gaffurius

Montecassino 871, fol. 42

3. Memento salutis Auctor,
   Quod nostri quondam corporis
   Ex illibata Virgine,
   Nascendo, formam sumpseris.

4. Sic praesens testatur dies,
   Currens per anni circulum,
   Quod solus a sede Patris
   Mundi salus adveneris.

5. Hunc caelum, terra, hunc mare,
   Hunc omne quod in eis est,
   Auctorem adventus tui,
   Laudans exsultat cantico.

6. Nos quoque, qui sancto tuo
   Redempti sanguine sumus,
   Ob diem natalis tui
   Hymnum novum concinimus.

7. Gloria tibi Domine,
   Qui natus es de Virgine,
   Cum Patre et Sancto Spiritu,
   In sempiterna saecula. Amen.

8. Pange lingua gloriosi

Anon.

3. In supremae noctae coenae Recumbens cum fratribus,
   Observata lege plene, Cibus in legalibus,
   Cibum turbae duodenae Sedet suis manibus.

4. Verbum caro, panem verum Verbo carnem efficit:
   Fitque sanguis Christi merum, Et si sensus deficit,
   Ad firmandum cor sincerum Sola fides sufficit.

5. Tantum ergo sacramentum Veneremur cernui:
   Et antiquum documentum Novo cedet ritui:
   Praestet fides supplementum Sensuum defectui.

6. Genitori, genitoque Laus et jubilatio,
   Salus, honor virtus quoque Sit et benedictio:
   Procedenti ab utroque Compar sit laudatio.
                                                  Amen.

9. Yerra con poco saber
Johannes Cornago

214

10. La pena sin ser sabida

Vincenet

216

218

11. [Textless]

Pere Oriola

12. Ora may, que ffora·n ço

Anon.

2. Soro mia: po' ca son suta,
    suta fora de l'inferno,
    damo ·nda festa e gaudimo
    bona vita e bon governo;
    que si campase en aterno
    non vollo esere piu monequa;
    que arça li sia la tonequa
    a quy se la vesta piu.

3. Soro mia: tu ay cagone;
    m'a' ben digcho la vertate:
    que no ·nx' a pejo presone
    que perder la libertate;
    an porder da quuyli frate
    si ·nxe stava piu, ero morta;
    veniano tocar la porta:
    "Abra-me, que frate Petro so."

4. Quando vano per la via
    sercando la caritate,
    con la votxe dotxa e pia:
    "Date-li pan, a li ffrate,"
    tanto ne a piatate
    e votcere complatxere,
    me de star en lur potere
    no me ·nxe colene piu.

5. Soro mia: voi que te diqua?
    ffrat' e prest' e saculare,
    cuy me vole per amica
    bazunya aga dinare;
    que ma vollo maritare,
    non vollo essere piu monequa;
    que arça li sia la tonequa
    a quy sse la vesta piu.

6. E fatxendo tala vita,
    non se mello paradisso
    qu'esser amata e ben servita
    com joc' e solas' e riço;
    e le jure en promisso,
    non vollo essere piu monequa;
    que arça li sia la tonecha
    a cuy se la veste piu.

7. Soro mia: io maritare
    me vorria, si potesse.
    Sense roba e dinare
    non se cantano le misse.
    Ora may, que scrit scrisse:
    non vollo essere piu monequa;
    que arça li sia la tonecqua
    a cuy se la vesta piu.

8. Soro mia: tu hay bon tempo;
    non te poy alamantare,
    que hay lo marito jovaneto,
    que te fay scotolare.
    Eu ne votxere pillare
    per a dar-me ·nde platxere,
    que de star en monasterio
    no me ·nxe colleno piu.

13. La morte che spavento de felice

Anon.

Seville 5-I-43/Paris 4379, fol. p9ᵛ

A l'homo che fortuna li desdice,
   fora assay meglio fosse sotterato.

Alboro che all'arena ha so radice,
   a mano a mano se vede sechato.

E senza focho tuta via se dice,
   tinczone morto may non fulumato.

14. Sufferir so disposto

Serafino dall'Aquila
(Music? – Text)

Reposo me sarria esser contento,
contento de l'Amor che porto ascuso.

Ascuso focho nel [mio] peto sento,
sento che me consuma el cor doglioso.

Doglioso vivo et del mio mal consento,
consento de morir, o glorïuso.

15. Cavalcha Sinisbaldo tuta la note

Anon.

Seville 5-I-43/Paris 4379,
fols. r3ʼ-r4ʳ

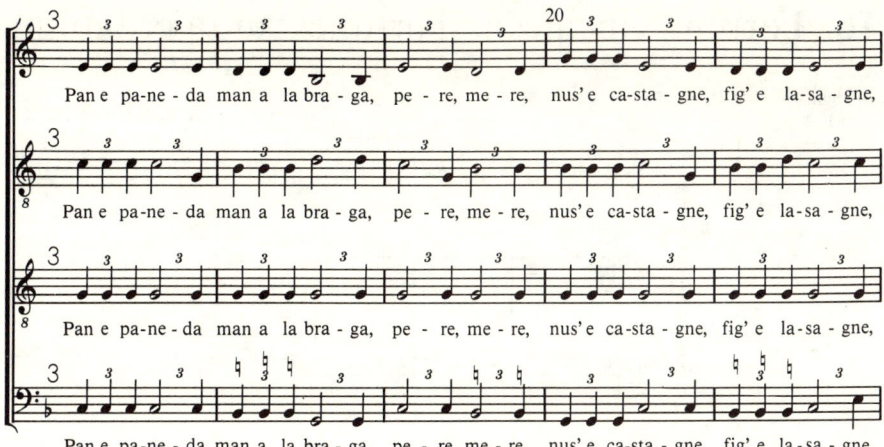

[2.] Trovò bella fantina, bosar la volse,
   fantina fo cortese bochim li sporse.
      Pan e paneda . . .

[3.] El cavalier vilan in terra la pose,
   fantina tenerella i ochi stravolse.
      Pan e paneda . . .

[4.] Diceva la badessa mo foss'io d'essa,
   diceva la priora et io ancora.
      Pan e paneda . . .

[5.] Che meneria el culo con tal vigoria,
   se havesse sassi sotto faria farina.
      Pan e paneda . . .

16. Fortuna vincinecta [Fortune, par ta cruaulté]

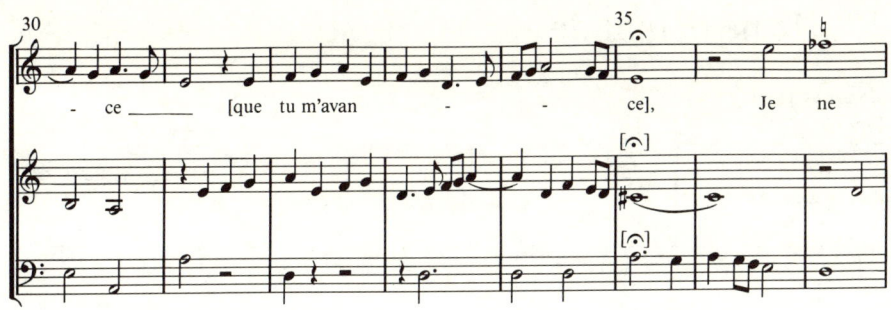

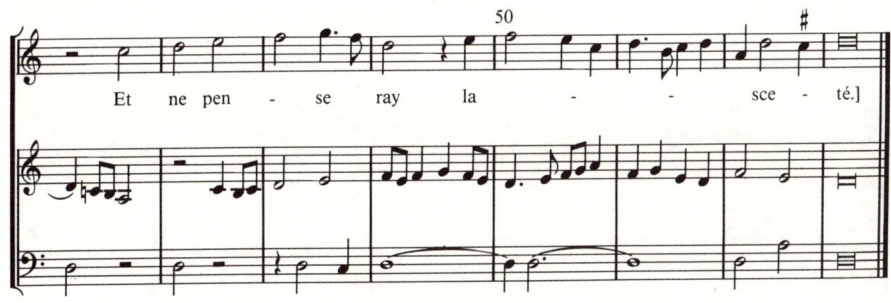

Plus tu as contre moy heurté
Moins suis doubteux, plus ay seurté,
Car j'ay le baston d'esperance.

    Fortune, par ta cruaulté . . .

J'ay bien malgré ta malheurté,
J'ay ris de ta diversité,
J'ay plaisir de ton agravance,
J'ay fierté contre ta puissance,
Car tout me vient de loyaulté.

    Fortune, par ta cruaulté . . .

17. Je ne demande

J.p.

Bologna Q16,
fols. lxxv^v-lxxvi^r

Je ne demano
de vos

Tenor Je ne
demano

Je ne demando

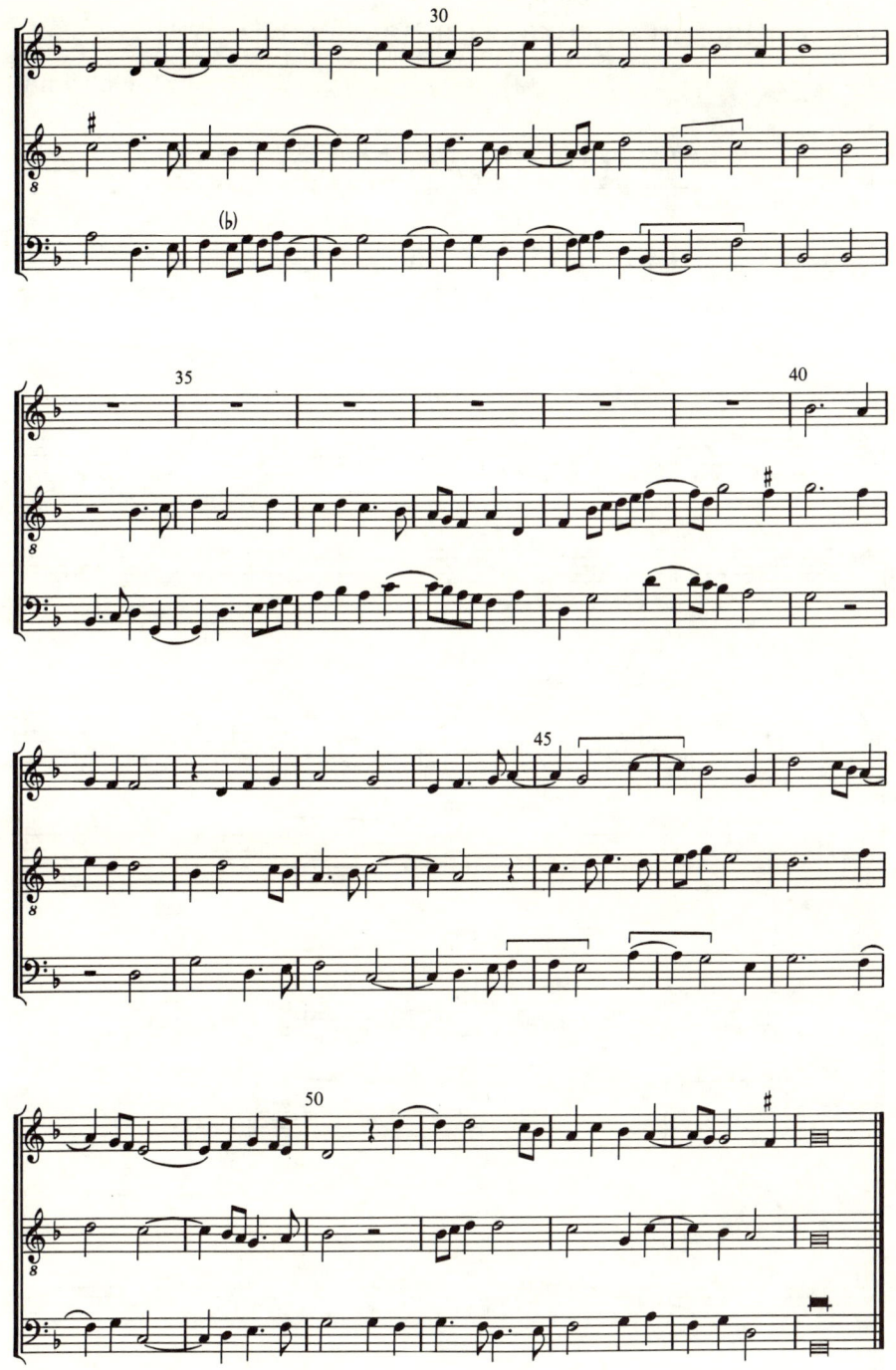

18. Falla con misuras [La bassa castiglya]

M. Gulielmus

Perugia 431, fols. 105ᵛ-106ʳ

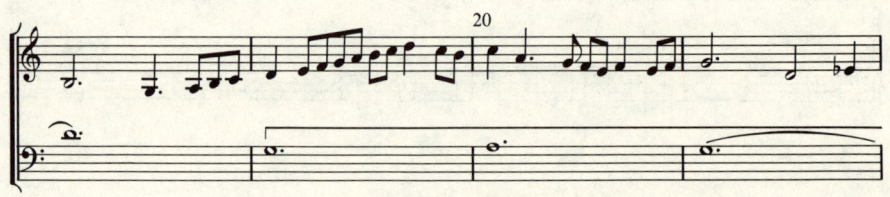

Critical Notes to the Edition

The Critical Notes for each piece begin by identifying the 'unique' or 'principal' source – that is, the source after which the transcription was made. In addition, the piece is located within the source, and the state of the text is described. The following bibliographical information is then provided: concordant sources (first those with music, then those with text only); facsimile editions; modern editions (again first those of the music, then those containing the text alone); errors in the unique or principal source; and variant musical readings in the concordant sources. If, for a given composition, a bibliographical category is not applicable, it is omitted entirely.

Both the errors in the unique or principal sources and the variants in the concordant sources are listed voice by voice, locating the error or variant by measure and beat numbers (the latter in terms of the quarter-note). Thus, '7:3–8:3' means that the reading registered begins at measure 7 beat 3 and extends through measure 8 beat 3. (Occasionally ² is used to designate the second half of a beat.)

The following abbreviations are used:

A	= altus	lig	= ligature
B	= bassus	M	= minim
Br	= breve	no t	= no text
col	= coloration	part t	= partial text
comp t	= complete text	S	= superius
CT	= contratenor	SB	= semibreve
dtd	= dotted	SM	= semiminim
inc	= incipit	T	= Tenor
L	= long		

1. Johannes Tinctoris, *O virgo, miserere mei*
    Unique source:
        New Haven 91   fols. 24^v–25^r/'Jo. Tinctoris'/'O virgo miserere mei'/S T CT: comp t/ above the S: 'Beatissime virgini d*omine* beatrici de Aragonia'
    Facsimile:
        Perkins and Garey, *The Mellon Chansonnier*, I, 84.
    Modern editions:
        Melin, *Johanni Tinctoris: Opera omnia*, 125–26; Perkins and Garey, *The Mellon Chansonnier*, I, 85.

2. Anon., *Viva, viva, rey Ferranddo*
   Principal source:
   Montecassino 871   fols. 161^r–161^v (pp. 393–94)/Anon./'Viva viva rey
                       Ferranddo'/S: comp t; A T B: inc
   Concordance:
   Berlin 78.C.28   fols. 37^v–39^r/Anon./'S' (prima pars), 'D' (secunda pars)/S:
                     initials; A T B: no t
   Facsimiles:
   Ghisi, 'Canzoni profane italiane', 9 (Montecassino 871); Pope and Kanazawa, *The Musical Manuscript Montecassino 871*, Pls. VII–VIIa; Reidemeister, *Die Handschrift 78C28 des Berliner Kupferstichkabinetts*, Appendix (Berlin 78.C.28 and Montecassino 871).
   Modern editions:
   Haberkamp, *Die weltlichen Vokalmusik in Spanien*, 284–87; Pope and Kanazawa, *The Musical Manuscript Montecassino 871*, 442–48; Reidemeister, *Die Handschrift 78C28 des Berliner Kupferstichkabinetts*, Appendix, No. 34.
   Errors in principal source:
   A: 15:1, L; 50:4–51:1, *g c b*-flat SB M M.
   B: flat in signature in first staff erased; 63:1, no corona.
   Variants in concordant source:
   S: 1:1–2, Br; 2:3–4, Br corona; 8:6, *g g f* M M M; 26:1–3^l, lig; 27:4, *b′ a′* M M; 32:2–3, lig; 40:1–41:2, lig; 42, no lig; 46, Br SB SB SB SB; 49:3–50:4, lig; 53:1–4, Br Br; 59:1–3^l, lig; 65:1–3^l, lig.
   A: 6:1, corona; 7:2^2, *c′* M; 7:3–8:3, lig; 11:1–3^l, lig; 19:1–3^l, lig; 24, L rest lacking; 33:3–34:2, lig; 35:1, L; 41:3–43:1, lig; 55:3–56:4, L Br; 59:1, *b*-flat; 64:3, dtdSB M.
   T: 2:3–4, Br; 4, L; 20:5–21:4, dtdBr dtdBr; 25:3–4, *c′* Br; 29–30, no lig; 33:1, no lig; 37:3–4, Br; 51:1, no lig; 63:1, no corona.
   B: 22:1, *d*; 27:3–29:4, Br Br–dtdL lig; 30:3–31:4, Br Br–Br lig; 33:4, no flat; 36:1–37:2, Br Br–Br lig; 41:2, *e*; 47:1–4, Br Br; 63, *c′ a* Br–Br lig.

3. Anon., *Missa L'homme armé*
   Unique source:
   Bologna Q 16   fols. lxxxvj^r–lxxxxvj^r (101^r–111^r)/Anon./'Missa de l'amormi'/
                   S T CT: part t or inc depending upon sub-section.
   Modern edition:
   Feininger, *Documenta majora polyphoniae liturgicae*, I.
   Errors in unique source:
   Kyrie: T: 6:1–2, *d′* SB.
             CT: 52:6, *d.*
   Gloria: CT: 108:1–2, *c.*
   Credo: S: 7:4–6, M M M.
             CT: 18:5–6, *f g*; 44:5–6, *d*; 53:4, SB; 54:6, *d*; 93:4 *a.*
   Sanctus: S: 8:3–5, SB; 17:1–18:1, *b′ a′ f′ f′ b′ a′* M dtdM SM SB M M; 39:6^2, M; 77:4–78:1, *a′ b′.*
             CT: 29:5^2, M.

4. Seraphinus, *Credo*
   Unique source:
       Perugia 431   fols. 22^v–26^r (12^v–16^r)/'Seraphinus'/'Patrem omnipotentem'/
                           S: comp t; T: inc/CT: no t
   Errors in unique source:
       CT 56:3–6, lacking.

4a. Anon., *Credo*
   Unique source:
       Perugia 431   fols. 19^v–22^r (9^v–12^r)/Anon./ 'Et in unum dominu*m*'/S:
                           comp t; T: part t or inc depending upon sub-section; CT: inc
                           or no t depending upon sub-section
   Errors in unique source:
       T: 88, SB SB.
       CT: 88, SB SB.

5. Bernardus Ycart, *Magnificat VI toni*
   Unique source:
       Faenza 117   fols. 6^v–7^r/'*bernardus* ycart'/'Et exultavit spiritus'/S: comp t; T
                           CT: inc
   Errors in unique source:
       S: 2:1–4, *f e f* Br Br Br.

6. Anon., *Adoramus te, Christe*
   Unique source:
       Perugia 431   fols. 168^v–169^r (158^v–159^r)/Anon./'Adoramus te *christe*'/S:
                           comp t; A T B: no t
   Errors in unique sources:
       S: after 28, line through staff.
       A: 24:4, *a*; 27:1–2, SB SB; after 28, line through staff.
       T: 21:1, superfluous SB rest.

7. Franchinus Gaffurius, *Christe redemptor omnium, Ex Patre Patris*
   Unique source:
       Montecassino 871   fol. 42^r (p. 329)/'F*r*anchin*us* Gaffurius'/'Christe
                                   redemptor o*mn*ium'/ S T: part t (first stanza); A B: inc
   Modern edition:
       Pope and Kanazawa, *The Musical Manuscript Montecassino 871*, 285–86.
   Errors in unique source:
       B: 6:2–3, SB M.

8. Anon., *Pange lingua*
   Unique source:
       Perugia 431   fols. 113^v–114^r (103^v–104^r)/Anon./'Pagne [*sic*] lingua
                           gloriosi'/S: inc; T CT: no t

Notes to the Edition 235

9. Johannes Cornago, *Yerra con poco saber*
   Principal source:
   Montecassino 871 fols. 11^v–12^r (pp. 268–69)/'Cornago'/'Yerra con poco saber'/S: no t; T: comp t; CT: inc
   Concordances:
   Escorial IV.a.24 fols. 107^v–109^r/Anon./'Yerra con poco saber'/S T (called contra): no t; CT (called tenor): comp t
   Trent 89 fol. 149^r/Anon./'Ex ore tuo sanctissima vir ego'/S: comp t; T CT inc
   Text concordances:
   Cancionero general fol. 178^v/'Pere Torroellas'/'Yerra con poco saber'
   London 10431 fol. 107^r/'Pere Torroellas'/'Yerra con poco saber'
   Modena XI.B.10 fol. 27^v/'Juan de Mena'/'Yerra con poco saber'
   Facsimile of text:
   A. Rodríguez-Moñino, *Cancionero general* (Madrid, 1958).
   Modern editions:
   Haberkamp, *Die weltliche Vokalmusik in Spanien*, 269–71; Hanen, *The Chansonnier El Escorial*, III, 372–76; Pope and Kanazawa, *The Musical Manuscript Montecassino 871*, 159–62.
   Modern editions of text:
   Bach y Rita, *The Works of Pere Torroellas*, 270; *Cancionero general*, II (Madrid, n.d.), No. 856.
   Errors in principal source:
   S: 67, lacking; 87, no corona.
   Variants in concordant sources:
   Escorial IV.a.24
      S: 40:2–4, *e' e' d'* M M M.
      T: 9:4, *e*; 13–15, lig; 61–62, lig; 66, *c'*; 76–80, lig; 87, *c'*-sharp.
      CT: 82–86:2, *d* rest *f e d c d c* Br Br SB dtdSB M SB–dtdM lig–SM col; 87–89, L without dot.
   Trent 89
      S: mensuration sign C; 21, lig; 25:3–4, *c'* SB; 31:3, no flat; 39:3–40:2, *f'* Br; 53, lig; 78:3–4, *c'* SB; 87, no repeat sign.
      T: mensuration sign C; 18–20, *a c*-natural *c*-natural Br-Br lig SB; 21:1, no lig; 30:3–31:2, Br; 38:3, no flat; 72, no lig; 73–75, lig; 87, no corona no repeat sign; 95, no lig; 97:1–2, *d e* dtdM SM.
      CT: 3, Br; 6:3–4, *g* SB; 7, no lig; 10:3–12:1, lig; 12:2–3, SB; 15, no lig; 64, lig; 82:1–2, *d* SB; 87, no repeat sign; 97:3–4, *d c* M M.

10. Vincenet, *La pena sin ser sabida*
    Unique source:
    New Haven 91 fols. 57^v–59^r/Vincenet/'La pena sin ser sabida'/S: comp t; T CT: inc
    Facsimile:
    Perkins and Garey, *The Mellon Chansonnier*, I, 150, 152.
    Modern editions:
    Davis, *The Collected Works of Vincenet*, 159–61; Perkins and Garey, *The Mellon Chansonnier*, I, 151, 153.

11. Pere Oriola, [Textless]
    Unique source:
        Perugia 431   fols. 76^v–77^r (66^v–67^r)/'Oriolus'/no text
    Errors in unique source:
        T: 7:2, flat appears after note.

12. Anon., *Ora may, que ffora·n ço*
    Unique source:
        Escorial IV.a.24   fols. 90^v–91^r/Anon./'Hora may che fora son'/S: part t; T CT: inc
    Text concordances:
        Barcelona 1   fols. 90^r–91^r/'Ora may que ffora·n ço'
        Florence 3   'Ora mai che fora sono'/(I was unable to consult this source)
        Milan 35 C sup   fols. 58^r–58^v/'Ora mai che fora suno'
        Paris 1069   fol. 55^r/'Ora mai che fora suno'
        Venice 9 CCIV   fols. 110^r–111^r/'Ora mai che fora so'
    Facsimile edition of text:
        Aramon i Serra, 'Dues cançons populars italianes', between pp. 178–79, and 182–83 (Barcelona 1).
    Modern editions:
        Cattin, 'Le poesie del Savonarola nelle fonti musicali', 279–80; Hanen, *The Chansonnier El Escorial*, III, 318–20; Pirrotta, 'Su alcuni testi italiani di composizioni polifoniche quattrocentesche', 155–56.
    Modern editions of text:
        Aramon i Serra, 'Dues cançons populars italianes', 22–27 (Barcelona 1); Bronzini, 'Poesia popolare del periodo aragonese', 260–66 (three versions); E. Pasquini, 'Il codice di Filippo Scarlatti (Firenze, Biblioteca Venturi Ginori Lisci, 3)', *Studi di filologia italiana*, XXII (1964), 538–39; R. Spongano, *Nozioni ed esempi di metrica italiana* (Bologna, 1966), 220 (Florence 3); G. Volpi, 'Poesie popolari italiane del sec. XV', *Biblioteca delle scuole italiane*, IV (1891), 36–40 (Florence 3).
    Errors in unique source:
        S: 2:1–2, a' g'.

13. Anon., *La morte che spavento de felice*
    Principal source:
        Seville 5-I-43/Paris 4379   fol. p9^v/Anon./"La morte che spavento de felice"/S: comp t; T CT: no t
    Concordance:
        Perugia 431   fols. 118^v–119^r (108^v–109^r)/Anon./'La morte che spavento de felice'/S: comp t; T CT: no t
    Facsimile:
        Plamenac, *Facsimile Reproduction of the Manuscripts Sevilla 5-I-43 & Paris N.A.Fr. 4379 (Pt. I)*, 89.
    Variants in concordant source:
        S: 5, lig; 7:3, d'; 8:1, Br rest; 8:3–6 c' d' e' f' e' e' d' M SM SM dtdSB M M M; 11:2, a' M; 12:4, b'-flat; 16:3–17:1, lig; 17:4^2, f' M.
        T: 6:3, sharp no lig; 7:1, no col; 7:2^2, b; 7:3 no lig; 12:5, sharp; 14:1–4, c' d' d' Br SB SB no lig; 15:1, c' c' M M; 15:3–4, g Br; 17:3, no lig.
        CT: 1:3, no lig; 3:1–4, dtdBr SB; 7:1–4, lig; 8:3–4, rest e d SB SB SB no lig; 10:3–11:2, lig; 12:3, no lig; 14 1–4, lig.

14. Anon. (Serafino dall'Aquila?), *Sufferir so disposto*
    Principal source:
       Perugia 431   fols. 126ᵛ–127ʳ (116ᵛ–117ᵛ)/Anon./'Sufferire so disposto'/S: comp t; A T B: no t
    Concordances:
       Florence 27   fol. 13ᵛ/Anon./'Ave regina virgo gloriosa'/S: comp t; A T B: no t; above the S: 'Sofrire son disposto'
       Florence 121 fols. 18ᵛ–19ʳ/Anon./'Sofferir son disposto'/S: comp t; A T B no t
       Paris 676   fols. 83ᵛ–84ʳ/Anon./'Soffrire io som disposto'/*a 3*, without A/ S: comp t; T B: inc
    Text concordances:
       Giunta, *Opere . . . Seraphino Aquilano*   fol. 190ʳ/'Seraphino Aquilano'/'Soffrire i' son disposto'
       Rome 5170   fol. 33ʳ/'Seraphinus'/'Soffrire son disposto'
    Modern editions of text:
       Bauer-Formiconi, *Die Strambotti des Serafino dall'Aquila*, No. 198; Menghini, *Le rime di Serafino de'Ciminelli dall'Aquila*, No. 174.
    Errors in principal source:
       A: 4:2–4, octave too high; 6:2², SB; 9:3, Br; 12:3, rest lacking.
       B: 5:3²–4, *c d* M SB; 7:1, *g*; 14:2, *c*.
    Variants in concordant sources:
       Florence 27:
          S: 8:1–3, dtdBr; 9:3, corona; 12:1, corona; 17, corona.
          A: 4:2–4, *g a* rest M M M; 6:2–7:2, *f a a a* SB Br SB SB corona; 8:3–9:4, *c' d' a a* SB SB Br Br; 10:1, lacking; 17, corona.
          T: 9:3, corona; 12:1 corona; 17, corona.
          B: 6, no lig; 7:1, *d*; 8:3–4, *d c*; 9:3, corona; 12:1, corona; 16:1, no lig; 17, corona.
       Florence 121:
          S: 7:3–4, no rest; 9:3–4, SB SB; 12:1, corona; 12:3, no rest; after 14:4, SB rest; 17:1, corona.
          A: clef is C³: 4:2–4, *g a* rest SB SB SB; 5:1, SB; 6:3–7:2, SB SB corona; 7:3–4, no rest; 9:1, *c'*; 10:1, *a*; after 14:4, SB rest.
          T: 7:3–4, no rest; 8:1–3, Br SB; 12:1, corona; 14:3, no corona; 17:1, corona.
          B: 3:4–4:1, SB SB; 6:1, no lig; 7:1, *d*; 7:3–4, no rest; 11:1, *f e* M M; 14:3, no corona; after 14:4, SB rest; 16:1, no lig.
       Paris 676:
          S: 9:3, corona; 12:1, corona; 12:3, Br rest; 14:1–2, *d' c' d' e'* M M M M.
          A: lacking.
          T: 1:1–3, dtdBr; 4:3–4, SB SB; 8:1–3, Br SB; 9:3, corona; 12:1, corona; 12:3, Br rest; 17:1, corona.
          B: 5:1, M M; 6:1–2, lig; 7:1, *d*; 9:3, corona; 10:2–3, SB SB; 11:1–4, lig; 12:1, *F/c*; 16:1–4, lig.

238 *Notes to the Edition*

15. Anon. *Cavalcha Sinisbaldo tuta la note*
    Unique source:
    Seville 5-1-43/Paris 4379   fols. r3^v–r4^r/Anon./'Cavalcha Sinisbaldo tuta la note'/S: comp t; A T B: part t
    Facsimile:
    Plamenac, *Facsimile Reproduction of the Manuscripts Sevilla 5-I-43 & Paris N.A.Fr. 4379 (Pt. I)*, 96.

16. Anon. arrangement of Vincenet, *Fortuna vincinecta (Fortune, par ta cruaulté)*
    Unique source:
    Bologna 596 H.H.2^4 fols 1^v–2^r/Anon./'Fortuna vincinecta'/S: inc; lute part: no t
    (For a list of sources that contain the polyphonic model, see Davis, *The Collected Works of Vincenet*, xxv; Perkins and Garey, *The Mellon Chansonnier*, II, 259.)
    Facsimile:
    Fallows, '15th-Century Tablatures for Plucked Instruments', Plates, 4–5.
    Errors in unique source:
    See Chapter VII, pp. 151–52.

17. J.P., *Je ne demande*
    Unique source:
    Bologna Q 16   fols. lxxv^v–lxxvi^r (89^v–90^r)/'.J.p:'/'Je ne demano de vos'/S, T, CT: inc
    Errors in unique source:
    T: 35:1, SB.
    CT: 28:4–29:1, M; 37:3, SM; 51: 1–2, *f e*.

18. Guglielmo Ebreo (Giovanni Ambrosio da Pesaro), *Falla con misuras (La Spagna)*
    Principal source:
    Perugia 431   fols. 105^v–106^r (95^v–96^r)/'M. Gulielmus'/'Falla con misuras'/S: inc; T: no t
    Concordance:
    Bologna Q 16   fols. lviiii^v–lx^r (74^v–75^r)/Anon./'La bassa castiglya'/S T: inc
    Modern edition:
    Bukofzer, *Studies in Medieval and Renaissance Music*, 199–200.
    Errors in principal source:
    S: 3:6, SM; 14:4, M M.
    Variants in concordant source:
    S: 1–3:4, mutilated; 5:6^2–8:1, mutilated; 21:6, no flat; 31:5^2–6, SM M M; 33:4^2–5, *g' f'* SM M.
    T: 15–18, lig; 43–44, lig.

Bibliography

Altamura, Antonio. *La lirica napoletana del Quattrocento*. Studi e testi di letteratura italiana, 14 (Naples, 1978).
'La letteratura volgare', *Storia di Napoli*, IV/2 (Naples, 1974), 501–71.
Napoli aragonese nei Ricordi di Loise de Rosa. Biblioteca napoletana, 3 (Naples, 1971).
Rimatori napoletani del Quattrocento. Collane di studi e testi di letteratura, 3 (Naples, 1962).
L'Umanesimo nel mezzogiorno d'Italia (Florence, 1941).
Ambros, August Wilhelm. *Geschichte der Musik*, 3rd ed. (Leipzig, 1891).
Anglés, Higinio. *Historia de la Musica en Navarra* (Pamplona, 1970).
'Alfonso V d'Aragona, mecenate della musica ed il suo ménestrel Jean Boisard', *Liber amicorum Charles van den Borren* (Brussels, 1964), 5–16 (references to rpt. in *Hygini Anglés: Scripta musicologica*, 3 vols., ed. Joseph López-Calo (Rome, 1975), II, 765–78).
'Die Instrumentalmusik bis zum 16. Jahrhundert in Spanien', *Natalicia musicologica Knud Jeppesen* (Copenhagen, 1962), 143–64 (references to rpt. in *Scripta musicologica*, III, 1415–42).
'La Música en la Corte Real de Aragón y de Nápoles durante el Reinado de Alfonso V el Magnánimo', *Cuadernos de trabajos de la Escuela Española de Historia y Arqueología en Roma*, XI (1961), 81–142 (references to rpt. in *Scripta musicologica*, II, 963–1028).
La Música en la Corte de los Reyes Católicos, I: *Polifonia religiosa*. Monumentos de la Música Española, 1, 2nd ed. (Barcelona, 1960).
'Cornago, Frater Johannes', *Die Musik in Geschichte und Gegenwart*, II (1952), cols. 1680–84.
'La Música en la Corte del Rey Don Alfonso V de Aragón, el Magnánimo (años 1413–1420)', *Spanische Forschungen*, Ser. I, Vol. VIII (1940), 339–80.
'El "Chansonnier français" de la Colombina de Sevilla', *Estudis universitas catalans*, XIV (1929) (references to rpt. in *Scripta musicologica*, III, 1357–92).
and Joaquín Pena. *Diccionario de la Música Labor* (Barcelona, 1954).
Aramon i Serra, R. 'Dues cancons populars italianes en un manuscrit catala quatrecentista', *Estudis romànics*, I (1947–48), 159–88.
Archi, Antonio. *Gli Aragona di Napoli* (Rocca San Casciano, 1968).
Arnese, Raffaele. *I codici notati della Biblioteca Nazionale di Napoli*. Biblioteca di bibliografia italiana, XLVII (Florence, 1967).
Atlas, Allan W. 'The Foligno Fragment: Another Source from Fifteenth-Century Naples', *Quellenstudien zur Musik der Renaissance: Datierung und Filiation von Musikhandschriften der Josquin-Zeit*, Wolfenbüttler Forschungen, 26, ed. Ludwig Finscher (Wiesbaden, 1984), 181–98.
Robert Morton: The Collected Works. Masters and Monuments of Renaissance Music, 2 (New York, 1981).

'La provenienza del manoscritto Berlin 78.C.28: Firenze o Napoli?', *Rivista italiana di musicologia*, XIII(1978), 10–29.

'Alexander Agricola and Ferrante I of Naples', *Journal of the American Musicological Society*, XXX (1977), 313–19.

'On the Neapolitan Provenance of the Manuscript Perugia, Biblioteca Comunale Augusta, 431 (G 20)', *Musica disciplina*, XXXI (1977), 45–105.

The Cappella Giulia Chansonnier: Rome Biblioteca Apostolica Vaticana, C.G. XIII. 27, 2 vols. Musicological Studies 27/1–2 (Brooklyn, 1975–76).

Bach y Rita, Pedro. *The Works of Pere Torroella* (New York, 1930).

Bagrow, Leo. *History of Cartography*, rev. ed. by R.A. Skelton (Cambridge, Mass., 1964).

Baines, Anthony. *Brass Instruments: Their History and Developments* (London, 1976).

'Fifteenth-Century Instruments in Tinctoris's *De Inventione et Usu Musicae*', *The Galpin Society Journal*, III (1950), 19–26.

Baldelló, Francisco de P. 'La Música en la Casa de los Reyes de Aragón', *Anuario musical*, XI (1956), 37–51.

Barblan, Guglielmo. 'Vita musicale alla corte sforzesca', *Storia di Milano*, IX (Milan, 1961), 787–852.

Barone, Nicola. 'Le filigrane delle antiche cartiere nei documenti dell'Archivio di Stato in Napoli dal XIII al XV secolo', *Archivio storico per le province napoletane*, XIV (1889), 69–96.

'Notizie storiche raccolte dai *Registri Curiae* della cancelleria aragonese', *Archivio storico per le province napoletane*, XIII (1888), 745–71; XIV (1889), 5–16, 177–203, 397–409; XV (1890), 209–32, 451–71, 703–23.

'Le cedole di tesoreria dell'Archivio di Stato di Napoli dell'anno 1460 al 1504', *Archivio storico per le province napoletane*, IX (1884), 4–34, 205–48, 387–429, 601–37; X (1885), 5–47 (references in this book are to Vol. IX (1884) unless noted).

Bauer-Formiconi, Barbara. *Die Strambotti des Serafino dall'Aquila*. Freiburger Schriften zur romanischen Philologie, 10 (Munich, 1967).

Baxandall, Michael. *Giotto and the Orators: Humanist Observers of Painting in Italy and the Discovery of Pictorial Composition, 1350–1450*. Oxford–Warburg Studies (Oxford, 1971).

'Bartholomaeus Facius on Painting: A Fifteenth-Century Manuscript of the *De viris illustribus*', *Journal of the Warburg & Courtauld Institutes*, XXVII (1964), 90–107.

Becherini, Bianca. 'Relazioni di musici fiamminghi con la corte dei Medici, nuovi documenti', *La Rinascità*, IV (1941), 84–112.

Bent, Ian and Margaret. 'Dufay, Dunstable, Plummer – A New Source', *Journal of the American Musicological Society*, XXII (1969), 394–424.

Benthem, Jaap van. 'Concerning Johannes Tinctoris and the Preparation of the Princess's Chansonnier', *Tijdschrift van de Vereeniging voor Nederlandse Muziekgeschiedenis*, XXXII (1982), 24–29.

Benton, Mary A., ed. *Fifteenth Century Anonymous Chansons*, II. Ogni Sorte Editions, SR 1 (n.p., 1981).

Bernstein, Jane A. 'Philip Van Wilder and the Netherlandish Chanson in England', *Musica disciplina*, XXXIII (1979), 55–75.

Bertolotti, Antonio. *Musici alla corte dei Gonzaga in Mantova dal secolo XV al XVIII* (Milan, 1890).

Bertoni, Giulio. 'Catalogo dei codici spagnuoli della Biblioteca Estense in Modena', *Romanische Forschungen*, XX (1905–06), 321–92.

Berzeviczy, Albert. 'Les Fiançailles successives de Béatrice d'Aragon', *Revue de Hongrie*, II (1909), 146–65.

Besomi, Ottavio, ed. *Laurentii Valle: Gesta Ferdinandi regis aragonum*. Thesauris mundi: Bibliotheca scriptorum latinorum mediae et recentioris aetatis, 10 (Padua, 1973).

Billanovich, Giuseppe, et al. 'Per la fortuna di Tito Livio nel rinascimento italiano', *Italia medioevale e umanistica*, I (1958), 245–81.

Bisticci, Vespasiano da. *Le vite*, I, ed. Aulo Greco (Florence, 1970); English transl. *The Vespasiano Memoirs: Lives of Illustrious Men of the XVth Century*, trans. William George and Emily Waters (London, 1926).

Blackburn, Bonnie J. 'A Lost Guide to Tinctoris's Teachings Recovered', *Early Music History*, I (1981), 29–116.

Bologna, Ferdinando. *Napoli e le rotte mediterranee della pittura da Alfonso il Magnanimo a Ferdinando il Cattolico* (Naples, 1977).

  I pittori alla corte angioina di Napoli, 1266–1414 (Rome, 1969).

  and Raffaello Causa. *Sculture lignee nella Campania* (Naples, 1950).

Boorman, Stanley. 'Limitations and Extensions of Filiation Technique', *Music in Medieval and Early Modern Europe*, ed. Iain Fenlon (Cambridge, 1981), 319–46.

Bottari, Stefano. *La Pittura del Quattrocento in Sicilia* (Messina, 1954).

Bouquet, Marie-Thérèse. 'La cappella musicale dei duchi di Savoia dal 1450 al 1500', *Rivista italiana di musicologia*, III (1968), 233–85.

Bowers, Roger. 'London: The Chapel Royal', *The New Grove*, XI, 151–53.

Bradshaw, Murray G. *The Falsobordone: A Study in Renaissance and Baroque Music*. Musicological Studies and Documents, 34 (American Institute of Musicology, 1978).

Brainard, Ingrid. 'Guglielmo Ebreo da Pesaro', *The New Grove*, VII, 798.

Bridgman, Nanie. *La Vie musicale au Quattrocento et jusqu'à la naissance du madrigal (1400–1530)* (Paris, 1964).

Bronzini, Giovanni B. 'Poesia popolare del periodo aragonese', *Archivio storico per le province napoletane*, Ser. III, Vol. XI (1973), 255–85.

Brovette, Emile. *Les 'Libri annatarum' pour les pontificats d'Eugène IV à Alexandre VI*, IV: *Pontificats d'Innocent VIII et Alexandre VI (1484–1503)*. Analecta vaticano-belgica, 24 (Brussels and Rome, 1963).

Brown, Howard Mayer. *Sixteenth-Century Instrumentation: The Music for the Florentine Intermedii*. Musicological Studies and Documents, 30 (American Institute of Musicology, 1973).

Bukofzer, Manfred F. *Studies in Medieval and Renaissance Music* (New York, 1951).

  'An Unknown Chansonnier of the 15th Century', *The Musical Quarterly*, XXVIII (1942), 14–49.

Camporeale, Salvatore I. *Lorenzo Valla: Umanesimo e teologia* (Florence, 1972).

Cannavale, Ercole. *Lo Studio di Napoli nel Rinascimento* (Naples, 1895).

Cardamone, Donna G. 'Cimello, Tomaso', *The New Grove*, IV, 403–4.

  'The Debut of the "*Canzone villanesca alla napolitana*"', *Studi musicali*, IV (1975), 65–130.

  'Forme musicali e metriche della canzone villanesca e della villanella alla napolitana', *Rivista italiana di musicologia*, XII (1977), 25–72.

Caretta, A., et al. *Franchino Gafori* (Lodi, 1951).

Carpenter, Nan Cooke. *Music in the Medieval and Renaissance Universities* (Norman, 1958).

Castelfranchi Vegas, Lina. 'I rapporti Italia–Fiandra', *Paragone/Arte*, XV/15 (1966), 9–24; XV/21 (1966), 42–69.

Cattin, Giulio. 'Il repertorio polifonico sacro nelle fonti napoletane del Quattrocento', *Musica e cultura a Napoli dal XV al XIX secolo*, ed. Lorenzo Bianconi and Renato Bossa (Florence, 1983).

  'Johannes de Quadris', *The New Grove*, IX, 667.

Italian Laude and Latin Unica in MS Capetown, Grey 3.b.12. Corpus mensurabilis musicae, 76 (American Institute of Musicology, 1977).
'Canti polifonici del repertorio benedettino in uno sconosciuto "Liber Quadragesimalis" e in altre fonti italiane dei secoli XV e XVI inc.', *Benedictina*, XIX (1972), 445–501.
'Le poesie del Savonarola nelle fonti musicale', *Quadrivium*, XII/1 (1971), 259–81.
Causa, Raffaello. *L'arte nella Certosa di San Martino a Napoli* (Naples, 1973).
Ceci, Giuseppe. 'Maestri organari a Napoli dal XV al XVIII secolo', *Scritti storici* (Naples, 1931), 1–10.
'Una famiglia di architetti napoletani del Rinascimento: I Mormanno', *Napoli nobilissima*, IX (1900), 167–72, 182–85.
Census-Catalogue of Manuscript Sources of Polyphonic Music, 1400–1550, 3 vols. Renaissance Manuscript Studies, 1 (American Institute of Musicology, 1979, 1981, forthcoming).
Cesari, Gaetano. 'Musica e musicisti alla corte sforzesca', *Rivista musicale italiana*, XXIX (1922), 1–52.
Chew, Geoffrey. 'The Early Cyclic Mass as an Expression of Royal and Papal Supremacy', *Music & Letters*, LIII (1972), 254–69.
Cianflone, G. F. *Galeota strambottista napoletana del '400* (Naples, 1955).
Cipolla, Carlo M. *Money, Prices, and Civilization in the Mediterranean World* (New York, 1962).
Cohen, Judith. *The Six Anonymous L'Homme Armé Masses in Naples, Biblioteca Nazionale, MS VI E 40*. Musicological Studies and Documents, 21 (American Institute of Musicology, 1968).
'Colantonio', *Enciclopedia universale dell'arte*, XV (Venice and Rome, 1967), 122
Corbin, Solange. *La Déposition liturgique du Christ au Vendredi Saint* (Lisbon, 1960).
Corti, Maria. *Pietro Jacopo de Jennaro: Rime e lettere*. Collezione di opere inedite o rare, 120 (Bologna, 1956).
Corvisieri, Constantino, ed. *Angelo Tummililo: Notabilia temporum di Angelo Tummulillis de Sant'Elia*. Fonti per la storia d'Italia: Scrittori, secolo XV (Rome and Livorno, 1890).
Coussemaker, C.-E.-H. de. *Scriptores de musica medii aevi*, 4 vols. (Paris, 1864–76).
Croce, Benedetto. *History of the Kingdom of Naples*, trans. Frances Frenaye, ed. H. Stuart Hughes (Chicago, 1970; originally pub. Bari, 1925).
La Spagna nella vita italiana durante la Rinascenza (Bari, 1917).
'Una lettera inedita di Alfonso I d'Aragona', *Napoli nobilissima*, I (1892), 127–28.
I teatri di Napoli, secolo XV–XVIII (Naples, 1891).
D'Accone, Frank A. 'The Performance of Sacred Music in Italy during Josquin's Time, c. 1475–1525', *Josquin des Prez: Proceedings of the International Josquin Festival–Conference*, ed. Edward E. Lowinsky and Bonnie J. Blackburn (London, 1976), 601–18.
'The Musical Chapels at the Florentine Cathedral and Baptistry during the First Half of the 16th Century', *Journal of the American Musicological Society*, XXIV (1971), 1–50.
'The Singers of San Giovanni in Florence during the 15th Century', *Journal of the American Musicological Society*, XIV (1961), 307–58.
D'Agostino, Guido. 'Il Mezzogiorno aragonese (Napoli dal 1458 al 1503)', *Storia di Napoli*, IV/1 (Naples, 1974), 233–313.
D'Ancona, Alessandro. *La poesia popolare italiana*, 2nd ed. (Livorno, 1906).
Davis, Bertran E., ed. *The Collected Works of Vincenet*. Recent Researches in Medieval and Early Renaissance Music, 9–10 (Madison, 1978).
Degenhart, Bernhard. 'Pisanello', *Enciclopedia universale dell'arte*, X (Venice and Rome, 1963), 611–16.
De Frede, C. *I lettori di Umanità nello Studio di Napoli durante il Rinascimento* (Naples, 1960).

De la Ville sur-Yllon, Ludovico. 'La chiesa di Santa Barbara in Castelnuovo', *Napoli nobilissima*, N.S., II (1923), 70–74.

De Marinis, Tammaro. *La biblioteca napoletana dei re d'Aragona*, 4 vols. (Milan, 1947–52).

De Robertis, Domenico. 'L'esperienza poetica del Quattrocento', *Storia della letteratura italiana*, III: *Il Quattrocento e l'Ariosto* (Milan, 1966), 357–784.

    ed. *Luigi Pulci: Morgante e lettere* (Florence, 1962).

Del Piazzo, Mario. *Protocolli del carteggio di Lorenzo il Magnifico per gli anni 1473–74, 1477–92* (Florence, 1956).

Del Treppo, M. 'The "Crown of Aragon" and the Mediterranean', *Journal of European Economic History*, II (1973), 161–85.

Dimier, Louis. 'Colantonio et le Saint Jérome du Musée de Naples', *Oud Holland*, L (1933), 263–70.

Diringer, David. *The Illuminated Book: Its History and Production* (London, 1967).

Dolmetsch, Mabel. *Dances of Spain and Italy from 1400 to 1600* (London, 1954).

Donato, Giuseppe. 'Contributo alla storia delle siciliane', *L'Ars nova italiana del Trecento*, IV (Certaldo, 1978), 183–209.

Doria, Gino. *Mostra del ritratto storico napoletano* (Naples, 1954).

    and Raffaello Causa. *La Reggia di Capodimonte. I tesori*, 4 (Florence, 1966).

Driscoll, Eileen R. 'Alfonso of Aragon as a Patron of Art', *Essays in Memory of Karl Lehmann*, ed. L. F. Sandler (New York, 1964), 87–96.

Dupire, Noël, ed. *Les Faictz et dictz de Jean Molinet*, 2 vols. (Paris, 1939).

Edwards, Warwick. 'Songs Without Words by Josquin and his Contemporaries', *Music in Medieval and Early Modern Europe*, ed. Iain Fenlon (Cambridge, 1981), 79–92.

Einstein, Alfred. *The Italian Madrigal* (Princeton, 1949).

Eitner, Robert. *Biographisch–bibliographisches Quellen-Lexikon*, 2nd ed. (Leipzig, 1900).

Fabriczy, Carel von. 'Summontes Brief am A. M. Michiel', *Repertorium für Kunstwissenschaft*, XXX (1907), 143–68.

Fallows, David. 'Three Neapolitan Repertories 1460–90: Three Recent Editions', *Early Music*, VIII (1980), 493–501.

    'Basin, Adrien', *The New Grove*, II, 240.

    '15th-Century Tablatures for Plucked Instruments: A Summary, a Revision and a Suggestion', *The Lute Society Journal*, XIX (1977), 7–32.

Faraglia, N. F. *Storia della lotta tra Alfonso V d'Aragona e Renato d'Angiò* (Lanciano, 1908).

    'Memorie artistiche della chiesa benedettina di SS Severino e Sossio di Napoli', *Archivio storico per le province napoletane*, III (1878), 236–52.

Federhofer, Hellmut. 'Trienter Codices', *Die Musik in Geschichte und Gegenwart*, XIII (1966), cols. 666–73.

Feininger, Laurence, ed. *Documenta majora polyphoniae liturgicae sanctae ecclesiae romanae*, No. 1: *Anonymus, Missa L'homme armé* (Trent, 1964).

Feldman, Fritz, ed. *Johannes Tinctoris: Opera omnia*, I. Corpus mensurabilis musicae, 18 (American Institute of Musicology, 1960).

Ferrante, Biagio. *Fonti aragonesi*, VIII (Naples, 1971).

Fétis, François-Joseph. *Biographie universelle des musiciens*, 2nd ed. (Paris, 1874).

Filangieri, Gaetano. *Documenti per la storia, le arti e le industrie delle provincie napoletane*, 6 vols. (Naples, 1883–91).

Filangieri, Riccardo. *Una cronaca napoletana figurata del Quattrocento* (Naples, 1956).

    'Report on the Destruction by the Germans, September 30, 1943, of the Depository of Priceless Historical Records of the Naples State Archives', *The American Archivist*, VII (1944), 252–55.

    Rassegna critica delle fonti per la storia di Castel Nuovo, 4 vols. (Naples, 1936–40).

Castel Nuovo: Reggia angioina ed aragonese (Naples, 1934).
'La Peinture flamande à Naples pendant le quinzième siècle', *Revue belge d'archéologie et d'histoire de l'art*, II (1932), 128–43.
'L'Arco di Trionfo di Alfonso d'Aragona', *Dedalo*, XII (1932), 439–66, 594–626.
'Les Origines de la peinture flamande à Naples au XVe siècle', *Actes du XIIe Congrès international d'histoire de l'art* (Brussels, 1930), 560–76.
Fiocco, Giuseppe. 'Colantonio e Antonello', *Emporium*, CXI (1950), 51–66.
Flamini, Francesco. 'F. Galeota, gentiluomo napolitano del Quattrocento e il suo inedite canzoniere', *Giornale storico della letteratura*, XX (1892), 1–90.
Fletcher, Jennifer. 'Marcantonio Michiel: His Friends and Collection', *The Burlington Magazine*, CXXIII (1981), 453–67.
Florimo, Francesco. *La scuola musicale di Napoli e i suoi conservatorii* (Naples, 1880).
Fois, Mario. *Il pensiero di Lorenzo Valla nel quadro storico–culturale del suo ambiente.* Analecta gregoriana, 174 (Rome, 1969).
Foucard, Cesare. 'Fonti di storia napoletana nell'Archivio di Stato di Modena, I', *Archivio storico per le province napoletane*, II (1877), 725–57.
Fuller, Sarah. 'Additional Notes on the 15th-Century Chansonnier Bologna Q 16', *Musica disciplina*, XXIII (1969), 81–99.
Gaffurio, Franchino. *De harmonia musicorum instrumentorum opus.* Biblioteca musica bononiensis, Ser. II vol. 7, ed. Giuseppe Vecchi (Bologna, 1972).
Galiano, Carlo. 'Nuove fonti per la storia musicale napoletana in età aragonese: I musicisti nei libri contabili del Banco Strozzi', *Musica e cultura a Napoli dal XV al XIX secolo*, ed. Lorenzo Bianconi and Renato Fossa (Florence, 1983), 1–11.
Gallo, F. Alberto. 'Il "ballare lombardo" (circa 1435–1475)', *Studi musicali*, VIII (1979), 61–85.
'Musica, poetica e retorica nel Quattrocento: L'*Illuminator* di Giacomo Borbo', *Rivista italiana di musicologia*, X (1975), 72–85.
Franchini Gafurii: Extractus parvus musice. Antiquae musicae italicae scriptores, IV (Bologna, 1969).
'Citazioni da un trattato di Dufay', *Collectanea historiae musicae*, IV (1966), 149–52.
Gaspari, Gaetano. *Catalogo della Biblioteca del Liceo Musicale di Bologna*, I (Bologna, 1890).
Gaye, Giovanni. *Carteggio inedito d'artisti dei secoli XIV, XV, XVI*, 3 vols. (Florence, 1839–40).
Geanokoplos, Deno John. *Interaction of the 'Sibling' Byzantine and Western Cultures in the Middle Ages and Italian Renaissance (330–1600)* (New Haven, 1976).
Gerber, Rudolf. 'Die Hymnen der Handschrift Monte Cassino 871', *Anuario Musical*, XI (1956), 1–21.
Ghisi, Federico. 'Strambotti e laude nel travestimento spirituale della poesia musicale del Quattrocento', *Collectanea historiae musicae*, I (1953), 45–78.
'Canzoni profane italiane del secondo Quattrocento in un codice musicale di Montecassino', *Revue belge de musicologie*, II (1948), 8–20.
Giazotto, Remo. 'Onde musicali nella corrente poetica di Serafino dall'Aquila', *Musurgia nova* (Milan, 1959), 3–119.
La musica a Genova nella vita pubblica e privata dal XIII al XVIII secolo (Genoa, 1951).
Gillers, Don. 'The Naples L'Homme armé Masses and Caron: A Study in Musical Relationships', *Current Musicology*, XXXII (1981), 7–28.
Gnecchi, Francesco and Ercole. *Le monete di Milano* (Milan, 1884).
Goldthwaite, Richard A. *Private Wealth in Renaissance Florence: A Study of Four Families* (Princeton, 1968).
Gombosi, Otto. *Compositione di messer Vincenzo Capirola* (Neuilly-sur-Seine, 1955).
Jacob Obrecht: Eine stilkritische Studie (Leipzig, 1925).

Gómez Muntané, Maria del Carmen. *La Música en la Casa Real catalano-aragonesa durante los años 1336–1432*. 2 vols. (Barcelona, 1977).

Gothein, Ernst. *Il Rinascimento nell'Italia meridionale*, trans. T. Persico (Florence, 1915).

Grandgent, Charles H. *From Latin to Italian: An Historical Outline of the Phonology and Morphology of the Italian Language* (Cambridge, Mass., 1927).

Gravier, Giovanni. *Raccolta di tutti i più rinomati scrittori dell'istoria generale del Regno di Napoli*. 22 vols. (Naples, 1769–72).

Grayson, Cecil. *Vincenzo Calmeta: Prose e lettere edite e inedite*. Collezione di opere inedite o rare, 123 (Bologna, 1959).

Gregori i Cifré, Josep M. 'Mateu Ferrer, *tenorista* i mestre de cant de la Seu de Barcelona (1477–1498)', *Recerca musicològica*, III (1983), 7–37.

Grohmann, Alberto. *Le fiere del regno di Napoli in età aragonese* (Naples, 1969).

Gundersheimer, Werner. *Ferrara: The Style of a Renaissance Despotism* (Princeton, 1973).

Günther, Ursula. 'Tailhandier, Pierre', *The New Grove*, XVIII, 527.

Haberkamp, Gertraut. *Die weltliche Vokalmusik in Spanien um 1500* (Tutzing, 1968).

Haberl, Fr. X. 'Die römische "schola cantorum" und die päpstlichen Kapellsänger bis zur Mitte des 16. Jahrhunderts', *Vierteljahrsschrift für Musikwissenschaft*, III (1887), 189–296.

'Wilhelm du Fay: Monographische Studie über dessen Leben und Werke', *Vierteljahrsschrift für Musikwissenschaft*, I (1885), 397–530.

Hanen, Martha Knight. *The Chansonnier El Escorial IV.a.24*, 3 vols. Musicological Studies, 36 (Binningen, 1983).

Hannas, Ruth. 'Concerning Deletions in the Polyphonic Mass Credo', *Journal of the American Musicological Society*, V (1952), 155–86.

Haraszti, Emile. 'Les Musiciens de Mathias Corvin et de Béatrice d'Aragon', *La Musique instrumentale de la Renaissance*, ed. Jean Jacquot (Paris, 1955), 35–59.

Harrán, Don. 'The Theorist Giovanni del Lago: A New View of his Music and his Writings', *Musica disciplina*, XXVII (1973), 107–51.

Hay, Denys. *The Church in Italy in the Fifteenth Century* (Cambridge, 1979).

Heartz, Daniel. 'Mary Magdalen, Lutenist', *Journal of the Lute Society of America*, V (1972), 52–67.

'Hoftanz and Basse Dance', *Journal of the American Musicological Society*, XIX (1966), 13–36.

Hernon, Michael A. 'Perugia MS 431 (G 20): A Study of the Secular Italian Pieces', Ph.D. Dissertation, George Peabody College For Teachers, 1972.

Hersey, George L. *The Aragonese Arch at Naples, 1443–1475* (New Haven, 1973).

Alfonso II and the Artistic Renewal of Naples: 1485–1495 (New Haven, 1969).

'Alfonso II, Benedetto e Giuliano da Maiano e la Porta Reale', *Napoli nobilissima*, Ser. III, Vol. IV (1964), 77–95.

Herzfeld, Marie, ed. *Alfonso I./Ferrante I. von Neapel: Schriften von Antonio Beccadelli, Tristano Caracciolo, Camillo Porzio*. Das Zeitalter der Renaissance: Ausgewählte Quellen zur Geschichte der italienischen Kultur, Ser. I vol. 4 (Jena, 1912).

Hill, G. F. *Italian Medals of the Renaissance*, I (London, 1930).

Hillgarth, J. N. *The Spanish Kingdoms, 1250–1516*, 2 vols. (Oxford, 1976–78).

Hucke, Helmut. 'Neapel', *Die Musik in Geschichte und Gegenwart*, IX (1961), cols 1307–42.

Hüschen, Heinrich. 'Tinctoris, Johannes', *The New Grove*, XVIII, 837–40.

'Ycart, Bernardus', *Die Musik in Geschichte und Gegenwart*, XIV (1968), col. 931.

'Tinctoris, Johannes', *Die Musik in Geschichte und Gegenwart*, XIII (1966), cols. 418–25.

Inglehearn, Madeleine. 'A Little-Known Fifteenth-Century Dance Treatise', *The Music Review*, XLII (1981), 174–81.

Jeppesen, Knud. *La frottola*, 3 vols. I: *Bemerkungen zur Bibliographie* . . .; II: *Zur Bibliographie*

. . .; III: *Frottola und Volkslied: Zur musikalischen Überlieferung des folkloristischen Guts in der Frottola.* Acta Jutlandica, XLI/1 (Aarhus, 1968–70).

Italia musica sacra, I (Copenhagen, 1962).

'Laude', *Die Musik in Geschichte und Gegenwart*, VIII (1960), cols. 313–23.

'Eine musiktheoretische Korrespondence des früheren Cinquecento', *Acta musicologica*, XIII (1941), 3–39.

Kenney, Sylvia. *Walter Frye and the Contenance Angloise* (New Haven, 1964).

Kimble, George H. T. *Geography in the Middle Ages* (London, 1938).

Kinkeldey, Otto. 'Dance Tunes of the Fifteenth Century', *Instrumental Music: A Conference at Isham Memorial Library, May 4, 1957*, ed. David Hughes (Cambridge, Mass., 1957), 3–30.

Orgel und Klavier in der Musik des 16. Jahrhunderts (Leipzig, 1910).

Kirsch, Winfried. 'Magnificat: 2. Polyphonic to 1600', *The New Grove*, XI, 495–97.

Die Quellen der mehrstimmigen Magnificat- und Te Deum-Vertonungen bis zur Mitte des 16. Jahrhunderts (Tutzing, 1966).

Kristeller, Paul Oskar. 'The Humanist Bartolomeo Facio and his Unknown Correspondence', *From the Renaissance to the Counter-Reformation: Essays in Honour of Garrett Mattingly*, ed. Charles H. Carter (London, 1966), 56–74.

Studies in Renaissance Thought and Letters (Rome, 1956).

La Fage, Adrien de. *Essais de dipthérographie musicale* (Paris, 1864).

Leone, A. *Il Giornale di banco Strozzi di Napoli (1473)* (Naples, 1981).

Lerner, Edward R. 'The Polyphonic Magnificat in 15th-Century Italy', *The Musical Quarterly*, L (1964), 44–58.

Lichtenthal, Pietro. *Dizionario e bibliografia della musica*, I (Milan, 1826).

Litterick, Louise. 'On Italian Instrumental Ensemble Music in the Late Fifteenth Century', *Music in Medieval and Early Modern Europe*, ed. Iain Fenlon (Cambridge, 1981), 117–30.

'Performing Franco–Netherlandish Secular Music of the Late 15th Century', *Early Music*, VIII (1980), 474–85.

Lockwood, Lewis. 'Strategies of Music Patronage in the Fifteenth Century: The *Cappella* of Ercole I d'Este', *Music in Medieval and Early Modern Europe*, ed. Iain Fenlon (Cambridge, 1981), 227–48.

'Josquin at Ferrara: New Documents and Letters', *Josquin des Prez: Proceedings of the International Josquin Festival–Conference*, ed. Edward E. Lowinsky and Bonnie J. Blackburn (London, 1976), 103–37.

'Dufay at Ferrara', *Papers Read at the Dufay Quincentenary Conference, Brooklyn College, December 6–7, 1974*, ed. Allan W. Atlas (Brooklyn, 1976), 1–25.

'Pietrobono and the Instrumental Tradition at Ferrara in the Fifteenth Century', *Rivista italiana di musicologia*, X (1975), 115–33.

'Aspects of the "L'Homme armé" Tradition', *Proceedings of the Royal Musical Association*, 100 (1973–74), 97–122.

'Music at Ferrara in the Period of Ercole I d'Este', *Studi musicali*, I (1972), 101–31.

Longhi, Roberto. 'Una "Crocifissione" di Colantonio', *Paragone/Arte*, VI/63 (1955), 3–10.

Lowinsky, Edward E. 'Laurence Feininger (1909–1976): Life, Work, Legacy', *The Musical Quarterly*, LXIII (1977), 327–66.

'Ascanio Sforza's Life: A Key to Josquin's Biography and an Aid to the Chronology of his Works', *Josquin des Prez: Proceedings of the International Josquin Festival–Conference*, ed. Edward E. Lowinsky and Bonnie J. Blackburn (London, 1976), 36–75.

Madurell Marimón, José M. *Mensajeros barceloneses en la corte de Nápoles de Alfonso V de Aragón, 1435–1458* (Barcelona, 1968).

Maïer, Ida. *Ange Politien: La Formation d'un poète humaniste (1469–1480)*. Travaux d'humanisme et Renaissance, 81 (Geneva, 1966).
Mancini, Girolamo. *Vita di Lorenzo Valla* (Florence, 1891).
Mandalari, Mario. *Rimatori napoletani del Quattrocento* (Caserta, 1885).
Manzi, Pietro. *La tipografia napoletana nel '500*. Biblioteca di bibliografia italiana, 62 (Florence, 1971).
Marix, Jeanne. *Histoire de la musique et des musiciens de la cour de Bourgogne sous le règne de Philippe le Bon* (Strasbourg, 1939).
Martines, Lauro. *The Social World of the Florentine Humanists, 1390–1460* (Princeton, 1963).
Martinori, Eduardo. *La moneta* (Rome, 1915).
Massenkeil, Günther. *Mehrstimmige Lamentationen aus der ersten Hälfte des 16. Jahrhunderts*. Musikalische Denkmäler, 6 (Mainz, 1965).
Mattingly, Garrett. *Renaissance Diplomacy* (Boston, 1955).
Mauro, Alfredo, ed. *Iacobo Sannazaro: Opere volgare* (Bari, 1961).
   ed. *Masuccio Salernitano: Il Novellino* (Bari, 1940).
Mayer, Elizabeth. 'Un umanista fiorentino alla corte di Mattia Corvino', *Studi e documenti italo-ungherese dell'Accademia d'Ungheria di Roma*, II (1938), 123–67.
Mazzoleni, Bianca. *Fonti aragonesi*, III, IV, VII. Testi e documenti di storia napoletana pubblicati dall'Accademia Pontaniana, Ser. II (Naples, 1963, 1967, 1979).
Mazzoleni, Jole. *Le fonti documentarie e bibliografiche dal sec. X al sec. XX conservate presso l'Archivio di Stato di Napoli* (Naples, 1974).
   Il 'Codice Chigi': Un registro della concelleria di Alfonso I d'Aragona re di Napoli per gli anni 1451–1453 (Naples, 1965).
   Il monastero benedettino dei SS Severino e Sossio, sede dell'Archivio di Stato di Napoli (Naples, 1964).
   Fonti aragonesi, I. Testi e documenti di storia napoletana pubblicati dall'Accademia Pontaniana, Ser. II (Naples, 1957).
   Regesto della cancelleria aragonese di Napoli (Naples, 1951).
Mele, Eugenio. 'Qualche nuovo dato sulla vita di Mossèn Pere Toroella e suoi rapporti con Giovanni Pontano', *La Rinascità*, I/4 (1938), 76–91.
Melin, William, ed. *Johanni Tinctoris: Opera omnia*. Corpus mensurabilis musicae, 18 (American Institute of Musicology, 1976).
Menghini, Mario. *Le rime di Serafino de' Ciminelli dall'Aquila*. Collezione di opera inedite o rare, 75 (Bologna, 1894).
Messer, Arm.-Ad. *Le Codice aragonese. Étude général. Publication du manuscrit de Paris. Contribution à l'histoire des aragonais de Naples* (Paris, 1912).
Michel, Artur. 'The Earliest Dance Manuals', *Medievalia et humanistica*, III (1945), 33–49.
Migliorini, Bruno. *Storia della lingua italiana*, 2nd ed. (Florence, 1968).
Miller, Clement A. 'Gaffurius, Franchinus', *The New Grove*, VII, 77–79.
   ed. *Franchinus Gaffurius: De harmonia musicorum instrumentorum opus* (American Institute of Musicology, 1977).
   'Early Gaffuriana: New Answers to Old Questions', *The Musical Quarterly*, LVI (1970), 367–88.
   'Erasmus on Music', *The Musical Quarterly*, LII (1966), 332–49.
Minieri Riccio, Camillo. 'Alcuni fatti di Alfonso I. di Aragona dal 15 aprile 1437 al 31 di maggio 1458', *Archivio storico per le province napoletane*, VI (1881), 1–36, 231–58, 411–61.
   Biografie degli accademici Alfonsini detti poi Pontaniani dal 1442 al 1543 (Naples, 1880; rpt. Italica gens: Repertori di bio-bibliografia italiana, 7 (Bologna, 1969)).

Cenni storici dell'Accademia Alfonsina (Naples, 1875).

Moerk, Alice Anne. 'The Seville Chansonnier: An Edition of Sevilla 5-I-43 and Paris N.A.Fr. 4379 (Part I)', Ph.D. Dissertation, University of West Virginia, 1971.

Molajoli, Bruno. *Il Museo di Capodimonte* (Cava dei Tirreni, 1961).

Monfisani, John. *George of Trebizond: A Biography and a Study of his Rhetoric and Logic* (Leiden, 1976).

Moores, J. D. 'New Light on Diomede Carafa and his "Perfect Loyalty" to Ferrante of Aragon', *Italian Studies*, XXVI (1971), 1–23.

Motta, Emilio. 'Musici alla corte degli Sforza: Ricerche e documenti milanesi, *Archivio storico lombardo*, Ser. II vol. 4 (1887), 29–64, 278–561.

Muratori, L.A. *Rerum italicarum scriptores*, XXIII (Milan, 1733).

Murray, Bain. 'New Light on Jacob Obrecht's Development – A Bibliographical Study', *The Musical Quarterly*, XLIII (1957), 500–16.

Musik in Geschichte und Gegenwart, Die, 16 vols., ed. F. Blume (Kassel, 1949–79).

Navarro, Tomás. *Repertorio de estrofas españolas* (New York, 1968).

New Grove Dictionary of Music and Musicians, The, 20 vols., ed. Stanley Sadie (London, 1980).

Nicolini, Fausto. *L'arte napoletana del Rinascimento e la lettera di Pietro Summonte a Marcantonio Michiel* (Naples, 1925).

  'Pietro Summonte, Marcantonio Michiel e l'arte napoletana del Rinascimento', *Napoli nobilissima*, N.S., III (1922), 42–59, 68–79, 98–105, 121–46, 159–72.

Noble, Jeremy. 'Josquin Desprez: [work list]', *The New Grove*, IX, 728–36.

  'New Light on Josquin's Benefices', *Josquin des Prez: Proceedings of the International Josquin Festival–Conference*, ed. Edward E. Lowinsky and Bonnie J. Blackburn (London, 1976), 76–102.

Oreste, G. 'Adorno, Prospero', *Dizionario biografico degli italiani*, I (Rome, 1960), 303–4.

Osthoff, Helmuth. *Josquin Desprez*, 2 vols. (Tutzing, 1962, 1965).

Osthoff, Wolfgang. *Theatergesang und darstellende Musik in der italienischen Renaissance*. Münchner Veröffentlichungen zur Musikgeschichte, 14 (Tutzing, 1969).

Ottolini, Angelo, ed. *Antonio Beccadelli: L'Ermafrodito – Pacifico Massimo: L'Ecatelegio* (Milan, 1922).

Paccagnini, Giovanni. *Pisanello e il ciclo cavalleresco di Mantova* (Milan, 1972).

Pane, Roberto. *Il Rinascimento nell'Italia meridionale*, 2 vols. (Milan, 1975, 1977).

  'Le Effemeridi di Joanpiero Leostello', *Napoli nobilissima*, Ser. III vol. 7 (1968), 77–85.

Parente, G. *Origini e vicende ecclesiastiche della città di Aversa* (Naples, 1858).

Passero, Giuliano. *Storia in forma di giornale*, ed. Vincenzo Maria Altobelli (Naples, 1785).

Pease, Edward. 'A Report on Codex Q16 of the Civico Museo Bibliografico Musicale (formerly of the Conservatorio statale di Musica "G. B. Martini"), Bologna', *Musica disciplina*, XX (1966), 57–94.

Pelliccia, Alessio Aurelio. *Raccolta di varie croniche, diarj, ed altri opuscoli così italiani, come latini appartenenti alla storia del regno di Napoli*, 5 vols. (Naples, 1780–82).

Pepe, Mario. 'Sul soggiorno napoletano di Mino da Fiesole', *Napoli nobilissima*, Ser. III, Vol. V (1966), 116–20.

Pèrcopo, Erasmo. 'Nuovi documenti su gli scrittori e gli artisti dei tempi aragonesi', *Archivio storico per le province napoletane*, XIX (1894), 376–409, 561–91, 740–49.

  Barzellette napoletane del Quattrocento (Naples, 1893),

  Le rime di Benedetto Gareth, detto il Chariteo, 2 vols. (Naples, 1892).

Perkins, Leeman L., and Howard Garey. *The Mellon Chansonnier*, 2 vols. (New Haven, 1979).

Perosa, Alessandro, ed. *Lorenzo Valla: Collatio novi testamenti*, Istituto Nazionale di Studi sul Rinascimento: Studi e testi, I (Florence, 1970).

Petrocchi, Giorgio. *Masuccio Guardati e la narrative napoletana del Quattrocento* (Florence, 1953).

Peverada, Enrico. 'Vita musicale nella cattedrale di Ferrara nel Quattrocento', *Rivista italiana di musicologia*, XV (1980), 3–30.

Pieraccini, Gaetano. *La stirpe de' Medici di Cafaggiolo*, 3 vols. (Florence, 1924).

Pietzsch, Gerhard. 'Die Beschreibungen deutscher Fürstenhochzeiten von der Mitte des 15. bis zum Beginn des 17. Jahrhunderts als musikgeschichtliche Quellen', *Anuario Musical*, XV (1960), 21–62.

Pirro, André. *Histoire de la musique de la fin du XIVe siècle à la fin du XVIe* (Paris, 1940).

'Un Manuscrit musical du XVe siècle au Mont-Cassin', *Cassinensia*, I (1929), 205–8.

Pirrotta, Nino. 'Su alcuni testi italiani di composizioni polifoniche quattrocentesche', *Quadrivium*, XIV/2 (1973), 133–57.

'Novelty and Renewal in Italy', *Studien zur Tradition in der Musik: Kurt von Fischer zum 60. Geburtstag* (Munich, 1973), 49–63.

'Two Anglo-Italian Pieces in the Manuscript Porto 714', *Speculum musicae artis: Festgabe für Heinrich Husmann* (Munich, 1970), 253–61.

Li due Orfei (Turin, 1969); English transl. *Music and Theatre from Poliziano to Monteverdi*, trans. Karen Eales (Cambridge, 1982).

'Music and Cultural Tendencies in 15th-Century Italy', *Journal of the American Musicological Society*, XIX (1966), 127–61.

Plamenac, Dragan. *Facsimile Reproduction of the Manuscripts Sevilla 5-I-43 and Paris N.A.Fr. 4379 (Pt. I)*. Publications of Medieval Music Manuscripts, VIII (Brooklyn, 1962).

'Excerpta Colombiniana: Items of Musical Interest in Fernando Colon's "Regestrum"', *Miscelánea en homenaje a Monseñor Higinio Anglés*, 2 vols. (Barcelona, 1958–61), II, 663–87.

'Faenza, Codex 117', *Die Musik in Geschichte und Gegenwart*, III (1954), cols. 1709–14.

'A Reconstruction of the French Chansonnier in the Biblioteca Colombina, Seville', *The Musical Quarterly*, XXXVII (1951), 501–42; XXXVIII (1952), 85–117, 245–77.

Planchart, Alejandro E. 'Fifteenth-Century Masses: Notes on Performances and Chronology', *Studi musicali*, X (1981), 3–30.

Polk, Keith, 'Ensemble Performance in Dufay's Time', *Papers Read at the Dufay Quincentenary Conference, Brooklyn College, December 6–7, 1974*, ed. Allan W. Atlas (Brooklyn, 1976), 61–75.

Pontieri, Ernesto. *La politica mediceo–fiorentina nella congiura dei baroni napoletani contro Ferrante d'Aragona, 1485–1492* (Naples, 1977).

'Dinastia, regno e capitale nel Mezzogiorno aragonese', *Storia di Napoli*, IV/1 (Naples, 1974), 3–230.

Per la storia del regno di Ferrante I d'Aragona, re di Napoli, 2nd ed. (Naples, 1969).

'La dinastia aragonese di Napoli e la casa de' Medici di Firenze', *Archivio storico per la province napoletana*, N.S., XXVI (1940), 274–342; XXVII (1941), 217–73.

Pope, Isabel. 'Cornago, Johannes', *The New Grove*, IV, 779–80.

'Oriola, Pere', *The New Grove*, XIII, 822.

'The Secular Compositions of Johannes Cornago, Pt. I', *Miscelánea en homenaje a Monseñor Higinio Anglés*, 2 vols. (Barcelona, 1958–61), II, 689–706.

'La Musique espagnole à la cour de Naples dans la seconde moitié du XVe siècle', *Musique et poésie au XVIe siècle*, ed. Jean Jacquot (Paris, 1954), 35–61.

and Masakata Kanazawa. *The Musical Manuscript Montecassino 871: A Neapolitan Repertory of Sacred and Secular Music of the Late 15th Century* (Oxford, 1978).

Pope-Hennessy, John. *The Portrait in the Renaissance*. Bollingen Series, 35 (New York, 1966).
Post, Chandler R. *A History of Spanish Painting*, VI: *The Valencian School in the Late Middle Ages and Early Renaissance* (Cambridge, Mass., 1935).
Previtali, Giovanni. *Giotto e la sua bottega* (Milan, 1967).
Prizer, William F. 'Bernardino Piffaro e i pifferi e tromboni di Mantova: Strumenti a fiato in una corte italiana', *Rivista italiana di musicologia*, XVI (1981), 151–84.
  Courtly Pastimes: The Frottole of Marchetto Cara (Ann Arbor, 1980).
Putaturo Murano, Antonella. *Miniature napoletane del Rinascimento*. Miniatura e arti minori in Campania, VIII (Naples, 1973).
Quartana, M. 'Un umanista minore della corte di Leone X', *Atti della Società italiana per il progresso delle scienze*, XX (1932), 464–72.
Quitin, José. 'Stokem, Johannes', *The New Grove*, XVIII (1980), 165–66.
Radetti, G. *L. Valla: Scritti filosofici e religiosi* (Florence, 1953).
Rao, Ennio I., ed. *Bartolomeo Facio: Invective in Laurentium Vallam, Critical Edition* (Naples, 1978).
Reese, Gustave. *Music in the Renaissance*, rev. ed. (New York, 1959).
Reidemeister, Peter. *Die Handschrift 78C28 des Berliner Kupferstichkabinetts: Studien zur Form der Chanson im 15. Jahrhundert*. Berliner musikwissenschaftliche Arbeiten, 4 (Munich, 1973).
Rennart, Hugo. 'Der spanische Cancionero des British Museums', *Romanische Forschungen*, X (1895–99), 1–176.
Resta, Gianvito. 'Beccadelli', *Dizionario biografico degli italiani*, VII (Rome, 1965), 400–406.
  L'Epistolario del Panormita: Studi per una edizione critica (Messina, 1957).
Riemann Musik Lexikon, 12th ed., ed. Willibald Gurlitt (Mainz, 1959).
Rohlfs, Gerhard. *Grammatica storica della lingua italiana e dei suoi dialetti*, 3 vols., trans. T. Franceschi, S. Persichino, and M. Caciagli Fancelli (Turin, 1969).
  Scavi linguistici nella Magna Grecia, trans. Bruno Tomasini. Collezione di studi meridionali, 20 (Halle and Rome, 1933).
Rokseth, Yvonne. *La Musique d'orgue au XVe siècle et au début du XVIe* (Paris, 1930).
Rolfs, Wilhelm. *Geschichte der Malerei Neapels* (Leipzig, 1910).
Romano, Stefano. *L'arte organaria a Napoli* (Naples, 1980).
Roth, Adalbert. 'Studien zum frühen Repertoire der päpstlichen Kapelle unter dem Pontifikat Sixtus IV. (1471–1484). Die Chorbücher 14 und 51 des Fondo Cappella Sistina der Biblioteca Apostolica Vaticana', Ph.D. dissertation, Johann Wolfgang Goethe-Universität (1982).
Rubsamen, Walter H. 'The Earliest French Lute Tablature', *Journal of the American Musicological Society*, XXI (1968), 286–99.
  Literary Sources of Secular Music in Italy (ca. 1500) (Berkeley and Los Angeles, 1943).
Ryder, Alan F. C. *The Kingdom of Naples under Alfonso the Magnanimous: The Making of a Modern State* (Oxford, 1976).
  'Antonio Beccadelli: A Humanist in Government', *Cultural Aspects of the Italian Renaissance: Essays in Honour of Paul Oskar Kristeller*, ed. Cecil H. Clough (Manchester, 1976), 123–40.
  'La politica italiana di Alfonso d'Aragona (1442–1458)', *Archivio storico per le province napoletane*, N.S., XXXVIII (1958), 43–106; XXXIX (1959), 235–94.
Salvati, Catello. *Misure e pesi nella documentazione storica dell'Italia del Mezzogiorno* (Naples, 1970).
  'Un conto dell'Introito e dell'Esito del Percettore Generale del Duca di Calabria per l'anno 1491', *Archivio storico per le province napoletane*, ser. III, vol. 9 (1971), 349–72.
Sanchis i Sivera, Josep. *Dietari del capellá d'Anfos el Magnànim* (Valencia, 1932).
  Pintores medievales en Valencia (Barcelona, 1914).

Santoro, Mario. 'La cultura umanistica', *Storia di Napoli*, IV/2 (Naples, 1974), 317–498.
Sartori, Claudio, 'Josquin des Prés cantore del Duomo di Milano (1459–1472)', *Annales musicologiques*, IV (1956), 55–83.
'Organs, Organ Builders, and Organists in Milan, 1450–1476: New and Unpublished Documents', *The Musical Quarterly*, XLIII (1957), 57–67.
Saviotti, Alfredo. 'Di un codice musicale del secolo XVI', *Giornale storico della letteratura italiana*, XIV (1889), 234–53.
Schäfke, Rudolf. *Geschichte der Musikästhetik in Umrissen*, 2nd ed. (Tutzing, 1964).
Schavran, Henrietta. 'The Manuscript Pavia, Biblioteca Universitaria, Codice Aldini 362: A Study of the Song Tradition in Italy circa 1440–1480', Ph.D. Dissertation, New York University, 1978.
Scherillo, M. 'Un uomo di stato del Rinascimento: gl'inizi e la vitalità di Giovanni Pontano', *Nuova anthologia*, Ser. VI, Vol. 206 (1920), 297–317.
Schuler, Manfred. 'Zur Geschichte der Kapelle Papst Martins V.', *Archiv für Musikwissenschaft*, XXV (1968), 30–45.
'Die Musik in Konstanz während des Konzils, 1414–1418', *Acta musicologica*, XXXVIII (1966), 150–68.
Sciascia, Leonardo, and Gabriele Mandel. *L'opera completa di Antonello da Messina*. Classici dell'Arte, 10 (Milan, 1967).
Seay, Albert. *Johannis Tinctoris: Opera theoretica*, 3 vols. Corpus scriptorum de musica, 22 (American Institute of Musicology, 1975–76).
Johannis Octobi: Tres tractatuli contra Bartholomeum Ramum. Corpus scriptorum de musica, 10 (American Institute of Musicology, 1964).
'The "Liber Musices" of Florentius de Faxolis', *Musik und Geschichte: Leo Schrade zum sechzigsten Geburtstag* (Cologne, 1963), 71–95.
Johannes Tinctoris (c. 1435–1511): the Art of Counterpoint. Musicological Studies and Documents, 5 (American Institute of Musicology, 1961).
'The *Proportionale musices* of Johannes Tinctoris', *Journal of Music Theory*, I (1957), 22–75.
'The *Dialogus Johannis Ottobi Anglici in arte musica*', *Journal of the American Musicological Society*, VIII (1955), 86–100.
Setz, Wolfram, ed. *Lorenzo Valla: De falso credita et ementita Constantini donatione*. Monumenta germaniae historica, 10 (Weimar, 1976).
Seymour, Charles. *Sculpture in Italy, 1400–1500*. Pelican History of Art (Baltimore, 1966).
Sherr, Richard. 'From the Diary of a 16th-Century Papal Singer', *Current Musicology*, XXV (1978), 83–98.
Slim, H. Colin. *A Gift of Madrigals and Motets*, 2 vols. (Chicago, 1976).
Snow, Robert J. 'The Manuscript Prague, Strahov Monastery, D.G.IV.47', Ph.D. Dissertation, University of Illinois, 1968.
Soria, Andres. *Los Humanistas de la Corte de Alfonso el Magnánimo* (Granada, 1956).
Southern, Eileen. 'El Escorial, Monastery Library, MS IV.a.24', *Musica disciplina*, XXIII (1969), 41–79.
The Buxheim Organ Book (Brooklyn, 1963).
Anonymous Pieces in the MS El Escorial IV.a.24. Corpus mensurabilis musicae, 88 (American Institute of Musicology, 1981).
Stäblein-Harder, Hanna. *Fourteenth-Century Mass Music in France: Critical Text*. Musicological Studies and Documents, 7 (American Institute of Musicology, 1962).
Staehelin, Martin. 'Isaac, Heinrich', *The New Grove*, IX, 329–37.
Stevenson, Robert. *Spanish Cathedral Music in the Golden Age* (Berkeley and Los Angeles, 1961).
Spanish Music in the Age of Columbus (The Hague, 1960).

Storia di Napoli, IV/1–2, ed. Ernesto Pontieri *et al.* (Naples, 1974).

Strohm, Reinhard. 'Die Missa super "Nos amis" von Johannes Tinctoris', *Die Musikforschung*, XXXII (1979), 34–51.

Tateo, Francesco. *L'Umanesimo meridionale*. Letteratura italiana Laterza, 16 (Bari, 1976).

   I centri culturali dell'umanesimo. Letteratura italiana Laterza, 10 (Bari, 1971).

   Giovanni Pontano: I trattati delle virtù sociali. Testi di letteratura italiana (Rome, 1965).

Thibault, Geneviève. 'Du rôle de l'ornementation dans la musique profane au Moyen-Age', *International Musicological Society: Report of the Eighth Congress*, I (New York, 1961), 450–63.

Tirro, Frank. 'Lorenzo di Giacomo da Prato's Organ at San Petronio and its Use during the Fifteenth and Sixteenth Centuries', *Essays Presented to Myron P. Gilmore*, II, ed. Sergio Bertelli and Gloria Ramakus (Florence, 1978), 489–97.

Torraca, Francesco. *Racconti di storia napoletana* (Naples, 1908).

   Teatro italiano dei secoli XIII, XIV, XV (Florence, 1885).

   Studi di storia letteraria napoletana (Livorno, 1884).

Torrefranca, Fausto. *Il segreto del Quattrocento* (Milan, 1939).

Trinchera, Francesco. *Codice aragonese o sia lettere regie, ordinamenti ed altri atti governati de' sovrani aragonesi in Napoli*, 3 vols. (Naples, 1866–74).

Valdrighi, L. F. 'Cappelle, concerti e musiche di casa d'Este (dal sec. XV al XVIII)', *Atti e memorie delle RR. Deputazioni di storia patria per le provincie modenesi e parmensi*, Ser. III, Vol. 2 (1883–84), 415–92.

Valentiner, W. R. 'Laurana's Portrait Busts of Women', *The Art Quarterly*, V (1942), 273–98.

Valentini, R. 'Le invettive di Bartolomeo Facio contro Lorenzo Valla', *Rendiconti delle Reale Accademia dei Lincei: Classe di Scienze morale, storiche e filologiche*, Ser. II, Vol. 5 (1906), 493–550, 660–62.

Van der Straeten, Edmond. *La Musique au Pays-Bas avant le XIXe siècle*, IV (Brussels, 1878).

Van Marle, Raymond. *The Development of the Italian Schools of Painting*, XV (The Hague, 1934).

Volpicella, Luigi. *Regis Ferdinandi Primi Instructionum liber (10 maggio 1486—10 maggio 1488* (Naples, 1916).

Walsh, Richard. 'Music and Quattrocento Diplomacy: The Singer Jean Cordier between Milan, Naples, and Burgundy in 1475', *Archiv für Kulturgeschichte*, LX (1978), 439–42.

Ward, Tom R. 'The Polyphonic Office Hymn and the Liturgy of Fifteenth-Century Italy', *Musica disciplina*, XXVI (1972), 161–85.

   'The Polyphonic Office Hymn from the Late Fourteenth Century until the Early Sixteenth Century', Ph.D. Dissertation, University of Pittsburgh, 1969.

Waters, W. G., trans. *The Novellino of Masuccio* (London, 1895).

Weinmann, Karl. *Johannes Tinctoris (1445–1511) und sein unbekannter Traktat 'De inventione et usu musicae': Historisch–kritische Untersuchung*, rev. ed. (Tutzing, 1961).

Weiss, Roberto. 'Jan van Eyck and the Italians', *Italian Studies*, XI (1956), 1–15.

   'Some Van Eyckian Illuminations from Italy', *Journal of the Warburg and Courtauld Institutes*, XVIII (1955), 319–21.

Wendland, John. '"Madre non mi far Monica": The Biography of a Renaissance Folksong', *Acta musicologica*, XLVIII (1976), 185–204.

Wexler, Richard. 'Priöris, Johannes', *The New Grove*, XV, 275–76.

Wilkins, Ernest Hatch. *A History of Italian Literature* (Cambridge, Mass., 1954).

Wolf, Johannes. *Heinrich Isaac: Weltliche Werke*. Denkmäler der Tonkunst in Österreich, 28 (Vienna, 1907).

Wolff, Christoph. 'Paumann, Conrad', *The New Grove*, XIV, 308–9.
Woodley, Ronald. 'Iohannes Tinctoris: A Review of the Documentary Biographical Evidence', *Journal of the American Musicological Society*, XXXIV (1981), 217–48.
Wright, Craig. *Music at the Court of Burgundy, 1364–1419: A Documentary History*. Musicological Studies, 28 (Binningen, 1979).
 'Performance Practices at the Cathedral of Cambrai 1475–1550', *The Musical Quarterly*, LXIV (1978), 295–324.
 'Dufay at Cambrai: Discoveries and Revisions', *Journal of the American Musicological Society*, XXVIII (1975), 175–229.

Index

Admiratis, Luigi de, 48, 49, 89
Adorno, Prospero, Doge of Genoa, 80
Adroner, Luys, 36, 89
Adzemar, Lambert, 29, 30, 35, 36, 37, 89
Aedvardus de Ortona, 121
Agricola, Alexander, 37, 49, 50, 52, 58, 60, 67, 85–86, 107, 121, 156
Alagno, Lucrezia d', 66
Alano, Petro d', 104
Albarells, Jaume, 28, 29, 30, 32, 55, 56, 75, 89
Alberti, Leon Battista, 17
Albertus, 89
Albizzi, Francesco degli, 144
Albrecht IV, Duke of Bavaria, 42n
Alegre, Gabriele, 89
Alexander VI, Pope, 5
Alfonso, Duke of Bisceglie, 54, 63
Alfonso, Duke of Calabria, then Alfonso II, King of Naples
 life and activities, 4, 5, 13, 39, 41, 54, 98–99, 101–102, 119n
 patronage of art and music, 20–21, 22, 45, 48, 50
Alfonso Galeco, 46, 89
Alfonso the Magnanimous, V of Aragon, I of Naples
 life, 1–3, 98
 patronage of humanism and literature, 6–9
 patronage of art and architecture, 11–16, 17–20
 patronage of chapel, 23–38, 51, 53, 54–55, 56, 57, 59, 69, 155–56
 patronage of organ-building, 31, 136
 musicality, 112
Allegretti, Allegretto, 144
Alos, Francisco, 36, 89
Aloth, Alon, 46, 89
Altavilla, Count of, 113
Altobello, 104
Amatore, 46, 89
Andrea, 89
Andrea dall'Aquila, 17n
Andrea d'Ascholi, 100
Angelo, Tommaso, 101
Angerran, Ffilion, 35, 89

Anna Inglese, Madama, 105–106
Anselmo, 46, 89
Antoine of Burgundy, 73
Antonello da Messina, 12, 13
Antonio, 29, 45, 89
Antonio da Venezia, 108
Antonius de Janua, 134, 137
Aragon, House of, *see under* Christian names
Aragon, Kingdom of, 1, 3
Argyropoulos, Isaac, 42
Avinyo, Jordi, 100
Azemar, *see* Adzemar

Baço, Jaime, 13, 15
Baldesaris, Seraphinus, 121, 131–33, 139
Bandini de' Baroncelli, Francesco, ix
Bartolo, Domenico, 48, 49, 89
Bartolomeo de Pistoja, 105, 106
Basin, Adrien, 58
Basin, Pierre, 58
Beatrice of Aragon, Queen of Hungary, 4, 22, 47, 71–72, 76, 103, 111–12, 116, 119–20, 128, 148–49
Beccadelli, Antonio ('Panormita'), 6, 7, 8, 98
Belardino venitiano, 100n
Belcari, Feo, 144
Bernardino d'Ascholi, 100
Bernardino of Mantua, 56, 110–11
Biondi, Tempesta, 124
Blanch, Guillem, 23n
Bonadies, Johannes, 79, 81n, 125
Bonnel, Pietrequin, 58, 69
Bonsenyore, Andrea, 100
Borbó, Jaume, 29, 32, 33, 35, 55, 89
Borbó, Joan, 32, 89
Botells, Jaume, 35, 89, 111
Brandano, Matteo, 36, 89
Brandolini, Aurelio, 54, 82, 102, 156
Brandolini, Raffaele, ix, 53–54, 102, 112
Brusca, Joan, 46–47, 48, 50, 89
Brusca, Pere, 35, 39, 43, 46, 52, 56, 75, 89–90, 111
Burgundy, Duchy of, 32
Busnois, Antoine, 58, 155

Calixtus III, Pope, 3

Index

Calmeta, Vincenzo, 102
Camilla (Marzani) of Aragon, 135
Campi, Giovanni, 39, 90, 117
Camtins, Genis, 32, 90
Cantelmo, Giovanni, Count of Popoli, 10, 11
Caracciolo, Giovan Francesco, 10, 144
Carafa, Caterina, 37
Carafa, Diomede, 108
Cardona, Luys, 67
Caritatus, Petrus, 121
Chariteo, Il, see Gareth, Benedetto
Carlo de Rugieri, 100n
Caron, Jehan le, 58, 116
Caron, Philippe, 116
Carrara, Michele, 151
Casanova, Giuliano, 34, 90
Castel Capuano, music at, 101, 105, 106
Castelnuovo, music at, 31, 42, 63, 101, 102, 105
Cava dei Tirreni, 113
Charles VIII, King of France, 5, 58, 60, 85
Charles the Bold, Duke of Burgundy, 58, 122
Chiaromonte, Isabella, Queen of Naples, 13
Chirardo, Giovanni, 48, 49, 90
Christofol de Sent' Steve, 27n
Cimello, Giovan Tomaso, 80n
Cini, Bernardo, 90
Cinico, Giovan Marco, 50n, 77
Citroli, Angelus Antonius, 91
Coch, Johan Io, 23n
Colantonio, 12–13
Coletta, 51, 91
Colinet de Lannoy, 58
Columbus, Ferdinand, 122, 123n
Compère, Loyset, 58, 155
Constantino de Tanti, 33, 41
Coppola, Giovanni Battista, 85–86
Corbató, Joan, 26–27, 36, 41, 52, 68
Cordier, Johannes, 41, 44, 52, 55, 91
Cornago, Joan, 35, 36–37, 39, 55, 62–69, 82, 91, 101, 119–23 passim, 126, 128, 140–41, 155
Corneul, Jean, 71
Cortes, Martin, 35, 37, 75, 91
Cortese, Paolo, 107
Coscia, Andrea, 102
Credencijs, Alberto de, 91
Credencijs, Roberto de, 51, 91

Damiano, Tommaso, 107
Damianus, 121, 139
Decembrio, Pier Candido, 8
Del Fiore, Gherardo di Giovanni, 119
Del Fiore, Monte di Giovanni, 119
Des Prez, Josquin, 49, 58, 67, 83–85, 122, 137, 153, 155
Dinantius, Johannes de Lotinis, 46, 47, 94
Donadio di Mormanno, Giovanni, 31, 101
Donatello, 17n
Donato da Tarj, 100
Donato di Andri, 117

Dornis, Antoni, 32, 91
Dortenche, Filippet, 39–40, 43, 44, 46, 48, 55, 67, 69, 75, 91, 117
Dragonexo, Johanne, 26, 91
Dufay, Guillaume, 81n, 137

Egidio di Martello, 91
Eleonora of Aragon, Duchess of Ferrara, 4, 13, 72, 103, 108
Elisio, Giovanni, 77n
Epo de Tropoya (Tropea), 47, 48, 50, 75, 91
Erfordia, Johannes de, 125
Este, Borso d', Marquis, then Duke, of Ferrara, 69
Este, Ercole I d', Duke of Ferrara, 4, 51, 60n, 108
Este, Isabella d', Marchesa of Mantua, 99n,
Este, Leonello d', Marquis of Ferrara, 32, 38, 53
Este, Sigismondo d', 108, 109
Eugene IV, Pope, 2, 7, 28
Evoli, Pietro d', 105
Exarch, Domingo, 24–30 passim, 32, 43, 56, 75, 91–92
Eyck, see Van Eyck, Jan

Facio, Bartolomeo, 7–8
Fayrfax, Robert, 135
Fede, Johannes, 59
Federico of Aragon, King of Naples, 5, 10, 50, 72, 77, 104–105
Felice, Matteo, 116
Felice da Nola, 51, 92
Fenice, Giovanni, 29, 92
Feragut, Beltrame, 59
Ferdinand the Catholic, King of Spain, 6, 62
Ferrante I of Aragon, King of Naples
  life, 3–5
  patronage of humanism and literature, 9–11
  patronage of art and architecture, 16–17, 21
  patronage of chapel, 25, 38–50, 51–55 passim, 59–60, 69, 73, 85–86, 155–56
  patronage of secular music, 107, 108, 110, 111, 112, 113
Ferrante II of Aragon (=Ferrandino), King of Naples, 5, 10, 50, 83
Ferrara, ix, 32, 53, 67, 69, 74, 155, 156
Ferrero, Giovanni, 92
Ferrero, Matteo, 32, 35, 92
Ferrilla, Juliano, 50, 92, 117
Ferrillo, Tommaso, 113
Figueras, Bartolome, 29, 92
Finero, Juliano, 50, 92
Florence, ix, 2, 4, 34, 52–54, 68, 113
Florentius de Faxolis, 83–85
Fogassot, Joan, 145
Fogliano, Jacopo, 138
Foliot, Philipoto, 23n
Francesco da Milano, 151
Frederick III, Holy Roman Emperor, 16, 69, 102

Fresneau, Jean, 58
Furtado, Pietro, 35, 92

Gaffurius, Franchinus, 59, 76–82 passim, 126, 134, 137–38
Gagini, Domenico, 17, 19, 21
Galderi de Madama Anna, 106
Galeota, Francesco, 10, 144, 146
Galiana, Pere, 61
Gareth, Benedetto, 'Il Chariteo', 10, 44, 82, 83, 102, 156
Garitxo, Gonsalvo (=Gonsalvo de Cordova, also Gonsalvo Garzia), 24–30 passim, 33, 35, 43, 48, 66, 92–93, 106–107
Garlon, Pasquale Diaz, 45n, 46
Garzia, Gonsalvo, see Garitxo, Gonsalvo
Garzia, Sancio, 29, 35, 93
Gerardo de Cimiterio, 34, 36, 93
Gerardo di Olanda, 101
Geronimo, 35, 44, 93
Ghiselin, Johannes, 58
Giacomo di Capua, 32, 93
Giannetti, Pietro, 84
Giglietto, 43, 93
Gil, Jacme, 31, 136
Giliardus, Arnulphus, 58
Giordi, 30, 31, 66, 93
Giotto di Bondone, 11, 16
Giovanna II, Queen of Naples, 1–2
Giovanni Ambrosio da Pesaro, see Guglielmo Ebreo da Pesaro
Giovanni da Gaeta, 42, 106
Giovanni de Angelo da Bari, 113
Giovanni de Lautis di Sicilia, 113
Giovanni di Brusselle, 36, 38, 67, 93
Giovanni di Sant'Angelo, 34, 93
Giustinian, Leonardo, 119n
Gonsalvo de Cordova, 'gran Capitano', 6
Gonsalvo de Cordova, see Garitxo, Gonsalvo
Gonzaga, Francesco, Marquis of Mantua, 37, 56, 110–11, 135
Gonzaga, Ludovico III, Marquis of Mantua, 43n, 61, 110
Guardati, Masuccio, 'Salernitano', 9, 35
Guarino, Silvestro, 51
Guarnerius, Guillelmus, 59, 81, 82, 111, 131
Guevara, Antonio de, Count of Potenza, 82
Guglielmo, 46, 93
Guglielmo Ebreo da Pesaro, 103, 122, 134n, 153
Guglielmo lo Monaco, 17n
Guinati, Antonio, 67
Gusto, Giovanni di, 63n
Guterrit, Gilet, 121n

Hayne van Ghizeghem, 58
Henry VI, King of England, 33
Hothby, Johannes, 79, 125
Hyeronimo de Manzo, 104

Innocent VIII, Pope, 4, 58

Isaac, Heinrich, 49, 58, 67
Isabella of Aragon, 22
Isaia da Pisa, 17n

'J.P.', 84–85, 122, 126, 153
Jachetto de Marvilla, 37–38, 40, 70, 93
Jacobo da Valenza, 50, 75, 93
Jacomart, see Baço, Jaime
Jacomo d'Ascholi, 100
Japart, Johannes, 85n, 153
Jean II of Anjou, 3–4, 38, 150
Jennaro, Pietro Jacopo de, 10, 144
Jeronimo Milecto, 'dicto Piovano', 44, 48, 53, 93
Joan de Ghianes, 46, 47, 93
Joan de Platea, 46, 94
Joan della Musica, 105, 107n
Joan Musico, 104, 107n
Joanna of Aragon, Queen of Naples, 99
Johan de Saragoza, 100
Johannes de Aragonia, 94
Johannes de Quadris, 137
Johannes presbyter, 85n
Joye, Gilles, 58
Juan II, King of Aragon and Navarre, 3
Juan de Epila, 36, 94
Juan of Aragon (nephew of Alfonso), 140
Juliano de Caiacza, 48, 49, 50, 56, 75, 94

Lagona, Antonio de, 104
Lascaris, Constantino, 8
Lassus, Roland de, 135
Laurana, Francesco, 17, 22
Laurentius of Cordova, ix, 107
Lenti, Antonio de, 35, 94
Leo X, Pope, ix, 53, 54, 113
León, Juan de, 124, 140
Leonardo egizio, 36, 94
Leostello, Joanpiero, 101
Liparolo, Girolamo, 21
Locha, Blasius, 94
Lombart, Johan, 100
Lomellini, Battista, 16
Lorenzo da Prato, 42
Loret, Joan, 32, 94
Louis III of Anjou, 2
Louis XII, King of France, 6
Lucca, 101n
Ludford, Nicholas, 135

M., Fra, de Ortona, 121
Maiano, Benedetto da, 20, 21
Maiano, Giuliano da, 20, 21
Maigret, Jehan, 71
Majorana, Cristoforo, 116
Maletta, Francesco, 52
Manetti, Gianozzo, 8
Mantua, 42n, 99n, 110–11, 156
manuscripts and contemporary printed sources
    Apt 16: 109

Barcelona 1: 63n, 145
Berlin 78.C.28: 118–19, 143, 148, 149–50
Bologna A 69: 82n
Bologna Q 16: 84–85, 104, 120, 121–22, 123, 128–30, 140, 148n, 152–53
Bologna 596 H.H.2[4]: 108, 124, 140, 151, 152
Cancionero general: 140n
Capetown 3.b.12: 138
Chantilly 564: 109
Dijon 517: 76
Escorial IV.a.24: 118–19, 140, 141, 143, 144–46, 148n
Faenza 117: 79, 81n, 124, 133–35
Florence 3: 144n
Florence 27: 147n
Florence 121: 147n
Florence 176: 76
Florence 204: 10n
Florence 2356: 138
Florence 2723: 10n
Foligno (MS without signature): 123, 124, 148n
London 10431: 140n
Milan 1, 2, 3, 4: 127n
Milan 35 C sup: 144n
Milan S.P.II.5: 145n
Modena α.M.1.2: 127n
Modena α.M.1.13: 127n
Modena XI.B.10: 140n
Modena AS: 127n
Montecassino 871: 62, 79, 82, 107, 118n, 120–21, 123, 133, 136–39, 140, 141, 147–50 passim, 155
Munich 352b: 43n
Naples VI.E.40: 112, 116, 128
Naples XII.F.50: 77n
Naples XIV.D.20: 77n
Naples XXI.C.22: 105n
Naples CF.III.4: 63n
Naples SM.XXVIII.4.22: 105n
New Haven 91 (Mellon chansonnier): 62, 70, 71, 76, 111, 116, 118n, 119–20, 128, 130, 140, 148, 149, 151
Oxford 213: 153
Paris 476: 134n
Paris 676: 147n
Paris 1035: 10, 147
Paris 1069: 103n
Paris 15123 (Pixérécourt chansonnier): 79, 117
Paris 16664: 144n, 146
Parma 1158: 81n
Perugia 431: 59n, 60, 62, 80, 83, 104, 120–24 passim, 128, 131–33, 136–39, 140, 143, 147–48, 151, 153–54, 155
Pesaro 1144: 108, 124, 151
Petrucci 1506[1]: 79, 127n
Prague D.G.IV.47: 63n, 76n
Rome 14: 127n
Rome 35: 128n
Rome 51: 127n
Rome 5170: 192n
Rome B.80: 127n
Seville 5-I-43/Paris 4379: 76, 81n, 120, 122–23, 147, 148
Trent 88: 63n
Trent 89: 76
Valencia 835: 116
Venice 9 CCIV: 236
Verona 755: 72
Washington L 25 (Laborde chansonnier): 76
Zwickau 78: 153

Margaret of Bavaria, Marchesa of Mantua, 99n
Marino della Falcuni, 51, 94
Marot, Jordi, 94
Marra, Alexander de, 48, 49, 94
Marrotta, Giorgio, 46, 94
Marti, Guillaum, 23n
Marti, Pere, 32, 94
Martini, Johannes, 58, 155
Martino nigro, 100n
Matteo di Capua, 32, 94
Matthias Corvinus, King of Hungary, 4, 47, 71, 76, 149
Matto, Nichollo, 74
Maximilian I, Holy Roman Emperor, 135
Mazzoni, Guido, 21–22
Medici, Giovanni de', *see* Leo X, Pope
Medici, Lorenzo de', ix, 4, 10, 37, 38, 40, 44, 53–54, 70, 107, 113, 117
Medici, Piero di Cosimo de', ix, 85
Melaguli, Pantaleone, 76, 77, 80, 82
Menaro, Menichello, 113
Meo, Giorgio, 100
Michele tedesco, 56, 110–11
Michelozzi, Niccolo, 85
Michiel, Marcantonio, 11
Milan, 2, 32, 40–41, 52, 58, 67, 68, 101n, 155
Mino da Fiesole, 17n
Miraballs, Jo. Franc., 48
Miro Benet, 32, 94
Molinet, Jean, 71
Montefeltro, Federigo, Duke of Urbino, 67
Mora, Pietro de, 23n
Morton, Robert, 58, 81n, 128, 130
Mossen Borra, *see* Tallender, Antoni
Muzi, Piero di Mariano, 144

Nacci, Francesco, 44
Nadal, Miguel, 24, 25, 26, 66, 94
Naples, Kingdom of, 64–65
  art and architecture, 11–22, 31, 33–34, 116
  bishoprics, 28
  currency, x
  education, 7, 54, 77, 83, 111–13
  literature and humanism, 6–11
  politics, 1–6, 51–52

Naples, chapel at, 23–57 passim
  compared to other chapels, ix, 32–33, 52–54
  constitution of, 30, 39, 49, 53, 59
  development of, 23, 51–52, 117
  liturgical books, 114–16
  liturgical music, 127–39 passim
  organ-building, 31, 42, 101, 106, 136
  recruiting, 31, 49, 60
  rosters, 29, 32, 46
  salaries and payments, 24, 25–26, 30–31, 36–37, 40, 64, 66–69, 100
  scribes, 117
  singers and chaplains, inventory of, 87–97
  size, 27, 33, 45, 55
  structure and function, 54–57
  use of wind instruments, 136
  visit to Florence, 34
Naples, churches and monasteries
  Duomo, 37
  San Martino, 28n
  San Pellegrino, 37
  Santa Maria del Popolo, 84
  Santa Maria della Pace, 13
  Santa Maria in Romania, 37
  Santa Maria Incoronata, 28
  Santa Maria Maddalena, 101n
  Sant'Anna dei Lombardi (Monteoliveto), 20–21, 48
  SS Annunziata, 80n
  SS Severino e Sossio, 16, 120
Naples, secular music at, 98–113, 140–54
  alta cappella, 110–11, 136
  chamber music, 105–109, 152–53
  dance, 102–104, 153–54
  harpists, 107–108
  improvisation, 83, 102
  lutenists, 108
  minstrels, 109–10
  processions, 98–99
  song repertory, 39, 101, 102, 140–52
  theater, 104
  trumpeters, 98, 99–100
  women musicians, 105–106
Nardello de Composta, 35, 94
Navarro, Luis, 32, 94
Nicola de Rinaldo, 34, 94

Obrecht, Jacob, 49, 60, 67
Ockeghem, Johannes, 58, 155
Oller, Joan, 42
Orbo, Johannes, 43n
Order of the Golden Fleece, 73, 77
Oriola, Juan, 43n, 61n
Oriola, Pere, 24–29 passim, 33, 35, 60–62, 94, 126, 133, 139, 143, 155
Orosco, Joan, 104, 106
Orto, Marbrianus de, 58
Ospato, Baldassare, 46, 94
Otranto, Battle of, 4, 130

Palumbo, Aniello, 108
Pando, Tancredus de, 94
Panormita, *see* Beccadelli, Antonio
Pappacoda, Francisco, 73, 74
Pascale, 29, 94
Passero, Giuliano, 99n
Patin, Luisot, 46, 56, 94
Paumann, Conrad, 42n
Pere the Ceremonious, King of Aragon, 54
Pere Joan, 17n
Perez, Berthomeo, 31, 94
Perez, Jaime, 36, 94
Perez de Corella, Eximen, 67
Pericho spagnolo, 100
Perleoni, Giuliano, 10
Perot de Vertoya, 46, 47, 94
Perrinetto, 100
Petrarch, 10
Petruciis, Giannantonio de, 144
Petrus de Pineda, 48, 95
Philip the Good, Duke of Burgundy, 32, 77
Picchart, Bernardo, *see* Ycart
Piccolomini, Maria, of Aragon, Duchess of Amalfi, 21
Pietro da Gaeta, 107
Pietro da Milano, 17
Pietro d'Alemagna, 107–108
Pietrobono de Burzellis, 108–109
Pinia, Salvatore, 46, 95
Pisanello, 15, 17, 21
Pius II, Pope, 8
Poggioreale, music at, 20, 102
Poliziano, Agnolo, 10
Pont, Antoni, 32, 45, 95
Pontano, Giovanni, 7, 8, 10–11, 16, 49, 109
Ponzo, Antonio, 40–41, 44, 52, 95, 138
Porcello, Felippo, 95
Prats, Luis, 47, 48, 95
Prebostel, Perrinet, *see* Torsel, Perinetto
Prioris, Johannes, 84, 153
Pronostrau, Perrinet, *see* Torsel, Perinetto
Puig, Pere, 108
Pulci, Luigi, 10
Pullois, Jehan, 84, 153

Rabaça, Joanet, 32, 95
Rabicano, Cola, 115, 116
Rafaele genovese, 100
Raganello, 100
Raynero, 40–41, 52, 95, 131
Recellani, Angelo, 34, 95
Regades, Pere, 32, 95
Rembert, Nicolaus, 71, 74
René of Anjou, 1, 2, 12
Rigo de Borgogna, 101
Risis, Esremus de, 48, 49, 95
Robert of Anjou, the Wise, King of Sicily, 11
Roberto, Francesco, 35, 95
Rocha, Antonius, 48, 49, 95
Rodolfo, 26, 27n
Rogeriis, Carlo de, 108

Romanello, 100
Rome, 32, 58
Romero, Blasius, 32, 84, 95
Romeu, Phelip, 24, 25, 26, 41, 66, 96
Rosa, Louise de, 9
Rosselino, Antonio, 21
Ruberto, 30, 31, 66, 96
Rugieri, 100n

Sagera, Guillermo, 17n
Salvatore de Capua, 32, 96
Sangallo, Giuliano da, 20
Sannazaro, Jacobo, 10–11, 104
Santa, Jaime/Jaume, 29, 96
Santa Creus, Cistercian monastery, 25, 27, 54, 56
Santillo, 38, 96
Sanya, Jaime/Jaume, 29, 35, 96
Savoy, 32, 43, 124n, 136
Schivegnola, Andrea, 99n
Sebastiani, Antonello, 42
Serafino dall'Aquila, 82–83, 102, 111, 126, 131, 147–48, 156
Seraphinus, Franciscus, 131
Sforza, Ascanio, 83–84, 153
Sforza, Bianca Maria, Duchess of Milan, 135
Sforza, Bona, Duchess of Milan, 103
Sforza, Constantine, Signore of Pesaro, 135
Sforza, Filippo Maria, 99
Sforza, Francesco, Duke of Milan, 41, 52
Sforza, Galeazzo Maria, Duke of Milan, ix, 23, 40–41, 42, 45, 52, 58, 67, 68, 106, 119n, 138, 155
Sforza, Ippolita, Duchess of Calabria, 4, 8, 20, 22, 39, 43, 45, 103, 119n, 144
Sforza, Ludovico, 'il Moro', Duke of Milan and of Bari, 5
Sigismund, Holy Roman Emperor, 109
Simon, Jan., 46, 96
Simplicianus, 48, 49, 96
Sixtus IV, Pope, 45, 55, 78
Socio de Montecatondo, 100n
Solario, Antonio, 'lo Zingaro', 15–16
Soler, Joan, 32, 96
Soto, Diego, de, 103
Squarcialupi, Antonio, ix, 34, 52–53, 113
Stefano del Paone, 47, 101
Steve, Joan, 32, 33, 36, 96
Stockem, Johannes, 74
Strozzi, Filippo, 26n

Strozzi, Lorenzo, 26n
Summonte, Pietro, 11–12
Suval, Fferrando, 24, 26, 27, 29, 30, 96
Symon le Breton, 130

Tabaria, Mateu, 24, 26, 96
Tailhandier, Leonardus, 109
Tailhandier, Pierre, 109
Tallender, Antoni, 109, 110
Tassinot, 36, 38, 96
Taxamor, Pirardo, 32, 96
Taxmet de Sancto Paolo, 32, 33, 96
Thomas de Alamanya, 39, 43, 96, 117
Tinctoris, Johannes
  compositions, 76, 81, 119–20, 122, 123, 126, 148–49
  life and activities, 37, 44, 46, 49, 51–52, 55, 59, 60, 71–77, 96, 111–12, 156
  treatises, 110, 116, 127, 128, 136
Torres, Jaime, 31, 75, 96
Torroella, Pere, 69, 140–141
Torsel, Perinetto, da Venezia, 26, 27n, 36, 66, 68
Trebizond, George of, 8
Trirades, Joan, 32, 96
Trithemius, Johannes, 75
Tuppo, Francesco, 9–10, 35, 96

Valentino, Jacobus de, 96
Valla, Lorenzo, 6–7, 67
Van der Weyden, Rogier, 16, 34
Van Eyck, Jan, 13, 16, 63n
Vaqueras, Bertrand, 58
Vasallo, Joanne, 51
Verardi, Carlo, 104n
Vesi, Giorgio de, 100n
Villette, Jacobus, 43–44, 46, 47, 56, 97
Vincenet, 40, 44, 55, 69–71, 97, 117, 120, 123, 124, 126, 141–42, 150–52
Vincinetti, Johannes (Vincenot), 70–71
Visconti, Filippo Maria, Duke of Milan, 2
Volpe, Nicolaus, 50, 97

Weerbecke, Gasper van, 58, 67

Ycart, Bernardus, 44, 46, 60, 76, 77–80, 81, 97, 121, 125, 126, 133–36
Ynnya, Jaume, 32, 97

Zamora, Alfonse, 48, 97